CW01260327

About the Author

Nathan Dylan Goodwin is a writer, genealogist and educator. He was born and raised in Hastings, East Sussex. Having attended school in the town, he then completed a Bachelor of Arts degree in Radio, Film and Television Studies, followed by a Master of Arts degree in Creative Writing at Canterbury Christ Church University. A member of the Society of Authors and the Crime Writers' Association, he has completed several local history books about Hastings, as well as several works of fiction, including the acclaimed *Forensic Genealogist* series, the *Mrs McDougall Investigates* series and the *Venator Cold Case* series. His other interests include theatre, reading, running, skiing, travelling and, of course, genealogy. He is a qualified teacher, member of the Guild of One-Name Studies and the Society of Genealogists, as well as being a member of the Sussex Family History Group, the Norfolk Family History Society and the Kent Family History Society. He lives in Kent with his husband, son, dog and an assortment of chickens.

NathanDylanGoodwin
@NathanDGoodwin

By the same author

nonfiction:
Hastings at War 1939-1945
Hastings Wartime Memories and Photographs
Hastings & St Leonards Through Time
Around Battle Through Time

fiction:
(The Forensic Genealogist series)
The Asylum - A Morton Farrier short story
Hiding the Past
The Lost Ancestor
The Orange Lilies – A Morton Farrier novella
The America Ground
The Spyglass File
The Missing Man – A Morton Farrier novella
The Suffragette's Secret – A Morton Farrier short story
The Wicked Trade
The Sterling Affair
The Foundlings
The Deserter's Tale – A Morton Farrier short story

(The Mrs McDougall Investigates series)
Ghost Swifts, Blue Poppies and the Red Star

(The Venator Cold Case series)
The Chester Creek Murders
The Sawtooth Slayer
The Hollywood Strangler

A Venator Cold Case

The Hollywood Strangler

An Investigative Genetic Genealogy Mystery

by Nathan Dylan Goodwin

Copyright © Nathan Dylan Goodwin 2024

Nathan Dylan Goodwin has asserted his right under the Copyright, Designs and Patents Act 1988 to be identified as the author of this work.

This story is a work of fiction. Names and characters are the product of the author's imagination and any resemblance to actual persons, living or dead, is entirely coincidental. Where the names of real people have been used, they appear with their consent.

All rights reserved. No part of this publication may be reproduced, stored in a retrieval system, or transmitted by any means, without the prior permission in writing of the author. This story is sold subject to the condition that it shall not, by way of trade or otherwise, be lent, resold, hired out, or otherwise circulated without the author's prior consent in any form of binding, cover or other format, including this condition being imposed on the subsequent purchaser.

Cover design: Patrick Dengate
www.patrickdengate.com

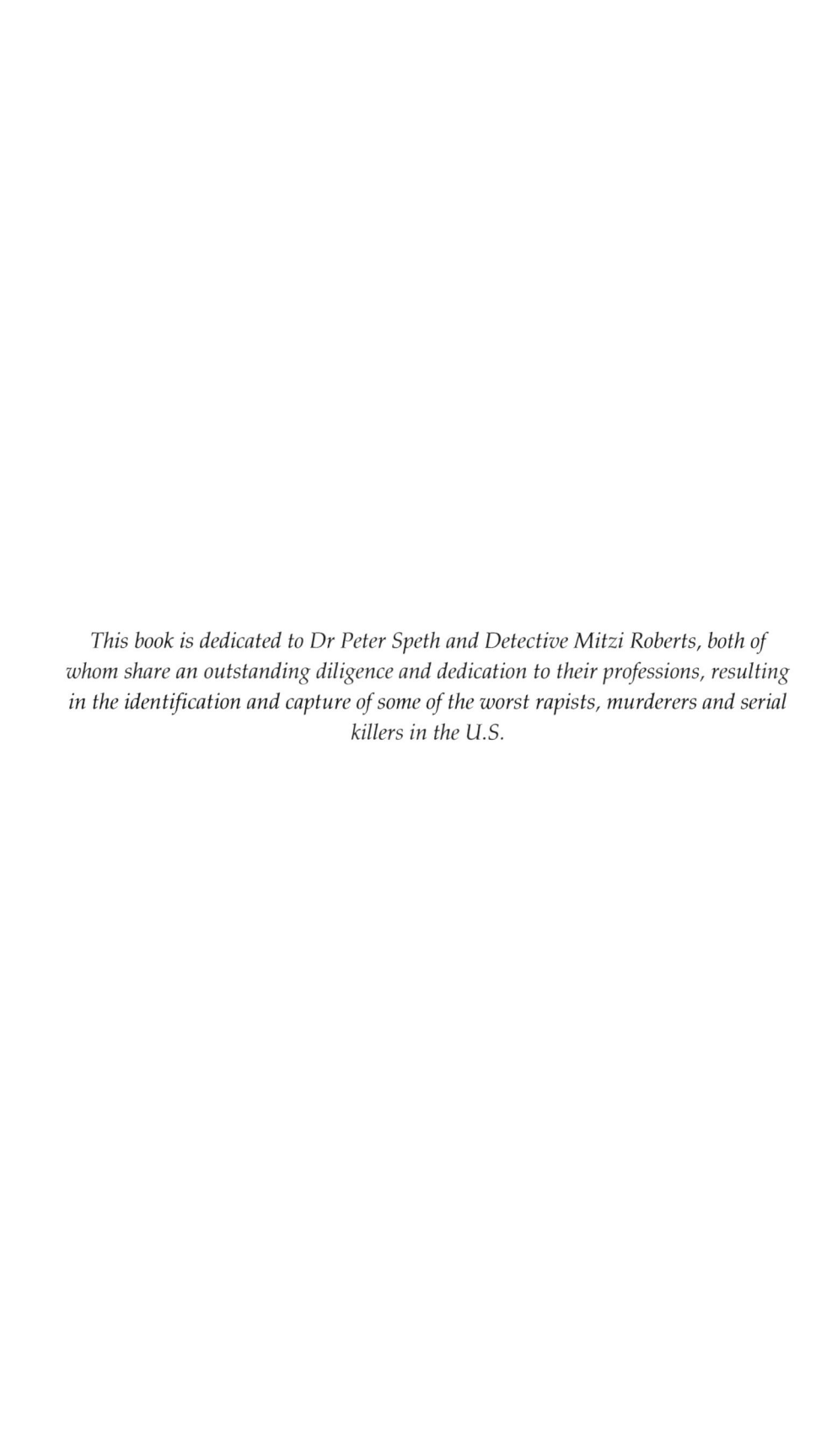

This book is dedicated to Dr Peter Speth and Detective Mitzi Roberts, both of whom share an outstanding diligence and dedication to their professions, resulting in the identification and capture of some of the worst rapists, murderers and serial killers in the U.S.

Prologue

Thursday, April 10, 1980, Ventura, Ventura County, California

The Medical Examiner's Office for the county of Ventura was a forlorn single-story converted toolshed with a tin roof. At the back of this rudimentary building, in his small office, was the Assistant Medical Examiner, Dr. Peter Speth. He was a tall, ambitious forty-four-year-old with a mop of dark hair pulled over from a side-parting. He had recently finished his one-year fellowship at the San Francisco Medical Examiner's Office and was now sitting at his desk, reviewing his dictated report of an autopsy that he had completed just the day before. All around him were the tools of his trade: well-thumbed textbooks and bound medical journals in the bookcase behind him; on one side of his desk, a Rolodex, note pads, a sizeable stack of case reports and a pen set inscribed with *American Academy of Forensic Sciences*; on the other side, a microscope, dictating equipment and several trays containing stained microscopic slides; and on the coat rack in the corner were his coveralls, boots and, perhaps most importantly, his small heavy-duty suitcase that he took out with him to crime scenes.

The air conditioner unit affixed to the window frame kicked in noisily, fluttering the stack of neat paperwork on the desk beside him. Dr. Speth picked up the silver-framed photograph of his wife, Helge, and placed it down on the papers with a smile. She was his absolute rock and stoically suffered the demands that the job was already heaping on their family, which had recently included using their home freezer to temporarily store a rape kit.

He was nearing the end of reviewing and signing the report in front of him, carefully preparing it for a countersignature from his boss, when the telephone out in the main office rang. It was answered almost immediately by Brian Metcalfe, the on-duty medical examiner investigator. Snippets of the short exchange filtered through the thin walls, enough to allow Dr. Speth to ascertain that he was about to be asked to attend a crime scene. He concluded reading the report, signed and dated it, and stood up just as Metcalfe delivered the anticipated knock on his door.

'So, where am I headed?' Dr. Speth preempted.

Metcalfe grinned. 'Nine ninety-nine Via Arroyo. A double homicide.'

'Another one,' Dr. Speth commented as he grabbed his leather suitcase, coveralls and boots before making for the door.

'Looks like it. I'll meet you at the scene,' Metcalfe responded.

Pushing open the front door, Dr. Speth stepped out of the building into a typical Ventura morning: blue skies and a temperature in the mid-sixties. Across the parking lot in the distance—equivalent to a three-block walk—was the Ventura County Medical Center. It was in that building's dingy, airless basement that Dr. Speth performed his autopsies.

He got into his small Renault 16, wound down the windows and began the short drive out to the crime scene. On his route, he passed several billboards promoting Ronald Reagan's bid for the White House later in the year.

Eight minutes later, Dr. Speth pulled onto Via Arroyo and began to ascend the steep hill. He eased off the gas, checking the house numbers as he went, but he quickly saw that there was no need. Just up ahead on the right-hand side, two police vehicles from the Ventura Police Department and one from the County Sheriff's Department were parked with their red and blue swirling lights broadcasting the crime scene location.

He pulled in behind the emergency vehicles, noticing the growing group of neighbors and passersby gathered behind the yellow tape that cordoned off the property. He climbed out of the Renault, pausing for a moment to take in the wider scene for context. He looked at his watch and noted that it was 10:32 a.m.

The house behind the tape was of a similar size and construction to the other middle-class homes on the street: single-story, detached with an adjacent garage. The properties were well taken care of and the small yards that fronted the street were all well-kept. Several mature trees dotted the yards along the road, the one in the front yard of number nine ninety-nine casting a long shadow over the blue Thunderbird on the driveway.

Dr. Speth strode toward the house and ducked under the crime scene tape, beelining for a detective alongside whom he'd worked in the past.

'That was quick, Dr. Speth,' Detective Turgenev, a short rotund man in an ill-fitting, brown shirt commented, a lit cigarette dangling from his left hand.

'What have we got?' Dr. Speth asked, noticing Brian Metcalfe approaching from his car with a notepad and pen in his hand. Wordlessly, Brian greeted the detective with a firm handshake and offered Dr. Speth a brief nod.

Detective Turgenev took a long drag on the cigarette, blew a torrent of smoke from his flared nostrils, and then replied: 'Married couple—David and Joyce Peck—murdered in their bed.' He took another drag, then added, 'Both smashed over the head with a lamp taken from the nightstand. Obviously, we've got a serial here. The same guy that killed Lyman and Charlene Smith.'

'How and when were you notified?' Metcalfe asked.

'Their cleaning woman arrived at her usual time,' Turgenev explained, 'but she couldn't get a response at the door. Unusually, the Thunderbird was still in the driveway and the newspaper lay beside it, so she figured something was wrong. We got the call for a welfare check at 9:51 a.m. Responding officers found all the doors and windows locked, except for a sliding glass door on the back side of the living room, which was unlocked. That's where we entered.'

Dr. Speth nodded grimly, now knowing what to expect inside. Last month, he had attended the double homicide of a couple who had been murdered in their beds, just three streets over. Charlene Smith had been raped, and then she and her husband, Lyman, had been bludgeoned to death with a log from a firewood pile outside the sliding door through which the assailant had gained entry. So far, nobody had been arrested for their murders and it seemed that their killer had just struck again.

A thin and wiry man, Detective Griffin, appeared from inside the house, a Canon F-1 camera dangling against his chest. He smiled from beneath a thick, salt-and-pepper mustache. 'Dr. Speth. Investigator Metcalfe. Ready to document what you find,' he announced, holding up his camera.

'Let's get on with it. Wait a second,' Detective Turgenev said, taking a final drag on the cigarette. He strode over to the sidewalk and tossed the cigarette down onto the road. 'Oh, one other thing, Doc,' he added, 'before you ask about the temperature: the air conditioner kicked in at six a.m. this morning, set to sixty degrees.'

'Thank you,' Dr. Speth replied, stepping inside the house. He observed a half-dozen police officers and plain-clothes detectives moving about the place, undertaking the initial investigation procedures: a bloody footprint was in the process of being cut from the cream carpet; purple powder was being brushed over probable fingerprint locations; and various household items were being bagged as evidence.

'Welcome to paradise,' Detective Griffin said, at the same time indicating for Dr. Speth to enter the bedroom.

'It's so beautiful,' Metcalfe muttered sarcastically, upon seeing the gruesome scene before them in the room.

Dr. Speth entered the bedroom, paying no heed to Griffin and Metcalfe's dark humor, knowing that such inappropriate jokes were often used to counter the otherwise excessive emotional stress of the job.

Joyce Peck was lying on the bed, naked, supine, with her eyes open and appearing to stare up at the torrent of blood spattered on the ceiling above her. The green, plush velvet headboard behind her was also dashed with multiple streaks of crimson. Her legs were outstretched and bound at the ankles, and her wrists tied and resting—perhaps defensively—over her groin. The left side of her skull was crushed, presenting just like Lyman and Charlene Smith, and as Turgenev had suggested.

Dr. Speth stepped to one side to take in an obese adult male victim, David Peck, who was also naked, lying crumpled up in a fetal position on his right side on the floor next to the bed. The left side of his skull had also clearly been shattered by blunt force trauma. Discarded, off to one side, was what appeared to be the murder weapon: a cracked, ceramic and metal lamp smothered in blood.

'Interesting,' Dr. Speth commented, crouching down beside

David Peck. He turned to address Detective Griffin. 'Did you get close-up shots of his bindings?'

'Yes,' he responded.

Dr. Speth pulled on a pair of latex gloves to take a closer look at the cords that bound David Peck's wrists and ankles and searched for any other trace evidence. 'This looks like telephone cord,' he observed, alternating his gaze between the two detectives. 'Was it taken from somewhere in this house?'

'Yeah,' Turgenev confirmed. 'From the living room.'

Dr. Speth got up and switched his attention back to the bed. 'But look at this,' he said, pointing now to Joyce's bindings. 'Skin-colored stockings. Were they hers?'

'We're not sure right now. We're trying to get prints from the closet.'

As Dr. Speth directed the close-up photography of Joyce Peck's bindings, he pondered on all that he was seeing. The knots on all the ligatures were basic noose knots, which concerned him somewhat. Lyman and Charlene Smith had been bound with drapery cord and a very complex diamond knot that was largely only used by people familiar with decorative pursuits such as macramé. The type of knot had been so complicated that Dr. Speth had been certain that the killer could not have worn gloves while tying it, as he appeared to have done for the rest of the time that he had been inside the Smith's property. Dr. Speth had cut the bindings from the previous victims, Charlene and Lyman, taking great pains to preserve the knots, which had then been submitted to the lab for enzyme testing. 'Does it not strike you that the knots here are very different from those used on Lyman and Charlene?' he asked, standing up and noticing that a young cop with MARSDEN on his brass name badge was hovering in the doorway.

Detective Griffin shrugged. 'Well, not all of theirs were diamond knots.'

'Any evidence of ransacking, like with their case?' Dr. Speth asked.

'No. Not so far,' Turgenev answered, before finally addressing the uniformed officer waiting awkwardly at the door. 'Look, what is it?'

The young cop held up a roll of film in a gloved hand. 'I just found this a little ways outside from the presumed point of entry.'

Detective Turgenev squinted. 'Be specific. What does 'a little ways' mean? And was it opened?'

Marsden shook his head uncertainly. 'About five yards away. It's not opened.'

'Bag it, just in case,' he directed, and the young cop disappeared from the room. 'Oh, and Marsden!' he called after him.

'Yes, sir?' Marsden said, hurriedly reappearing at the doorway.

'You still want to be a detective when you grow up?' Turgenev asked with a derisive laugh.

Marsden nodded.

'Good. Then you just come back in here when you're done and watch this guy in action,' Turgenev said, indicating Dr. Speth with his thumb. 'Your first lesson in detection: get every medical examiner you work with to copy exactly what you see happening right here.' He faced Dr. Speth and added, 'That is, if that's okay with you, Doc?'

Dr. Speth smiled. 'Of course, I'll talk him through it.'

Marsden beamed. 'Thanks.'

Dr. Speth leaned in for a closer look at Joyce Peck. Beyond the severe trauma to the side of her head, she had what appeared to be light bruising around her neck. A full autopsy would reveal the true extent of her injuries but, right now, he had a more pressing task. 'So, guys, can I proceed with my time of death determinations?'

'Over to you,' Detective Turgenev said. 'Work your magic.'

'Glad to oblige,' Dr. Speth answered with a smirk as he removed a battery-operated digital probe from his suitcase. He was known by detectives as being a maverick, but his methods, while unconventional, were considerably more accurate than those of his peers.

'I'm back,' the rookie cop, Marsden, announced, slightly out of breath.

'We missed you,' Turgenev quipped.

Dr. Speth turned to face Marsden. 'The first thing is temperature determinations. The rate at which a body temperature changes after death is dependent on three things: the ambient temperature—so, in here it's sixty degrees Fahrenheit; body habitus, meaning the size of the person—and he's obese—which we'll have to factor in; and lastly, clothing, or lack thereof in this case.'

Marsden nodded but said nothing, observing closely as Dr. Speth crouched down and gently lifted David Peck's head off the floor. Then he carefully inserted the probe into David's right ear, pushing it in until it reached the tympanic membrane. He held it still for several seconds, then removed it. 'Eighty-five degrees Fahrenheit,' he noted, doing his best to repeat the process with the left ear. However, due to the complex skull fracture on that side of his head, he wasn't certain if the reading would be accurate. 'Also eighty-five degrees. And that gives me an approximate central temperature of the brain.'

'Okay,' Marsden said quietly.

Dr. Speth rummaged in his suitcase. 'These,' he said, holding up three laminated sheets of paper, 'are my customized nomograms.'

'What does that mean?' Marsden asked.

'They contain data from over fifty of my previous cases where the exact times of death were known. Watch.'

Dr. Speth ruled a single line in red marker between the tympanic membrane temperature and the ambient room temperature. Next, he ruled a yellow line that took account of the body habitus and clothing. He pointed at the data where the two lines intersected. 'This gives a mean time since death of about ten hours.'

Griffin looked at his wristwatch. 'So, they were killed around…1 a.m.'

'Well, as you know, Detective Griffin, there are other factors to be taken into account yet,' Dr. Speth said with a wry smile, removing a small pressure gauge from his suitcase before turning to Marsden. 'My second time-of-death determination is to assess what I call the blanchability of lividity.' He beckoned Marsden over for a closer look and then carefully rolled David Peck's body up to reveal the underside parts. 'This bluish-purple discoloration—right down here—is caused by the deoxygenated blood no longer circulating and instead settling through gravity in the lowest vessels in areas that are not pressing down onto supporting surfaces. Applying pressure to the most-dependent areas, then the intermediary-dependent and then the least-dependent of lividity can also give an approximate time of death. Watch.'

Marsden silently observed as Dr. Speth pressed the gauge at a preset amount of pressure against the three areas of skin, testing the lowest part, then moving slightly higher and higher still, to see if the blood would move out of the spots. Then, he stood up to address the keen observers. 'So, the most-dependent lividity did not blanche, but, despite the victim's obesity, both the following areas of intermediary- and least-dependent lividity *did* blanche, meaning, in those two, that the blood was still liquid, therefore allowing it to be pressed up out of those dependent vessels.'

'Okay, but how does that help determine the time of death?' Marsden asked.

'In the lowest, most-dependent area, the liquid component of the blood had already leaked out of the vessels due to degradation of the body. The timeframe at which the lividity is no longer blanchable is again co-determined by the ambient temperature, body temperature, body habitus and clothing. Plotting all this on my second nomogram will give me a further mean time since death.'

Returning to his suitcase, Dr. Speth took out the nomogram, this one specifically for lividity, drawing two dissecting lines across this set of data points from his past cases. 'Ten hours since death,' he declared.

'Same as the first,' Detective Griffin noted. 'Around 1 a.m.'

'You're gonna like the next test,' Detective Turgenev said, shoving his elbow into Marsden's side. 'It's cool.'

Dr. Speth removed a 5 ml syringe with a 22-gauge needle from his suitcase and then carefully inserted it into the lateral third of David Peck's right eye at an angle of forty-five degrees. As he slowly withdrew the gel, he explained: 'We're looking here at vitreous potassium levels—that's the gel in the eyeballs. Potassium from the lining cells of the eyeball progressively leaks into the vitreous as the body begins to deteriorate after death.'

Marsden nodded, visibly fascinated by the process.

Once Dr. Speth had withdrawn around 2 ml of the eyeball gel, he removed the needle. 'Now, we need to get this transported to the local hospital immediately for an analysis of the potassium level. I'll repeat the process with his other eye in an hour and then, when I get the results back, I can apply them to another nomogram for an approximate time of death.'

'Do you not measure rigor, like I've seen on the cop shows?' Marsden asked.

'Second lesson in detection: never watch cop shows,' Turgenev interjected with a laugh. 'They'll make you want to smash up your TV.'

Dr. Speth screwed up his face and replied, 'Rigor is too unpredictable; there are too many variables and there is no progressive change that you can measure—unlike what you've just observed me doing here.'

Dr. Speth then repeated the time-of-death assessments on Joyce's body. The only differences were that her tympanic temperatures were two degrees lower, and the lividity blanched in the intermediary-dependent areas. 'It's a similar time of death for her, taking into account that she is stretched out and not obese, but also naked,' he advised the detectives.

'So, the killer got in, tied the pair of them up, killed David, then raped and killed Joyce,' Detective Griffin mused.

'Well, as of yet, we don't know that she was raped,' Dr. Speth reminded them as he cut her ankle bindings at a distance from the knots and allowed the detective to take close-up photographs of her unbound legs. 'But we're about to find out. Would one of you mind closing the curtains, please?'

Marsden moved over to the window and pulled the heavy material tightly shut as Dr. Speth took a hand-held lamp from his bag and switched it on, bathing the room in ultraviolet light.

'There's your answer, right there,' Detective Griffin stated, moving closer and taking a series of photographs of the bright blue fluorescence around Joyce Peck's groin and on the bed sheet beneath her.

'Not so fast, Detective. That could well be from prior consensual sex,' Dr. Speth warned, handing Marsden the ultraviolet light.

As with his other approaches to the job, Dr. Speth's own rape examination protocol was viewed as unconventional but tended, once again, to produce more accurate, scientific results than those of his peers. From his suitcase he took out an array of scientific equipment, which he spent several minutes carefully setting on a secured table at the far side of the bedroom. Finally, he placed a cap lamp on his head and, putting on a fresh pair of latex gloves, took five unwrapped swab sticks from Metcalfe. Holding them tightly together, he swabbed the introitus, taking care to ensure that all five swabs were being applied uniformly and then handed them to Metcalfe.

Metcalfe placed two of the swabs into one test tube and another two into a second tube, cotton tips up, and then placed both of those into a tube rack to have the swabs air-dried in front of a fan. The fifth swab was placed in a separate tube but not air-dried.

In the meantime, Dr. Speth carefully inserted a speculum into the vagina and looked for any injuries. 'Now look at that,' he declared. 'There's a rounded, pale pinkish bruise, about three-quarters of an inch in diameter, at between two and three o'clock in the proximal vagina.'

'Does that prove rape?' Marsden asked.

'Not necessarily,' Dr. Speth responded. 'It could have been from rather rough consensual sex.'

Continuing with his examination through the speculum, Dr. Speth took additional swabbings in the same manner: five in the middle of the vagina, five in the fundus and, finally, five in the cervical os, taking great care not to touch the other compartments on insertion and withdrawal. Each time, Metcalfe handled the swabs in the same careful manner.

'Why are you taking so many samples?' Marsden asked. 'I mean, don't you just need the one?'

'By separating the compartments, I may be able to distinguish consensual seminal deposits—even as far back as seventy-two hours—from rapist deposits. They'll be tested for enzymes.'

'Enzymes?' Marsden asked.

Dr. Speth then became very studied. 'Enzymes are specific proteins found in seminal fluid and they can differ between individuals. They are subject to deterioration when left at room temperature, exposed to moisture or freeze-thawing. That's why I air-dry them, put desiccants into the tubes and have them transported on dry ice to the freezers. And for all these reasons, out of abundance of care, I make duplicate kits.'

'Makes sense, I guess,' Marsden commented.

'It does to *me*,' Dr. Speth agreed with a smile. 'And yet, many—if not *most*—medical examiners simply take general swabbings of the vaginal tract; or at best, two swabbings. I'm also the only medical examiner—that I know of, that is—who conducts the rape examinations at the scenes. The minute you begin to roll and move the body around at the scene and the multiple times that it takes to get it from one place to the morgue, there will be mixing of the seminal deposits that liquefy after about twenty minutes and become subject to gravity flow.' Dr. Speth became very earnest, looking Marsden directly in the eyes. 'Conducting the rape exams at the scene is essential to evaluating the motility and preservation of the sperm cells, which is my next task. Look, come with me.'

Marsden followed Dr. Speth over to the table, where the microscope was set up and waiting. After adding saline solution into the concave depression of a slide, Dr. Speth swished the fifth swab that he had taken from the introitus in the solution and examined it under the microscope.

'Aha,' he said, stepping back and encouraging Marsden to take a look for himself. 'Do you see? There are a few intact motile sperm cells swimming around in the saline—they look like tadpoles with tails.'

'Oh, yeah. I do,' Marsden answered.

'Now we do the same thing with the deposits from the other compartments,' Dr. Speth explained, repeating the task and allowing Marsden to look each time.

Once done, he concluded, 'So, guys, I found abundant motile sperm in the mid-vagina. In the fundus I found abundant motile sperm cells, but also a few immobile sperm cells; some with, some without tails. In the cervical os, I only found immobile sperm cells and also some without tails. So, it does appear that a rape has occurred. However, there was also consensual sex within twenty-four to seventy-two hours before. And…the timing of the rape fits well into the preliminary time-of-death range.'

'Just like in the case of Lyman and Charlene Smith,' Detective Turgenev commented.

'Similar, yes,' Dr. Speth agreed, despite not being convinced that this was the same perpetrator.

Finally, Dr. Speth took duplicate swabbings from the breasts, from the inner aspects of the lips in the mouth and from the rectum and air-dried them in the same way as the others. He provided the detectives with fingernail clippings, plucked scalp and pubic hairs, which were all placed into individually labeled evidence bags, along with any other loose hairs that had been found around the body during the examination. The same attention was paid to David Peck, but there was no evidence of sexual assault.

'Thank you,' Marsden said to Dr. Speth, once he had completed the examinations.

'Pleasure,' he answered. Then, he turned to face Turgenev. 'Well, guys, I'll draw the other vitreous and will drop it off at the lab on my way back. I'll let you know as soon as I get the vitreous potassium results and provide you with my formal estimate of the time-of-death range. I can do the autopsies at 2 p.m. tomorrow.'

'Yeah, that works,' Turgenev confirmed.

'Listen, Detective.' Dr. Speth said as he packed up his suitcase. 'Something isn't quite right, here. I'm just not getting the impression that this is the same guy who killed Lyman and Charlene Smith...'

'What do you mean?' Detective Turgenev asked with a snort. 'You think it's a coincidence that we got two married couples with their skulls smashed in, three streets away from one another and one month apart?'

'No, not a *coincidence*,' Dr. Speth said with a slight scowl. 'Just...maybe not the same guy.'

The detective laughed. 'Based on what? The different bindings?' he said.

'They're totally different knots,' Dr. Speth answered, packing away his suitcase. 'And Lyman and Charlene were on their bed with a sheet covering them, Charlene lying face-down and with the initial knots on Lyman thought to have been tied by his wife. Compare that to what we have here—look at the evidence.'

Dr. Speth watched a look of scorn pass between the two detectives.

'You're concentrating on the finer details, Doc,' Detective Griffin said. 'Look at the bigger picture: a killer targeting couples in the middle-class suburbs of Ventura. He doesn't pay much attention to type or methods, just ties the couple up with whatever comes to hand, kills the guy first by bludgeoning him over the head, then rapes and kills the wife. It's that simple.'

'It just doesn't feel the same to me,' Dr. Speth countered. 'But, hey, you're the detectives and I'm just the Assistant Medical Examiner.'

'And we value your opinion, Dr. Speth,' Detective Griffin replied.

'Well, my opinion is that I'm thinking perhaps the Peck's killer didn't expect to find David here,' Dr. Speth said to the detectives as he prepared to leave. 'He had to use a makeshift cord to bind him. And… I need to wait for the post-mortem, but it does also appear to me that the killer tried to strangle Joyce. Maybe when that failed, he resorted to the lamp on the nightstand.'

Detective Turgenev waved his hand dismissively. 'This'll turn out to be the same guy, for sure. I promise you.'

'Well, we'll see,' Dr. Speth muttered, packing the last of his things, picking up his suitcase and making for the door.

As he walked away, he heard Turgenev say to Marsden, 'And that's your third lesson: trust your gut instinct and right now mine is telling me we've got a series on our hands.'

'Time will tell…always,' Dr. Speth muttered to himself as he got into his Renault 16 and started the engine. He took one final look up at nine ninety-nine Via Arroyo, almost certain that there were two distinct killers at large in Ventura.

Chapter One

Monday, September 12, 2022, Los Angeles, California

Retired detective, Reserve Police Officer Ted Marsden sauntered into the grand, ten-story LAPD Headquarters Facility on 100 West First Street in downtown Los Angeles with a swagger in his step. Beside him was his partner, Reserve Police Officer Travis Powers, walking with an air of equal satisfaction. They passed through security and took the elevator up to the fifth floor, home to the elite Robbery-Homicide Division of the Los Angeles Police Department. The floor was a perpetually busy labyrinth of offices and cubicles, roughly divided into the four discrete units of Robbery, Homicide, Gang Homicide and Special Investigation Sections, which employed almost one hundred personnel between them.

Marsden and Powers entered the main office of the Special Investigation Section, heading to a smaller office that was the center for the Cold Case Homicide Unit. Upon its creation in April 2020, it had made LAPD history by becoming the only unit to be entirely staffed by reserve officers. Six retired detectives had been paired up with six young reservists and tasked with attempting to solve some of the more than four thousand cold homicide cases in the department's vaults. The novel system worked well, and each pair had been solving an average of four cases per year. Marsden and Powers were one such pairing and had just returned from court, having successfully concluded a long-standing cold case.

'Life without parole!' Powers, a muscular and good-looking Asian American, yelled to the other half-dozen reservists sitting down in their cubicles in the open-plan office.

Most looked up. Some clapped. A couple cheered, and one, Detective Supervisor Mitzi Roberts, who oversaw the unit, stood from her desk and called, 'Good job, guys. You worked hard on it.'

'Thanks, boss. Those boys deserved justice,' Marsden replied, making his way over to his workstation. He sat at his desk, loosened his tie and exhaled. His close-cropped hair and goatee made him appear less than his sixty-seven years. But he was exhausted. Despite jogging five miles almost every day and keeping himself trim, in the past few weeks he had started to feel his age. Getting this last case over the line had taken its toll on him. Five black boys—all under the age of ten—had been sexually assaulted, murdered and mutilated back in the late 1980s. Although Marsden wouldn't admit to it publicly, the original investigation had lacked anything like the rigor that should have been applied. The cold case, filed in three binders known as murder books, had received scant review over the years until he and Powers had first looked at it last year. The evidence that they had found in the Property Room amounted to just one banker's box. Their painstaking work, practically starting from scratch, had all been worth it, culminating in the arrest, conviction and now the life-imprisonment of one Peter Ray Maddox II.

Marsden sighed again as he stared at the photographs of his wife and twin daughters, pinned to the green soft-wall cubicle divider that separated his booth from that of his partner. His wife, Judith, had recently been diagnosed with breast cancer and every time he left her to go to work voluntarily in a job that had consumed his whole life, it tore at his conscience.

In Marsden's peripheral vision, Powers slid his chair back and stared at him. 'What's with all the sighing, man? Jesus, we won. Come on. Maddox is never getting out.'

He forced a smile. Of course, he was delighted and relieved about the conviction, but he was also damned tired, and his family needed more of him. 'I think I'm going to retire—like, for real this time.'

Powers rolled his eyes. 'Wow, you've never said *that* before. Oh…no…wait. You said it last week. And the week before that and the week before that and—'

'Hey, this wasn't what I had in mind for my retirement,' Marsden protested. 'Golf. Extended vacations in Europe. Time with my grandkids. *That* was my vision for my twilight years, I'll have you know.'

Powers laughed. 'Twilight years… Jesus, listen to you. Okay, one more case and I'll let you go. We'll make it a good one to go out on.'

This time, it was Marsden's turn to roll his eyes. He knew exactly the case that Powers wanted them to work.

'Come on, it'll be like in the movies,' Powers pleaded. 'Twenty-six-year-old charismatic, ethnically diverse and handsome cop, partnered with miserable old white dude who keeps insisting he'll retire but doesn't. They take on one last case and it just so happens to be the biggest of both their careers. Bigger than Golden State, bigger than BTK, Bundy, Gacy or Dahmer. *You know* what I'm talking about.'

'Not as big as Sam Little, though,' Mitzi Roberts said with a smile, appearing from the other side of Marsden's booth.

'Yeah, whatever,' Powers replied. 'So, you nailed the worst serial killer in U.S. history—what about it?'

'And thank God you did,' Marsden said, acknowledging Roberts's tenacious tracking down and capture of the man who had confessed to murdering at least ninety-three women.

Roberts was attractive with sympathetic eyes and a gentle-but-tough demeanor that commanded authority. 'All in a day's work,' she said with a casual shrug.

Powers extended his arm toward Marsden and said, 'Hey, maybe if you take on this case *you* might get a character in a book based on you.'

Marsden grinned at the reference to the author Michael Connelly's having based Renée Ballard, an LAPD detective, on Roberts. He sat up straight in his chair and nodded. 'Yeah, I could see that.'

'I mean, you'd never be as cool as Renée Ballard or Harry Bosch, of course,' Roberts countered.

'Whatever,' Marsden muttered.

'So, come on,' Powers enthused. 'Let's take it on. End your career on the sexiest murder book in Robbery-Homicide Division history. Can we do it, Mitzi?'

Without it being spelled out, Marsden could see that Roberts knew exactly to which case they were referring. He could also see that she wasn't convinced. As Reserve Police Officers, they worked without remuneration, so were usually permitted to take on any cold case that interested them. But this one was different.

Finally, Roberts answered. 'This case has been pulled up so many times in the twenty-seven years that I've worked in RHD, and nobody has managed to crack it; it's the department's great white whale. Just what do you two think you're going to do differently this time around, may I ask?'

Roberts and Marsden looked at Powers for the magic answer.

'DNA,' he said with exaggerated enthusiasm.

'Wow,' Roberts replied. 'If only we'd thought of that before now.'

Marsden laughed at seeing Powers's face fall.

'His DNA has been tested *so many* times,' Roberts said.

'But has anyone tried investigative genetic genealogy before?' Powers countered.

'No,' Roberts answered. 'But do you know how much of his DNA is left?'

Powers shook his head.

'Thirty picograms. That's it,' she answered. 'And you know how much one picogram is?'

'A spoonful?' Powers guessed.

'Okay. Let me tell you. So, one picogram is equal to about one trillionth of a gram,' Roberts explained. 'To put it another way, we have about half the weight of a single grain of table salt of this guy's DNA left.'

'Not enough to test, then?' Powers intuited with a sigh.

'It *could* be enough to test,' Roberts revealed. 'But it would consume the entire sample. If it's degraded or insufficient, then we've got nothing left to ever test against in the future.'

'So, that's a no, then?' Powers said.

'It's…not a no. It's a big consideration. Let me take it to the captain,' she replied. 'I'm meeting with him this morning, so I'll ask.'

Powers grinned. 'Can we look at the murder book while we wait?'

'Sure, go ahead,' Roberts said.

Powers looked at Marsden. 'Let me guess. You wanna go look at the original murder book rather than the more easily navigated digitized version?'

'I just prefer to see it right in front of me—it feels more real that way,' Marsden said.

Powers jumped up. 'Let's go.'

Marsden exhaled at length, cast an uncertain look at Roberts, then followed Powers to the file room at the far end of the fifth floor. The windowless room was dominated by bookshelves filled with blue three-ring binders, all of them containing LA cold cases back to their first in 1899. Murder books were the heart and soul of a case, holding records, photos, documents, recordings, witness statements and lists of what evidence existed in the Property Room.

'After you,' Powers said, taking a deferential step back and silently acknowledging Marsden's long-standing history with the department.

Marsden knew the vault intimately. He'd been working here as a detective in the elite Robbery-Homicide Division since the cold case unit was first established back in November 2001 when there had been over 10,000 unsolved murders in LA just for the period of 1960 to 1997.

Marsden ignored the first few shelves of bound volumes that contained single-page summations of all the murders that had occurred in the city and walked down a narrow passage between two tall shelves of murder books, coming to a stop partway down. He reluctantly raised his left hand and indicated four blue plastic binders.

Powers lifted down the first file. 'We can catch this guy. One final case for the dynamic duo, Marsden and Powers, and it happens to be the sexiest, biggest case of all time: the Hollywood Strangler.'

For what felt like the hundredth time that day, Marsden sighed, finding himself lifting down the three remaining murder books and piling them up in Powers's hands. 'We don't even know if we're cleared to work it yet. And I swear to God, this will be my last case, whether we close it or not.'

Powers winked at him. 'Let's get to work.'

Marsden led the way back to their workstations, where they set about reviewing one of the toughest unsolved serial murders in the Cold Case Homicide Unit, starting with the short case summary report.

The Hollywood Strangler
Active 1980-1986
6 victims, 2 male, 4 female
Victims all bit-part actors and actresses in the movie industry. Perpetrator entered their homes at night. Victims strangled and then displayed in a tableau from movies they had appeared in.

Marsden then moved on to the chronological record of the case, the opening document for each murder book in the department, which charted every action taken by the detectives running the original investigation, as well as the subsequent reviews that had taken place over the years.

Almost two hours later, Roberts appeared at Marsden's desk. 'Okay, you've got one last roll of the DNA dice.'

'Yes!' Powers exclaimed, flexing his biceps.

'But,' Roberts added, 'you know this is going to consume the whole sample, so please make it count.'

'Thanks,' Marsden said uncertainly. He knew that they were fortunate even to be permitted to run a final test that would exhaust the whole sample; some states prohibited doing so without a court order. Despite his reluctance, it would be an amazing end to his career if they could solve the Hollywood Strangler case, but it was way more than a big *if*. The case had defeated dozens of his colleagues over the past forty-two years and had been the subject of numerous films, documentaries, podcasts, and true crime investigations. It was way more than a big *if*.

Chapter Two

Tuesday, September 13, 2022, Los Angeles, California

It was day two of Marsden and Powers's review of the Hollywood Strangler case. Neither man needed to familiarize themselves with the basics of the investigation. It was one that any detective who had worked in RHD for more than a few years knew well. Like several other infamous serial killers in the U.S., this one rose above the thousands of other unsolved homicides, partly because of its uniqueness and partly because of its intimate connection to the industry that gave the unknown killer his sensational alias. The case was a big hitter among true crime aficionados and armchair detectives. A slew of potential suspect names had been bandied around over the years, ranging from famous directors, major Hollywood actors and even some of the other serial killers operating in LA at that time, such as the Grim Sleeper or the Scorecard Killer. But, owing to the very specific M.O. of the Hollywood Strangler, it was the belief among most detectives who had reviewed the case over the years, that none of these people was in fact the killer.

Marsden was in the process of making a request through the LAPD Lab's Forensic Science Division to have the tiny remaining DNA sample sent out to Gene by Gene, the parent company of Family Tree DNA, in readiness for the investigative genetic genealogy process.

'This guy sure is one sick puppy,' Powers mumbled from his adjacent desk.

Marsden peered over the half-wall and saw Powers looking at copies of the Polaroids that had been left at each crime scene.

'Jesus,' Powers said, looking at a photograph of the first victim, Babette Monroe, sitting down on a sofa with a cigarette in one hand poised at the mouth and a glass in the other hand. Her legs were crossed at the ankles and her immaculately made-up face was looking directly at the camera. She was wearing an exact copy of the glamorous, black evening dress that she had worn in her final appearance in the B-Movie, *Fleeing to France*. The Polaroid was a typical still shot from a Hollywood movie. The only trouble was that Babette Monroe had been dead when that picture had been taken. Powers leaned in to take a closer look. 'How'd he make it look so realistic?'

'Fluorocarbon fishing line—tough and near invisible for the lighter body parts—then some kind of polycarbonate wire for the heavy parts. All that, suspended from a wooden frame that he built.'

'Wow,' Powers muttered.

'You know, honestly, it's way worse when you see it for real. I mean, in the room with the bodies right there,' Marsden commented.

Powers shot him an incredulous look. 'What? You were *on* this case?'

'No,' Marsden replied. 'I was still over in Ventura for the first victims. But in 1986, I was temporarily partnered with a guy who was working it. I was with him on the call to Tracie Satchell's house and saw the final two victims.'

'What was it like seeing it for real?' Powers asked, setting down the binder and giving Marsden his undivided attention.

Marsden drew in a long breath. 'I don't even know how many murders I've been to over the years… Or how many victims of serial killers I've seen in my career… But this one… Well, this one, still to this day, sends shivers right down my spine. This might sound weird, but… If Tracie Satchell and Christian Lofthouse hadn't been dead—like, if this guy'd actually used mannequins or some such—it would have been a real work of art. You see, he had recreated a love scene from the movie, *Garbo's Wishes*. Tracie was sitting astride Christian, hands raised in the air—like she was surrendering—and him holding onto her shoulders.' Marsden paused. '*Every single* one of their fingers was tied up with wire in a perfect position. I mean, not a *single* digit seemed to be out of place.'

'Jesus,' Powers mumbled. 'So, how did he manage to get Tracie and Christian in the same place at the same time to kill them?'

'Oh, they were actually a couple in real life. Got together on the set of *Garbo's Wishes*. According to friends and neighbors, Christian stayed at her place most of the time.'

Powers seemed confused again and referred to the open murder books on his desk as he asked, 'And he sexually assaulted *both* of them?'

Marsden nodded. 'Uh-huh.'

'And then he just stopped?' Powers questioned. 'Just like that?'

'Yeah, they were his last known victims. No other murders even *remotely* similar occurred after Tracie and Christian.'

'Entered into HITMAN?' Powers asked.

'Yeah,' Marsden confirmed, impressed that Powers had even heard of the now obsolete Homicide Information Tracking and Management Automation Network, an early in-house computer program that compared local crimes. 'That's why everyone assumes the guy must have died.'

'And no idea at all about who he was?' Powers asked, flipping open one of the murder books and searching for a specific page. 'Weren't there…wasn't it like eighty-something suspects?'

'Uh-huh, something like that, yeah,' Marsden confirmed.

'I take it puppeteers in the movie industry were looked at?'

Marsden nodded. 'Very closely. Some of them made the suspect list.'

'One-nineties?'

'One-nineties all eliminated over the years by DNA,' Marsden confirmed, referencing the California law which gave convicted sex offenders the numerical nickname.

'So, what else was the DNA tested for?' Powers asked.

'Wait. Let me find the breakdown,' Marsden said, sitting back down at his own desk. He pushed his keyboard to one side and opened the fourth murder book, flicking through to the summary of evidence. Having found what he was looking for, he read it out to Powers: '*1996. Autopsy swabs sent to Intermountain Forensic Laboratories. Results back with a DNA profile of an unidentified male. CODIS checked with no results. Several suspects re-interviewed and DNA tested against the sample—all ruled out. June 2000, evidence re-tested. More suspects eliminated. February 2017, evidence tested for Y-DNA. Match found on fifty-three of sixty-seven markers—*'

'That sounds positive,' Powers interjected.

Marsden looked up. 'Yeah, it sounds it. But while it does imply a common ancestor between the killer and the person he matched, that common ancestor would be about eight hundred or so years ago. So…'

'Right.'

'Um, *March 2020, California Department of Justice approved Familial*

Searches of the statewide database. No kinship arrests for violent felonies.' Marsden shrugged.

'Meaning?'

'Meaning…that none of the killer's first-degree family members—parent, sibling or child—were in the database.'

'And now we have the final scrap of DNA left for IGG,' Powers noted. 'No pressure, then, huh?'

'Nope,' Marsden muttered, sitting back in his chair, staring at the murder books that contained over four thousand pages, almost nine hundred contacts and interviews and more than eighty suspects. What was he even doing taking on *one final case*? His wife, Judith, was at home quietly dealing with her cancer, and here *he* was, working a job that had nearly killed him several times over; all for a meager stipend of $650 a year. He looked at the photo of his wife and kids. Then, not for the first time in his career, he put himself in the position of the victims' families, imagining just for a few seconds the anguish and grief that they had endured for the past four decades.

On the computer screen was the email for the DNA request. As Roberts had said, this was the final chance for the Hollywood Strangler case. If he clicked send, he knew that he would have to give it everything he had to do justice to the victims and to the thousands of hours that his colleagues before him had already poured into the case over the last forty-two years.

He had to try.

He clicked send and the request was gone.

One final roll of the DNA dice.

Chapter Three

Tuesday, September 20, 2022, Salt Lake City, Utah

Madison Scott-Barnhart stood up from her desk and walked over to the printer, watching as the final page spewed out from the indefatigable machine. She looked out of her fifth-floor window which overlooked Salt Lake City's Main Street, heaving with the usual early-morning commuter traffic pouring from the TRAX train. Although fall was fast-approaching, it was still comfortable outside with temperatures in the high seventies.

She gathered up the papers from the printer, opened her office door and entered the open-plan space occupied by the team of her investigative genetic genealogy company, Venator. 'Okay, quick team briefing, please, guys,' she called out.

Kenyatta, her second-in-command, looked up from her workstation. 'Team briefing? Didn't we have one last thing yesterday?'

'Uh-huh,' Maddie said, moving to the front of the office with the paperwork pressed to her chest. She positioned herself in front of the three large boards that were the working hub of the company's operation. The center board was a six-foot-wide, interactive digital whiteboard which was largely used by her staff to present their findings during briefings. To the left, and with equivalent dimensions, was a glass writing board, and to the right, a regular whiteboard.

'Well, I hope you're not expecting to see any progress,' Kenyatta muttered as she finished typing something into her computer.

Maddie ran a hand through her blonde, shoulder-length hair, waiting until she had the attention of the whole team, currently consisting of just her receptionist, Ross, her deputy, Kenyatta, and one of her expert genetic genealogists, Hudson.

'Okay…' Maddie began. 'Now, before I say anything else, I'm going to need you to sign these.' She walked quickly to the three members of staff, placing a two-page document in front of each of them.

'NDAs?' Kenyatta exclaimed. 'Are you serious?'

'We've never had to sign non-disclosure agreements before…'

Hudson commented, skim-reading the document.

'I have to sign it, too?' Ross asked incredulously.

'Yes. You *all* do.'

'What's it all about?' Hudson asked.

'I can't comment until you've signed it,' Maddie said, enjoying the air of mystery that she was creating.

'Well, looking at the bottom, I can see it's LAPD,' Kenyatta observed, shooting a look at Maddie. 'Wait. Zodiac?'

'I don't think Zodiac was LA, was he? More Northern California,' Hudson said. 'What about…the Southside Slayer?'

'My lips are NDA-sealed,' Maddie said with a light laugh.

'The Westside Rapist?' Ross suggested.

Maddie laughed. 'I quite literally cannot and will not confirm or deny anything until you've all signed the document.'

'Wow,' Kenyatta said, quickly adding her signature to the bottom of the document and handing it to Maddie. 'Done. Now, tell me! Come on, out with it!'

Hudson and Ross followed suit and waved their forms aloft, ready for Maddie to collect them.

Although Maddie trusted her team implicitly, she quickly checked the signature lines before taking each of them in, one at a time.

'Oh, come on… For heaven's sake!' Kenyatta said. 'This isn't *American Idol*, you know. We don't need a dramatic pause to build up the suspense.'

'Oh, I think you do,' she replied wryly. 'The case is…' She gave them the dramatic pause, looking at them each in turn.

'Maddie! Enough already,' Kenyatta called.

'The Hollywood Strangler,' she finally revealed with a smile, receiving a collective gasp from the team.

'No way, José!' Hudson muttered. 'That's awesome.'

'Hang on. I heard a podcast talking about this case and I thought all the DNA had been used up.' Ross said.

'There's a tiny amount left. And, yes, this will use up the last sample. It's being processed right now, and the results should be through on FTDNA any day. Two detectives from LAPD are coming up tomorrow to brief us on the case.'

'Wait, you're saying this is starting right away?' Kenyatta asked. Maddie nodded.

'Can we cope?' Hudson asked. 'I guess we should have Becky's replacement on the team by then?'

'Exactly. I've narrowed it down to three excellent candidates,' Maddie answered. 'They've all been interviewed and are definitely up to the job. So, it's now coming down to them demonstrating their IGG skills in the mock assignment, which is due in at noon today.'

'Well, you're the boss,' Kenyatta said, returning to her work.

'Sounds to me like we're going to be *mighty* busy,' Hudson commented.

As Maddie headed back to her office, she knew that the small team didn't share her confidence that they could cope with such a huge additional case. Maybe they were right. The Hollywood Strangler would be their biggest, most high-profile case ever. Maybe that was why she had been reluctant to turn it down, even though she had declined plenty of others recently. It didn't help that a key member of her staff, Becky, was on a sabbatical with no date confirmed for her return. Although she was out of the country, Becky still undertook some work for Venator when she could and because of that, Maddie had also had her sign an NDA.

In the company's small kitchenette, Maddie made herself some coffee, then walked back into her office. She put the cup on her desk beside the framed photographs of her husband, Michael, and her three kids; then she placed the NDAs back on the printer and hit the scan button. Since she had founded Venator in June 2018 she'd never encountered the need to sign an NDA for a case. If they could close this one, it would be huge for the company and huge for the burgeoning IGG industry. But simply having a suspect's DNA did not mean that they could close the case. Although Venator's success rate was above the industry average of around eighty-five percent, they had their own fair share of cold cases that—for a variety of reasons— remained currently unsolvable.

Maddie sipped her coffee, watching as the documents passed in and out of the scanner, then she sat down and sent them as attachments to the detective in charge of the case.

She took a cursory glance at her emails, seeing that she had sixty-seven unread. She would get to them at some point, but since she was short-staffed, she needed to prioritize around working on her current case.

Maddie was ten days into working on a set of unidentified human remains, dubbed Wind River Doe, for the area in Wyoming state where the remains of a man had been discovered five years ago. Detectives had recently reopened the case, hoping to learn more about who the man might have been. The remains belonged to a biological male, believed to have been in his twenties or thirties. His cause of death had not been established. Fragments of surviving clothing—including a Chemise Lacoste shirt that had ceased being manufactured in 1980—pointed to a date of death around the late 1970s or early 1980s.

Up until Wind River Doe's DNA had been uploaded to FTDNA and GEDmatch Pro, that was almost all that had been known about him. Maddie's first discovery about the Doe had been his ethnicity, which had suggested very strongly that he had been African American. At FTDNA, his estimate for Guinea & Sierra Leone had been 49%, with lower ranges given for Nigeria and North Mexico.

Maddie hated the Doe appellation that was routinely ascribed to unidentified human remains; she felt that it was no better than an impersonal number imposed on a prisoner. Where possible, she named her Does something more humane. In Wind River Doe's case, she had named him Leon Sierra, as a fitting twist on his suggested ethnicity.

The high likelihood that Leon was of African American descent was evidenced in the severely low number of DNA cousin matches that Maddie had found in the databases. Leon's highest cousin match was with a man named Malik Johnson. The two men shared just seventy-nine centimorgans of DNA, meaning that the common ancestor for whom Maddie was searching could be several generations in the past. The process of finding a common ancestor was a difficult and often highly complex task, but with African American heritage was often much harder still. It was the often-overlooked paradox in the investigative genetic genealogy field. Though most U.S. murder victims were black men, the vast majority of cold cases, including those picked up by Venator, were for young white women.

Maddie had read a study in *The Atlantic* last year which had troubled her. They had reported that out of more than one hundred investigative genetic genealogy cases from April 2018 to April 2020, just four had been for a black victim. The article went on to explore the myriad of complicated reasons behind this fact, pointing out that people of color had been generally more cautious about uploading their DNA to databases to which law enforcement would have access. Therefore, there had been fewer cousin matches within the genealogy databases, thus making cases all the harder to be solved. Maddie had also heard of many people of color losing trust and taking down their DNA tests from consumer websites in the aftermath of George Floyd's death in May 2020.

'Then there's the huge vacuum of documentary evidence for most African Americans before 1870,' Hudson had added when the point had come up in a team briefing to discuss their various findings.

Kenyatta had drawn an imaginary circle in the air with her finger as she'd said, 'Which comes back round to detectives prioritizing cases with higher solvability and picking a more newsworthy pretty young white girl.'

'And so, it goes on,' Maddie had agreed.

'We're over-policed when we don't need to be and we're under-policed when we do,' Kenyatta had summarized. 'And, you know, forty percent of missing persons cases in the U.S. are Black people, despite the fact we only make up about thirteen percent of the population.'

Maddie had solemnly nodded her agreement, resolving to try and seek more balance in the cases that Venator would take on in the future.

Despite the inherent difficulties in the research, Maddie had easily identified Malik Johnson's parents, all four grandparents and all eight great-grandparents. She now clicked to open the 1870 U.S. Census entry—the first to have recorded the names of all African American inhabitants—that she had saved to the profile of Wyatt Johnson, one of Malik's sixteen great-great-grandparents.

Wyatt Johnson had been recorded on the census as an eight-year-old boy living in Houston, Texas, with his farm-laborer father, James, and his mother, Caroline. All three family members were stated to have been born in Texas.

Not for the first time, Maddie studied the entry, searching for any additional clues that could help her track down James and Caroline Johnson on the 1860 census, a task that had so far eluded her. In all likelihood, they would have been among the 90% of African Americans still enslaved at that point in history and, therefore, had not been named alongside the rest of the free population. The Slave Schedules for the same year provided no additional information, simply naming the slave owners and giving the enslaved person's age, sex and color.

The solution was obvious: to pass Leon Sierra over to Kenyatta who specialized in African American genealogical research and often presented for the Afro-American Historical and Genealogical Society. But Maddie was stubborn and wanted to crack this one for herself.

Turning her attention to James Johnson, she opened *Texas Death Certificates 1903-1982* at Ancestry and typed in his details. She spent some time wading through the search results, none of them apparently correct. Then, as she neared the bottom of the page, she viewed the scan of an original death certificate which looked as though it could be right.

Full Name: James Johnson
Date of Death: Nov 7, 1909
Place of Death: Freemen's Town, Houston, Texas
Residence: 1311 Andrews Street, Freemen's Town, Houston, Texas
Length of Residence in Texas: whole life
Date of Birth: 1841
Sex: Male
Color or Race: Colored
Alien or Citizen: Citizen
Single, Married, Widowed or Divorced: Widowed
Birthplace: Texas
Name of Father: Spencer Johnson
Birthplace of Father: Unknown
Maiden name of Mother: Mary Henry
Birthplace of Mother: Unknown

The information on the certificate fit with the facts that Maddie already knew about James; that he had died by 1910, was predeceased by his wife, and that he had resided at Andrews Street in Freemen's Town, an area largely created by African Americans following Emancipation in 1863.

Maddie added the names of James Johnson's parents to Malik's family tree, then repeated the death search for Wyatt and his mother.

Ross, Maddie's receptionist, appeared at her office door, drawing her out of over two and a half hours' worth of engrossing but frustratingly fruitless research.

'Maddie, I've got the candidates' case studies in,' he informed her, holding up three manilla envelopes.

'Great. Thank you,' Maddie said, standing up to take the documents before placing them down on her desk, secretly grateful to have a break from the endless brick walls that she had been encountering while trying to build a family tree for Leon Sierra.

Maddie opened the top-most file from the first candidate, Shelby Davis Griffin. Shelby had interviewed well and possessed a wealth of genetic genealogy experience, as had the other two applicants, Annette Crafton Corbell and Hudson's roommate, Reggie Snowwolf. It would all come down to how they had interpreted and possibly solved the mini-investigation Maddie always set for the job applicants.

Giving them just four days to complete the task, Maddie had sent the prospective candidates a newspaper article with the very simple brief: *Who was Roland T. Owen?* The story was about a man named Roland T. Owen who had died in mysterious circumstances in a hotel in 1935. He had been found naked in his room in the Hotel President, tied by the wrists and ankles to the bed and strangled to death. The newspaper had stated that his clothing, comprising a wool suit, collared shirt and tie, trilby hat, underwear and socks had all been neatly folded and placed in a pile at the foot of the bed. Beside the stack of clothing had been the man's shoes, silver pocket watch, wallet containing twelve dollars cash, and a pair of cufflinks with purple violets imprinted on them. A single-breasted jacket with the initials RE had been found hanging behind the door. The victim had been found to have an appendix-removal scar.

And that was all that Maddie had given them to go on, deliberately giving them little time, no clue as to where the story had come from and no further details beyond that which the story presented. Past successful candidates—including Kenyatta and Hudson—had been able to sift through a range of online documents, newspaper articles and family trees to work out that Roland T. Owen was actually a man named Roger Eisenhower.

Maddie flicked through Shelby Davis Griffin's submitted response to the task, smiling at the familiar records which showed that she had worked along exactly the right lines. The final page in her submission was a neat and concise conclusion of her findings which correctly identified Roger Eisenhower. 'Well, you've passed,' Maddie said, closing the folder and setting it to the side.

Next, she opened Annette Crafton Corbell's file, seeing from the very first line that she had also correctly named Roger Eisenhower as being the man featured in the story. There then followed a long list of source documents which definitely met the threshold for Genealogical Proof Standard. 'And you have passed, also.'

She opened the final file, from Reggie Snowwolf, and saw from his opening conclusions that he had incorrectly identified Roland T. Owen as another man, one named Jackson Miller. At least that was one candidate eliminated, Maddie thought, starting to worry that perhaps the test had somehow become too easy. She was about to close Reggie's file when the sheer volume of supporting documents that he had included suddenly piqued her interest. It was *a lot* of information for an incorrect response. She returned to his conclusion, reading it in more detail.

Roland T. Owen was a pseudonym for a man whose birth name was Jackson Miller. Jackson was born May 20, 1900, in New Brunswick, Canada. He died in mysterious circumstances on June 10, 1935. This case study, which includes references and sources, gives an outline of his complicated life.

As Maddie read on, checking all Reggie's meticulous sourcing as she went, she became increasingly confused. Everything that she was reading pointed to his actually being correct. She stood up from her desk, walked over to her office door and called Hudson over.

'Your roommate,' Maddie began when he arrived.

'Yeah?'

'Be honest. And I really don't know how else to ask you this. But...did you help him at all with his job application?' Maddie asked, holding up the manilla file.

Hudson shook his head. 'No, not in the slightest. I jokingly said I wasn't going to help, and he said that he didn't want me to help him because if he couldn't do it by himself, then the job wasn't for him. I mean, I can tell you he worked *real* hard on it, but nothing at all came from me. Not even a clue.'

'Okay,' Maddie said, instantly believing him.

'I take it, then, that he worked out that the guy was Roger Eisenhower?' Hudson said with a smirk, evidently recalling his own application where he had worked the exact same case.

'No...actually,' Maddie replied.

Hudson looked surprised. 'I don't get it. You think I might have helped him give the *wrong* name?'

'I haven't finished reading his submission yet, but he's proposing that Roger Owen was really a guy named Jackson Miller.'

'What?'

'Uh-huh. I need to finish reading it all to see just where he went wrong. He has clearly put so much effort into this, so I owe him that much,' Maddie said, twisting around and heading back into her office.

She sat down at her desk with a sigh, suddenly feeling daunted by the scale of the work she now had in front of her. She loved her job and wasn't afraid of hard work, but it felt right now as though everything had become more complicated than it needed to be.

Looking down at the three files in front of her, Maddie half-wondered about *not* bothering to finish reading through Reggie Snowwolf's application after all. The other two candidates had identified the correct answer, had interviewed well and would fit right in with the Venator team, so why bother trying to unstitch Reggie's incorrect conclusions just to offer him insight into where and how he'd gone wrong? But her gut instinct—something that she relied on so heavily in her job—was telling her to continue reading through his submission for clarity. But first, she needed a drink.

Maddie picked up her empty mug, headed out into the kitchen area and poured herself some fresh coffee. She carried it back to her office, casting a quick glance over the floor as she went, smiling at the diligence of her staff and, not for the first time, feeling grateful to have such an outstanding team. This was why getting the right candidate for the job would be so critical. She could envisage each of the three applicants fitting into the team just fine in their own way; but she only had one job to offer.

She sighed, sipped her coffee and picked up Reggie Snowwolf's file again, continuing to read where she had left off. If nothing else, she wanted to see how on earth he'd managed to produce so many documents which ultimately led to a false conclusion.

Maddie ended a phone call and rose from her desk at 4:45 p.m., feeling somewhat floored by Reggie Snowwolf's findings, which she had just finished reading and cross-checking. She carried his manilla folder out to the main office, making her way to the front of the room and positioning herself in front of the digital whiteboard. 'Okay, team,' she called out. 'Can I grab you all for just a few minutes, please?'

'Almost done,' Kenyatta said.

'With you,' Hudson said, swiveling his chair to face Maddie.

While she waited for Kenyatta to finish up, Maddie took a glance down at the folder in her hand, still somewhat bemused.

'Okay, done,' Kenyatta said.

'Right,' Maddie began, 'I just wanted to update you on the vacancy. I just got off the phone with the successful candidate and offered the job…which was duly accepted. I'm pleased to announce that Reggie Snowwolf—Hudson's roommate—will be starting work here with us, first thing tomorrow.'

'You gave him the job?' Hudson asked incredulously. 'But you said he'd messed up and got the wrong name for Roland Owen.'

Maddie shook her head. 'Actually… *We* got the wrong name for Roland Owen. All of us.'

'What?' Kenyatta stammered. 'It's Roger Eisenhower. I should know, I had to identify the man to get my job here!'

'Me too,' Hudson concurred.

Maddie shook her head again. 'Nope.' She held up Reggie's folder. 'Everything in here proves pretty conclusively that Roland T. Owen was actually a man called Jackson Miller.'

'But… But how?' Kenyatta mumbled. 'Now, I'm going to need to see that file.'

Maddie rubbed her eyes, still flummoxed as to how she had been blindsided by Reggie's work. 'You're welcome to comb through his findings but, basically, everybody who's successfully—or so I thought—worked this case, has followed the paper trail through various newspaper articles to the official police reports, which are available online, and included a headshot of his corpse and, crucially, a signed confession that his name was Roger Eisenhower. That in turn leads back to finding Roger on the 1910 census and a birth record. Case closed.'

'And Reggie didn't find that, or what?' Hudson said.

'Oh, he found all that, alright,' Maddie replied. 'Then, he somehow managed to get a death certificate from the courthouse that showed that Roger Eisenhower had died in 1913.'

'So, wait a minute. How did he work out that Roland was Jackson Miller?'

'The cufflinks that were found in the hotel room,' Maddie answered.

'What about them?' Hudson asked.

'They had purple violets on them,' Maddie said. 'Nothing I've ever found documented anything more about them, but Reggie investigated them and found that they're—'

'—The provincial flower of New Brunswick, Canada,' Hudson interjected, nodding in recognition as he spoke. 'I should have gotten that. Damn it.'

Kenyatta shot him a look of uncertainty. 'Why should *you* have gotten it?'

'I grew up in Madawaska, Maine, right across the St John's River is New Brunswick. From my grandpa's grave, I can literally see the town of Edmundston. I *know* the provincial flower is a purple violet.

Jeez!'

'Right,' Kenyatta said. 'But knowing that it might be related to New Brunswick doesn't mean much on its own. That narrows it down to—what—a few hundred thousand people?'

'Then, he searched the First World War Canadian Expeditionary Force attestation records for anyone with a scar and cross-checked them all until he found ones with just an appendix scar,' Maddie explained. 'He then ran that list through the St Albans records which list land crossings between Canada and the U.S., finally giving him one name: Jackson Miller.'

'That *is* impressive,' Ross said.

'Then, he tracked him to Chicago,' Maddie continued, 'where Jackson married and had two kids. The final piece of evidence is this.' Maddie held up a newspaper print out. The story would be illegible from where her team were sitting, but that wasn't what she was trying to show them.

Kenyatta gasped. 'It's him,' she said, leaning to get a closer look at the photograph that accompanied the story under the headline: MISSING PERSON.

'Oh yeah. It is him,' Maddie confirmed.

'So, then what happened?' Kenyatta asked.

'Then, for reasons unknown, Jackson Miller took on the identity of one Roger Eisenhower,' Maddie explained.

'Oh my gosh. He's a *way* better researcher than us phonies,' Hudson conceded with a laugh.

Maddie smiled and lowered the folder. 'Well, let's see how he fits in with the team. Thanks for your efforts. See you in the morning.'

'Don't forget the job's only temporary,' Ross reminded her.

'Yeah, I know. The job's his until Becky decides to come back,' Maddie replied, returning to her office and immediately feeling daunted all over again by her huge, remaining workload. On top of preparing for a new member of staff starting tomorrow, she had two detectives arriving from LA with Venator's most high-profile case to date.

Chapter Four

Tuesday, September 20, 2022, Los Angeles, California

Reserve Police Officer Ted Marsden was sitting down at his desk in the LAPD Police Headquarters Facility. The fifth floor was practically deserted and those who were working were either on the graveyard shift engaged in an urgent case or simply had no real reason to go home.

Marsden was putting the final touches on a presentation that he'd been asked to create for Venator, the investigative genetic genealogy company that was going to analyze the DNA in the Hollywood Strangler case. He and Powers would fly to Salt Lake City tomorrow morning to talk through the investigation with the team. In truth, he couldn't really grasp the process and, at this point in his career, he really didn't much care to try; he just wanted to close the case and finally get to retire.

To the side of his desk was the fourth and final murder book for the cold case, open at the Investigator's Chronology which he'd read countless times already. He and Powers had been working almost non-stop for the past week reviewing the files. As Marsden had warned Powers before they had begun, there were very few avenues or leads that hadn't already been picked up in previous reviews. Although he wouldn't vocalize it, Marsden felt as though he was just going through the motions of ticking boxes. He knew that these murder books had been churned over a half dozen times since the original investigation—which he deemed to have been rigorous—and nothing new of any value had come up.

'Eat!' Powers suddenly instructed from behind him, thrusting a McDonalds bag down on the desk.

'Thanks,' Marsden replied, opening it up and pulling out a double cheeseburger. 'Smells good.'

'I'm literally starving to death,' Powers commented from his booth, shaking numerous packets of salt onto his fries. 'Hey, isn't this weird?'

'What?' Marsden said, taking a bite from the burger before

looking across.

Powers held up his index finger, at the end of which was a single grain of salt. 'We're relying on a DNA sample *half* the size of this?'

'Yeah, it is weird. Science has come a long way.'

'Let's hope it's come far enough to finally nail this guy,' Powers said, stuffing a handful of fries into his mouth. 'Is the presentation good to go?'

'Uh-huh,' Marsden confirmed. 'I mean, I think so. I know they've signed the NDAs, but just how much of this sicko's work do we need to share with them? Do they *need* to see evidence of his handiwork just for them to be able to draw his family tree?'

'Probably not, but then most of the crime scene photos are on the internet, anyway,' Powers pointed out. 'Besides, it might be a good way to get them on board—motivate them—do you know what I mean?'

'Uh-huh,' Marsden managed to agree with his mouth full of burger.

'You ready to watch these?' Powers asked, holding up a thumb drive.

Marsden nodded, grabbing his container of fries and wheeling his chair over next to Powers, who was plugging the thumb-drive into his computer. A technician from the Electronics Unit working out of the Piper Tech building had digitized a bunch of old VHS tapes with a tangential link to the case.

'Did you get anywhere with those?' Marsden asked, nodding his head to the Field Interview Cards on Powers's desk. They were three-by-five index cards that patrol officers had filled out on people they had stopped while out on routine patrol. Marsden had already been through those created on the nights around the murders with a fine-tooth comb and was now expanding his search for the days running up to each murder.

'Not yet,' Powers admitted. He hovered his mouse over the play button but turned to Marsden without clicking it. 'The answer is somewhere in those murder books, I'm damn sure of it.'

Marsden shrugged. 'Okay, play the first video.'

Powers clicked play, stuffing yet more salty fries into his mouth as he sat back to watch the screen.

White noise briefly filled the screen, then jaunty, daytime TV music accompanied a slow zoom in to a mock-up of a comfortable living-room scene from the early 1980s, complete with a fake tree outside of a fake window. Sitting cross-legged on a tan, leather sofa was the host, wearing a blue suit, red tie and white shirt. He smiled as the camera moved in for a close-up and he picked up with the script: *'Hi, I'm Gary Collins. Welcome to* Hour Magazine.*'* He was a man with a charismatic smile, in his forties with side-parted blond hair. *'Today we're going to be talking to a mother who has just given birth to her* third *set of triplets. That's right, third. We'll be finding out about how she and her husband cope with nine children under the age of six. But, first up, we've got an exclusive interview with the devastated father of Babette Monroe, believed to have been the first victim of the so-called Hollywood Strangler. Ladies and Gentlemen, please welcome Glenn Stoltman to the stage.'* The unseen audience clapped vigorously as a middle-aged man in a cream suit ambled onto the set with a haunting look of detachment that Marsden had seen time and again in the faces of victims' families who were unable to comprehend what had happened to their loved one.

As Marsden watched the victim's father take the seat next to the host, he was disappointed to discover that he'd reached the end of his French fries and reached over for a handful of Powers's.

'Hey, knock it off,' Powers complained. 'I'm trying to watch trashy daytime TV…which is what you'll be doing all the time if you retire, by the way.'

'That's *when* I retire,' Marsden corrected.

'*Thank you for joining us, Glenn,*' Gary Collins said solemnly. The camera cut to a close-up of Gary as he continued, '*It's coming up on three years since your daughter, Babette, was so brutally murdered and, despite a lot of publicity, nobody has been caught for her murder and just last week, the Hollywood Strangler apparently struck again with his third victim. How are you feeling right now?*'

'Pretty peachy, I should think,' Powers muttered, rolling his eyes.

Marsden watched as Glenn Stoltman took in a long breath. The camera zoomed in for a tight close-up of his grief-ravaged face. '*I'm numb, Gary, just absolutely numb. I'm in utter disbelief. I… I can't believe that my only daughter is gone. I can't believe the way in which she was taken from me.*

And…I just can't believe that this monster is still out there. It's totally unfathomable, it really is.'

Gary Collins nodded. *'Are you aware of any enemies your daughter might have had? Perhaps an old flame who might have struggled with their breakup? Or an ex-colleague jealous of her rise to fame?'*

'No…' Glenn answered, emotion cracking his voice. *'I know this gets said a lot, but everyone loved her. There's not one person that I can think of that even had a bad word to say about her.'*

The camera cut to a close-up of Gary Collins nodding sagely. *'Now, Robyn—or Babette, to use her stage name—was an ambitious actress. She was a rising star in Hollywood and—as I'm sure all of our viewers are aware—a scene from the movie,* Fleeing to France, *which she had a part in, was directly recreated after her death by her killer. Do you think that her death could have occurred because of her involvement in the movie industry?'*

'Yes, I do,' Glenn Stoltman confirmed. *'I think if she hadn't taken that part, she would still be with us here today. She was very security-conscious; always locked her doors and would rather roast in her bed than leave a window open at night.'*

Gary Collins gave a weak but compassionate smile. *'And the detectives working the case said the guy that did it would really have had to work hard to get into her apartment.'*

'Oh, yeah,' Glenn Stoltman said. *'She had a near miss over in Ventura and, since then, kept everything triple-locked. Lights on outside the property. Everything. This wasn't a chance opportunity; she was targeted by someone who'd got obsessed after watching that movie.'*

Marsden leaned across the desk and hit pause. 'What did that mean? What he said… A near miss in Ventura?'

'I don't know,' Powers replied.

'Make a note of that. See if somehow we missed her reporting a previous attack.'

Powers jotted something on his notepad and then clicked play again. Gary Collins resumed his interview. *'It's coming up to the third anniversary and we've now had a third death linked to this monster. How are you and your family coping without answers or reasons or justice for your daughter?'*

'We're really not,' Glenn Stoltman replied. *'My wife and I are simply existing. We're not living. Her brother, Caleb, is… Well, he's just not dealing with*

it well. Not at all.'

Marsden sighed, slumping back in his chair. Although he continued to watch Gary Collins interview the bereaved father of Babette Monroe, he couldn't stop thinking about this near miss in Ventura. There was nothing in the case files that related to any previous attack or attempted attack on her.

The interview ended with Glenn Stoltman leaving the stage to sympathetic audience applause and Gary Collins swiftly moving on with an introduction to the mother from Indiana who had given birth to three sets of triplets.

Powers killed the video and turned to Marsden. 'Shall I call up Ventura and ask if they have any previous cases relating to Robyn Stoltman?'

Marsden nodded. 'Good idea. I'm going to have a quick final check of this presentation for tomorrow, and then let's take a look at the next video.'

'Okay,' Powers agreed, picking up his phone and calling the Detective Bureau at Ventura PD to find out if Robyn Stoltman had filed any previous complaint or been involved in a crime in some way over there.

Marsden flicked through the presentation, still unsure of whether he was conveying too much or too little information. By the time he reached the end, he was satisfied that he had struck the right balance but, tomorrow, he would find out either way.

Powers hung up. 'Nothing at all recorded in Ventura for Robyn Stoltman. They even checked their cold cases…and nothing.'

'What about her alter-ego, Babette Monroe?' Marsden asked.

'Yeah, they checked both names and still nothing. Another dead end. Looks like it really does all come down to the DNA.'

'We gotta hope this Venator team is up to the job,' Marsden commented, saving the presentation to his thumb drive. 'Okay, come on. Let's watch the next video.'

Powers clicked play on the next digitized video, an appeal that had been broadcast nationwide on the *Unsolved Mysteries* program in 1986, after the final murders had taken place.

'It's going to be a long night,' Marsden complained.

Chapter Five

Wednesday, September 21, 2022, Salt Lake City, Utah

Maddie stepped out of her white RAV4 in the underground parking garage beneath the Kearns Building. She was wearing ripped, stone-washed jeans and a loose lumberjack shirt. She took her purse from the passenger seat, locked the car and strolled over to the elevator, slightly tense about the busy day ahead. She breathed out noisily, tucked her blonde curly hair behind her ears as she entered the elevator and then rode it up to the fifth floor.

'Well, hi. You're certainly eager,' Maddie said, seeing Ross and her newest member of staff, Reggie, chatting outside the Venator office.

'Gotta make a good impression,' Reggie answered with a grin. He was a handsome African American in his late twenties with bleached-blonde hair.

'Oh, trust me. You've already done that,' Maddie said, unlocking the office door. She faced Ross and asked, 'And how are you coping, living alone?'

'Yeah, I'm missing Becks,' Ross admitted, 'but…also rather enjoying having the apartment to myself.'

'I bet you are,' Maddie replied, knowing that Becky's place, paid for by her parents, was in an expensive part of town. 'Ross, could you show Reggie around the kitchen and point out the restroom, then show him to his desk, please?'

'Sure thing,' Ross said. 'Follow me.'

Maddie entered her office, put down her purse, started up her computer, then headed out to the kitchen area to make herself some coffee. She looked over at Reggie sitting down at his new workstation and laughing at something that Ross was saying or doing. She had a good feeling about her newest employee and hoped that he would fit right in with the Venator team.

Maddie sipped the coffee, printed off another non-disclosure agreement and opened a Zoom meeting. She left her office just as Hudson entered the main door with a smile on his face. 'Good morning,' he said. 'Are you all set to solve one of the country's biggest serial-killer cases?'

'Morning,' Maddie replied. '*If* we can solve it.'

'Oh, we can do it,' he said confidently.

The door opened again, and Kenyatta walked in with an air of confidence and enthusiasm. 'Good morning, team,' she called. 'How are we all doing today?' Before she had time for a response, she gasped and pointed at Reggie. 'There he is! The golden man of the hour! We are not worthy!'

Reggie laughed but Maddie could tell that he was mystified by the adoration. 'Ignore her. She's just plain jealous,' Maddie explained. 'You see, you're the only one of us to identify Roland T. Owen as Jackson Miller.'

'Really?' Reggie said.

'All in a day's work for you, though, huh?' Kenyatta said with a laugh, sitting down at her computer station.

'Yeah, you did well,' Maddie confirmed. 'But let's see how you get on with your first case. Oh…which reminds me… NDA coming right up.'

Maddie set down her coffee and grabbed the blank non-disclosure agreement from the printer and carried it over to Reggie. 'Assuming your discreet housemate hasn't gossiped to you already about it—' she shot a mock-serious look at Hudson '—we've got a pretty big case starting today, and you need to sign this before I can tell you any more about it.'

'It's not a big case; it's *huge*,' Hudson said. 'And, no. I haven't told him anything at all about it, obviously… Oh, I *wanted* to.'

Reggie signed the paper and Maddie whispered, 'The Hollywood Strangler.'

'No way!' Reggie exclaimed. 'Are you serious? Is this for real or some sort of initiation joke you're all having at my expense?'

Maddie shook her head and walked over to the front of the office, switching on the large digital whiteboard. She addressed the team. 'Now, I'm expecting the detectives here at any moment, so go get yourselves some coffee and be ready to take a lot of notes. Kenyatta, do you mind showing Reggie the ropes?'

'Sure,' Kenyatta agreed. 'But I'm really not sure who'll be teaching whom.'

Maddie smiled and returned to her office. She picked up her laptop and saw that Becky Larkin, her employee currently on sabbatical, had joined the Zoom meeting. 'Hey, Becky. Good to see you,' Maddie said. 'How's it going out there?'

'Hi, Maddie!' Becky greeted her enthusiastically. 'It's going great, thank you.' She pulled her mousey hair back into a band and glanced upward. 'But it would be much better if my ceiling fan actually worked.'

'Is it hot?'

'You could say that. It's over ninety most of the time at the moment. But it's really the humidity,' Becky replied.

'Right, sure,' Maddie said.

'Listen, I hope my internet connection holds out for this meeting, but I'll just rejoin if it drops out…and if it will let me. And, oh my God, I cannot believe you've landed the Hollywood Strangler. Thank you so much for bringing me in on it. I've always been totally fascinated by this case.'

'Well, you're the only person qualified to do geo-profiling and it might be important on this one,' Maddie said. This was largely true, although she was also holding out some hope that Becky might reveal how her own investigations had been going in Port-au-Prince. She had gone out to the Haitian capital over nine months ago to try and find out more about her father's business enterprises there, which also seemed to have involved Maddie's husband, Michael. In January 2015, Michael and two of his business associates, Artemon Bruce and Jay Craig, had visited Haiti as part of an infrastructure finance package created by Becky's father's company, The Larkin Investment and Finance Group. Within eleven months of the trip, Artemon Bruce and Jay Craig had been found dead in suspicious circumstances and Michael himself had disappeared from the face of the earth. In the intervening years, the trail to the truth about what had happened to Michael had gone cold and Maddie had resorted to looking for answers herself. Thus far, Becky had been evasive about her findings, telling Maddie only that she had been making slow progress.

'How's everyone else?' Becky asked.

'Good. Let me take you out to see them. They'll be really excited to see you,' Maddie said, carrying the laptop out to the main office. 'Hey, everyone, look who's dropped in.'

Kenyatta's eyes widened when she saw Becky on-screen, and Hudson came rushing over from his desk. At that moment, the main reception door opened and two thick-set men—one younger and one older, both recognizably detectives—entered the office.

'Here, take Becky. Introduce her to Reggie,' Maddie said, handing Hudson the laptop before walking over to the detectives and shaking their hands. 'Good morning, I'm Madison Scott-Barnhart. Maddie.'

'Good to meet you, Maddie,' said the older man with short hair and a goatee. 'I'm Reserve Police Officer Ted Marsden and this is Reserve Police Officer Travis Powers.'

'Come on in. Can we get you some coffee?' Maddie asked.

'No, we've just come from breakfast, thanks. So, we're good to go when you are,' Marsden answered.

'Nice set up you've got here,' Powers commented, glancing around the office floor.

'Thanks. We've got everything we need here; most important being my excellent team,' she said, turning to introduce her staff but instead finding them all huddled around her laptop, chatting to Becky. Maddie turned back to face the two detectives, 'Sorry. One of our team is currently on sabbatical in Haiti and is joining us on Zoom. They're just excitable and having a little catch up.'

Marsden offered a polite smile, held up a small thumb drive and asked, 'The presentation you wanted is on here. Where do you want us?'

Maddie directed him to the main computer that fed the interactive digital whiteboard. She took the thumb drive and opened up the PowerPoint presentation, which started with a pixelated image that Maddie had seen used on the internet multiple times over the years. Above a photo of the famous Hollywood sign was the word *The* and below it was the word *Strangler*, the letter *g* appearing as a noose rope. Maddie said nothing about it but felt that it was a little crass, and she found it sloppy to have merely copied and pasted the first image that would have cropped up on the internet.

With the presentation loaded, she turned to see that her team was back in professional mode, waiting and ready, with Becky positioned just in front of the detectives. 'Okay, Detectives, take it away,' Maddie said, handing Marsden the remote clicker and then sitting down on the other side of Kenyatta.

The two detectives introduced themselves, then Marsden pointed to the image on-screen and said, 'So, I'm guessing you've all heard of the Hollywood Strangler case, right?'

Maddie and her team nodded their heads and murmured their agreement that they were fully apprised of the case. Or at least, they knew as much as had been circulated in the news and social media over the years.

'I'm just going to give you a brief summary of the case; the full details that you asked for, like crime scene photos, victim biographies, etcetera are all on the thumb drive,' Marsden explained. 'Just before I begin, and to put you in the picture of what LA was like at the time, up to six serial killers are believed to have been operating independently there from the late 80s to the early 90s.'

'What?' Kenyatta said. 'Are you serious? Six?'

'Yes, ma'am. That's why it was known as the Killing Fields. The Hollywood Strangler was one of these six.'

Marsden moved the presentation on to a slide headed *VICTIM #1 ROBYN STOLTMAN / BABETTE MONROE*. Below the title was a photograph of the victim posed on a sofa, drinking and smoking and gazing at the camera. Owing to its shocking execution, it was the one main image associated with the case, shown time and again as a representation of the whole.

Powers stepped forward to talk. 'Robyn Stoltman was the first known victim of the Hollywood Strangler. She was murdered on October thirteenth, 1980. As with all the victims, the killer broke into her home while she slept, tied her up and changed—or forced her to change—into what she wore in her last movie, *Fleeing to France*. He styled her hair, put make-up on her and then, when she looked like she did in the movie, sexually assaulted her. Then he strangled her to death. After she was dead, he used types of fishing line and wire to create this horrific image that you see before you now, taken by the killer himself and left at the crime scene.'

'One thing I've never understood…' Kenyatta interrupted. 'Where was all that wire attached to? The ceiling?'

Powers shook his head. 'He built a wood frame to suspend all the wires from.'

'What?' Kenyatta stammered. 'So, he was literally in her apartment building a human marionette show? Dear God. Did the neighbors not hear anything…or see someone coming back and forth with a ton of wood and tools in the middle of the night?'

'Nope,' Marsden answered. 'I mean, yes, some of them heard noise but it was during the daytime after he'd already killed her, so nobody suspected there might be a problem.'

'I'm assuming people who worked on the film sets with Robyn were looked into?' Maddie asked.

'Yeah, pretty exhaustively,' Powers replied. 'There were a few persons of interest, but the main ones were ruled out by DNA and any others had good alibis for some of the murders.'

Marsden moved the presentation forward. *VICTIM #2 TIFFANY WINTERS* headed the new slide, along with an accompanying photograph, which was also a post-mortem re-creation from a film that she had appeared in. Maddie had not seen this particular photo before, and if Tiffany had indeed been deceased and strung up when the picture had been taken, then it was all the more horrendously remarkable. Tiffany was lying on her side on a bed, her head propped up on her clenched fist, gazing slightly off camera. Although the pose would easily pass for having been taken when she'd been alive, there was something missing from her eyes and her back was arched in a way that looked uncomfortable.

'So, Tiffany was found like this around three days after her murder on June second, 1981, eight months after Robyn Stoltman. The M.O. was identical—dressed up and made to look like her fleeting appearance in a scene from *Moonlit Desires*—raped, strangled and then posed like this. Exactly like the movie.'

'Hello. Sorry… Can I ask a question,' Becky said from Maddie's laptop.

'Sure, fire away,' Powers said.

'Was any connection ever made between these actresses and actors? Like, did they know each other, or act together at some point?' Becky asked.

'Apart from Tracie Satchell and Christian Lofthouse, no,' Marsden answered. 'But it's possible that they may have crossed paths as uncredited extras at some point.'

'Was any reason ever deduced as to why he chose these B-movie, less-well-known actors and actresses?' she asked.

'No,' Marsden responded with a shrug. 'It's always been assumed that the sicko just saw a movie, became instantly obsessed with one of the actors or actresses, then stalked them until he knew enough about their lives to take the chance to do what he did.'

Marsden paused for a moment, looking at the team expectantly before clicking on to the next slide, titled *VICTIM #3 JACK FAIRBANKS / KEVIN HOANG.*

Maddie leaned forward to study the image. For some reason, the addition of a male victim intrigued her. As Kenyatta had pointed out, most cases picked up for investigative genetic genealogy were for young white girls. On the whiteboard in front of them, however, was a young Asian man. He was sitting down at a desk, hands on a vintage typewriter, lit only by the muted yellow light from a desk lamp, looking up coyly at the camera.

'This is Kevin Hoang, AKA Jack Fairbanks and this is a re-creation of a scene from his final movie, a film noir entitled *Diamonds in the Rough*,' Powers explained. 'Tied up, dressed up, sexually assaulted and then posed like this.'

'This was August seventh, 1982,' Marsden added.

'I guess that must have appeared a little left field in the investigation up to that point?' Hudson surmised. 'It being a male victim, I mean.'

'Yeah,' Marsden agreed. 'Right up until the DNA from all the victims was put into CODIS, it was strongly believed that this couldn't have been the work of one guy by himself, but rather some kind of a crazed, movie-sex-cult thing. But, no, it was all the same guy.'

'Interesting,' Hudson said.

'Moving on to victim four,' Powers said, nodding to Marsden to change the slide. 'This is Natalie Van Derlyn in a re-creation of her role in *Echoes of Yesterday*. She was murdered April twenty-fourth, 1984.'

The photograph showed a white woman in her early twenties, sitting in a kitchen, appearing to stir a wooden spoon in a large silver pot. She was wearing silk lingerie with her hair up in rollers.

'How *on earth* is she sitting down like that?' Maddie asked nobody in particular.

'Just a lot of very strong wire,' Marsden answered.

'Oh no,' Kenyatta mumbled. 'Unbelievable.'

'It really is,' Powers agreed.

'Which brings us to the fifth and sixth victims—also believed to be his last,' Marsden said, bringing up a slide headed with *VICTIMS #5 & #6 TRACIE SATCHELL & CHRISTIAN LOFTHOUSE*. 'They were murdered November nineteenth, 1986, and this is them in a pose from *Garbo's Wishes.*'

Maddie had seen this image before. It was of the two lovers, naked and entwined, both totally dead but appearing in the image as if very much alive. Maddie blew out a mouthful of air, feeling somewhat nauseous. She was glad that there were no more victim photos to have to endure.

'It defies all belief,' Kenyatta said. 'We've worked on some really deranged folk in this office, but I think this guy takes first prize.'

'That's why there have been so many books, documentaries, films and podcasts about the case,' Marsden said. 'It's really messed up. It involves one of the biggest and most glamorous industries in the U.S. and it remains unsolved. It's true-crime heaven.'

Maddie nodded her silent agreement.

Marsden clasped his hands together and addressed the team. 'I don't want to put too much pressure on you all, but this really is the last chance for this case. There are no avenues left to explore, there is no more DNA to test; this will consume the last sample. That's it then. If we don't get a result from this, it's game over.'

'Have you heard from Gene by Gene yet?' Maddie asked the detectives. 'It's taking longer than I would have expected.'

'No, not yet,' Marsden replied. 'I'll chase it down as soon as we're done here. For now, does anyone have any other questions?'

Becky asked several questions concerning the locations of the crimes and more of the psychological aspects that she needed to know in order to do her part of the job. The rest of the team appeared dumbfounded by what they'd just heard and couldn't bring themselves to say anything.

'Interesting first case for you,' Maddie whispered to Reggie.

'Mind-blowing,' he answered.

'Well,' Marsden said, 'before we leave, I do just need to remind you all that you've signed NDAs. A lot of the material on that thumb drive has never been made public and it needs to stay that way.'

'Noted,' Maddie said, standing up. 'If there are no more questions, you can all get back to what you were currently assigned, at least until the DNA profile comes through on this case.' She walked over to the two detectives. 'Thanks for coming all this way. I'd have liked to discuss the DNA and the case's solvability with you, but we need the file uploaded to be able to consider that meaningfully.'

'I'll give them a call and if I get anywhere before our return flight to Burbank tonight, we'll come back to you,' Powers suggested. 'We'll do some work in the café across the street for a couple of hours. I think it was called Evie's Bakery?'

'Eva's,' Maddie corrected, shaking their hands. 'I recommend the brunch flatbread.'

'That's my lunch choice taken care of, then,' Marsden said with a grin. 'Anyway, goodbye for now.'

Maddie saw them to the door, then headed over to the kitchen area. 'Anyone needs any coffee?'

'No, thanks,' Hudson replied.

'Decaf for me!' Becky called out of the laptop, reminding Maddie that she was still there.

Maddie bent down to face the screen. 'Sorry, Becky. I forgot you were trapped in there. Did you get all that?'

'I think so. At least the connection didn't drop,' Becky confirmed. 'Can you save all the files to the shared drive, and I'll get on with the psychological and geo-profiling.'

'Yes. I'll get Ross to save it in the active cases file for you,' Maddie said.

'Thanks, I'd better go. Lunch break over.'

'Thanks for joining us, Becky,' Maddie said. 'You take care.'

'Goodbye,' Becky said, not giving away any clue as to what she was doing in Port-au-Prince that required a lunch break. The mystery was eating at Maddie.

The team shouted their goodbyes and then Maddie ended the Zoom meeting.

'Is it just me,' Kenyatta asked, 'or does anyone else feel woozy and sick in the stomach after that little presentation of theirs?'

'Uh-huh,' Maddie agreed.

'And now we're switching back to more murder victims,' she said to Reggie, who was sitting down keenly beside her. 'The world really is a very bad place from where I'm sitting.'

'But it's made all the better for people like you,' Reggie said with a smile.

'Creep,' Kenyatta responded. 'Come on, let me show you how it's done here and take you through some of our processes.'

Maddie made some coffee and headed back into her office. She sat down with a sigh. Her emails, open in front of her, now numbered ninety-three unread. Right at the top, was the one that she'd been waiting for from Gene by Gene, regarding the Hollywood Strangler DNA sample. She read it quickly. And then again more slowly. It was not good news. The sample had not proceeded beyond the extraction and quality control phases. Maddie read the final sentence with a despairing sense of disappointment.

Poor nuclear DNA presentation. NOT recommended for whole genome sequencing.

The extraction phase had consumed the very last remaining and apparently unviable sample in the Hollywood Strangler case.

It was all over, and before it had even begun.

Chapter Six

Thursday, September 22, 2022, Salt Lake City, Utah

Maddie was waiting at the counter at Eva's Bakery. It was one of her favorite places to eat and was right across the street from her office in the Kearns Building. While she waited for her food, she checked her emails on her phone. Close to the top was the one from the lab, informing her that the DNA sample had not been viable for generating a profile. Reserve Police Officer Marsden had received the same email and he'd called her up late last night, desperately asking if there was anything else that could be done. But there was nothing more: the DNA hadn't been a good enough sample to be tested and now it was all gone. Although she was disappointed that it was case closed, there had also been some degree of relief at the pressure that it had immediately lifted from the Venator team. They'd all been visibly disheartened when she broke the news to them first thing this morning, but Kenyatta had been right when she had said that it would allow them time to focus fully on some of their other cases.

'Brunch Flatbread to go,' the server called from behind the counter, handing her the food in a paper bag.

Maddie thanked her and then left the bakery, stepping out into the lunchtime bustle of Salt Lake City's Main Street. She walked slowly to the crossing, enjoying the warm sun on her face during this, the first day of fall.

She approached the entrance to the Kearns Building, its name in bold, Art Deco gold lettering above the glass doors. She walked over to the elevator and rode to the fifth floor. Back in the Venator office, she headed directly to her desk, sat down, and tucked into her lunch as she woke up her computer.

Having spent most of the morning working through her backlog of emails, Maddie was now ready to continue with her research into Leon Sierra. She took a bite of the flatbread and pulled up the tree that she'd been creating for Leon's closest DNA match, Malik Johnson. She'd only managed to identify half of his sixteen great-great-grandparents; the rest were either impossible or would take far more hours than she could justify giving over to them, which meant that she had a fifty percent chance at best of working out the most recent common ancestor or ancestors shared by Malik Johnson and Leon Sierra. They were not great odds.

She now returned to Family Tree DNA, logged in to Leon Sierra's kit and then accessed his autosomal DNA matches. Clicking the *In Common With* button beside Malik Johnson's name, Maddie was presented with a short list of just six people who were related to both Malik and Leon. The match in the list with the next highest amount of shared DNA was a man named Elijah Benton, but the quantity of DNA was a paltry twenty-nine centimorgans. She now faced an uphill battle to identify as many of Elijah Benton's direct ancestors as she could in the hope that, among them, she would find an overlap with Malik Johnson's ancestors. The person or persons who ascended from both Elijah Benton and Malik Johnson should also be the direct ancestor of Leon Sierra.

Thankfully, Elijah Benton had given Maddie a leg up by providing the names of his parents and four grandparents, all of whom were African Americans from Mississippi.

Maddie transferred the information from Elijah Benton's tree to a speculative tree that she had created in Ancestry. She studied the vital records for each of his four grandparents carefully, hoping to see that one of them might have come from the same area as one of Malik Johnson's known ancestors; but she couldn't see anything obvious. Since Elijah Benton's paternal line should technically be easier to spot but had not yet appeared in any of her searches, Maddie opted to begin her research with his maternal grandmother.

As she ate more of her flatbread and began the search, Maddie very much hoped that the rest of the Venator team was having more luck with their cases than she was.

Several hours later, Maddie stood from her desk with a deep feeling of frustration at her afternoon's work. She had achieved very little on Elijah Benton's tree, with almost all lines crashing to a screaming halt at the 1870 census. She walked out to the kitchen area, craving some caffeine and a screen break. 'Anyone for coffee?' she called across the office.

'Oh, I'm over here, pretending I'm good with just my water,' Kenyatta called over to her with a broad smile. 'How are you getting on with Leon?'

Maddie exhaled with exaggeration. 'Well, it's safe to say that I'm nowhere near finding out who he really was. I'm really struggling to triangulate between Leon's matches. I've done all I can with his closest match and, with the next, I've pinned down all but two of his great-grandparents and they're all from Alabama or Mississippi with no links as of yet to Malik Johnson's tree, which, apart from the Belling line in Mississippi, is predominantly in Texas.' Maddie shrugged.

'Have you tried the Mapping The Freedmen's Bureau website?' Reggie asked.

'Uh, no I have not,' Maddie admitted.

'It's pretty good for helping research enslaved people,' he said. 'The website basically points researchers to potential resources for the period just after the Civil War ended. Institutions set up for survivors of slavery like the Freedmen's Bureau Offices were dotted all around the south. Plus, the Freedmen's Savings Bank, Freedmen's Schools... I learned all about it from Dr Shelley Murphy. Murphy's Rule—a spin on Murphy's Law—is this: follow the money, land, water, communities and the faith of the people.'

'Right,' Maddie said, pausing to think for a moment. 'Okay, that's it. I admit defeat. I'm passing Leon Sierra over to you, Reggie. Come into my office and I'll bring you up to speed.'

Reggie grinned. 'Okay, cool.'

With Reggie following behind, Maddie returned to her office and spent some time explaining the basics of the Wind River Doe case and her work so far. She was midway through demonstrating how to access all the files on the internal drive when Kenyatta appeared at her door, wearing her coat. 'It's after five,' she pointed out.

Maddie looked at her computer clock in disbelief. 'Right. Okay. Sure. Time to go, Reggie.'

'Time for you to go, too,' Kenyatta said pointedly.

Maddie nodded. 'I'm going. I'm going.'

'I want to see you actually shutting down that computer. I'm watching,' Kenyatta said.

Maddie shut the lid. 'There.'

'Good girl. Now, you have a great evening,' Kenyatta said.

'See you tomorrow,' Maddie replied, picking up her purse and leaving the office. She waited until all the team had gone, then switched off the lights, locked up and headed to the basement garage to her car.

Maddie arrived at her home on Jordan Bend Road, twenty-five minutes south of the city, feeling significantly less stressed than when she'd left first thing this morning. Along with lifting the pressure from the Hollywood Strangler case, she felt much better for having passed Leon Sierra over to Reggie. Although she was stubborn and liked to imagine that she would eventually have identified him, she knew that the case was best placed with her newest member of staff and his undoubted experience in this area.

Having parked her RAV4 in the driveway, Maddie approached and unlocked the front door and entered her spacious home, making sure to lock the door behind her again.

As always, her first job was to check in on her mom who was suffering from Alzheimer's. Last year, the illness had gotten bad enough to necessitate her mom moving into assisted living accommodation with a focus on memory care. Maddie had spent hours researching the best facilities nearby, visiting almost every one of them within a twenty-mile range, finally settling on Legacy House Assisted Living of South Jordan, just a short distance from her home. Her mom, in her moments of lucidity, had fully understood and supported the decision, but during the increasingly lengthy periods where the disease ravaged her mind, she violently and vehemently fought against the decision. Just as Maddie had begun the painful task of sorting through her mom's belongings, deciding what from sixty-four years of life should be kept or discarded, she abruptly changed her own mind. The weight of the decision had just been too much for her to bear, and Maddie decided at the last moment to employ a live-in caregiver instead.

'Hi,' Maddie greeted, entering the kitchen and seeing her mom sitting down at the table beside her caregiver, Katie, doing a jigsaw puzzle.

'Hey,' Katie said, smiling. She was in her early thirties, petite with black hair pulled back into a ponytail. She had a no-nonsense attitude but with deep compassion and an understanding of what her mom needed beyond her personal care. 'She's doing so well,' Katie said to Maddie, indicating the partially completed jigsaw puzzle on the table. 'She did all this by herself.'

'Great job, Mom,' Maddie praised, and in return receiving a customary glare from her mother.

The jigsaws, Maddie noted, were an agonizing metaphor for her mom's condition, getting simpler and more child-like as time went on. Her mom's passion and skill for complex word problems and puzzles had diminished to the point that she was now struggling with a twelve-piece jigsaw of two kittens.

'I hate cats,' her mom said, trying to place a piece of puzzle containing one of the kittens' faces where its tail should go.

'Well, you used to love them,' Maddie said.

'No, I did not,' her mom countered, tossing the puzzle piece to the floor, picking up another and trying to force it into the tail spot. 'Why do they make these things so darn hard?' She then threw this piece to the floor and started to walk toward the front door. 'That's it. That's enough. I'm going home.'

'Mom, this is your home,' Maddie called after her. 'Come and sit down, and I'll get you a drink.'

Her mom reached the door and tried the handle. 'This thing's always shut,' she complained, whipping around to face Maddie. 'Have you found the key yet, Madison?'

Maddie shook her head. 'It'll turn up. Why don't we sit down together, and I'll fix you a nice drink.'

Her mom sighed, taking another reproachful glance at the locked door. 'I'll have a drink, and then maybe the key will show up. And… I need to get home. My mom will definitely be worried…'

Maddie smiled, taking her mom's hand and leading her back into the kitchen.

'I want wine,' her mom insisted.

'Sure thing,' Maddie replied, having no intention of giving her mom any alcohol.

'You still here?' her mom said to Katie. 'The key's gone and I need to get home.'

Katie shrugged. 'Make yourself comfortable here. It's a nice place.'

Her mom looked around the room, saying nothing as Maddie pulled out a chair at the dining room table for her.

'Come on over here and take a seat,' Maddie said, then headed over to the refrigerator and took out a bottle of non-alcoholic wine. She poured out a glass for herself and a plastic beaker for her mom. 'Are the kids—' she stopped and corrected herself. 'Is Trenton home?'

'Yeah, he's in his room,' Katie replied.

Maddie was missing her daughter, Nikki, who had just started as a sophomore at Brigham Young University, living on campus. She'd only been gone three weeks, but it already felt like three months. With her absence, the house had lost its balance and Maddie was struggling to navigate the difficult waters between her demanding sixteen-year-old son, Trenton, and the unrecognizable person that her mom was becoming.

'Here you go,' Maddie said, handing her mom the drink.

'Thank you,' her mom responded before taking a big gulp and then violently coughing, as she had developed some difficulty with swallowing.

'Are you okay, Mom?' Maddie asked, jumping up and rubbing her back.

Her mom scowled. 'This wine's far too strong.'

'I'll go get you a weaker one,' Maddie replied, carrying the beaker into the kitchen, pouring the drink down the sink and then filling it with exactly the same non-alcoholic wine as before.

'Oh, that's much better,' her mom commented.

'I'm going to go check on Trenton,' Maddie said, leaving the kitchen and heading upstairs. She knocked lightly on his bedroom door.

'Come in,' he called.

She found him sitting down at his desk, appearing to be doing his homework…miraculously. 'Hey, how's it going?' she asked, taking a seat on his unmade bed.

Trenton put down his pen and twisted his chair to face her. He seemed to be more grown up every time she looked at him. It seemed a lifetime ago that she and Michael had adopted him and Nikki from South Korea, a decision that she had been so grateful for every day since.

'Okay, I guess,' he answered. 'How was your day?'

'Uh, good, thank you,' Maddie replied, taken slightly aback by his reciprocally asking after her.

'Great,' Trenton said.

Maddie stood up, walked over and planted a kiss on the top of his head. 'I'll call you when dinner's ready,' she said, heading back out of his room.

Closing the door to Trenton's bedroom, Maddie stood still for an instant and closed her eyes. Although the family was going through a period of challenge, change and uncertainty, moments like this let her know that they would come through the other side.

Chapter Seven

Thursday, September 22, 2022, Pasadena, California

Ted Marsden was sitting down in his backyard drinking an Angel City IPA. He'd just finished mowing what little grass hadn't been killed off by the recent drought in the LA basin. He was on a wooden bench, staring at the white fence that separated his property from the neighbor's behind him.

'You all done, Teddy?' his wife, Judith, asked, stepping out of the house and placing her hand on his shoulder.

'Yeah. All done,' he replied, turning to face her. She was smiling but he could see the pain the cancer treatment was giving her. Earlier on, he had seen her bent double, trying to conceal her agony from him. He also knew that she was losing thick clumps of her hair every day but was wearing it so as to try to hide it from him.

'Shall I fix us some dinner?' she asked.

'No,' he said, jumping up. 'I'll do it. Is there anything you particularly want? Or…we could go out? Parkway Grill or Bistro 45?'

Judith shook her head. 'No, honestly, Teddy. I'll make us something. I need to keep busy. It helps. I'm fine.'

Marsden touched her arm. 'Just don't go doing too much, okay?'

'I won't,' she said, heading back into the kitchen. 'I meant to ask… Did you officially resign yet, Teddy?'

'Not yet,' he called back, swigging the last remnants of the beer.

He put the bottle on the patio beside him and returned his gaze to the back fence, all the while his preoccupied mind raked over the Hollywood Strangler case, looking for any oversight in their review. He'd been unable to sleep last night and had got up, spending the rest of the night at his computer, searching the hundreds of articles, blogs, websites and social media posts that had been written about the case over the past forty years. He'd discovered almost every type of outlandish theory that existed but nothing whatsoever that he felt warranted any further investigation.

Marsden stared unblinking, wondering if his entire retirement that he'd worked so hard to achieve would be like this; gazing blankly at the fence while his brain overrode his desire to slow down and instead plowed back over all the cases in his career that had failed to end in a successful prosecution. His Achilles heel had always been his compassion. If he could just switch that off or turn it down a gear, he could retire in some peace, knowing that he'd done all that he could have, and it was now time for other, younger, and fitter officers to take the reins. But he couldn't help thinking about the victims' families, held in perpetual uncertainty and pain.

In his mind, he had a very clear mental image of Glenn Stoltman as he had appeared on *Hour Magazine*, cocooned in a disorienting shell of grief. He knew from the files that Glenn and his wife had long-since died, going to the grave not knowing who had killed their beloved daughter. But there was a brother, Caleb, mentioned in the interview.

'I got you a fresh one. Here you go,' Judith said, handing him another beer and taking away the empty bottle.

'Thanks, honey,' he called after her.

He took out his cellphone and pulled up Facebook, searching for Caleb Stoltman. There were only two profiles that matched that name precisely. Marsden clicked the first name, finding that it belonged to someone who appeared to be a teenager. He backed out and clicked the second. It was for a man who appeared to be in his late fifties to mid-sixties, just the right age to be Robyn's younger brother. Marsden noted that his location was given as Los Angeles and the few posts that Caleb had made suggested that he might be the right guy. Marsden continued scrolling through his profile, hitting on a photograph that confirmed him to be Robyn Stoltman's brother. It was of her headstone—shared on the anniversary of her death—with the caption *Still loved and still missed.*

Marsden looked at the headstone for a long time, then he returned to Caleb's profile and clicked *Message*. He wasn't sure if contacting Caleb was the right thing to do, since the case had collapsed and he was about to retire, but, despite his reservations, he typed out a message, opening with a brief introduction and an apology for contacting him in this way. Then Marsden asked if Caleb knew what his father had been referring to on the *Hour Magazine* about some sort of near miss in Ventura. He hit send and then pocketed his cell phone.

He drank some more beer and stared at the back fence.

Moments later, his phone pinged in his pocket, and he took it out to see that he had a message back from Caleb Stoltman.

The incident in Ventura that my dad was referring to was a homicide that happened in a place my sister was living six months before. It wasn't actually a near miss for her. Are you reviewing the case?

Marsden quickly tapped out a reply. *Thank you. Do you know the address or any further details? We're just checking again to see if there are any avenues that haven't been explored yet.*

He drank the rest of the beer, impatiently watching as his phone told him that *Caleb is typing…*

No idea, sorry, came his short response.

Marsden stood up and went inside the house, finding Judith peeling potatoes. 'Honey, would you mind if I shot back downtown for something?'

'To hand in your resignation?' she asked.

Marsden laughed. 'Not yet. Just a loose end I need to tie up on the strangler case.'

'Sure,' she replied. 'I'll hold dinner until you're home.'

He kissed her on the lips. 'You're amazing. I'll be back soon.'

As he headed out to his car, he sent a message to Powers, telling him to meet him back at the unit.

Powers was already at his desk in the Cold Case Homicide Unit when Marsden arrived. On the drive down, he'd called him up and asked him to look up Robyn's address in Ventura.

'Here,' Powers said, handing Marsden a sheet of paper. 'Found it.'

Marsden took the paper. 'Thanks. Wait a minute… Holy crap.'

'What is it?'

'The address… Nine-ninety-nine Via Arroyo,' Marsden said.

'Uh-huh. What of it? Does it mean something to you?' Powers asked.

'I was there…on that case…as a rookie cop. It was a double homicide and the detectives working it thought that the murdered couple were linked to Lyman and Charlene Smith who were killed a few streets away a month before.'

'Weren't Lyman and Charlene Smith Golden State Killer victims?' Powers asked.

'Yeah, they were,' Marsden confirmed. 'But this couple—at Via Arroyo—they weren't the same killer, although detectives at the time thought they were.'

'That's a bit of a weird coincidence, isn't it? Robyn Stoltman previously living at that address?' Powers asked. 'When was this?'

Marsden blew air from his cheeks, his mind searching. 'Nineteen eighty. March or April, I would guess.'

'What was the M.O.?'

Marsden sat down, took a long breath and tried to pull the case out through forty-two years of work stored up in his mind. 'Married couple…bludgeoned to death in their beds. She was raped. No sign of sexual assault of the husband.'

Powers seemed disappointed. 'So, nothing similar to the Hollywood Strangler?'

Marsden shook his head, resting his elbows on his thighs, thinking. 'The detectives there gave me three pieces of advice that I haven't forgotten to this day: one, don't watch cop shows—I never have since; two, trust your instincts—always have; three, get every medical examiner to perform a crime scene investigation just like how I saw Dr. Speth doing it that day—easier said than done.'

'What did he do that was so amazing?' Powers asked.

'Just crazily thorough,' Marsden replied.

Powers stood up and suddenly marched away with an urgency to his gait.

'Hey, where are you going?' Marsden called out, but Powers just kept on walking.

'You look like you could use a vacation,' a voice said from in front of him. It was Detective Supervisor Mitzi Roberts. 'You okay? Pissed because of the case?'

'It was always going to be a long shot,' Marsden responded. 'And yes, I desperately need a vacation.'

Roberts smiled. 'So, take one, then. Go take Judith off on some world cruise. It's not like you haven't earned it.'

'Yeah,' he replied absent-mindedly.

'Where's Powers rushing off to?' Roberts asked.

Marsden gave Roberts a brief rundown of what had just occurred. He ended by saying that he had no idea where Powers had gone, just as he reappeared with a murder book open in his hands.

'Look at that,' Powers said, thrusting it in front of Marsden. '*Fleeing to France*, starring—well, kinda starring—Robyn Stoltman, aka Babette Monroe, was released in March 1980. If you're right with the date of the homicides, then this movie came out right before this couple was killed.'

'What's your point?' Marsden asked.

'What if it's the same guy?' Powers suggested. 'He watched the movie, became obsessed by Robyn Stoltman, found out her address, then went over to do what he eventually did, but found she wasn't living there—it was this other couple—and killed them instead.'

Roberts and Marsden exchanged glances.

'Was there anything you can remember from the Ventura case that was similar to the strangler case?' Roberts asked.

Marsden closed his eyes, focused and thought really hard. Almost everything had been different between that crime scene and the ones that he'd been reviewing in the Hollywood Strangler case. He broke his silence: 'Nothing comes to mind, no.'

'So, you think it was just a coincidence?' Powers asked.

Marsden shrugged. 'Don't forget what we told the guys at Venator: there were multiple killers operating at the same time in LA in the 1980s.'

'Did the DNA from the Ventura couple's attacker get entered into CODIS?' Roberts asked.

'I don't know,' Marsden answered. 'But CODIS didn't exist at the time. I guess it depends on if it remained unsolved and was picked up in a review.'

'It's worth checking, right?' Powers pushed.

'Sure, it's worth checking,' Marsden said. 'I'll call up Ventura right now.'

'I'll leave you guys to it,' Roberts said. 'Good luck.'

Marsden called Ventura Police Department and spent some time being passed around until finally he reached a detective who used to work at RHD. The detective didn't take long to confirm that the murders of David and Joyce Peck had remained unsolved. He promised to pull the file from the cold case vault, scan it and email it over.

Marsden relayed the pertinent details, holding back to the last moment a potential bombshell from the case file. 'And…get this. The killer's DNA never made it to CODIS.'

'What?' Powers cried.

'According to the file, the sample was sent to a lab to be tested back in 2015 but it never made it,' Marsden explained. 'Lost somewhere along the way.'

'The whole goddamn sample?'

'The whole sample,' Marsden confirmed.

'So, yet another dead end…'

'Not necessarily,' Marsden said.

'What do you mean? It's gone, right?'

'Yeah, it's gone. But, like I told you, one of the reasons I remember that case so well is because the M.E., Dr. Speth, was so totally thorough in his job. Unlike any other medical examiner that I've ever worked with, he took a duplicate rape kit.'

'So, there's another kit out there somewhere?' Powers stammered.

'Possibly. We just need to find it.'

Chapter Eight

Thursday, September 22, 2022, Los Angeles, California

Powers was standing close to him, staring intently.

'It's ringing,' Marsden whispered. After a few seconds, a male voice answered the phone at the other end of the line.

'Hello?'

'Hi, there. My name is Detective Ted Marsden. I'm working with the Cold Case Homicide Unit in the Special Investigation Section of LAPD and I'm looking for a Dr. Peter Speth.'

'Speaking…' the man replied.

'Holy cow! You're still alive!' Marsden said, immediately regretting his choice of words but unable to reel them back.

'I think so. Well, last time I checked that is,' Dr. Speth answered him with a cheery chuckle.

'You're probably not going to remember me, but, back in Ventura in 1980 I was a rookie cop working on the double homicide of David and Joyce Peck. You taught me all about rape exams and time of death calculations—' Marsden said, trying to aid the doctor's recall.

'Oh, yes. I sure do remember you,' Dr. Speth confirmed. 'I also recollect that the detectives working the case were wearing blinders about the killer.'

'Yes. You weren't really convinced at the time, were you?' Marsden asked.

'It just didn't feel right to me. All the dots have to line up. If they don't, then something's wrong with the case. They were fixated on trying to link the Peck murders to Lyman and Charlene Smith who, of course, turned out to be victims of the Golden State Killer, Joseph DeAngelo.'

'And, as I understand it, DeAngelo was only caught because of a duplicate rape kit you did on Charlene Smith. Is that right?' Marsden asked.

'Yes, that's right,' Dr. Speth confirmed. 'The DNA in evidence had all been used up until they found my second kit.'

'I'm sorry, I can't remember… Can you refresh me again as to why you always prepared two kits?' Marsden questioned.

'It's simple really,' he explained. 'In the days before DNA, when one relied on fragile proteins called enzymes, the specimens had to be kept frozen. Every time they got a suspect, they thawed out the swabbings in order to conduct the tests. They not only used up the specimens, but they couldn't reuse any remaining specimen because they couldn't refreeze the swabbings; just like you can't refreeze a thanksgiving turkey. My duplicate kits were backups for the future.'

'That was so very insightful,' Marsden commented. 'And you prepared a duplicate kit at nine ninety-nine Via Arroyo, right?'

'Yes, you have a good memory,' Dr. Speth confirmed.

'Any idea where that duplicate kit went? The original sample is gone, and we desperately need it.'

Dr. Speth laughed. 'Well, the last time I saw it forty-plus years ago, the kit was in the freezer at the Ventura County Medical Examiner's Office.'

Marsden shot a look at Powers. 'And do you think it's still likely to be there? Is there any chance?'

'That I just couldn't say. It *should* be there unless someone's taken it out for some reason,' Dr. Speth answered.

'Thank you so much, Dr. Speth,' Marsden said.

'Let me know how things turn out.'

'Oh, I will. I can't tell you much more, but you might just be the catalyst for solving one of the biggest serial killer cases in the U.S. Thanks again. Goodbye.' Marsden ended the call and addressed Powers. 'So… He took a duplicate rape kit. And the last he saw it, it was in the freezer at the Ventura County Medical Examiner's Office.'

Powers's eyes lit up. 'Well, what the hell are we waiting for? Call them up. I'll get the number.' Powers wheeled his chair to his computer and ran a Google search for the Ventura County Medical Examiner's Office. 'Eight zero five, six four one, four four, zero zero.'

Marsden punched in the number and then, when the call was answered, he put the phone on speaker. Having clarified who he was, he asked to be put through to the Medical Examiner, to whom he then explained that the offender who murdered David and Joyce Peck was also suspected of other murders in LA. Marsden was careful, though, not to refer to the Hollywood Strangler case at all.

'I'm happy to take a look in the freezer for you,' the Medical Examiner said. 'Obviously, you'll have to implement the chain of transfer for the release of the sample out of county. And that's if it's still here.'

'I'll get everything you need, expedited,' Marsden said, at the same time noticing a new email from Ventura PD pop into his inbox in front of him.

'I'll give you a call back when I've taken a look,' the Medical Examiner promised.

'Thank you,' Marsden said, ending the call and clicking on the email attachment. He beckoned Powers over, telling him, 'The scanned file from Ventura is here.'

Powers slid his chair over and the two of them began to read through the cold case files of David and Joyce Peck, noting any similarities to the Hollywood Strangler case.

'Zoom in to her wrists,' Powers said, referring to the crime scene photograph of Joyce Peck's body. 'You can barely see the stockings binding her wrists. But her husband was tied up with telephone cord from the house, like maybe the killer wasn't expecting him to be home and had to improvise. Does it say if the stockings were hers?'

'I'm not sure,' Marsden said, reading through the evidence log and the summary reports from the detective in charge. As they continued reading through the file, Powers's theory that Robyn Stoltman had been the killer's intended victim gained more traction in Marsden's mind.

'Look,' Powers said, pointing at a line in Detective Turgenev's report. '*The stockings used to bind Joyce Peck were believed to have been brought to the house by the killer...*' He looked at Marsden. 'I think he could be our guy.'

Marsden nodded agreement but said nothing.

Almost an hour later, Marsden's cell phone began to ring. 'It's the M.E.,' he said, before answering the call.

'Good news, Detective. It's your lucky day. The rape kit is still here,' the Medical Examiner confirmed. 'Of course, I can't look inside to see if it is still preserved because it has Dr. Speth's and the investigating detective's signatures across the intact seal.'

'Oh my God, that's amazing,' Marsden said. 'I'll get on with the transfer of evidence paperwork right now. Thank you for looking. I'll be in touch.'

The two men stared wordlessly at one another as the reality of the situation dawned on them both. They might just have found a plentiful supply of the Hollywood Strangler's DNA. But only a match in CODIS would be able to confirm it.

Five weeks, four days later

Chapter Nine

Monday, October 31, 2022, Salt Lake City, Utah

Maddie had just finished eating her lunch and couldn't help but smile at the email that had just landed in her inbox from Gene by Gene, confirming that the Hollywood Strangler profile had been uploaded to Family Tree DNA. Last night, while she was sitting at home with Trenton watching Netflix, Ted Marsden from LAPD had called her with the surprising news that a duplicate rape kit had been found for the case and that the profile uploaded to CODIS had been a definite match to the Hollywood Strangler. They were back in business. After the previous disappointment, Maddie had not yet informed the rest of her staff that the case was back on the table.

Carrying her laptop through to the main Venator office, she strode to the front of the room, placed her laptop down on a vacant desk and clicked to mirror her screen. The log-in page for FTDNA appeared on the six-foot-wide digital whiteboard, instantly garnering the attention of the team, as she had well known it would.

'What's going on?' Hudson called over.

Maddie smiled. 'Team briefing in about thirty seconds. Ross, can you come over and take notes, please?'

'Sure,' he replied, picking up his laptop and walking over so that he too could see the whiteboard.

'New case?' Kenyatta asked, swiveling her chair to face front.

'Something like that,' Maddie said, being deliberately vague as she feigned concentration and typed in the kit details, bringing up the FTDNA dashboard. 'Everybody ready?' She looked up and saw that the team was facing front, eager to find out what this new case was all about.

'Are we not getting background, here?' Hudson asked.

'You already had it,' Maddie answered. 'Welcome to…the Hollywood Strangler.'

'What?' Kenyatta said. 'I thought the final sample had been consumed?'

'They found a duplicate rape kit in a freezer in the Ventura County Medical Examiner's Office.'

'Wow, that's amazing,' Hudson commented. 'Have you looked at the autosomal matches yet? Are they good?'

'Not yet, no,' Maddie answered. 'I thought we'd all like to take a look together.'

'Well, let's do it, then,' Kenyatta said with a laugh.

From the FTDNA dashboard, Maddie clicked on *Family Finder Matches*, which brought up the Hollywood Strangler's autosomal cousin matches—regular people who had uploaded their DNA to the website and who were somehow related to the serial killer.

'That's pretty good,' Maddie commented, seeing that the highest result was two hundred and twenty-three centimorgans of DNA.

'So, the generation of connection is likely somewhere in the second-cousin region,' Reggie noted. 'But could still be closer or further away.'

'It's a good list,' Maddie said, scrolling down and seeing that, at the end of the first page of twenty-five matches, the amount of shared DNA had just fallen below one hundred centimorgans.

'I can't believe we're actually looking at the Hollywood Strangler's cousin matches,' Hudson said. 'And they're really strong.'

Maddie smiled. 'Okay, let's finally bring this guy out of the shadows. Let's do this. Hudson, can I put you on Y-DNA and phenotypes? Kenyatta on clustering. Reggie on ethnicity. And I'll get the kit up onto GEDmatch Pro. I'll email Becky and ask if she can pick up on geo-profiling. I know we've only got about four hours until the end of the day, but if we can meet at that point to see where we're at? Everyone good with that?'

The team confirmed that they were happy to proceed, and the office atmosphere suddenly shifted to one of bubbling excitement. They had a lot of hard work ahead of them but Maddie, like her team, felt optimistic about their chances of identifying one of America's most high-profile serial killers.

Returning to her office with her laptop, Maddie's first job was to email Becky and ask her to start work on geo-profiling the case—a task that was her strong suit with her having a bachelor's and a master's degree in criminology.

Next, she returned to the main FTDNA dashboard, and below *Family Finder Matches*, she clicked *Data Download*, then followed the instructions until the CSV Zip file was in her downloads folder. Logging in on the GEDmatch Pro website, Maddie entered the Venator credentials to access the law enforcement arm of the company. *Your Kits* was written in white lettering on a blue tab and below that was a search box to help sift through the many kits that her company had uploaded there. Beside it was the option to *View All Kits* and the button that Maddie now clicked, *Upload New Kit +*. Accessing the CSV file in her downloads, she proceeded to upload the kit to GEDmatch Pro, paying the $550 to purchase a credit in order to do so. Certain functionality, including accessing the list of matches who had opted in to assist law enforcement, took up to twenty-four hours, but some tools, including Admixture, were instantly available. Maddie sent an email to Reggie, informing him that he could now look at the killer's ethnicity—or admixture or geo-ancestry as some called it—on both websites.

Until Kenyatta had gone through the match lists and created clusters of individuals who were related to each other and the killer for the team to work on, there was little direct work that Maddie could do for the case right now. She pulled up the notes file that Ross maintained for each case, printed out the contents and took the sheets of paper back out to the main office.

Standing in front of the non-digital whiteboard, Maddie picked up the red marker pen that was only used for verified facts and wrote THE HOLLYWOOD STRANGLER at the top of the board. Beneath that, she affixed a photograph of each of the six victims, annotating these with their names and ages underneath. She opted to use photographs that showed the victims in happier circumstances, rather than the grotesque post-mortem tableaus that were to be found all over the internet.

Maddie read through the case documents carefully, adding pieces of relevant information to the whiteboard as she went.

At just before 4:30 p.m., she called the team together for their first briefing on the case. She stood beside the whiteboard, armed with the red marker pen, hoping that her team would have some general but concrete facts about the killer. 'Hudson, do you want to kick us off?'

'Sure,' he said, standing up with his notepad. 'Let's start with the EVCs.'

Of all the excitement in the opening phase of a case, the EVCs—externally visible characteristics, or phenotypes as they were also known—were the part that Maddie liked the most. After decades of hiding anonymously in the shadows, the EVCs would provide a general, physical description of the man who had plagued Hollywood for several years.

'So, from the data inputted into the Hirisplex website, it appears that the killer had brown eyes, brown hair and intermediate skin color,' he relayed.

'Oh, good. Here we go. Another middle-aged white guy,' Kenyatta commented. 'Jeez, these guys sure need to get some better hobbies.'

Maddie grinned as she noted the information on the whiteboard. Although it was fairly generic, it had often helped their cases in the past when it came to narrowing down a pool of suspects. 'Good work, Hudson. And on the Y-DNA?'

He looked down at his notes. 'As usual, it was tested at Y-111 and, as usual, the results aren't especially enlightening. In fact, there are no matches at all at 111 markers. He has eighteen matches at 67 markers, but they're all at least six genetic steps away. The top surnames to keep a look out for are: Weston, Shaul, Danton, Miller, Smith—obviously—Hunt and Crisp.'

'Thanks,' Maddie said, noting them on the whiteboard. 'And the haplogroup?'

'Is R-M269—a common one.'

'Great. Anything else?'

'That's all for the moment,' Hudson answered, sitting back down.

'Reggie, do you want to go next with ethnicity?'

'Sure. Can I share my screen?' he asked.

'Go ahead,' Maddie said, and watched as the familiar *MyOrigins* interface at FTDNA appeared on the large digital whiteboard.

'Pretty standard admixture for someone with white European heritage,' Reggie reported. 'West and Central Europe accounts for 62%, Southeast Europe 21%, Scandinavia 11%, then a little Ireland and

Asia Minor making up the rest. It's similar on GEDmatch Pro.' He clicked on a different tab, which showed a colorful pie chart from that website.

Although the locations and percentages weren't particularly enlightening, Maddie wrote them onto the whiteboard in red marker, then thanked Reggie. 'Kenyatta, your turn.'

Kenyatta stood up and smiled. 'I'm obviously waiting on the kit to clear at GEDmatch Pro before I can analyze the clusters there, but at FTDNA we've got seven strong genetic network groups and three slightly weaker ones. I've saved them all to the shared drive, so for tomorrow we're all good to go.'

'Excellent, thank you, Kenyatta. And thank you all for your efforts this afternoon. Let's pick up tomorrow with the clusters and try and identify this monster,' Maddie said, switching off the digital whiteboard and returning to her office.

As the Venator staff slowly filed out, saying goodbye as they left, Maddie sent an email to the LAPD detectives, informing them that she judged the case as having a high probability of being solved. With the email sent, Maddie closed her laptop and then left the office, heading down to her car in the garage. Before she set off for home, she started playing one of her favorite podcasts, DNA: ID. She enjoyed keeping up to date with cold cases solved with investigative genetic genealogy and liked that this podcast was as much focused on the victim as the perpetrator or the crime itself.

'Thank God you're home, Madison,' her mom said as soon as she entered the front door. 'I was worried sick. It's almost dark out there.' Her mom was wearing her beige bathrobe over her nightdress, which usually meant that Katie had not been able to get her dressed.

'Sorry,' Maddie said, locking the door behind her and removing the key.

Her mom sighed. 'And there's no sign of your father, either. Probably out with his work friends. He thinks I can't smell the whiskey on his breath. He's going to walk right in here sucking a Peppermint Place Mint any moment. Just you wait…'

'He said he was going to be late tonight, Mom,' Maddie said, playing along. 'There's really no point standing there, staring at the door.'

Her mom thought for a moment. 'I guess you're right. I'll get the dinner on. If his spoils, well, it's his own fault.'

'I'll fix dinner tonight, Mom,' Maddie replied. 'I've got all the ingredients for a chicken casserole. Why don't you sit down and do some of your memory games?'

'Because I don't need to do memory games,' her mom retorted, folding her arms. 'There is nothing wrong with my memory. Ask me anything you like.'

Maddie hated this exchange. If she asked questions about her mom's childhood, she'd almost always get the right answer. If she asked questions about the past twenty years, she'd almost always get the wrong answer. 'What's your name and birth date?' Maddie asked.

'Patricia Scott and I was born February third, 1958, in Portland, Oregon,' her mom announced. 'I was one of five children born to Frank and Betsy Ellwood. Do you want to hear about where I went to school?'

Maddie nodded her head. 'Come with me into the kitchen. I'll make us a drink while you tell me all about it.'

'Hi, Maddie,' Katie greeted. 'Good day at work?'

'Hi. Yes, we're starting a new case and it's off to a very positive start. How has your day been?' Maddie asked with a subtle nod toward her mom. 'She's about to tell me all about her school.'

'Great,' Katie said. Then, she lowered her voice. 'It's been a challenging one today. But she ate her lunch and took a short walk in the yard this afternoon, which is good news.'

'Hmm,' Maddie said, trying to muster some enthusiasm for these tiny glimmers of light in her mom's deterioration into darkness.

'I attended Woodrow Wilson High School,' her mom announced. 'I was in the top class for everything. Everything. My teachers will tell that you if you ask them.'

'I believe you,' Maddie replied. 'You're a smart cookie.'

'That I am,' she agreed, folding her arms.

'Hey, Mom,' Trenton said, entering the kitchen.

'Hi, you. How was school?' she replied quietly, trying to give the impression that she was still listening to her mom.

Trenton shrugged. 'What's for dinner?'

'Chicken casserole.'

'Oh,' he said, turning around and leaving the room.

Maddie looked at Katie and asked, 'Is it too early for wine, do we think?'

Katie shook her head. 'I'll pour you a glass.'

'Thanks,' Maddie said, sitting down at the counter and looking at her cell phone. She had two unread text messages. The first was from Nikki.

Loving my Hist 388 class!

Maddie smiled. Nikki was taking a bachelors in Family History at BYU—the only degree major in genealogy in the U.S. Her current class was using DNA evidence in genealogical and family research. Nikki's career goals changed with the wind, but her current plan was to become an intern at Venator—a role she had presumptuously told Maddie that she would have to create for her when the time came—and then get a full-time, paid role at the company.

That's great! Maddie replied, looking at her other unread message. It was from Clayton Tyler, a detective whom she'd met two years ago when he'd visited the Venator office to present a cold case for IGG.

I can't wait to see you on Saturday, Maddie, he wrote.

'One white wine,' Katie said, placing a glass in front of Maddie.

'Thank you,' she said, taking a sip as she stared at the message from Clayton. She was looking forward to seeing him, too; but it was complicated. Back in March 2020 they'd kind of flirted but nothing had happened. And then, a few months later, Maddie had been visiting a girlfriend in his hometown of Philadelphia and they had met up for dinner, something she felt that she had owed him after he'd gone to such great lengths to help her work out what had happened to her husband, Michael. Clayton had been responsible for a fresh CSI sweep of Michael's truck, the result of which had been the discovery of one solitary fingerprint on the trunk catch, which belonged to an employee of The Larkin Investment and Finance Group, Emmanuel Gribbin. Clayton had then procured security footage from College Park Airport in Maryland, which had shown Gribbin bundling a large object from his Pilatus PC-12 turboprop airplane into the back of a waiting SUV.

So, feeling as though she had had a huge debt of gratitude to repay, Maddie had gone out for a Philly cheesesteak and an AleSmith Speedway Stout with him, not really expecting to enjoy the evening as much as she had. She'd seen him again the following two nights that she had been in Philadelphia and then he'd visited Salt Lake City a few weeks later, at which point Maddie had come to accept something. They were dating.

I'm really looking forward to seeing you, too, she sent back.

Chapter Ten

Tuesday, November 1, 2022, Salt Lake City, Utah

Hudson Édouard sat at his desk in the Venator office with a smile on his face. At twenty-seven years old, he was finally starting to feel settled within himself. The past few years had been difficult for him with various problems in his personal life. But the one constant had been his job at Venator. He was a biology major and loved the science that underpinned investigative genetic genealogy. He was good-looking with dark hair and olive skin that he'd proudly inherited from his French Guianan grandparents.

He took a sip of coffee as he opened up the shared drive on his computer, navigating through ACTIVE CASES to THE HOLLYWOOD STRANGLER subfolder. Inside it was another folder containing everything received from the detectives, the main file that Ross maintained with all relevant names, dates, places and information uncovered as the investigation proceeded and, finally, a list of ten CSV files, each containing a distinct genetic network. Hudson had been assigned clusters one and six. He clicked to select *Cluster One* and a spreadsheet opened in front of him with several columns of data, many of which were only partially completed. The left-most column contained the names of nine individuals who shared DNA with one another and also with the killer. His task was to work out *how* they were related.

At the top of the list, matching the killer with two hundred and twenty-three centimorgans, was a person with the username *Gurmany*. Typically, there was no further information beyond a Gmail address and several predicted relationships to the killer: *1st Cousin-3rd Cousin, Great/Half Uncle/Aunt/Niece/Nephew, Great Grandparent/Grandchild.*

Hudson logged in at the FTDNA website and clicked through *Family Finder Matches* to find Gurmany and to see if they'd uploaded any kind of a family tree. They had not. So, Hudson copied their email address and then opened the background-check website, Spokeo. Pasting the email address into the search box, Hudson was presented with one result: *Yannis Gurman, 41. Resides in Winston-Salem, North*

Carolina. Hudson clicked to view the full background check. It listed Yannis's current address, four past addresses, phone number and email, which in turn matched the one used at FTDNA.

Scrolling past information about the size of Yannis's property, its value, and last time sold, Hudson reached the section titled *Family Members*. Two people were listed:

William R. Gurman, 82
William, 82, has previously lived with Yannis, 41, in Mobile, Al.
Born Aug 1940. Married. 1 Phone number. 2 Addresses

Cecilia Gurman, 40
Cecilia, 40, has previously lived with Yannis, 41, in Mobile, Al.
Born Jun 1983. Married. 1 Social Match. 4 Phone numbers

Hudson's working assumption was that William R. Gurman was Yannis's father and Cecilia was his wife; but he needed more proof. Clicking on Cecilia's name, Hudson scrolled down to *Social Profiles*, where her email address was associated with a Facebook page that he clicked to view.

The profile and header photographs for Cecilia Gurman were of two young kids smiling at the camera. Hudson moved down the page, noting that her hometown was given as Winston-Salem, her occupation listed as *at home*, and that she was married—although no partner was named. Looking at Cecilia's 303 friends, Hudson found that there were two others with the surname Gurman, which he noted down on some scrap paper to the side of his keyboard. Then, he clicked *Photos*, seeing that the vast majority were of the same two young kids in the profile pictures. Other photos were of group gatherings, a motorbike and a backyard. One image stood out, appearing somewhat dated by comparison to the rest. It was a close-up of a woman who looked to Hudson to be in her seventies. She had curly hair and large glasses and was smiling at someone or something to the left of the photographer. Her clothing dated the picture to the 1980s. Hudson clicked the image, bringing up all the public comments.

Kathy Znidersic: I really miss her…
Judy Darrington: Is that your mom?
    Cecilia Gurman: Mother in law
Marie Grundy: the best cook(e) ever!
    Cecilia Gurman: lol but true
Roger Cooke: lovely photo of Auntie Irene

Taking Roger Cooke's and Marie Grundy's comments together, Hudson made the assumption that the photograph was of Yannis Gurman's mother, Irene Cooke. He jotted down the information on the scrap paper and then opened a new internet tab, accessing the GenealogyBank website. He typed *Irene Gurman* in the search box with *Cooke* as a keyword, then clicked search. There was one result: an obituary from the *Mobile Register*, December 31, 1989.

GURMAN, IRENE
Mrs. Irene Gurman—A resident of Mobile, AL for all her short lifetime, died in a local hospital on Saturday, December 28, 1989. She is survived by her husband, William; young sons Yannis and Peter; parents Warren and Ethel Cooke; brother James and many nieces, nephews and good friends.

Hudson scanned over the rest of the obituary, which detailed the funeral arrangements but offered no further genealogical information. It was succinct, but it was enough for him to be able to create a new speculative family tree with Yannis Gurman as the home person. He added William Gurman as his father and Irene Cooke as his mother, and her parents, Warren and Ethel Cooke.

For what felt like the first time in several hours, Hudson looked up from his computer as he finished his coffee. Despite Kenyatta and Reggie working not far away, the office was almost silent. 'How's it going with you two?' he asked.

Kenyatta glanced up and nodded. 'Not bad. I think I've established who Mary Poppins really is.'

'What?' Hudson said.

'The lead name for cluster two is Mary Poppins—as in the movie—but I think her real name is actually Margaret Jones,' Kenyatta said with a laugh.

'That's pretty boring by comparison,' Hudson replied with a smile.

'And I'm *really* struggling with establishing my cluster lead,' Reggie said.

'Oh dear,' Kenyatta commented. 'Has the bubble burst for the new golden boy already?'

'I think so,' he conceded. 'I'll be lucky if I can tell you anything about my cluster lead by the time of the team briefing this afternoon.'

'Just switch him or her out,' Kenyatta said. 'Take the next closest match and work on them instead.'

'I might just do that.'

'What about you, Hudson?' Kenyatta asked.

'Good so far. I've figured out enough information about my cluster lead to get the names of his parents and one set of grandparents.'

'Good work,' she said.

Hudson returned his focus to his computer. Since he had no idea which side of Yannis Gurman's family tree was connected to the killer, he opted to continue working on the maternal line. Knowing that Irene Cooke had been born in 1942, he began to search for her parents' marriage prior to that point. He started with a vital records check at FamilySearch, finding that there were numerous datasets in various guises online.

Hudson spent some time sifting through the marriage records, but the best that he could find was simply an index at FindMyPast, which stated that Warren Cooke had married Ethel Webster in 1940. He searched all the major companies but was unable to find any further details of the marriage.

Returning to the FamilySearch homepage, Hudson clicked to SEARCH THE LIBRARY CATALOG, wondering if perhaps the FamilySearch Library housed any physical documents that could provide additional information. There were several results for his inquiry, but even inside the building the marriage records for Mobile County only ran as far as 1931. Short of contacting the relevant Probate Court for a copy of the full marriage license, Hudson had to set this search to one side, opting instead to look for the family on the 1950 U.S. Census.

He found them easily, living in Mobile, Alabama. The entry confirmed Hudson's findings so far and also added a birth year and the birth state of Alabama to Warren Cooke's and Ethel Webster's profiles. Not knowing at which point in 1940 the couple had married, Hudson jumped back to the census of that year and searched for Warren Cooke. There were 586 results with various spellings of first name and surname—but only one was living in Mobile, Alabama. Hudson jotted down the pertinent information and then saved the entry to Warren's family tree profile.

Leslie Cooke, 44, born Mobile, Alabama
Carrie Cooke, 44, born Knoxville, Tennessee
Warren Cooke, 21, born Mobile, Alabama
MaryAnn Cooke, 19, born Mobile, Alabama

Hudson returned to his Alabama marriage inquiry, entering Leslie Cooke's details. This time, FindMyPast had a scanned copy of the original record. The page was headed with the word *WHITE*, causing Hudson to assume that a separate ledger existed for Black marriages. Although the document was rich with biographical information for the two parties concerned—including descriptions of their age, height, weight, occupation, religious beliefs and residence—it failed to include details of their parents, which would have helped Hudson to push their lines back a generation. He added the new information of the precise date and location of their marriage and Carrie's maiden name of Cox to the family tree.

In just a short time, Hudson had succeeded in identifying two out of eight of Yannis Gurman's great-grandparents. There was a strong possibility that he actually did not need to progress any further back to find the important generation of connection, but he wanted to be certain, and so set about finding Leslie Cooke's and Carrie Cox's parents.

Hudson remained in his research rabbit hole until lunchtime, when Maddie drew him out of it by asking if anyone wanted anything from Eva's Bakery across the street.

'I'd say that's getting to be a daily habit of yours, Madison,' Kenyatta commented with a wry smile.

Maddie grimaced. 'Yeah, I know. I need to be better at making a packed lunch, but the mornings in our household right now are worse than when the kids were little.'

'I'll have a Boulange BLT, merci,' Hudson called over.

'Sure. Reggie?'

'I got a sandwich, thanks,' he replied.

Hudson watched as Maddie checked in with Ross on her way out of the office. Then he stood up, stretched, used the bathroom and made some fresh coffee, which he carried directly over to Ross's desk.

'Hey, how's it going?' Hudson asked him.

Ross looked up and smiled. 'Good, thanks. You?'

'Not bad, thank you,' Hudson replied, feeling slightly awkward. For no reason that had ever been established, he and Ross had never really hit it off. Although, if Hudson were really being honest with himself, he would have to admit that his own background had probably made him generally hold Ross at arm's length.

'Have you heard from Becky lately?' Hudson asked.

Ross nodded. 'I hear from her fairly regularly—though, I have a suspicion she's checking up on the apartment more than she's actually worrying about me.'

Hudson laughed. 'Do you know what it is that's keeping her in Haiti? It seems a pretty strange place to be for so long.'

'She never really goes into what she's doing out there…except to say charity work,' he answered with a shrug.

'Any idea when she'll be back?'

'Nope, no idea.'

'Well, I guess she knows what she's doing, and she'll come home when she's good and ready,' Hudson said.

'Yeah,' Ross agreed.

'Right, I better get back to work. See you later.'

'See you.'

Back at his desk, Hudson continued his research into Yannis Gurman's maternal grandmother, Ethel Webster. He'd already confirmed the names of her parents and was now working on the generation above.

A few minutes later, Maddie returned with his food and Hudson ate while he continued to work. Despite Maddie constantly nagging the team to take proper breaks, in practice they very rarely did, especially when they were working a big case.

When Maddie called the afternoon briefing at 4:30 p.m., Hudson sat back in his chair, satisfied with his day's work.

'Okay,' Maddie said, addressing the team as she shared her screen on the digital whiteboard. 'I'll start with my progress on cluster three.'

Hudson looked at the displayed pedigree chart, scanning it for any overlap with his own genetic network.

'So, my cluster lead is a lady called Hope Beal from San Diego, which, given the relative proximity to LA, could be an interesting lead. As you can see, I've identified her parents, all four grandparents and all eight great-grandparents, but I've still got the generation above to complete. The majority are California-based, but I have two of the great-greats from Arizona. Surnames to watch out for so far are…Beal, Hughes, Hernandez, Moreno, Garcia, Berrycloth—'

'Cool name,' Reggie interrupted Maddie's list.

Hudson turned to him and said, 'Right. So says the person with one of the best surnames ever.'

Reggie smiled and shrugged. 'To be frank, it's the one and only thing I can thank my parents for.'

'Reggie Snowwolf is an *amazing* name,' Maddie added. 'Anyway, getting back to my cluster. Last two names to be on the lookout for are Kinnan and Pace. That's kind of it from me. Kenyatta, your turn.'

Kenyatta stood up with a broad smile. 'First of all, GEDmatch Pro came up with the goods, providing us with another cluster with a strong lead of one hundred and twenty centimorgans, so I've added that to the shared file. As for my research today… I've been working on—one second—' she leaned over to her computer and then mirrored a pedigree chart onto the digital whiteboard '—cluster two, Mary Poppins!'

'I love that movie,' Maddie commented. 'But I never thought I'd see the day we'd be working on *her* genealogy. Practically perfect?'

'Well, you'd hope so,' Kenyatta replied. 'But the truth is a little more boring, I'm afraid. Real name, Margaret Jones, from Charlottesville, Virginia, and not a sign of Dick Van Dyke or a flying nanny. Instead, we have her father not showing up on *any* official records and Margaret taking her surname from her mom. So, I could have a big problem with the whole paternal side. I'm going to keep going and see how it goes. Right now, these are the names and places to watch out for: Jones, Wilcox, Sweran and Bonifay in Maryland, White and Fellows in South Carolina, Anderson in Texas and Goodrich in Pennsylvania.'

'Thanks, Kenyatta,' Maddie said. 'Hudson, what delights do you bring to us today?'

'Good progress, actually,' he announced, standing up with enthusiasm as he clicked to override Kenyatta's screen. 'I've gone to the great-great-grandparent level on my cluster lead's maternal side. Cooke, Trotter, Cox, McLemore, Webster, O'Carroll, Phillips and Boicourt are all in and around the South: Alabama, Tennessee, Georgia and the Carolinas,' he said.

'Thank you,' Maddie said. 'Last but not least, Reggie. And I'm expecting you to have wrapped up the whole case, or otherwise…you're fired.'

Reggie grinned as he stood up and shared his screen. 'Yeah, it's all done. I know who the Hollywood Strangler is but I'm not going to tell you all. You need to keep on working on it for yourselves. It's good practice.' He laughed and then continued. 'But for now, here's my progress on cluster four. I spent a long while trying to work out who my cluster lead was. It was worse than Mary Poppins; their username and email address is XT39 with no additional information. So, I've switched them out and here's the work I've done on the second match, Jennifer Hatter. I've traced all paternal lines back to the great-great-great-grandparent level. Surnames are Hatter, DeFrieze, Reed, Crass, Haunsom, Glenn, Stockstill and Flaherty. Mostly California, but some Ohio, Ireland, Wisconsin, Kansas and Norway.'

He sat back down, and Maddie moved to the front of the room.

'Great work today, guys,' she said. 'We've made really good progress on this case already. Some potential overlaps in the Carolinas and California to keep an eye out for.'

'Are we going to hear from Becky with the geo-profiling?' Kenyatta asked. 'That might help narrow our focus.'

'She's *hoping* to come to the briefing on Monday,' Maddie replied. 'Between her work out there—whatever that is—and spotty internet, it's not easy. But I do know that she is working on it.'

'I miss her,' Kenyatta said.

'Me too,' Maddie agreed. 'I'm really not sure it's that safe for her to be down there alone.'

'I think she's made a few friends who are looking out for her,' Ross said. 'Not as good as *me*, obviously.'

'Obviously,' Maddie agreed. 'She'll come back when she's good and ready, I guess.' She switched off the digital whiteboard. 'Okay. Home time, folks. See you all tomorrow, bright and early.'

Hudson brought up Yannis Gurman's father's family tree profile, ready to begin work on him tomorrow. Then, he closed his computer and packed up his bag. 'Coming home?' he asked Reggie. 'Or are you out with your mysterious date again, tonight?'

'I'm home, man. Let's go,' Reggie replied.

They said goodbye to the rest of the team and walked the forty-five minutes back to Hudson's house on Milton Avenue in the Liberty Wells district. Not long after Hudson's former wife, Abigail, had left the home during the pandemic, Reggie had moved in to the guest room. Hudson's initial reluctance to have a housemate had quickly dissipated and he'd enjoyed having the company and the distraction from his marriage ending.

'Should I cook, or do you have plans?' Hudson asked as he closed the front door, hoping to elicit an inkling about Reggie's latest conquest.

'I'll make my fried chicken special, if you like?' Reggie suggested.

'Perfect,' Hudson replied from the hallway. During the more than two years that he'd been living with him, Reggie had had no fewer than two boyfriends and three girlfriends, followed by a period of avowed celibacy that had ended around two months ago when he'd started dating someone that Hudson had yet to meet. 'I want to take this one slow,' Reggie had told him. 'Try and make it work.'

Hudson had viewed the carousel of Reggie's relationships with a mixture of awe and bewilderment; his confidence was boundless. 'Well, unless you need any help, I'm going to sit and watch some basketball.'

'I'm good, man,' Reggie replied. 'Are your team playing?'

'Not until next week,' Hudson answered, referring to his home-state team, the Maine Black Bears. 'Against the Nebraska Cornhuskers.'

'Astounding,' Reggie said with his usual lack of enthusiasm for the sport. 'Have you downloaded Fiorry yet?' Reggie added.

'No,' Hudson answered, rolling his eyes as he sat down in the living room and switched on the TV. Fiorry was a dating app that Reggie and some of Hudson's other friends had tried to encourage him to use to get back onto the dating scene.

'Do it now!' he called.

'I don't know…'

'Hudson!'

Hudson sighed, took out his cell phone and downloaded the app. Then he sat staring at it, his thumb hovering over the icon. He just couldn't do it. He wasn't ready. Instead, he opened up the KARE11.com website to check the news.

Two years ago, Hudson had been approached by a woman called Wanda Chabala, who had procured—by illegal means—a DNA sample from the suspect who had raped and murdered her daughter, Francesca. For a significant amount of money, Hudson had undertaken private investigative genetic genealogy on the illegal sample. The work had almost cost Hudson his job at Venator and things had gotten worse when one of the two brothers that he'd identified as prime suspects had turned out to be Wanda Chabala's husband, Warren Mercaldo, who was eventually arrested for the crime. Last year, after a lengthy trial, Warren had been convicted of Francesca's rape and murder and sentenced to life in prison. A man previously convicted for the crime, Brandon Blake, was still serving time in prison for a crime that he hadn't committed. A fresh appeal at the Minnesota Supreme Court was currently in the oral argument phase, but there was nothing new on the news website about the case.

Hudson closed his cell phone and turned on the TV to watch some basketball.

Chapter Eleven

Wednesday, November 2, 2022, Salt Lake City, Utah

It was 6:13 a.m. and Reggie Snowwolf was sitting down at the kitchen counter, drinking coffee. It was pitch black outside and the only light came from the soft strip lighting under the cupboards and from his laptop which was open in front of him, softly playing some Carrie Underwood.

His busy mind rarely allowed him to sleep much past five o'clock in the morning and, for the most part, he put this time to good use working on his cases.

He'd spent the past hour working on Leon Sierra, attempting to triangulate between the family trees of Malik Johnson and Elijah Benton. But it was an absurd task. Elijah Benton only matched Leon Sierra with twenty-nine centimorgans of DNA, meaning that their common ancestors could be anything from fourth to eighth cousins, or possibly even more distant. The chance of finding this ancestral person or couple was close to zero.

But still Reggie persisted.

He was looking at one of Elijah Benton's great-great-grandparents, Thomas Cristmas, on the 1870 census for Yazoo, Warren County, Mississippi. The entry wasn't particularly revealing.

Green, Alexander, 32 years old, male, mulatto, farmer, born Mississippi
Cristmas, Thomas, 22 years old, male, mulatto, farm hand, born Mississippi

Reggie saved the document to Thomas Cristmas's profile page and ran searches for him on the previous censuses. As Reggie had fully expected, there was no sign of him, likely because he and his family had been enslaved and, therefore, remained unnamed.

He drank some coffee as he stared at the screen, still and in thought.

Reggie opened a new web browser tab, loaded the Mapping The Freedmen's Bureau website and navigated to their records on Mississippi. He scrolled down, pausing when he spotted a record titled

Register of Freedmen at Home Colony, Davis Bend, MS. From his previous research, he knew that Davis Bend—now Davis Island—was just diagonally across the Mississippi River from Yazoo. It was worth a look. He clicked the link and then read the document description.

The Home Colony at Davis Bend, Mississippi was established by the Freedmen's Bureau in 1863-64 on land formerly owned by Jefferson Davis and his brother...

Reggie entered the surname Cristmas into the search box.
'Boom!' Reggie said with a grin as he pored over the results.

Henrietta Cristmas, female, age 36, brown, house servant, owner: James Woods
Thomas Cristmas, male, age 16, brown, field hand, owner: James Woods
Joseph Cristmas, male, age 15, brown, field hand, owner: James Woods

Despite the current lack of evidence, Reggie suspected that Henrietta Cristmas had been the mother to Thomas and Joseph.

Switching to the 1860 U.S. Federal Census Slave Schedules, Reggie entered James Woods' name and Warren County, Mississippi, into the search box. *One Result.*

Name of slave owner: James Woods
Slave, aged 56, female, black
Slave, aged 44, female, black
Slave, aged 33, female, mulatto
Slave, aged 13, male, mulatto
Slave, aged 12, male, mulatto

Reggie saved the entry against Thomas Cristmas's profile despite the fact that it was insufficient evidence. Even if he could confirm with certainty that the final three slaves belonging to James Woods had indeed been Henrietta, Thomas and Joseph Cristmas, it actually did nothing to push the family back another generation, which was what he needed to do.

Since marriages between enslaved people had been illegal at that time, there was little sense in Reggie running a search for Henrietta.

The same was true for trying to find a birth certificate for Thomas and Joseph.

He closed his eyes and tried to switch off to allow his brain to mull over the problem. Reggie was a keen and talented chess player, his mind able to play forward several moves across multiple permutations. He applied the same parts of his brain to genealogical research, allowing his mind to work systematically several paces ahead of his current position.

'Do you *ever* sleep?' Hudson suddenly asked, waltzing into the kitchen, showered, dressed and ready for his day.

Reggie opened his eyes. 'When my body permits it,' he replied with a smile. 'I'm working on Leon Sierra.'

'And? Getting anywhere?'

Reggie nodded. 'Slowly but surely, yeah.'

'Coffee?' Hudson asked.

Reggie quickly looked at the time: 7:32 a.m. 'No thanks, man. I'd better get ready for work.' He shut his laptop and carried his empty cup over to the sink, gazing out of the window for a moment. The first signs of dawn were appearing over the distant Wasatch Mountain range. Although he could see nothing more than the gnarled outline against the paling sky, he knew that the snow line was creeping down the mountain ready for this winter's ski season. Reggie was a snowboarder and couldn't wait to hit the slopes at Brighton or Powder Mountain, his favorite resorts in the area.

He took a quick shower, and by 8:15 a.m., he and Hudson were ready to walk into the city together.

Although they arrived just before 9 a.m., Hudson and Reggie were the last to arrive at the Venator office.

'You're all very eager,' Maddie commented from the kitchen area when she saw that everyone was working quietly at their desks before they were even due to be in the office. 'I guess you're all desperate to catch the Hollywood Strangler,' she added with a laugh.

'Sssh! We're busy,' Kenyatta mock-rebuked.

Maddie grinned as she disappeared inside her office.

Reggie was working on cluster four. Having substituted the

designated lead for the second highest match, Jennifer Hatter, he had identified all eight of her paternal great-great-grandparents and was now focusing on her maternal line.

He returned to Jennifer Hatter's birth record, pulling it up from the family tree profile that he'd created for her. She'd been born in 1965 in Los Angeles, California, and her mother's name was given as Peggy Dee Waldon. Reggie had found Peggy's marriage to Jennifer's father, Clifford Hatter, in 1959 in Los Angeles. The 1950 census had given Peggy Dee Waldon's birth details as 1934, California, so Reggie opened the *California Birth Index 1905-1995* on FamilySearch and entered those particulars. Despite receiving over ten thousand possible results, the top of the list appeared to be correct.

Name: Peggy Dee Waldon
Birth Date: 13 Sep 1934
Gender: Female
Mother's Maiden Name: Schaw
Birth County: Sacramento

Although it looked as though it might be right, the brevity of the record—as with almost all the results from the California birth index—meant that it was impossible to be certain. The absence of the father's name meant that Reggie could not confirm right now that this was the correct record.

Copying down the details onto scrap paper, Reggie looked at the family on the 1940 census, which revealed that Peggy Dee's father had been named as Sherman Waldon, born 1910 in Wyoming.

Although Reggie was trying to build a quick and simple tree for Jennifer Hatter, pushing back on every family line possible, a mistake at this point would result in the creation of an incorrect tree which he'd never be able to connect to the killer. He thought for a moment about other resources that might confirm Peggy Dee Waldon's parents' names, then opened *U.S., Social Security Applications and Claims Index, 1936-2007* and entered her name and the date stated on the California birth index. One result.

Name: Peggy Dee Waldon
Gender: Female
Race: White
Birth Date: 13 Sep 1934
Birth Place: Sacramento, California
Death Date: 14 Feb 2003
Father: Sherman Waldon
Mother: Helen Schaw
SSN: 250071178

The record tied what he'd found together, and Reggie now felt adequately assured to save the new information to Jennifer Hatter's growing family tree. His next step was to try and find the marriage record between Sherman Waldon and Helen Schaw. With luck, it would name both sets of their parents.

He started with the Research Wiki at FamilySearch, which listed several options for Wyoming marriages. It looked promising. Working his way down the list, he found a scanned copy of the original marriage certificate at FindMyPast. The couple had married on April 23, 1930, in Lander, Fremont, Wyoming. The record confirmed the bride's and groom's ages and their residence at the time of marriage, but there were no additional family members named.

Reggie downloaded the marriage certificate and added it to Sherman and Helen's profile before switching over to the 1920 U.S. Census, searching for Sherman Waldon, born 1910 in Lander, Fremont, Wyoming. After a moment of trawling, he found what appeared to be the right person.

Waldon, Edward, head of household, white, married, age 32, born Colorado, father born Colorado, mother born Arkansas
Waldon, Elsie, wife, white, married, age 32, born Wyoming, father born Switzerland, mother born Switzerland
Waldon, Sherman, son, white, 10, born Wyoming, father born Colorado, mother born Wyoming
Schoettlin, Susette, mother-in-law, white, widow, age 62, born Switzerland, father born Switzerland, mother born Switzerland

Reggie added the information to Jennifer Hatter's tree and followed it up by stepping back a decade to find the family in 1910. He located them easily, living in Lander, Fremont, Wyoming, and the information it contained correlated to that which he'd already found. It also supplied the additional information that Edward Waldon and Elsie Schoettlin had married in 1907, and that the union had produced three children, all of whom had been recorded as still being alive in 1910.

Reggie was about to save the census page to the relevant parties' profiles when he spotted a familiar name two households above the Waldons.

Schoettlin, Fred, head of household, white, married, age 52, married 35 years, born Switzerland, father born Switzerland, mother born Switzerland, immigration 1882, naturalized
Schoettlin, Susette, wife, white, married, age 52, married 35 years, two children born and still living, born Switzerland, father born Switzerland, mother born Switzerland, immigration 1882, naturalized
Schoettlin, Margaret, daughter, white, single, age 30, born Switzerland, father born Switzerland, mother born Switzerland, immigration 1882, naturalized

Reggie smiled at the new information as he saved the census page to the Waldon and Schoettlin families. Then, he checked to see if naturalization records existed for Wyoming. They did, but only for Laramie County, which Reggie checked just to be sure, finding nothing for the family.

Knowing that Edward Waldon had been born in 1888 in the state of Colorado, Reggie looked for birth records on the Research Wiki at FamilySearch. He groaned when he spotted that instead of the usual list of dates, places and options to view digital records, there was just a simple statement.

A law was passed in 1876 requiring counties and towns in Colorado to record births and deaths. In those counties where the clerks complied, the records are available at the local courthouse. Most early files are incomplete.

It didn't sound promising, he thought, as he ran a search for Edward Waldon's birth. Unsurprisingly, there were no results.

He next looked at church records for the state, receiving a similar announcement.

Church records vary significantly depending on the denomination and the record keeper.

Reggie followed the link to *Colorado, Church Records, 1692-1942* but found no mention of the Waldon family within the record set.

He sat back, sighed and stretched.

'Are you stuck, my golden boy?' Kenyatta teased.

Reggie looked over at her and smiled. 'I'm never stuck, just waiting for my brain to recalibrate and direct me down the correct path.' He smiled, clicked his fingers and said, 'Probate! That's where I'm headed next.'

He turned back to his computer and opened *Colorado, U.S., Wills and Probate Records, 1875-1974,* running a search for anyone in the state with the surname Waldon.

He found one Waldon, several Waldens, two Weldons and a bunch of Waltons.

He started with the Waldon entry, intending to look at the others with the minor spelling variations. A scanned copy of an original will, dated 1923, loaded on-screen. It was a typed form with space for handwritten answers. He zoomed in to get a better read.

In the Matter of the Last Will and Testament of Jack Waldon, deceased, to the Hon Geo. Longford, Judge of the County Court of the City and County of Denver, in the State of Colorado. The petition of the undersigned Laura Waldon respectfully represents that Jack Waldon, late of the City and County of Denver, in the State of Colorado, departed this life on or about the 6th day of January A.D. 1923.

The document continued on in legal speak until the key part that Reggie was most eager to read.

Your petitioner would further show that said deceased left him surviving as his sole

and only heirs at law, devisees and legatees as follows, to-wit:
Laura Waldon, widow, of Grove St, Denver, CO
Mr. Edward Waldon, son, of Lander, Fremont, WY
Mrs. Helen Hazelwood, daughter, Irving Street, Denver, CO
His only children

'I'll take that. Thank you very much,' Reggie said to his computer as he saved the document and updated Jennifer Hatter's tree with the new information. He was now in possession of the names of eleven out of sixteen of her great-great-grandparents. He just needed to identify Laura Waldon's maiden name, and he'd have his twelfth.

He sat back and stretched again, momentarily pulled out of his Jennifer Hatter research and noticing that Kenyatta and Maddie were milling around in the kitchen area. He looked at the time: 12:32 p.m. And, as if by magic, his stomach began to growl. He stood up and wandered over to them.

'Had a productive morning?' Maddie asked.

He nodded as he made himself some coffee. 'Yeah, really good, thanks. I think, by the time we get to the briefing, I should have all of my cluster lead's great-greats in place.'

'Good job,' Maddie said, taking a lunchbox from the refrigerator.

'You not going to Eva's today?' Kenyatta asked, exaggerating her shock at this revelation.

'No. I am *not*,' she confirmed. 'I happen to have made myself a very healthy chicken salad instead.'

'Well, welcome to the convince-yourself-that-you-like-eating-salad club,' Kenyatta responded, taking out her own salad box.

'Well, you enjoy that,' Hudson commented with a laugh, 'I'm going out for a Boulange BLT, and I don't care what any of you think.'

Maddie scowled at him as he headed to the door.

Reggie stood for a moment, holding his sandwiches, then wandered over to chat to Ross. 'Hey. How's your morning been?'

Ross looked up from his computer and ran a hand through his floppy blond hair. 'It's been busy as usual,' he replied with a smile, noticing Reggie's sandwiches. 'You want to eat lunch together?'

Reggie looked across the office, seeing that the general policy appeared to be that everyone ate at their own desks and continued working. He shook his head. 'It looks like I'd better get back to it.'

'Maddie keeps nagging at everyone to take their breaks,' Ross countered.

'Yeah, but…by the looks of things, it doesn't seem to be working,' Reggie commented. 'It's okay, I'm good having a working lunch.'

'Tomorrow… Let's go out for lunch, yeah?' Ross asked.

Reggie nodded. 'Sure. Okay.' Then he returned to his desk.

In truth, he really was more than happy to eat his lunch while he continued with Jennifer Hatter's tree. He loved doing genetic genealogy, so it was hardly a chore for him anyway; a sentiment he surmised that the rest of the Venator team also shared.

He took a bite of his cheese and ham sandwich as he set about finding Laura Waldon's maiden name. Within a few seconds, he was back in his own world, a genealogical multiverse.

The afternoon briefing arrived as it usually did, without warning. Maddie gave them a five-minute heads-up and then stood beside the digital whiteboard while she waited for them all to finish off whatever they were in the middle of working on.

Reggie prepared his screen to share and then turned to face front.

'Okay, any volunteers to kick off the briefing?' Maddie asked.

'Sure,' Reggie said, standing up and mirroring his screen so that Jennifer Hatter's pedigree was displayed for the team. 'I've managed to pin down all of this cluster lead's great-great-grandparents, except one: I can't find Laura Waldon's maiden name. Nothing on the census or birth records for where she claims to have been born.' He zoomed in to the top sixteen ancestors so that the full surnames became legible. 'In addition to California, Ohio, Ireland, Wisconsin, Kansas and Norway, we've also got Arkansas, Colorado, Wyoming and Switzerland.'

'Half the world, in other words,' Hudson said, smiling.

'Pretty much, yeah,' Reggie agreed. 'I may need to go a generation higher, but I'm going to focus on triangulating with another match first.'

'Smart move,' Maddie said. 'Well done. Who wants to go next?'

'I will,' Hudson volunteered, standing up as his computer screen overrode Reggie's with a similar pedigree chart for his cluster lead, Yannis Gurman. 'So, I've just finished working on Yannis's paternal line, but I've hit a wall with his grandfather's father who's absent from the records. The surname Gurman actually came from Yannis's great-grandmother,' he said, zooming in to this section of the pedigree. 'Still mainly focused on the Deep South. So, with fourteen out of sixteen great-greats, I'm done with this guy and now also need to concentrate on triangulation.'

'Excellent. Good work,' Maddie said. 'Kenyatta?'

Kenyatta mirrored her screen, which appeared not to have changed since yesterday's briefing. 'Not so much progress from me. Mary Poppins, here, is really trying my patience.'

'Have you tried a spoonful of sugar?' Reggie asked.

Kenyatta glowered at him. 'I've pushed back a little further on the maternal lines, but Miss Poppins's paternal line is a non-starter. I'm also ready to switch to triangulation and need to hope that the match is on the maternal side.'

'Great going, troops,' Maddie said, typing into the free computer close to the digital whiteboard and bringing up her own screen. She was also almost done with the great-great-grandparent generation. 'As you can see, I'm almost there. Although, I may need to go back a generation further. Ironically, I'm having trouble pushing back the Berrycloth line. I think the more unusual the surname, the more ways it gets spelled. Location-wise, we're still looking at the Wild West: California, Nevada, Arizona, Utah up to Oregon.' She looked around the room, then clapped her hands together. 'Okay. Thanks, everyone. You're dismissed. Have a great evening.'

Reggie turned back to his computer and opened the CSV file for cluster four. The top match was XT39, which he'd switched out after being able to glean nothing about the person's identity, and the second was Jennifer Hatter. There were six other names, all matching the killer with a lessening amount of DNA as the list progressed. Next on the list was someone called Jonas Crawford.

On the FTDNA website, Reggie logged in using the Hollywood

Strangler kit details and navigated through the dashboard into the autosomal matches. He found Jonas Crawford, who matched the killer with one hundred and one centimorgans. Under the heading *Ancestral Surnames*, Jonas had added Crawford, Morris, Best and Castelejin. Reggie noted that the family tree icon was dark blue, meaning that Jonas had included some kind of a tree. Oftentimes, he found that the information uploaded was minimal, private or inaccurate, but he was pleased to see that the pedigree ran from Jonas, through two parents—named only as *Private*—to grandparents who held the same four surnames as those listed under *Ancestral Surnames*. It was an excellent place to start his research tomorrow.

'You coming?' Hudson asked, standing beside Reggie's desk with his jacket on and bag slung over his shoulder.

'Yeah, sure,' Reggie replied, shutting down his computer.

'Goodbye, all,' Kenyatta called as she headed for the door.

'Oh, Kenyatta!' Reggie called after her, causing her to stop and turn. 'Don't get that song stuck in your head now.'

'Which song?' she questioned, confused.

He sang *Supercalifragilisticexpialidocious*.

Kenyatta growled at him, covered her ears and continued walking. 'I'm not listening. I can't hear you.'

Reggie laughed, collected his jacket, called goodbye to Maddie and walked beside Hudson toward the door.

'Are you out with your hot date tonight, or playing it cool?' Hudson asked as they left.

'Playing it cool,' he confirmed. 'I don't like to give too much of the Snowwolf away in one go.'

'Cheesy,' Ross said, as they passed him.

Reggie grinned and left the office, already planning to spend his evening continuing to try to work out Leon Sierra's identity.

Chapter Twelve

Thursday, November 3, 2022, Salt Lake City, Utah

Kenyatta Nelson was nibbling on a carrot stick, something she'd unexpectedly grown to enjoy eating since going on a diet two years ago. Despite a few setbacks along the way and severe overindulging at Thanksgiving and Christmas last year, she'd stuck to her weight-loss plan and was now a very comfortable and happy one hundred and seventy pounds. Her weight loss had coincided with a positive upturn in her personal life, and she was now happier than she'd been in a very long time.

She was sitting at her desk, having just opened the family tree for the lead of cluster two, Mary Poppins, aka Margaret Jones. Now it was time to choose another individual from within this cluster who was a DNA match to both the killer and Margaret. She'd picked the next person with the highest amount of shared DNA in the CSV file: someone with the username Timothy K. Schwartz and who matched the killer with one hundred and twenty-nine centimorgans.

Before she did anything further, she needed to verify that Timothy K. Schwartz was actually the person's real name and not another pseudonym like Mary Poppins. At FTDNA, she checked to see what information he had included in his profile. There was almost nothing there except for a headshot photo, his mandatory email address, which was at Gmail, and a combination of his first and last name and the number 1982. Kenyatta copied the email address, wondering if there was any significance in those numbers, and pasted it into the background-checking website, BeenVerified.

The presented results—which were sometimes wildly inaccurate—suggested that Timothy K. Schwartz was indeed a real person, born in February 1982. Several potential addresses and phone numbers for Timothy were included, all within the city of Indianapolis. Kenyatta scrolled down to *Social Media*, finding one match to a LinkedIn account which she now clicked to view.

The profile photo for the account holder matched the one on Timothy's FTDNA page. Kenyatta was sure that she had found the right person. According to his business profile, his occupation was a *Financial Technology Recruitment Consultant* for a large company in Indianapolis.

Kenyatta hit *See all posts* and slowly began scrutinizing everything that Timothy K. Schwartz had posted. The vast majority related to the company and industry in which he worked, which Kenyatta didn't really understand. The more she read, the more confused she was over what Timothy's job actually was. She checked the comments on every post, looking for anyone with the surname Schwartz or who might have declared a familial connection to Timothy.

She got back to September 5, when he had shared an image with the words *Happy Labor Day* emblazoned over the stars and stripes. The accompanying text read, *For everyone celebrating in the US, enjoy time with your friends and family. #Laborday #Americanworkers.* Underneath were six comments, one of which was from someone named Martin James Schwartz, who wrote, *Happy Labor Day, son. Proud of all you've achieved.*

Was this Martin James Schwartz using *son* to reflect their relationship, or in the way that some older guys sometimes spoke to younger ones, and the connection between them actually not at all patrilineal?

Kenyatta looked at Martin James Schwartz's own LinkedIn profile to try and determine the answer. It seemed that Martin had a similarly nebulous job description to Timothy. His profile photo dated him to be in his sixties and very plausibly a generation older than Timothy. There was also a distinct similarity between the two men, but Kenyatta was always wary of drawing comparisons like that.

Martin wasn't a regular poster on LinkedIn and Kenyatta quickly reached his first post in July 2021. All that she gleaned was that he too was from Indianapolis. She still didn't have proof that they were father and son, so she returned to BeenVerified and ran a search for Martin James Schwartz in the city of Indianapolis. The inquiry gave just a single result for a man born in June 1946. Under the *Relatives* tab, one person was listed: Janet Schwartz. Kenyatta clicked her name, finding a link to her Facebook account.

It took Kenyatta four minutes of snooping in Janet's open profile to find several photographs that showed her with Martin in a way that confirmed that they were indeed a couple. Other family events, including a recent barbecue, showed Janet and Martin together with Timothy.

Satisfied that she had found the correct Timothy K. Schwartz and his parents, Martin and Janet, Kenyatta turned back to Ancestry and the speculative family tree that she had created for Mary Poppins. Clicking on her real name of Margaret Jones, Kenyatta added Timothy K. Schwartz as her son. Even though this was certainly *not* their relationship, it allowed Kenyatta to create a new floating tree within Margaret Jones's, which she would hopefully connect up later after more research.

Clicking into Timothy K. Schwartz's profile, Kenyatta selected *Edit relationships*, removing Margaret Jones as his mother and leaving him as an orphan. She then hit the *Add father* button and typed in Martin James Schwartz's name and birth year. Then she added Timothy's mother as Janet with no surname. Hopefully it wouldn't take too long to find out how Margaret Jones and Timothy K. Schwartz were really related, and then she could link the two trees together. The Hollywood Strangler should also descend from the point where these two families converged.

Kenyatta returned to Janet Schwartz's Facebook page and began a systematic scrutiny of each of her posts, harvesting several names of family members and key dates of births, marriages and deaths.

Just over an hour later, Kenyatta had built up a detailed picture of Timothy K. Schwartz's family up to all four grandparents. So far, there was no sign of an overlap with Margaret Jones's family.

'Kenyatta?' Ross called over. 'Phone call for you. East High School.'

'The school?' Kenyatta checked, picking up her cell and wondering why they hadn't called her there. She found that her phone was on silent, and she had three missed calls from them. Their persistence could only mean that there was a problem.

She got up, hurried over to Ross's desk and took the phone. 'Hello?'

Ross tactfully slid backward, got up from his seat and wandered over to talk to Reggie for a moment.

'Hi, is this Mrs. Nelson?' asked a voice Kenyatta recognized as belonging to Mr. Reeves, the school principal. He would not be delivering good news.

'Yes, speaking,' she confirmed, bracing herself.

'This is Principal Reeves from East High School. I'm calling about Troy.'

'Oh,' she said, not in the least bit surprised that of her three sons, he would be the reason for this call. He was sixteen years old and the polar opposite of his twin brother, Gabe, and older brother, Jon.

'I'm afraid he's been bullying another student…quite severely. It's been going on a while apparently, mainly verbal, but today it became physical, and the other student wound up needing to go to the hospital.'

'Oh, that's awful,' Kenyatta said, then lowered her voice when she saw Hudson and Reggie turn to look over. 'What happened?'

'He twisted the student's arm up behind his back until his shoulder popped out,' the principal said.

Kenyatta gasped. 'What? Was he provoked in any way? Did this other student do something to Troy?' she asked, vainly hoping that she could find a justification for such excessive violence. Although, really, she knew that nothing could warrant snapping someone's arm out of joint.

The principal was quiet for a moment. 'No, I'm afraid not. Several witnesses have confirmed that the student did nothing more than look at Troy.'

'But… But why did he…? Why would he do that?' Kenyatta asked. 'Why did he say he did it?'

'He's only said that the other student deserved it.'

'My goodness. I am so sorry. How's the other student doing? I hope he's okay. Is he?' she asked.

'I'm not sure, but he was in a lot of pain when the ambulance took him to the hospital.'

Kenyatta fought back against the emotion rising inside her. To think that her own son had behaved in such a barbaric way. 'I take it he'll have a suspension?'

Principal Reeves cleared his throat. 'I'm afraid not this time, Mrs.

Nelson. Taking the seriousness of this assault into account, and the fact that Troy has been in trouble with us before, means that, unfortunately, we're left with no choice but to expel him from the school.'

'Oh, no,' Kenyatta interrupted with a sob. 'Please don't do that. I'll talk with him. We'll do a restorative justice program and a behavior contract... Anything but expel him. Please, no.'

'It's too late, Mrs. Nelson. I'm sorry.'

'But...where will he go?'

'I'm looking at alternative education programs, but I don't feel that Troy should be moved to another high school. Mrs. Nelson, we think that he needs educating somewhere better equipped to cope with his specific behavioral issues.'

Kenyatta was floored.

'I know this is hard for you to hear, Mrs. Nelson, but we just can't have Troy in our school environment any longer. I'll talk with him some more before he gets dismissed.'

'Okay,' Kenyatta stammered.

'Can you come and collect him?'

'I'm at work right now, but I'll ask my neighbor to come and get him.'

'Thank you. And I'm sorry.'

She ended the call, took in a deep breath and ran her forefingers under her eyes. She breathed slowly for a few seconds, then sent a message to her neighbor asking if she could collect Troy. A few moments later, she turned with a mask of normality and returned to her desk.

'Everything...okay?' Hudson asked.

Kenyatta smiled and nodded. 'Just Troy getting into a fight.'

'Is he okay?'

'Yeah, he's fine,' she replied, feigning deep interest in her computer screen, while trying to stop her mind from going into freefall with countless questions about Troy's education and the potentially damaging implications of the decision to expel him. But the part of it all that she kept coming back to was what he'd done. This was *not* a fight. Troy had snapped someone's arm out of joint. Troy. Her son.

Her phone lit up with a reply from her neighbor confirming that she would head over to the school and collect him.

Kenyatta sent a message to thank her and then pushed her phone to one side, trying to steady her breathing. She wondered about going into Maddie's office, explaining the situation and asking for the rest of the day off. But she knew that if she confronted Troy right now, it would not go down well. He needed time alone. She should also notify her ex-husband, Otis, but knew that he'd fly straight off the handle and would probably beat Troy.

Kenyatta sighed for her own weakness. Given Otis's temper, was it any wonder that Troy was the way he was? Witnessing his father's verbal and sometimes physical abuse over the years of their marriage had obviously deeply affected him. Deep down, she knew that it wasn't as simple as that. Troy's twin brother, Gabe, had witnessed everything, too, and he had absolutely no anger issues whatsoever, even when Troy had turned on him. She reflected on their childhood skirmishes, squabbles and fall outs. The balance of blame had always been heavily tipped toward Troy. Despite Otis's objections, Troy had seen a therapist on several occasions in the past and she now regretted not continuing to get him help. She was sure that it was Otis's warped DNA in Troy that had made him snap that poor boy's arm. Her thoughts jumped into a bleak place as she recalled the stoning to death of the family dog, Dougie, two years ago, and her son Jon's insistence that Troy had been the person responsible. She'd believed Troy's denial at the time, but now she wasn't so sure. Something had to be done about it, but she needed a clear head to think. Now was not the time.

Kenyatta did something that her own therapist, Tabitha, had advised her against doing, and pushed the problem into a recess in her mind and shut the door. Then, she allowed her eyes to focus on the content of the screen in front of her that she'd been staring at for the past few minutes. Now, where was she?

Timothy K. Schwartz's maternal grandmother, that was where. Kenyatta had been trying to find Marianne Eisenhut's maiden name. The 1950 census showed her living with her husband, Cornelius, and daughter, Janet, in Logan, Hocking County, Ohio, and that she had been born in the same state.

Kenyatta ran a search for vital records for the county in the

FamilySearch Wiki, selecting the top of several possible links to *Ohio, Marriages, 1800-1942*, where she inputted just Cornelius Eisenhut's name. There was just one result and it appeared to be correct. Kenyatta clicked the camera icon and waited a few seconds while a black-and-white scan of an open page appeared in front of her. It looked like a thick tome with one marriage entry per page, exactly the kind of rich detail that she was hoping to find.

In the matter of Cornelius Eisenhut and Marianne Burch, the undersigned respectfully make their application for a marriage license for said parties, and upon oath state...; That said Cornelius Eisenhut is 24 years of age on the 29 June 1941. His residence is 515 Linden Street. His place of birth is Degraff, Ohio. His occupation is laborer. Color white. His father's name is Charles Allison Eisenhut. His mother's maiden name was Flossie P. Decker. That he was not previously married.

Kenyatta smiled at the level of information as she carefully added it to Timothy K. Schwartz's tree before returning to the document for the bride's details.

That said Marianne Burch is 22 years of age on the 30 day of October 1941. Her residence is 509 Beaufontaine, Logan County. Her place of birth is Westerville, Ohio. Her occupation is clerk. Color white. Her father's name is Ben Burch. Her mother's maiden name was Della Fellows. That she was not previously married.

As Kenyatta added the information to the family tree, her eyes rested on the name of Della Fellows. Although she couldn't hold each and every name in her head that she came across, she was fairly sure that the name Fellows *had* cropped up in her research, so she entered the surname into the *Tree search* box. Sure enough, one of Margaret Jones's maternal great-great-grandparents had been a man named Walter Fellows from Virginia. It wasn't a particularly unusual name, so it could well be a coincidence, especially as the two families appeared to be from different states. But it was certainly worth checking out.

Kenyatta looked at Walter Fellows's profile. There were eleven hints for his name, which she clicked to view. Knowing that Margaret

Jones's great-grandmother, Betty Fellows, had been born in 1899 in Virginia, Kenyatta opted to pick the 1900 census from the list of hints. The document, taken in Staunton City, Augusta County, Virginia, loaded on-screen.

Fellows, Walter, Head, born April 1876
Fellows, Mary, Wife, born Sep 1877
Fellows, James, Son, born Mar 1896
Fellows, Della, Daughter, born Jun 1897
Fellows, John, Son, born Jul 1898
Fellows, Betty, Daughter, born Dec 1899

Kenyatta grinned. Della and Betty Fellows appeared to be sisters, making Walter Fellows and his wife, Mary Goodrich, common ancestors to Margaret Jones, aka Mary Poppins, and Timothy K. Schwartz. If she was correct, then Walter and Mary would also be the Hollywood Strangler's direct ancestors.

Although she was certain that she'd found the correct connection, Kenyatta wanted further evidence. Her hope that she might find birth certificates for Della and Betty to confirm that they had the same parents was thwarted when she found that records for Augusta County only ran to 1896.

She now needed to follow Della's and Betty's lives through vital records, the censuses and any other documentation that she could find to substantiate her findings.

At 4:30 p.m., as Maddie asked the team to prepare for the afternoon briefing, Kenyatta sat back and managed a momentary smile.

'You look like you've had a good day,' Maddie said to her.

Kenyatta shrugged. 'We'll have to wait and see.'

While the rest of the team got themselves ready, Kenyatta briefly allowed her thoughts to return to Troy. She'd checked her cell phone regularly throughout the day, but he hadn't responded to her message asking him to notify her when he got home. She quickly typed out a message to his twin brother, Gabe.

Are you home, Gabe? Is Troy with you?

'Okay,' Maddie said, positioning herself beside the digital whiteboard. 'Is everyone ready? Ross, are you good to record?'

'Ready and waiting,' he confirmed.

'Well, I don't think I can stand the anticipation of what Kenyatta has to tell us,' Maddie said. 'So, why don't you go first.'

'It will be my pleasure,' Kenyatta said. She shared her screen, which showed a descendancy tree from Walter Fellows and Mary Goodrich, down through their children to Margaret Jones. 'So, this is Mary Poppins's line, descending through Walter and Mary's daughter, Betty.' Kenyatta scrolled across to Betty's sister, Della, and clicked to expand her descendants. 'And this line descends to Timothy K. Schwartz.' Kenyatta thrust a small orange piece of paper in the air, waving it around over her head. 'Cluster closed, and the first orange slip for the Hollywood Strangler case!' she declared.

'Oh, wow,' Maddie said. 'Well done. Come and collect your prize.'

Kenyatta sauntered up to the whiteboard and took down the twenty-dollar bill that was fixed there as a light-hearted incentive for the first person to establish the common ancestors in their genetic network.

Kenyatta moved to the front of the room and stuck the orange piece of paper, which showed Walter and Mary's names and key locations, to the whiteboard.

'Good job,' Hudson congratulated. 'The first known relatives of the Hollywood Strangler—ever!'

Kenyatta winked as she walked back to her desk, saying, 'So, keep your eyes open for the Fellows name in Virginia or Ohio.' She sat down and put the twenty dollars into her wallet.

'Okay, what an excellent start to the briefing,' Maddie said. 'Who thinks that they can follow that?'

'I will,' Hudson volunteered. 'Although I can't claim an orange slip as of yet.'

'Go ahead,' Maddie said.

Hudson's screen overrode Kenyatta's, displaying a pedigree chart for a woman named Lorna Woodhouse. He stood up as he explained,

'As you can see, I've got Lorna's parents and all four grandparents pinned down, but they're really proving a hard family to research. So far, I haven't got any overlaps with the cluster lead, Yannis Gurman, and I've got this horrible feeling the link might be on Yannis's paternal side where I've hit a brick wall.'

'What locations are you seeing for Lorna Woodhouse's tree so far?' Reggie asked.

'They're very firmly rooted in New England: Maine, Vermont and Massachusetts. Yannis Gurman's line is all Deep South.'

'Keep going,' Maddie encouraged. 'Well done. Reggie, you want to go next?'

Reggie nodded and mirrored his computer screen on the digital whiteboard, displaying a pedigree chart for Jonas Crawford. 'So, I've managed to pin down six out of the eight great-grandparents. Two are proving elusive, but I think I'm on to something with this person here,' he said, circling the mouse around one of Jonas Crawford's maternal great-grandmothers. 'Agnetta Hartmann. She was born in Chicago, but her name is distinctly Germanic and I'm wondering if she connects up to the cluster lead, Jennifer Hatter, via her Swiss line. Right now, it's just a hunch which I'll focus on tomorrow.'

Maddie smiled. 'Good job, Reggie. Okay, me now,' she said, pulling up the pedigree chart for her cluster lead, Hope Beal. 'According to the Shared Centimorgan Project, there's more than a fifty percent chance that the generation of connection between Hope Beal and the killer is at the great-grandparent level, or closer. So, I've concentrated on getting as much information on this generation as possible, which has included the names of ten out of sixteen great-great-grandparents. Still no luck with the Berrycloth line, though. Tomorrow, I'm going to switch to triangulation.'

'We're going to nail this guy,' Hudson commented. 'I can feel it.'

'Well, even if we do ID him, don't forget what the detectives said: he's very likely deceased,' Maddie reminded him.

'We'd still have cracked one of the biggest serial cases ever in U.S. history,' Hudson countered.

'I just hope we're not hounded by the press,' Kenyatta replied, receiving a laugh from both Reggie and Hudson. But she was being serious. Some of these big cases drew a lot of media attention, which was the last thing she wanted.

'We've still got a long way to go,' Maddie said. 'And right now, the way you all need to go…is home.' She smiled, switched off the whiteboard and headed into her office.

Kenyatta turned her cell phone over to see that she'd received a text from Gabe.

I have no idea where Troy is. After what he did to Cal, I don't care.

Kenyatta sighed as she shut down her computer and got her things ready to leave. She stood from her desk, called goodbye to Hudson and Reggie, then tapped on Maddie's open office door.

'Come in,' she said.

Kenyatta entered and pushed the door shut behind her. 'Um, I just wanted to ask you something.'

'Sure, go ahead.'

'When we crack this case and it all blows up in the media, can my name be kept out of it?' Kenyatta asked.

Maddie nodded slowly. 'I'll certainly do my best, but I don't think I can guarantee it. You're on the website as a member of staff and you've appeared in press releases for some of the other cases. It wouldn't be too hard for them to get your name.'

'Okay,' Kenyatta replied.

'Is there a problem with this case?'

'No, just a couple of issues at home with Troy. I could just do without any extra attention being drawn to my family, that's all.'

'I'll do my best to keep your name away from the case. *If* we solve it,' Maddie said.

'Thank you. And…we *will* solve it.'

'Let me know if there's anything I can do to help,' Maddie said. 'Or if you just want to talk things over.'

'Thanks,' Kenyatta replied. 'See you tomorrow. Don't work too hard.'

'I'll try not to.'

Kenyatta left Maddie's office, said goodbye to Ross and left the building. Outside, Kenyatta bustled across the crowded sidewalk to the Green Line TRAX stop, where she waited for the train to take her back home.

She took out her cell phone. Nothing at all from any of the boys, only a confirmation from her neighbor that she'd collected Troy and taken him home. She took a moment to compose herself, then dialed Troy. The call went straight to voicemail. 'Hi, Troy. Can you give me a call, please. I'm waiting for my train, then I'll be home so we can talk about what happened today.'

She thought for a moment. Just like she did every Thursday night, tonight she was supposed to be helping out at the SLC Homeless Kitchen. It was also her regular date night with Jim, her partner of two years. But given what had happened today and that there was still no sign of Troy, she would have to cancel. She typed out a quick message to Jim, apologizing and asking if she could postpone her shift and their date to Sunday.

Kenyatta replayed the conversation with Mr. Reeves, the East High School Principal. He'd said that the other student had done nothing but look at Troy. What on earth could have possessed him to push this boy's arm so hard up his back that it popped out of its socket? That was some anger. Although there was no justifying Troy's actions, Kenyatta desperately hoped that there was more to the story than she'd been told.

The train arrived and instantly filled to capacity so that Kenyatta had to stand all the way to her stop.

She hurried to the front door of her small house on East Seventh Street, finding Jon and Gabe watching TV in the living room.

'Hey, is Troy back yet?' Kenyatta asked, kicking off her shoes.

Gabe shook his head.

'He hasn't been home,' Jon confirmed. 'I can't believe what he did, Mom. You should have heard Cal screaming in agony. It was awful. Where's he going to go to school now?'

Kenyatta felt a tightening in her chest. 'I don't know. The first problem is to find him. Gabe, can you text his friends, please?'

Gabe gave a mock laugh. 'What friends? He doesn't have any.'

'Well, *your* friends, then. Just to see if anyone's seen him,'

Kenyatta directed, shocked by what she was hearing. He'd always struggled to make friends, and he had never had people over like Gabe and Jon did, but she hadn't realized it was this bad.

Just as Gabe took out his cell phone to message his friends, Otis called her. Literally, the last person that she wanted to talk to right now.

'Otis,' she said, trying to hold her voice at neutral.

'Just letting you know…I've got Troy, here,' he said bluntly.

'Oh. Can I talk to him?'

'He doesn't want to talk to you right now.'

'Did he tell you what happened at school today?' Kenyatta asked.

'Yeah, some nasty little kid always snarking at Troy finally got what was coming to him,' Otis said.

'What? I spoke with the principal, and he said the other student had done nothing wrong.'

'Of course they're going to say that,' Otis responded. 'They've never liked Troy. And the kid deserved it.'

'Wait. Deserved his arm being popped out of its socket? Are you serious?' Kenyatta stammered.

'Well, it'll be the last time he picks on Troy, that's for sure.'

'I don't think he was picked on. I want to talk to him,' Kenyatta pushed, realizing that there was little point in arguing the rights and wrongs of the situation with her psychopathic ex-husband.

'I told you… He doesn't want to talk,' Otis said, ending the call.

Kenyatta took in a breath and then burst into tears.

Chapter Thirteen

Friday, November 4, 2022, Pétion-Ville, Port-au-Prince, Haiti

Becky Larkin finally had the magic combination of time and stable internet to be able to focus on the latest Venator case. She'd managed to download all of the key documents from the secure, shared Venator drive yesterday and had spent much of last night reviewing them.

She could hardly believe that she was working on the Hollywood Strangler case; it was one that she had studied as part of her master's degree in criminology, a part of which had involved creating a psychological profile of the killer. She had taken it upon herself to visit the key locations from the case and, while in Los Angeles, had even undertaken her own investigations. Working on the police theory that the killer's murder-spree had abruptly ended because he had died, Becky had completed a systematic review of every male who fit her psychological profile and had died in the three years following his last known victims in 1986. Despite the final list being unwieldy and huge, she had handed it to a detective working the case but had never heard anything back and had always assumed that her work hadn't thrown up any cross-checked matches with their own list of suspects.

Becky was sitting down at her small wooden desk in the two-room apartment that she was renting on the top floor of a five-story building on Rue Stephan Archer in the reasonably affluent Pétion-Ville suburb of the Haitian capital, Port-au-Prince. The area was one of the few places in the capital that still managed to attract a limited number of tourists and some business, while the rest of the city and country rapidly descended into severe poverty and political chaos. Following last year's assassination of the country's prime minister at his home in Pétion-Ville, control of well over half of Port-au-Prince now resided with various rival criminal gangs and not with the defective and disintegrating government.

Becky liked to reassure friends and family back home of her safety by sending them photos and videos of the view outside of her window of ordinary daily life. Normal people going about their normal lives. But in truth, every moment that she spent outside, she felt exceptionally vulnerable and unsafe. As an American in Haiti, Becky often felt like an outsider; a foreigner both in appearance and culture. Her light skin and mousy hair, her manner of speaking and even the clothes she wore all marked her as a potential target. She was desperate to go home but she still had work to do here, and a big part of that work involved traveling to the very center of the gang-controlled slums in Port-au-Prince.

Six months ago, Becky had taken a voluntary position with a small charity dealing with women and children who had suffered sexual exploitation and abuse at the hands of United Nations troops stationed here. From 2004 until 2017, thousands of peacekeepers were sent to the country as part of the United Nations Stabilization Mission in Haiti, also known as MINUSTAH. Their humanitarian role in the country had been to restore law, public order and safety, but the organization's presence there had had a hidden, dark and sinister element to it; namely, the sexual exploitation and abuse of women and children by the very people who had been sent to protect them. Becky and her four colleagues were painstakingly working to confirm the paternity of dozens of children who had been fathered by these peacekeepers, and then to hold those men and the UN accountable for their actions. It was a mammoth task, and they were really just dealing with the tip of the iceberg. More and more women and children, now living in abject poverty, were coming forward every week seeking their help.

Becky sipped her cold mango juice and glanced at the open window, hoping that by looking at it, a fresh breeze might just materialize and cool the apartment. It didn't, and Becky ran the back of her hand over her sticky forehead.

Her first task on the Hollywood Strangler case was to prepare a report of the kind of killer they were dealing with. It was all work that she'd done before. The only problem was that it was boxed up in her parents' attic and, due to her taking the job in Haiti, they weren't currently speaking to her. So, she needed to start over. But it was probably better to view the case with fresh eyes and with the additional benefit of the files shared by the detectives than to rely on notes and observations that she'd made several years ago.

As always, Becky began by looking at the FBI's *Serial Murder*

Pathways for Investigations document, starting with possible motives. The FBI file proffered five main categories for motivation in serial murders: *sexual, anger, mental illness, profit* or *other*. Although mental illness could not be ruled out, there had been a clear sexual motivation in each case, something that the detectives had noted in their own reports. In this section, Becky was surprised to see that the detectives had included that the killer had taken each of the victims' underwear as a trophy, stressing, too, that this piece of information was a hold-back and not out in the public domain.

Moving on to the next section in the document, Becky examined the possible relationship between the killer and victims, defined as one of either *stranger, targeted stranger, acquaintance, relative / familial* or *customer / client*.

It was a tough one to call. If the killer had worked in the movie industry, as some people suspected, then all of the victims could have been acquaintances. The police had never found a link between the separate murders beyond them all being actors and actresses. The most likely relationship between the killer and the victims was *targeted stranger*, which was categorized as *a situation where the offender knew who the victim was, but the victim had no knowledge or familiarity with the offender.*

The method of body disposal was very clear-cut: *Displayed* was defined as *the offender intentionally positioning the victim's body after death to shock the police, the victim's family, or the general public; or to provide a message concerning the offender's opinion of the victim or class of victims.* But the killer's rationale for displaying the bodies as he had was indeterminate. Becky felt his reasoning behind the graphic displays tied back to his own sexual gratification rather than a desire to shock others.

Having typed up a report on her findings so far, Becky turned to geo-profiling, which involved examining the locations where the victims had been abducted or murdered and then applying a psychological theory known as the circle hypothesis. The theory suggested that in over eighty-five percent of serial murder cases, the killer lived within a circle defined by a diameter drawn between his two furthest offences. It was one of her favorite parts of the job, which really came into its own in the concluding stages of Venator's investigation.

Becky sipped her juice, then opened Google Maps to start plotting the locations of each of the victims' homes. For the final two victims, Tracie Satchell and Christian Lofthouse, Becky opted to only use the female victim's house, where the murders had actually taken place.

Once all of the properties were marked clearly on the map, Becky took a screenshot. Then, opening the image in Preview, she carefully drew a semi-transparent purple circle over the demarcated victims' homes between the two furthest offences. The resultant geographical area where the killer might have resided was substantial, covering much of downtown Hollywood.

Becky had a few hours left until the briefing, so she spent some time pulling her research together and uploading it to the Venator drive, just in case her internet should give out before the meeting.

Satisfied with her work, she decided to fight her inner voice of caution and go for a short walk. She longed to get back to her running and climbing, neither of which she could do here.

The sunsets in Haiti were like none that Becky had ever seen before. Every evening, she would position a chair next to the window and stare out until the light faded behind the tall trees in the Place Saint-Pierre Park. Today, though, Becky had to satisfy herself with a passing glance outside because it was time to join the Venator briefing.

She dragged the chair to her dining table and took in a few long breaths and, as she clicked on the Zoom link that Maddie had sent earlier in the day, she pasted on the veneer of a smile.

'Hey, Becky!' Maddie greeted. 'How's it going out there?'

Becky's fake smile widened. 'Great, thank you. Just the heat that I'm still not yet acclimatized to.'

'How's work?' Maddie asked, carrying the laptop into the main office.

'Yeah, it's going great, thank you,' Becky answered, knowing full well that Maddie was fishing for answers regarding what she might have discovered about what had happened in Haiti with various employees from Becky's father's company, including Maddie's husband, Michael. The truth was, Becky had made some progress, but wasn't yet ready to share it. And her investigations were far from over.

'Becks!' Ross called, pushing his face close to the camera. 'How are you?'

'Good. You? I hope you're looking after the apartment.'

Ross frowned. 'What apartment?' He mocked a dawning understanding. 'Oh, right. *That* apartment. I trashed it, sold it and kept the money.'

Becky grinned. 'Hope you got a good price for it.'

'Hi, Becky,' Hudson and Kenyatta chanted together, peering at the laptop camera.

'Hi,' she responded, aware of how much she missed working alongside them all. It felt great to be back among them, albeit virtually.

'Maddie, do you mind if I start? The internet is considerably worse in the evenings, and I might get cut off.'

'Sure,' Maddie agreed. 'Let's get started right away. I'll put you on the digital whiteboard and give you permission to share your screen.'

'Thanks,' Becky said, pulling up the map of Hollywood with the purple circle covering the five annotated houses where the victims had lived and died. 'Sorry to say, but due to the population density of downtown Hollywood, I think the Circle Theory of Environmental Range is probably the least helpful that it's ever been on a case we've had. But, for what it's worth, the killer likely lived somewhere on this map in the 1980s.'

'I'll print it out afterward and stick it to the board,' Maddie said. 'Thank you for that.'

'Next up,' she said, sharing her profile of the killer, 'is what kind of a person he might have been.'

'Oh, I hear he was real nice,' Kenyatta said with a chuckle.

Becky grinned. 'So, the fact that he had a sexual motivation is pretty clear-cut. Interestingly, the detectives included some hold-back information that I'm not sure we should have been privy to; that is that the killer kept the underwear from each victim.'

'I noticed that, too,' Hudson commented.

'Yeah, I'm not sure we should have seen that either,' Maddie agreed.

'What's not clear is the killer's relationship to the victims.

Obviously, given those awful posthumous tableaus he created, the killer knew the victims. But did he know them personally—perhaps because he was in the film industry and, therefore, could be a stranger or an acquaintance—or had he simply watched the movies that they had acted in? In which case, they were targeted strangers.'

'What's your gut feeling on this?' Maddie asked.

'My gut feeling...is that we're dealing with a psychopath who targeted the victims after seeing—'

The Zoom meeting connection dropped.

Becky checked her internet. Nothing. It was the same most evenings and would likely stay disconnected until the early hours, when she had no intention of still being awake.

She sighed with deep disappointment. Not only had she not got to tell the rest of the team all of her findings, but she also hadn't gotten to hear how their investigations were proceeding.

She waited a while longer, trying to reconnect to the internet, but then gave up and headed over to the small kitchenette where she took out a plate of *Diri ak Pwa*, a Haitian rice dish with spices, black beans and a side of plantain.

Sitting back down at the table, Becky picked up a manila folder from a pile of more than a dozen and opened it up. It contained a thick stack of paperwork pertaining to a girl only identified in the files as *V38*—Victim 38. She was now seventeen years old and the child of a Haitian girl repeatedly raped by various UN peacekeepers between 2004 and 2007. Becky and her four colleagues were painstakingly applying investigative genetic genealogy techniques to try and identify V38's biological father.

Becky sifted through the file to ascertain the progress so far. V38 had taken voluntary DNA tests at Ancestry, MyHeritage, 23andMe and FTDNA. The paternal matches were few in number across all the sites but did corroborate the allegations made by V38's mother, who had given evidence that she and several other girls had been forcibly part of a child sex ring. As a result of an internal UN investigation, 134 Sri Lankan peacekeepers were returned to their country of origin, but none were ever charged or held accountable for their crimes or made responsible for any children that they had fathered. Similar work, using investigative genetic genealogy to identify the fathers of abuse victims, was being undertaken in Sierra Leone and the sex slums of Manila.

But, it was hard going. Not only were the databases severely lacking cousin matches from the Sri Lanka area, but once paternity had been confirmed, getting anyone in authority to take action was damned near impossible.

Becky ate her food as she re-read V38's case file, making sure everything was in her head prior to another meeting on Sunday. Because of security concerns, she could take nothing with her to the meeting more than a notepad and pencil and had never even been told V38's or her mother's real names.

She was just finishing the last of her dinner when the apartment door was unlocked. Becky was momentarily startled, but then smiled when the door opened. 'Hey. How was it?'

Aidan—a tall, athletic man with broad shoulders and short cropped hair—exhaled as he shut the door and ran the three bolts across. 'Okay, I guess,' he answered in his Australian accent. He kicked off his boots, walked over and slumped down at the table. 'No. Actually, it was bloody hard.'

'What happened?' Becky asked.

He stood staring at the stack of manila files in the center of the table. 'Just the usual bureaucratic BS.' His tone changed to mock-imperious, where his accent shifted from Australian to some kind of odd-sounding British-American hybrid. 'We cannot comment on individual cases. Following several investigations and reviews, practices have been changed and lessons learned.'

Becky rolled her eyes, having also heard that a million times before. Aidan was the business face of their organization and spent much of his time dealing with various government and humanitarian officials, trying to push for compensation for the victims of sexual exploitation and abuse at the hands of the aid workers.

He strolled over and kissed Becky on the lips. Aidan was also her boyfriend and, despite having only been together for four months, she felt something for him that she'd never felt for anyone ever before. He opened his thick arms and pulled her tight to him. In that moment, in his arms, nothing mattered, and she felt safe.

Chapter Fourteen

Saturday, November 5, 2022, Los Angeles, California

Ted Marsden was sitting down at his cubicle desk on the fifth floor of the LAPD Police Headquarters Facility in downtown Los Angeles, rolling his cell phone over and over in his left hand.

In his peripheral vision, Powers slid back in his chair. 'Just call her already,' he snapped.

Marsden turned to face him. 'What?'

'Call her. The genetic genealogy lady,' he clarified. 'Why don't you just call her and ask for an update?'

'I don't know. Feels too pushy,' Marsden replied. 'I feel like we need to just leave her to get on with it.'

'Yeah, but maybe she's already found something out that might help us to review the suspect list. You know, get to the answer faster. Which, by the way, would mean that you get to retire faster.'

Marsden scratched his head. He'd been wanting to call Madison Scott-Barnhart since the day that she had confirmed she'd accessed the DNA kit. Her only words to him had been, 'It's a good match list. I'll be in touch when we've got something to say.' She hadn't been in touch and, therefore, had nothing to say, which bothered Marsden more with every passing day. Did it mean that their work wasn't going well?

He was aware that Powers was still staring at him.

'It's a Saturday,' Marsden countered. 'She won't even be in the office.'

'But you've got her cell, right?'

Marsden nodded.

'So, call it.'

'Hey guys,' Detective Supervisor Mitzi Roberts said, passing behind their cubicles. 'How's it going? Any updates on the case?'

Marsden shook his head.

'I'm telling him to call the genealogy lady to ask,' Powers complained.

'Okay. Okay, I'll do it,' Marsden finally conceded, pulling up

Madison's name from his contacts. He touched her cell number and then put the call on loudspeaker for the benefit of Powers and Roberts.

She answered within three rings. 'Officer Marsden. How can I help?'

He suddenly regretted having called her. He could at least have waited until Monday, or thought about how he could frame the question. 'Hi. I'm sorry to call on a Saturday like this. I... I was just wondering how the IGG was progressing on the Strangler case? I'm getting pressure from my pushy boss.'

'What?' Roberts mouthed, opening her palms skyward.

'Well, it's a general policy of mine not to give a running commentary of our cases,' Madison said. 'I will say that it's going well and I'm confident that we can get a decent suspect list for you soon.'

'Okay, that's great,' Marsden said. 'Um, anything concrete already that I could give my boss, you know, to get her off my back?'

Roberts screwed up her face and shrugged.

'What you need to understand is that most of what we're doing in this phase right now is crucial to the process but won't mean anything to you or indeed to the final result. It's building trees for his match list. These are people who have nothing to do with him other than a few shared bits of DNA.' She paused. 'I guess I could give you the phenotype and geo-ancestry, which are also *not* guaranteed at this point. We *estimate* that he is of European heritage, brown eyes, brown hair and intermediate skin color.'

'Wow,' Marsden said, glancing from Powers to Roberts. 'That's good and, actually, we can cross several people off the suspect list already with this.'

'Please don't do that, Officer Marsden,' she insisted. 'These are estimates, not scientific proof.'

'Sure,' Marsden said. 'But what kind of percentage accuracy are we running on here?'

Madison took a while to answer. 'It's about seventy-five percent.'

Marsden glanced at Powers and grinned. 'Okay. Anything else?'

'Not right now, no.'

'Okay, thank you so much for your time,' Marsden said. 'Goodbye.'

She said goodbye and ended the call.

'Go get the murder book,' Marsden directed Powers.

'It's good information,' Roberts said. 'Just remember what she said, though: it's not scientific proof.'

'I know,' Marsden said.

'Good luck. And a little less of the *pushy*, maybe,' Roberts said, walking away.

Powers returned a few moments later, carrying the four cold case files for the Hollywood Strangler case. He placed them down on his desk. 'What are we looking for?'

'Get the suspect list—we're going to cross-check skin, hair and eye color for everyone on there against DMV records.'

'That could take a while,' Powers mumbled.

Ignoring his comment, Marsden continued, 'We're not eliminating anyone at this stage, just making a short list. Okay?'

Powers nodded and opened the first murder book.

Marsden pulled up the Department of Motor Vehicles database online, which listed physical data for everyone issued with a California driver's license and steeled himself for the first name of many in the suspect list.

Although this wouldn't be conclusive, Marsden was pretty confident—or at least seventy-five-percent confident—that he could now bring the suspect list down below fifty for the first time ever.

Hudson Édouard was working on his laptop at the kitchen counter. He was continuing with the progress he'd made yesterday on Lorna Woodhouse's tree. He knew the names of all of her paternal great-great-grandparents and was now working on her maternal side, hoping to find a link to the cluster lead Yannis Gurman's tree.

He drank some coffee and looked out of the window at the snow-covered Wasatch Mountains in the distance.

'Six days, man! Just six days,' Reggie said, slapping his hands on Hudson's back and making him jump.

'Jeez, Reggie. You nearly gave me a heart attack,' Hudson complained. 'What's in six days?'

'Brighton opens its slopes,' he clarified. 'And the Snowwolf will be the first to hit that fresh powder.'

'Rather you than me,' Hudson said, noticing that Reggie was dressed smartly. 'Where are you off to?'

'Saturdate,' he replied.

Hudson rolled his eyes. 'Am I going to get any clues yet?'

Reggie shook his head. 'I can confirm that it's an adult human. That's about all you need to know for now.' Reggie squinted at Hudson's computer screen. 'Come on, man. Work? Do you really have nothing better to do? Work to live!'

'I want to solve this case,' Hudson countered. 'It's the Hollywood Strangler, for God's sake. Can you imagine if we end up identifying him?'

Reggie grabbed Hudson by the cheeks. 'Hudson. He's dead. It can wait until Monday, man.' He let go of Hudson's face and smoothly closed his laptop lid. 'Get off this and onto Fiorry. Go get yourself a Saturdate.'

'Sure,' Hudson said, doing his best to humor him. He'd learned fast not to challenge Reggie when he was in one of his exuberant moods.

'Cool!' Reggie said, swinging around and heading for the door. 'See you tomorrow at some point.'

'Bye,' Hudson mumbled, reopening his laptop and trying to remember where he'd left off. He was working on pushing back Lorna Woodhouse's maternal great-grandfather, George Terrell, who, according to various censuses, had been born in Boston, Massachusetts, in 1895. But, so far, Hudson had been unsuccessful in his attempts to find any official sign of George Terrell prior to his marriage in 1919. His record in the *U.S., World War II Draft Registration Cards, 1942* gave his full date of birth as June 25, 1895, in Manchester, Massachusetts.

Hudson searched for George Terrell in the *Massachusetts, U.S. Town and Vital Records, 1620-1988* record set on Ancestry, receiving five results, only one of which was for the correct name. Hudson clicked to see the original record, finding that it was a death certificate for a man who had died in 1972 and was definitely not the right person.

Hudson amended the search by removing the surname. *73,776 results.* It was a ridiculous figure to check, so he edited the search parameters for George's precise date of birth. Although he received the same astronomical number of hits, the top three were the only ones with that exact date of birth. George B. Hoffman, George R. McGregor and George T. Boicourt.

Hovering his mouse over the *View Record* option, Hudson checked the birth location of each of the three men. The first was born in South Hadley, the second in Framingham and the last in Manchester. Hudson stared at the entry. Boicourt. It was a name he'd already come across.

With a rush of excitement, Hudson whipped the cursor over to *View Images* and clicked to load a black and white scan of the original entry.

Date of Birth: June 25, 1895
Name and Surname of Child: George Terrell Boicourt
Sex: Male
Place of Birth: Manchester
Name of Parents: Agnes Boicourt (base born)
Occupation of Father: -
Birthplace of Father: -
Birthplace of Mother: Virginia

'Boicourts in Virginia,' Hudson said to himself with a smile. 'Gotcha.'

He hurriedly opened the speculative tree that he had created for Yannis Gurman and entered the name Boicourt. Sure enough, Yannis's maternal great-great-grandmother was named as Lillie Boicourt, born in 1872 to Jacob Boicourt and Elizabeth Rhodes.

Clicking on Jacob's profile, Hudson looked him up on the 1880 census.

Jacob Boicourt, head, 30, oyster planter, born Virginia
Elizabeth Boicourt, wife, 29, born Virginia
Peter Boicourt, son, 9, born Virginia
Lillie Boicourt, daughter, 8, born Virginia

Agnes Boicourt, daughter, 6, born Virginia
Daniel Boicourt, son, 4, born Virginia
Lewis Boicourt, son, 2, born Virginia

'Yes!' Hudson said, jubilantly thumping the air. The record confirmed that both Yannis Gurman and Lorna Woodhouse had descended from Jacob and Elizabeth Boicourt. Therefore, so had the Hollywood Strangler.

Hudson picked up his cell phone, wondering about texting the Venator group to share his news but quickly realized that Reggie had been right. It was Saturday and the case had been cold for almost forty years. It could wait until Monday.

He stared at his phone, wondering. As the screen began to go dark, Hudson swiped across to the Fiorry app and opened it up. It was a dating app specifically designed for transgender individuals and their allies, yet something was holding him back.

He put the phone down and returned to his laptop to continue his work. But he couldn't concentrate, picked his cell back up again and, before he changed his mind, quickly entered his basic personal details, completed the compatibility survey and then promptly closed the app.

Maddie was drinking decaf coffee with her mom and Trenton at the kitchen counter. Her mom was having a bittersweet moment of lucidity, granting them a rare glimpse at the woman who she had once been.

'How's Nikki enjoying school?' her mom asked. 'Remind me what she's studying?'

'Genealogy…of all things,' Maddie replied, rolling her eyes. 'She's loving it, though. And getting straight As as usual.'

Her mom smiled. 'That will be your influence, no doubt.'

Maddie shrugged.

'She was adopted, right?' her mom checked.

'That's right. From Korea.'

'And Trenton,' her mom said tentatively. 'But not the older one. Wait. Jenna.'

Maddie smiled and placed her hand on her mom's. 'That's right.' She'd been about to congratulate her mom but remembered that the last time she had done that, it had caused great upset. She really had to choose her words carefully right now.

'Are you going out again tonight, Mom?' Trenton asked.

Maddie took a moment to answer, trying to interpret his internal feelings through his currently expressionless face. She'd kept the early days of her relationship with Clayton to herself and had actually returned from her first visit to Philly feeling guilty that she was betraying Michael. She'd sat Trenton and Nikki down just before his last visit to Salt Lake City and asked how they'd feel if she started dating again. Much to her relief, both had been overwhelmingly supportive, so she'd told them a little about Clayton. This time around, she'd said that he was in town and that she'd be out for a couple of evenings with him. 'Yes, I am,' she finally replied.

'I'm not judging, Mom,' Trenton added. 'Invite him here if you want. I'd really like to meet him.'

A surge of emotion rose from Maddie's heart. 'Are you sure?'

'Sure, I'm sure. Why not?' Trenton answered.

'Is this Michael you're talking about?' her mom asked.

'No, Michael is…no longer in the picture, Mom. This is Clayton Tyler. I'll get him over so you can meet him.'

'That would be nice; although, you know, I did like Michael.'

'Yeah, me too,' Maddie agreed, drinking the last of her coffee.

The conversation went quiet, and Trenton moved into the living room and switched on the TV. Maddie still had to get ready, but she couldn't bring herself to take her hand away from her mom's.

The precious moment ended a few seconds later anyway when her mom abruptly stood up and said, 'Right, I need to get the dinner on. Your father will be home soon.'

'Don't worry, Mom. Katie's going to cook for you.'

'Katie? Who's Katie? Katie Couric?'

'No. Katie. She lives here with us, like a home caregiver,' Maddie explained.

Her mom frowned. 'Madison, I'm sixty-four years old. I do *not* need a caregiver, thank you very much. Does your father know about this Katie girl?'

'No,' Maddie answered. 'But he'd be happy. He'd want you to get some rest and let her help with the chores. Why don't you go sit with Trenton in the living room?'

Her mom thought for a moment, then conceded with a sigh before joining Trenton in the living room to watch TV.

'I'm going to get ready,' Maddie told Trenton, then headed upstairs to her bedroom, where she sat on the edge of her bed and cried.

Maddie entered a smart, six-story building with the words *westgate lofts* above the sidewalk entrance. To the right of the door was a small grocery store, Vosen's Bakery, and to the left was Maxwell's Little Bar, where Maddie now entered.

She spotted Clayton right away. 'Hey,' she greeted him with a warm smile.

'Hey, you,' he replied, standing from the bar stool and kissing her on the lips. 'You look amazing.'

Maddie thanked him and glanced down at her outfit. She was wearing an elegant, black evening dress with a white, fake-fur shawl over her shoulders. For someone most comfortable in jeans and an oversized sweater, she really had made an effort. 'You don't look so bad yourself,' she responded, perching opposite him at the wooden, two-person table at which he was seated.

Clayton laughed. He was wearing dark pants and a green shirt that matched his eyes. He'd put some kind of product in his short dark hair and was wearing a pleasing potent aftershave. Since their first meeting in 2020, he'd gotten into good shape. He'd told her that he was eating healthy, going to the gym after work every day, and was even seeing a personal trainer.

'It's so good to see you, Maddie,' he said, grinning. 'I've missed you.'

'You, too,' she replied.

Clayton reached out to hold Maddie's hand. She turned her hand to hold his. It was a sensation that she was now able to embrace fully and enjoy, but it had taken a long time to get to this point and a lot of patience on Clayton's part.

Now he was here again, staying at the Hyatt House Hotel in downtown Salt Lake City for two weeks.

'What would madam like to drink?' he asked her, rotating the menu that was on the table between them so that it faced her. He had it open at the wine page, his finger resting on their most expensive white, Rodney Strong Chardonnay. 'This one?'

'Perfect,' she said.

Clayton smiled. 'What about to eat?' he asked, turning the page to the food menu. 'I'm having the Untouchables.'

Maddie scanned down the pizza list just as a young waitress with black hair, heavy black eye shadow and a nose stud came over to take their order.

'I'll have a large glass of the Rodney Strong Chardonnay, please,' Maddie ordered.

'And can I get a Moab Johnny's IPA, please?' Clayton added.

'Sure,' the waitress said. 'Anything to eat?'

'A Bronx Tale pizza for me, please,' Maddie said.

'And an Untouchables pizza for me,' Clayton added.

'Great,' the waitress said, heading off to the kitchen.

Maddie glanced around the small bar. It was an industrial-chic type of place, with concrete and exposed pipework everywhere. Above a central bar were several TV screens showing a game of football to the suited and beer-drinking clientele seated over at the bar.

'So, come on,' Clayton said. 'Bring me up to speed. Work. Family. Michael. I want the whole lot.'

Maddie took a breath. Each of those things was incredibly complicated and one or two almost ineffable. 'So, work…I can't talk too much about, actually. For the first time ever, I've had to sign an NDA.'

Clayton's eyes widened. 'What? That must be a well-known case.'

Maddie nodded as the waitress arrived and placed the drinks down on the table.

They chinked glasses, and then Maddie took a long gulp of the wine.

'Which state?' Clayton asked.

'Non-disclosure agreement,' Maddie replied with a grin.

'Oh, you spoilsport,' he replied.

'Family,' Maddie continued, 'are all okay, I guess. Nikki is loving life at BYU. Trenton is…Trenton. And my mom is being slowly and painfully replaced by an interloper who looks just like her but with a completely different—and, frankly, most of the time, unlikable—personality.' She paused to sip her drink. 'Jenna is doing really well down in Florida, and all loved up. I'm hoping she'll come here for a vacation soon. And on the Michael front… Well, there's not much to report.'

'What about whatever Becky's working on out in Haiti?' Clayton asked.

'Your guess is as good as mine. I don't know what she's doing out there and it's driving me half-crazy. All I know is that she felt the answers to what happened to Michael and his two coworkers, Artemon Bruce and Jay Craig, were to be found in Haiti, where they had all been in the months prior to their deaths or disappearance. She's working for some humanitarian charity; but which one and what they're doing, I don't know. I tried to get it out of Ross—he's her roomie—but he claims to not know, either.'

Clayton drank some of his beer. 'You *will* get your answers,' he said, trying to sound reassuring.

'I don't even know if I want the answers anymore,' Maddie countered. She'd spent the past seven years clinging to the slim hope that Michael was still alive. But now, the circumstances that would permit that version of reality—that he'd deliberately left his old life behind or had suffered some terrible kind of amnesia—were either too painful or too unimaginable to bear. With little evidence to support it, Maddie was coming to terms with the fact that Michael was dead. By accepting it on those terms, she was giving herself permission to live and explore a relationship with Clayton.

Maddie's desire not to dwell any longer on the tired subject coincided with the arrival of their pizzas.

'Okay. Well, that's huge,' Maddie commented as the waitress placed hers down on the table in front of her.

'Listen, my personal trainer can seriously *never* know about this,'

Clayton said with a laugh.

'Well,' Maddie began, 'How would you feel about getting something a little healthier at my place Monday night? The kids are eager to meet you.'

Clayton nodded. 'I'd really like that. If you're sure...?'

Maddie nodded firmly as she tore off a piece of pizza. 'I'm sure.'

Chapter Fifteen

Sunday, November 6, 2022, Salt Lake City, Utah

Reggie Snowwolf was holding a cup of coffee, staring out of the balcony windows at the snow-covered Wasatch Mountain Range. Just five days until the Brighton slopes would be open for the season and he could not wait. Although he'd like to have gotten up there on Friday, as he would have done when he had been working freelance, there was no way that he was going to ask for the day off. There was also probably no way that he'd be given the day off, since the team was in the middle of their highest profile case to date. He had to face up to the fact that snowboarding on the fresh powdered slopes of Brighton would just have to wait until Saturday.

He sipped his coffee, feeling a steady contentment deep inside that he'd not felt in a long time.

Reggie crossed the open-plan living area of the swanky Sugar House Apartment to the kitchen, sat down at the counter and opened up his laptop, navigating to the speculative tree that he'd created for Thomas Cristmas. He hadn't actively worked on the case since Wednesday morning, but a part of his brain that never seemed to be off-line had come up with several avenues worth exploring.

Using data from the 1860 census, Reggie created a speculative tree for the slave owner, James Woods. Then, he jumped back to 1850 where he found him as a twenty-one-year-old living in the household of his planter father, David Woods, a widower. For James to be the slave owner in 1860, it suggested that his father, David, had died in the intervening decade.

Reggie pulled up the *Mississippi, Warren County general probate court docket, 1810-1940* record set on FamilySearch and then began a painstaking trawl of the unindexed records there. The search took a lot of time, but, once he'd gotten used to the format of the records, he was able to move slightly faster through the digitized images.

After almost two solid hours of diligent searching through the records, Reggie cried out, 'Yes! Thank you!'

On-screen in front of him was the probate record for David

Woods, late of Warren County, Mississippi, who had died in 1857. Reggie moved past the legal preamble, finding that David had essentially split up his estate and holdings and divided it all between his two sons. The first of the two siblings, James Woods, was the one for whom Reggie searched.

'What was all that about?' Ross asked, appearing from the bedroom in his boxer shorts. He leaned on the door frame and yawned.

'Sorry, man,' Reggie said. 'Working on Leon Sierra.'

'Reggie, it's not even nine o'clock in the morning...on a *Sunday*. You're worse than Becky,' he complained with a sigh. He entered the kitchen and kissed Reggie on his way, beelining for the coffee machine. 'Need a refill?'

'Yes, thank you very much,' Reggie replied, returning his attention to the document in front of him. Sandwiched uncomfortably between a description of farm buildings and livestock was a list of people, headed simply *Negroe's Names and Ages*.

Henrietta Cristmas, 30
Thomas Cristmas, 10
Joseph Cristmas, 9

The probate record confirmed that Henrietta, Thomas and Joseph Cristmas were bequeathed to James Woods by his father, David, but it did not provide Reggie with any information to help him push the line backward.

'So, what do you want to do today?' Ross asked as he made the drinks.

'Uh, I was going to work some more on Leon—' he noticed Ross's face fall '—but...I'm open to suggestions.'

'And you said you were telling Hudson off yesterday for all work and no play,' Ross commented. 'How about we head down to The Gateway for some shopping, grab dinner and a movie?'

Reggie looked over with a smile. 'That sounds perfect. While we're out, I need to go visit the Church of the Sacred Whale.'

'Is that some kind of a joke?' Ross replied.

'What? You haven't heard of the huge whale sculpture on the roundabout down at ninth and ninth?'

Ross looked baffled, as though he were still waiting for the punchline.

'Really? It's got a cult following. People are literally making pilgrimages there to leave offerings. And to take selfies.'

'Why?'

'To bring snow, Ross! Lots of snow! That's why it's known as the Church of the Sacred Whale.'

Ross shook his head. 'I have no words.'

'Right,' Reggie began. 'Today we'll go and leave an offering to the whale and go shopping, and then next week—after heavy snow—we're gonna go to Brighton. And I'm going to teach you how to snowboard.'

Ross grimaced as he placed Reggie's coffee down. 'Uh, *no*, you're not. I would literally break. I'll come to Brighton, though, and sit in a nice coffee shop with my book.'

'We'll see,' Reggie said.

'*No*, we won't,' Ross insisted, taking his cell phone off the charger and tapping at the screen. A few moments later, he leaned on the counter opposite Reggie and said, 'I've narrowed it down to two movie choices: *Prey for the Devil* or *Till*.'

Reggie shrugged. 'Honestly… Never heard of either of them. What are they about? Sound any good?'

Ross read the blurb for each movie and then summarized. '*Till* is about the 1955 murder of a black boy—'

'Emmet Till,' Reggie interrupted.

Ross nodded and continued, '—in Mississippi, which became a pivotal moment in the civil rights movement. And *Prey for the Devil* is about a nun exorcising the same demon from a young girl that possessed her own mother.'

Reggie burst out laughing. 'What a tough choice.'

'It really is,' Ross agreed, 'but I think we'll go with *Till*.'

'I think so,' Reggie said.

'Okay, I'm going to grab a shower.'

'Cool, I'll wrap up with Leon, then get ready to hit the shops,' Reggie said, watching as Ross headed to the bathroom.

He sat back with his coffee, another wave of contentment washing over him. Life was good. And next week, when the slopes opened again, it would be even better.

Putting down his coffee, Reggie downloaded the probate document and quickly ran his eyes down the remainder of the page. He was about to close the file when he noticed a familiar name among the slaves bequeathed to James Woods's brother, Richard.

Negroe's Names and Ages
Frances Brown, 18
Hannah Brown, 16
Sally Belling, 10
Betsy Adley, 6

Belling. Reggie had seen that name somewhere on the speculative tree that he'd created for Malik Johnson. He was also sure that Maddie had mentioned it when she had still been working on the case.

He clicked *Find in tree* and searched for the surname Belling.

Sally Belling, 1847 -
Noah Belling, 1865 - 1919
Matilda Belling, 1899 - 1974

Sally Belling was Malik Johnson's great-great-grandmother, a woman enslaved to Richard Woods.

Reggie's mind was running away with itself.

'Time's up,' Ross said, appearing from the bedroom, dressed and ready to go out.

'Give me twenty minutes and I'll be good to go,' Reggie said, shutting the laptop lid but allowing his brain to continue to puzzle over Leon Sierra.

Becky's heart was racing wildly as she and Aidan cowered behind a thick guava tree, looking out across to Rue Hubert where an elderly man lay slumped at the edge of the road, dying. Moments before, a gunshot had rung out and everybody in the vicinity had taken cover, knowing this was yet another random sniper attack.

'Where did it come from?' Becky managed to ask.

Aidan pointed to a three-story building farther along the street that towered above the one-room tin shacks which dominated the area. 'My guess would be up there.'

'What about that poor man?' Becky asked, watching him writhing in pain.

Aidan shrugged. 'There's nothing we can do for the guy without getting ourselves killed in the process.'

Becky hated feeling so helpless. There was no point in calling the police because they wouldn't come. 'Let's try and get someone from the Médecins Sans Frontières building,' she said. 'It's only just down the street.'

Aidan nodded. 'Good idea. I'll do that. You go to the meeting point.'

'Are we safe to run?' Becky asked.

'Yeah, just keep your head down and keep going,' Aidan said. 'Go.'

Becky followed him, running at full pelt down the road running perpendicular to Rue Hubert, where they were due to meet V38 in about ten minutes. Once they were well clear of the main road, they slowed their pace to a jog but still didn't stop until they reached the venue, a make-shift community center almost directly opposite the Médecins Sans Frontières, Hôpital de Brûlures.

Aidan entered the room first, checking that it was safe, then called for Becky to follow. 'Wait in here for V38 and I'll nip across the street and see if anyone can go up and help the old man. I reckon he's a goner, though.'

Becky nodded, unable to talk. She watched Aidan leave the building and attempted to stabilize her breathing. She sat down on the dirty wooden floor, trying to convince herself that she was safe here. This place had been specifically chosen because it was bordered by the hospital on one side, a green wasteland to another and lower density housing on the other two sides. But the stark and terrifying reality was that nowhere in Port-au-Prince was safe right now.

During these regular moments of high anxiety, Becky retreated inside her memories of home. She imagined herself being back in her Sugar House Apartment with its beautiful views out to the mountains that surrounded Salt Lake City. The ski resorts must be about to open up any day for the winter season, she thought. Right now, in this oppressive heat and with the constant threat of danger, Becky would have given anything to be up at her parents' second home in Park City.

Her breathing started to calm, and her heart rate became steadier, as she wondered how her parents were doing. Although she missed them, she knew that the fact that they had ceased all contact with her meant that her presence in Haiti had caused a stir. There was something here that her father did not want her to find. Becky didn't have enough evidence yet, but she hoped that V38 might be able provide some.

Right on cue, V38 and the translator, Fabienne, cautiously entered the room.

'*Bonjou*,' Becky said in Haitian Creole. '*Koman ou ye?*'

V38 smiled and replied, '*Mwen byen mèsi, ak ou?*'

'*Gran mèsi*,' she lied, observing from V38's demeanor that she too was lying about how she was. She was dark-skinned with black braided hair, a simple white t-shirt and dirty jeans. She spoke again and, although Becky didn't understand her, she could tell that what she'd said contained sadness.

'She said her mother has cholera,' Fabienne explained. 'She is bad with it.'

'I'm sorry to hear that,' Becky said.

'Another gift from the UN,' Fabienne added.

Becky nodded and sighed. Following the devastating earthquake in Haiti in 2010, UN peacekeepers introduced cholera to the country by knowingly pumping raw sewage from the peacekeeper camps directly into the rivers used by Haitians for drinking and cooking. More than 10,000 people had died from the outbreak, which continued to blight the island. The U.S. Federal Court of Appeals rejected a case for victim compensation on account of UN immunity under U.S. law. And so, the Haitians were left to die.

'Let's sit down,' Becky said, directing V38 and the translator over to a small table with four chairs around it. 'Aidan will be here in a moment.'

As they sat down, Becky took out her notepad and pencil. 'Before we get on to your case, the last time we met, you mentioned a group of women from Pétion-Ville who were victims of an international abuse ring?'

V38 nodded, glancing over at the door.

'And this group had nothing to do with the UN peacekeepers?' Becky checked.

V38 shook her head, then spoke in Haitian Creole.

'She said that no, the abusers were white men, mainly from America,' Fabienne translated. 'The girls were raped and abused, but their children were not *pitit MINUSTAH* or *bébés casques bleus* as they are also known.'

'So, not children of the peacekeepers,' Becky confirmed, making deliberately cryptic notes on her pad. 'When was this going on?'

'From some time after the earthquake until 2020,' Fabienne told her. 'When the pandemic hit, the abusers couldn't come anymore.'

'Can you put me in touch with some of these women?' Becky asked.

V38 took in a long breath. She was clearly reluctant. '*Mwen ka eseye.*'

Fabienne said, 'She can try.'

The three women jumped as the main door opened with a crack. It was Aidan.

'Did you get help?' Becky asked him.

'Yeah, but the poor bugger was dead by the time they got there, and no sign of the cops,' he said. He took the last seat and greeted V38 and Fabienne. 'What've I missed?'

'Nothing,' Becky answered. 'We were waiting for you.'

'Yes. And talking about the fair-skinned abusers in Pétion-Ville,' Fabienne said rather pointedly.

Aidan shot a look at Becky. 'That's not what we're here for.'

'Let's get on with it, then,' Becky said, addressing V38. 'We're still working on identifying your biological father. We haven't found him yet, but we've got a fairly good idea of the family name and geographical area.' She paused, allowing Fabienne to translate, then continued. 'We think the surname is Fonseka and that he came from the area around Jaffna in Northern Sri Lanka.'

'*Ou ka jwenn li,*' V38 asked softly.

'Can you find him?' Fabienne said.

'I'm having meetings with representatives from the UN,' Aidan confirmed. 'So far, they're denying that there was a peacekeeper matching these details in Haiti during the time that your mother alleges the rape happened.'

V38 slammed her fist down onto the table, tears in her eyes. '*Se pa yon akizasyon. Li viola li.*'

'It's not an allegation; he raped her.'

Becky reached for V38's shaking hand, just as another gunshot rang out nearby.

Kenyatta was standing behind a long folding table that was set back from the sidewalk in Pioneer Park in downtown Salt Lake City. A small group of the local homeless population had gathered around, eating soup and bread served by Jim Stanley, a man she now proudly called her partner. After a few weeks of dating, he'd become her boyfriend; but then, once she'd told her sons about him, they had unilaterally agreed that 'a woman of her age' couldn't have someone whom she was dating described as a boyfriend. They said it made him sound like a twentysomething, rather than his actual age of sixty. But, although the boys were being supportive of her dating, they had been unable to settle on an acceptable term to describe his relationship to their mom, so Kenyatta had opted for the word *partner* because of its sense of permanence. After a horrific end to her marriage with Otis, she needed something with longevity, preferably a relationship that ran right to the end, God willing. With Jim, it was so far, so good.

She smiled at him as he served David, an elderly African American with curly gray hair who'd been a regular visitor to the SLC Homeless Kitchen for many years.

'What?' Jim asked Kenyatta. 'Have I got something on my face?'

David leaned closer and stared at Jim. 'No. Not that I can see from here.'

'I was just smiling at you, is all,' Kenyatta said, making David a coffee.

'Black with two,' David reminded her.

Kenyatta rolled her eyes. 'I've been making your coffee for a long time; I know exactly how you like it. The day I forget...is the day I need to go home, put my feet up and retire.'

'I got news for you. You're never doing that,' David said, taking the drink and wandering off.

For the first time that afternoon, Kenyatta and Jim were left alone together. He returned her smile and took her hand in his.

'Say, do you want to go on vacation?' Jim suddenly asked.

Kenyatta's eyes widened. 'Desperately. Hawaii, perhaps?'

Jim nodded. 'Okay. I'll get something booked. Do you have any preferences for location?'

Kenyatta let go of his hand and stared at him. 'What? I was only kidding.'

'Well, I'm being serious,' he said. 'We've been together now for...what...two and half years, and we've not been away anywhere together.'

Kenyatta thought for a moment. A vacation sure would be welcome. With all that had gone on with her sons, the divorce, the pandemic and a very limited budget, she hadn't been outside of Utah for many years. But she knew she didn't want any funny business going on until they were married.

'Separate rooms,' he said, correctly intuiting her reluctance to jump at the idea.

'Yeah, okay,' she agreed. 'But my budget won't quite stretch to Hawaii. For sure, though, somewhere outside of the Beehive State should be manageable. Let's look into it.'

Jim grinned, then planted a big kiss on her lips.

'That's plain disgusting,' a familiar voice barked. 'Why would you come down to a public park and do *that*.'

Kenyatta smiled warmly. Standing in front of her was her old friend, Lonnie, with his trademark ratty gray beard and the same grimy mismatched clothes that he always wore. He was as dependable in his appearance as he was in his inability to filter his thoughts before opening his mouth. 'Hey, Lonnie. How's it going?'

'Listen to me. It's November. Heavy snow is due. I'm homeless. Now, how do you think it's going?'

'He's got a point,' Jim agreed.

'Well, maybe this delicious, fortifying turkey soup will warm you up,' Kenyatta said, indicating the silver pot gently simmering the food.

'Turkey? That s'posed to be some sort of early thanksgiving present?'

'Yeah, exactly that,' Kenyatta said. 'Want some?'

Lonnie shrugged. 'I guess so.' He watched carefully for a moment, as Jim ladled the soup into a bowl, before he turned back to face Kenyatta and asked, 'So, what is it you working on right now?'

'Oh, this one is *big*, Lonnie. Real big. I've even had to sign an NDA, so you'll have to wait until this one gets solved to find out,' she said.

'Not that Hollywood Strangler, is it?' Lonnie asked.

Kenyatta was taken aback and swiftly swallowed down her surprise. 'What? Why do you, uh... Well, why would you think it's that one?'

Lonnie's mouth opened into a wide toothless grin. 'I'm on the money! It IS the Hollywood Strangler! Old Lonnie guessed it right first time. Well, ain't that a turn up for the books, Kenny.'

Kenyatta raised her finger to her lips and tried to be admonishing: 'Sshh!'

Lonnie chuckled. 'You know your name's going to be all over the newspapers if you catch him, right. We won't see little Kenny down here doing her bit for the community no more. She'll be a bright star.'

Kenyatta glanced at Jim, who was pulling a face that screamed *Is this right?!* She responded with an uncertain look that confirmed it.

'Wow,' Jim muttered under his breath as he handed Lonnie his soup.

Lonnie chuckled again as he walked away, saying, 'The Hollywood Strangler. She ain't gonna know what's hit her, that one.'

'If he did guess correctly,' Jim said quietly. 'Then he's also right about your name being plastered everywhere. This is huge, Kenyatta.

Let's get that vacation booked, can we?'

'I don't know,' she said, suddenly seeing reality, thinking about Troy and not liking the idea of being away from home right now.

They were interrupted as Candice, a painfully thin young woman with a shaved head, wandered over to the table. 'I'm literally starving to death,' she announced.

'Turkey soup and a roll?' Jim replied.

'You see, here's the thing,' she said, rolling her hands over themselves and pulling an odd facial expression. 'I'm an *actual* vegetarian. So, if you could just fix it to give me the money instead, and I'll go buy something for myself?'

'You know it doesn't work like that, Candice,' Kenyatta answered. 'Just take the roll, if you don't want the soup. You gotta be...what...ninety pounds. I don't think you can afford to be too fussy, sweetheart.'

'I'm not fussy. I have allergies. I'm also gluten intolerant. Are you literally just going to stand there and watch me die of starvation in front of you, rather than hand over a measly five bucks?'

Kenyatta patted her pockets. 'I don't have a dime on me, Candice.'

'What about you?' she demanded, looking at Jim.

'I don't carry cash. But if you're hungry and really can't eat this, then I'll happily walk you over to Caputo's and get you something nourishing and vegetarian to eat,' Jim replied.

Candice sneered, spat on the ground, then turned around and walked away, calling over to David and asking if he had any money she could borrow.

'On Thursday night, we had vegetable soup and she didn't want that, either,' Jim said to Kenyatta.

'Let me guess, she was allergic to one of the ingredients?'

'Uh-huh,' Jim confirmed. 'Carrots. They make her see too much and it hurts her eyes if she eats them.'

Kenyatta couldn't help but smile in spite of the likely sadder truth. 'I just wish these kids would take the help they're offered.'

'Me too,' Jim agreed ruefully. 'Oh, yeah. That reminds me... Have you heard anything from Troy yet?'

Kenyatta wasn't sure she liked the link between the two conversations, but she didn't say anything about that and answered his question. 'Not a single word. He's ghosted us all—even his brothers.'

'So, what's he planning on doing with himself? Just staying over at Otis's house?'

'That's about the size of it, yeah,' Kenyatta confirmed.

'But you have joint custody, right?'

'Uh-huh,' she confirmed. 'But I'd rather this didn't have to go through the courts again.'

'What are you going to do?'

'Be patient,' she answered. 'It's the one good thing that my complicated relationship with Otis has taught me. Patience will prevail.'

Chapter Sixteen

Monday, November 7, 2022, Salt Lake City, Utah

'Okay. Usual Monday morning question,' Maddie asked as she poured herself some coffee. 'Did anyone defy me and work on the weekend?' Although she spoke projecting a feigned displeasure, she really did *not* want her staff to be working on the weekends. She recognized that it stood as a testament to their professional dedication and personal commitment to achieving justice that they often did, however.

Hudson sheepishly raised his hand. 'I... did a tiny bit,' he confessed.

'I worked on Leon Sierra,' Reggie called from his workstation. 'But not on the Strangler case.'

'I did a little on my Boys under the Bridge,' Kenyatta chipped in.

'While *I*... had the weekend off,' Maddie said. 'Clayton's in town.'

Suddenly the team was staring at her.

'I'm going to need details!' Kenyatta called.

'He's here on vacation. We've been hanging out. He's coming to the house for dinner tonight for the first time. That's it,' Maddie said.

Kenyatta gasped. 'This is so exciting! I'm so happy for you, Maddie. Oh, you deserve someone nice like him.'

Maddie shrugged, not too sure of what she did or did not deserve. 'Okay, anyway... Moving back to the case. We won't have a full briefing; but, Hudson, if you can bring us up to speed with what you've discovered, we'll get on and have a full briefing this afternoon. Anyone else need some coffee before we start?'

When nobody spoke up, Maddie took her drink over to the spare desk, close to the front, and sat down, waiting for Hudson to share his screen to the digital whiteboard.

He stood up at his desk as a scanned image from the 1880 census appeared in front of the team. He ran his cursor around the head of household, Jacob Boicourt, and his wife, Elizabeth. 'This couple had five children.' He moved the cursor to their daughter, Lillie. '*She* is my cluster lead Yannis Gurman's great-great-grandmother, and *she*—' he circled Lillie's sister, Agnes Boicourt, '—is Lorna Woodhouse's great-

great-grandmother.'

'Another common ancestral couple,' Maddie declared. 'Excellent work. Get that orange slip filled in and added to the board.'

'Well done,' Kenyatta said. 'So, one of Lillie and Agnes's siblings is likely to be the direct ancestor of the Hollywood Strangler.'

'Yeah,' Hudson agreed.

'So, we now have two confirmed direct sets of ancestors,' Maddie said, walking over to the whiteboard and reading the names on the other orange slip. 'As a reminder, keep an eye out for Fellows, Goodrich, and now, also Boicourt and Rhodes. What a great start to the week. Let's keep going.'

Hudson walked over to the front with an orange slip of paper with the names, dates and locations for his cluster and stuck it onto the whiteboard.

'I would honestly rather you weren't working your weekends,' Maddie said to him. 'But, great work, all the same.'

'Thanks,' he replied.

Maddie smiled as she glanced around the office, seeing that everyone was immediately focused on their work.

She returned to her office and sat down at her laptop. As was constantly the case, she was drowning in emails. Ross did his level best to field the ones directed at Venator, but when it came down to approaches from law enforcement with requests to take on a case, the decision had to rest solely with Maddie. At the top of her inbox was a new inquiry from a detective in Michigan.

Dear Ms Scott-Barnhart

My name is Detective Peters and I'm reaching out to you regarding a cold case and the possibility of your company using IGG to track down the suspect for prosecution. The case is a Baby Doe, born in a gas station restroom in 1991 and left by the mother to die. We have a workable DNA sample from the baby, and we'd like you to track down the mother.

Please let me know how to proceed.

Yours,

Ron Peters

Maddie sighed and typed out her standard reply to such cases.

Dear Detective Peters
Thank you for your inquiry. Regarding Baby Doe cases, Venator's policy is not to work on such cases if prosecution of the mother is the desired or otherwise intended outcome. If the purpose is to provide a name for the Baby Doe and / or support for both of the child's parents, then we would be happy to look into the case.
Regards
Madison Scott-Barnhart

In ninety-nine percent of these inquiries, the detective had never come back. They were rarely altruistically interested in the mother's mental health or background story that had commonly led to such a sorry outcome and almost never interested in the identity of the father, much less holding him accountable for his part in the baby's story.

Maddie worked through another bunch of emails, drinking her coffee as she went. When she had cleared her priority messages, she switched back to working on cluster three. By the time of the briefing last Friday, she had managed to identify all but four of Hope Beal's great-great-grandparents. Now, it was time to triangulate within the cluster.

Opening up the CSV file labeled *Cluster Three* in the Venator shared drive, Maddie looked down the list of fourteen names that ran below Hope Beal's in descending order by the quantity of DNA shared with the killer. Next on the list was a person named Andrew Mathison, who matched with 134 centimorgans of DNA.

Maddie logged in on the FTDNA website using the Hollywood Strangler's kit number, then navigated through the autosomal matches until she saw Andrew Mathison. She smiled when she saw several names listed under the heading *Ancestral Surnames*. Maddie clicked *View Details* and a box popped up in the middle of the screen.

'Thanks,' Maddie said to Andrew Mathison, as she took a screenshot of all the names he'd included. She hoped that, because the family tree icon was colored blue rather than gray, he would also have included these names on his actual family tree.

Maddie's joy quickly faded. Andrew Mathison had indeed

included a lot of names in his family tree, but every single one of them pertained to his paternal side, which ran back on every line to the great-great-grandparent generation. She looked at the names and locations but none of them were familiar. Just to be absolutely certain, Maddie pulled up the general case file that Ross maintained, and which included every name and location found during their research. She cross-checked each surname on Andrew Mathison's pedigree against the master list. There was no overlap at all and the locations dominating the tree were Wales, Denmark and the Netherlands, none of which had come up anywhere else in the investigation so far.

If Maddie were to trust Andrew Mathison's own research, then the only conclusion that she could draw was that the connection between him and the Hollywood Strangler was via his maternal side, which consisted of just one name: Helena Wilde, his mother. Not a single other piece of information about Helena had been included.

Andrew Mathison appeared to have worked extensively on his paternal line, yet done nothing at all on his maternal ancestry. Maddie's gut feeling was that, given the amount of work he'd done on his paternal side, it probably wouldn't have been for lack of trying.

She returned to the match list for cluster three and looked for someone who could replace Andrew Mathison for triangulation, but the amount of shared DNA fell rapidly below fifty centimorgans and nobody else within the cluster had included ancestral names or a family tree to give her research a helpful starting point.

With some reluctance, Maddie created a floating tree within Hope Beal's, starting with Andrew Mathison. She then copied the as-yet-unverified information regarding Andrew's father, Coben Mathison, to the tree. Her plan was to build a profile for Coben, which would hopefully include some information about his wife, Helena Wilde.

According to Andrew's tree, Coben Mathison had been born in Wales in 1914 and had died in 1989 in Tucson, Arizona. Maddie opened the GenealogyBank website and ran a search for an obituary. The top result of twenty appeared to be correct.

The Arizona Daily Star - October 12, 1989
Coben Mathison, a former sports teacher at the Northern Arizona University's

sports department, died Wednesday at his Tucson home from a severe asthma attack. He was 75.
Mathison was born June 14, 1914, in Wales. His family moved to Tucson in 1920, which Coben happily made his life home. He graduated from Tucson High School and went on to study physical education at the University of Arizona, a subject he continued to teach until his retirement in 1978.
Mathison is survived by his wife, Helena; two sons, Andrew and James, both of Tucson; one sister, Mrs. Rita Wright; and 8 grandchildren.

The obituary went on to record details of the funeral but contained no more genealogical information. Maddie saved the data to Andrew Mathison's tree. As far as his maternal side was concerned, the obit really only told Maddie that Helena had still been alive at the time of her husband's death in October 1989.

Maddie edited the search parameters for Helena's death from 1989 onward. She found it easily.

The Arizona Daily Star - August 1, 1994
Helena Mathison, a retired teacher died at her home in Tucson following a long battle with cancer.
Surviving are two sons, Andrew and James; and ten grandchildren.

'Short,' Maddie commented, pulling out the key information and adding it to Helena's profile.

Next, she turned to the Research Wiki at FamilySearch, looking for Arizona marriages, specifically for Tucson. Vital records for the state were distributed across most of the major genealogy companies, but Maddie clicked on *Arizona, County Marriages, 1871-1964* within the FamilySearch website. She entered just Coben's name and used a broad search timeframe, then hit enter. Once again, the top result looked correct, making Maddie suspicious that it was all going too well. She clicked to view a black-and-white scan of the original marriage register, which was broken up into three parts: the marriage license, the marriage certificate and the certificate of record. Despite the lengthy appearance of the document, it contained more legal speak than useful information. Just one paragraph contained the key names, ages and date.

I do hereby certify that Coben Mathison, 22 and Helena Wilde, 21 were joined in marriage by me at Tucson in the County of Pima, State of Arizona, on the 6th day of November, 1936.

Despite its brevity, Maddie downloaded the certificate and added it to Helena and Coben's profiles. She then ran a search for the couple in the 1940 census, finding them living in Tucson with a one-year-old Andrew Mathison. Once she had confirmed that she had the correct family, the part of most interest to Maddie was Helena's place of birth, which was stated to have been California.

Maddie saved the entry, her instinct telling her to pursue the connection to California, from where several of the ancestors of Hope Beal, the cluster lead, had hailed.

As Maddie opened *California Births and Christenings, 1812-1988*, her cell phone pinged with a message from Clayton. It was a selfie of him sitting down at a three-computer setup with a wide grin on his face. The accompanying text read, *Guess where I am?!*

Maddie smiled. She knew exactly where he was. The third floor of the FamilySearch Library.

Where isn't the question; why is, she responded.

While she waited for him to reply, Maddie entered Helena Wilde's details into the search boxes. One result.

Name: Helena Wilde
Sex: Female
Race: Caucasian
Birth Date: 21 Nov 1915
Birth Place: Los Angeles, Los Angeles, California
Father's Name: John Walter Wilde
Father's Age: 22
Father's Birthplace: Arkansas
Mother's Name: Maude Flora Trilby

Mother's Age: 20
Mother's Birthplace: California

Another message from Clayton came through: *Genealogy is why! Mom always said that a cousin had traced the Tylers back to the Mayflower. And on dad's side we descend from a Navajo tribe leader. Should be interesting.*

Maddie couldn't help but laugh out loud. *Good luck finding all that out*, she replied with an accompanying laughing face emoji.

Since Arkansas had not come up in Hope Beal's tree, Maddie opted to prioritize her research into Helena's maternal line. She edited the California birth search with Maude Flora Trilby's details, receiving a long list of results, none of which looked correct.

She spent time checking the top entries and adapting the search criteria but still found no sign of Maude Flora Trilby's birth. Checking each of the major genealogy websites one after another produced the same negative result.

Maddie's run of luck on this tree was over, she conceded, hoping that Maude's slightly unusual name might make her stand out on the 1910 census. But there was no sign of her, so Maddie jumped back a decade.

'Is that you?' she muttered, reading an entry which could have been correct.

Trilbie, Maria, head of household, white, female, single, born Jan 1878, California. Boarding Housekeeper.
Trilbie, Maud, daughter, white, female, single, born Jul 1895, California.

The record was not good enough evidence for Maddie to save it to Maude's profile. There were spelling inconsistencies, a lack of corroborating data and the fact that Maude was recorded under her single mother's surname. Instead of saving the entry, Maddie jotted it down on some scrap paper off to her side. Since there was no surviving census for 1890, Maddie ran a search for Maria Trilby / Trilbie in 1880. There were three results which Maddie checked, one after the other. The final entry, for a girl living with her parents on Fernando Street, looked to be the most likely.

Charles Trillbie, head of household, white, male, married, age 30, born California. Traveling salesman.
Lucinda Trillbie, wife, white, female, married, age 30, born California.
Maria Trillbie, daughter, white, female, single, age 2, born California.

It was another very tenuous link. Could this Maria, with a third spelling of Trilby, really be Andrew Mathison's great-grandmother? It was no wonder he'd left his maternal line blank.

Maddie stretched. She needed coffee. As she stood up, she caught sight of a surname in the neighboring property that made her look more closely and sink back to her seat.

Samuel Moreno, head of household, white, male, married, age 30, born California. Hotel cook.
Elena Moreno, wife, white, female, married age 27, born California.

Samuel and Elena Moreno were one set of Hope Beal's great-great-grandparents. And they were living right next door to Maria Trilby.

Something was off.

Maddie studied the document carefully. Her research in getting from Andrew Mathison to Charles and Lucinda Trilby was paper-thin to say the least. It would never stand up to the Genealogical Proof Standard in a million years. And yet, it could not be a coincidence that these people were neighbors. She looked hard at the names and ages, reaching another tentative conclusion without an ounce of proof. Could Maria Trilby's biological father have been Samuel Moreno? Conceived while Charles Trilby was out of town as a traveling salesman? If she were correct, then it would mean that only Samuel Moreno was the common ancestor between the Hollywood Strangler, Hope Beal and Andrew Mathison.

Maddie went over it all again, feeling more and more sure. But she needed more evidence before she presented it as probable fact at this afternoon's briefing.

There was a cough followed by a light tap on her office door.

Maddie glanced up to see Ross.

'Hey, Ross. What can I do for you?' she asked.

'Everyone's ready and kinda waiting for the briefing,' he replied with a slight grimace.

'What?' Maddie stammered, looking at her laptop clock, finding that it was 4:35 p.m. 'I'll be right there.' She hastily saved the record that she'd just found, then hurried with her laptop out into the main office. 'So sorry, guys,' she apologized. 'Slipped headfirst into quite a rabbit hole, there.'

'That's a relief. We thought maybe you'd fallen asleep,' Kenyatta quipped.

'If only,' Maddie replied, setting her computer down and then sharing her screen. 'I'll go first.' She held up a blank orange piece of paper, which precipitated immediate praise from the team. 'Don't get ahead of yourselves. I *think* I'm going to fill this in, but I'd like you all to tell me what your thoughts are before I go ahead and do it.'

Maddie talked them through her day's work and the conclusions that she had reached. In the past few hours, she had found additional evidence to support her theory that Samuel Moreno was Maria Trilby's biological father.

'I think the coincidence is too great to ignore,' Kenyatta said when Maddie had finished. 'And I think, once we've worked out who the killer is, the amount of centimorgans will either add up or they won't.'

'I think you're good to write it up,' Hudson agreed. 'Although you can't apply the GPS to the theory, you don't absolutely need to at this stage.'

Maddie nodded. 'Yeah, I had reached that conclusion, but I guess I just wanted your opinions. Okay, I'll go ahead and get Samuel Moreno onto an orange slip. Who wants to go next?'

Hudson stood up and declared, 'Good people of the Venator team, I do hereby present to you the first great-grandparent couple!' He took a blue piece of paper from his desk and held it aloft.

'No way!' Kenyatta gasped.

Hudson's laptop screen overrode Maddie's, showing the same 1880 census entry that he had shown this morning.

'You'll remember Lillie and her sister, Agnes Boicourt, from this morning? Well, their eldest brother, Peter—shown here in 1880—married and had a daughter called Florence Boicourt.' Hudson closed the census and then brought up Florence's profile. 'Florence—' he said, clicking her profile '—married a guy called James Fellows.'

'Oh!' Kenyatta exclaimed. 'The brother of Betty and Della Fellows from my cluster two.'

'Correct,' Hudson confirmed.

'Bravo. Great job, especially at this stage of the game,' Maddie congratulated.

'Thanks,' Hudson said. 'It was kind of accidental, actually. I know we're not supposed to be working that generation yet, but I was searching for a record and saw Florence and James together and I couldn't not confirm it.'

'Did they have many kids?' Maddie asked.

'Yep,' he replied. 'Twelve.'

'Wow. Okay. One of those twelve is highly likely to be the Hollywood Strangler's grandparent,' Maddie said.

The team fell quiet for a moment. Maddie guessed they were reflecting on how close they were getting to catching one of America's most notorious serial killers. She broke the silence by asking, 'What have you found today, Reggie?'

Reggie stood up and sighed. 'As you know, I'm trying to triangulate cluster four between Jennifer Hatter and Jonas Crawford. I spent most of Friday working on a hunch that they were linked via the Schoettlin or Schmidt line from Switzerland, but I just can't find the link. So, today, I went back to square one and pulled up a *third* person from the cluster.' Reggie mirrored his computer. 'Allow me to introduce Clement Easton. Born in 1982 in Sydney, Australia, which—since there are very few publicly available vital records for the country—has proven to be another headache. His social media has given me all four grandparents, all born and bred in Sydney or Melbourne. That's it so far. I'm hoping for fairly recent immigration to the country rather than convicts from the 1780s.'

Maddie frowned. 'Is he really the next best person to pick from cluster four?'

Reggie nodded. 'Yeah, the others are significantly worse.'

'Okay, well, keep going with it,' Maddie encouraged. 'Kenyatta? Have you had any better luck?'

'Well, I've made a good start on this young lady who is the lead person for cluster eight,' she replied, displaying her screen which showed a pedigree chart for someone called Jean Adams. 'She was born in New Mexico, but her parents were from Louisiana. I've pushed back on the maternal line to the great-grandparent level, but I can't see any connections to any other cluster or surname, so far.'

'Great work,' Maddie said, stepping up and moving to the front of the office. 'You're all doing fantastic. Keep it up, but don't work yourselves too hard. Have a good evening *off*, everyone.'

'Good luck with *your* evening,' Kenyatta said.

Maddie felt a sudden and sharp stab of anxiety in the pit of her stomach at the prospect of introducing Clayton to her family. With the complexity of her research today, she'd managed to push all thoughts of the evening to the back of her mind. But now it was time to head home and face the challenge of introducing a new man to her family. As she packed up her things to leave, the sense of guilt that she felt toward Michael grew to the point that it overwhelmed her thoughts.

Taking out her cell phone, she typed out a message to Clayton.

I can't do tonight, sorry.

Maddie's finger hovered over the blue send icon. She looked at the photographs of Michael, Jenna, Nikki and Trenton on her desk, an undeniable ache of grief and guilt consuming her. Was seven years too soon to move on? Would Michael have forgiven her?

She took a breath, deleted the message and put her cell phone in her purse.

The drive home on I-15 had quieted Maddie's mind. She needed to remind herself that she had the full support of all her three kids and that she was only having Clayton over for a family dinner, not inviting him to move in. Once she had resolved to go ahead with the evening, she switched on her favorite podcast, DNA: ID, and allowed her mind to focus on absorbing the details of another cold murder case solved by IGG.

As she pulled into her driveway, the front door opened, and Nikki stood with a wide grin on her face.

Maddie hurriedly switched off the engine, got out, leaving her door open, and ran into her daughter's arms. 'Oh, Nikki. It's so good to have you home.' After a long embrace, she stepped back. 'Look at you, all grown up.'

Nikki laughed. 'Mom, I've only been gone a few weeks. I don't think I've grown in that time.'

'Oh, I think you have,' Maddie said, stroking her hair and sighing. 'The house just isn't the same without you.'

'Yeah, it's much more peaceful,' Trenton called from inside the house.

Nikki rolled her eyes. 'Are you all ready for tonight?'

Maddie shrugged as she knocked the car door shut and headed into the house. 'Not really, but then…I don't think I ever will be.'

Nikki put her arm around Maddie's waist. 'What is it you're worrying about exactly? Clayton's reaction to our dysfunctional family or that Dad might not have approved?'

Maddie smiled as she locked the front door. 'Both, I guess.'

'It'll be fine,' Nikki tried to reassure her. 'You just need to relax.'

'Dad would've moved on…if it would have been the other way around,' Trenton commented from the kitchen. 'He'd have a wife and three kids by now.'

'Trenton!' Nikki rebuked. 'Stop.'

'I'm just saying.'

'Jenna!' Maddie's mom shouted from the kitchen. 'Come here.'

Maddie's eyes widened and she whispered to Nikki, 'Jenna's here?'

Nikki shook her head. 'No, she's not. She's been calling me Jenna since I've been back.'

Maddie slipped off her shoes and followed Nikki into the kitchen. Trenton was sitting up at the counter, appearing to be doing homework, while her mom was sitting down at the table, studiously drawing in a kids' coloring book.

'What are we having for dinner?' Trenton asked.

'Jambalaya,' she replied.

'Cool. What time's he getting here?'

'In about an hour, give or take. So, I need to get moving. Trenton, can you move your stuff up to your room, please?'

He leaned back in the chair and stretched. 'Sure,' he replied, scooping up his books into one pile and carrying them from the room. 'Call me when my new stepdad gets here, okay?' he shouted back.

'Trenton!' Nikki yelled. 'You're so not funny.'

'It's okay,' Maddie said. 'Honestly... I'd rather that he was making his inappropriate jokes than being against the whole situation.'

'He's an idiot,' Nikki said in reply. She rolled up her sleeves. 'Give me a job. In fact, let me do the cooking. You go and take a shower and get ready.'

Maddie looked at her daughter with gratitude. 'Are you sure?'

'Sure, I'm sure. Go,' Nikki insisted, wafting her hand toward Maddie.

Maddie kissed Nikki on the head, thanked her and headed up to her bedroom. She sat down on her bed and took in a long breath as she looked around the room, noting all the things that still existed from when Michael had been here. Her eyes finally settled on the silver-framed photograph of their wedding in the summer of 2005. She walked over to the dresser and picked up the photo, staring at Michael in his sharp navy suit. He was so young and fresh-faced back then; but then, so was she. But Maddie had aged, whereas Michael was stuck, freeze-framed at forty-one years old. She wondered what the last seven years might have done to his features. Would he have started to go gray by now? Maybe grown the middle-aged paunch that Clayton Tyler was working hard to try and shift? Knowing Michael and his love of sport and the great outdoors, he would have fought getting old with a determined passion.

Tears pooled in her eyes. And as she set the frame back down on the dresser, it hit her that she had done far more than her fair share of crying in this room; and she resolved in that moment that it was high time to change that.

It was time to get herself ready and to take Nikki's advice and try to relax.

'Damn!' Maddie muttered, rushing from her bedroom while trying to put in a gold hoop earring. The doorbell had just rung, and she had listened in horror as Trenton had been the one to answer the door and let Clayton into the house. 'You're five minutes early!' she called as she dashed down the stairs to meet him.

Clayton smiled. 'Well... I can go back outside and wait?'

'No,' Maddie replied, a tenseness visiting all of her muscles as he leaned in and pecked her on the cheek. 'Come on in.'

'I got you these,' he said, handing her a bunch of white roses.

'They're beautiful. Thank you,' she said, leading the way into the kitchen. 'Clayton, this is my youngest daughter, Nikki, and my mom, Patricia. You've just met Trenton.'

'Yeah. And just so you know... I'm her favorite,' Trenton chipped in.

Clayton shook Nikki's hand and then moved toward Maddie's mom, who met his approach with a scowl.

'Who is this man?' her mom asked.

'His name is Clayton. He's come for dinner.'

Her mom reluctantly shook his proffered hand. 'And why's he here?'

'He's come for dinner,' Maddie repeated.

'He and Mom are dating,' Trenton said.

'And what will Michael have to say about that?' her mom demanded, thrusting her hands onto her hips. 'Does he even know?'

'He would be absolutely fine with it, Grandma,' Nikki said softly. 'Do you remember, he disappeared seven years ago.'

'Of course I remember. I just can't imagine that he'd approve of whatever *this* is going on here.'

Maddie flushed red with embarrassment, wondering yet again if she was making a terrible mistake.

'Should I go?' Clayton whispered to Maddie. 'I can just go...'

She shook her head, vehemently trying to reassure him about the situation. 'Mom, could you help set the table for dinner, please?'

Her mom took another disapproving look at Clayton, then walked over to Nikki. 'Remind me where those—oh, the—those things we eat with. Where are they kept, Jenna?'

'Right here, Grandma,' Nikki answered, pulling open the cutlery drawer.

Maddie watched nervously as her mom took out handfuls of knives and spoons and began laying them arbitrarily around the table.

'So, I went to the FamilySearch Library today,' Clayton said in a clear attempt to ease the tension.

'Did you find your link to the Mayflower and the Navajo tribe that you were seeking?' Maddie asked with a grin.

'No,' Clayton admitted. 'Genealogy is much harder than it looks on *Finding Your Roots*, don't you know?'

Maddie and Nikki laughed.

'You should have asked for help,' Nikki said. 'The staff and volunteers there are super knowledgeable.'

'I did and I managed to work on my dad's line that came over from Italy. I found some interesting facts that my family will love to hear.'

'Like what?' Nikki asked as she pulled the jambalaya from the oven.

Maddie smiled at Clayton's genuine enthusiasm as he animatedly shared his genealogical findings from the day. While he did so, she went around the table, surreptitiously trying to rearrange the cutlery so that it made sense.

'Dinner is served,' Nikki declared, carrying the Dutch oven to the center of the table, lifting the lid to reveal the steaming shrimp-covered rice dish.

'That looks incredible, Nikki,' Clayton complimented.

'Take a seat,' Maddie said. 'I'll get us a glass of white wine.'

Clayton, Trenton, Nikki and her mom all sat down at the kitchen table as she poured two glasses of wine. She looked on at the assembled group, thinking that maybe things might just turn out okay. She did just need to relax.

'Hey, Jenna,' her mom said to Nikki. 'You think your real dad will approve?'

Nikki smiled as she served her a portion of jambalaya. 'Grandma—like I told you—he disappeared.'

'No, not Michael,' her mom responded. 'Your *real* dad. You know, the English boy your mom met when she was over there. I don't think he knows anything about all of *this*,' she said, waving her fork over the dinner table.

Maddie flushed with embarrassment. This *had* turned out to be a truly terrible idea.

Chapter Seventeen

Tuesday, November 8, 2022, Salt Lake City, Utah

Hudson Édouard was working in the FamilySearch Library, sitting down at his favorite workstation, 2-041. It was a two-computer set up at the back of the second floor. He liked it because it was quiet and tucked out of the way from the main banks of computers, facing a line of gray nondescript filing cabinets that offered him no distractions.

He was just starting work on cluster six, building up the family tree for one George Whitlock. Hudson's initial research this morning had led him to Wirt County, West Virginia, where the vital records had not yet been digitized. Fortunately for him, a large portion of these documents had been transcribed and were on the open shelves of the FamilySearch Library.

He put his notepad, pencil and a pedigree chart down on the desk and walked over to the bookshelves relating to U.S. and Canadian records that ran in rows behind the filing cabinets. He wandered through a middle aisle that dissected the long avenues, checking the library reference numbers and locations as he went. *West Virginia*. He stopped and headed up the row jam-packed with six shelves of books on each side. He paused at several points to check the reference numbers printed on the front of each spine.

He stopped again. *975.426. Wirt County, West Virginia.*

Hudson examined the range of multi-colored tomes that lined the shelf, sliding out several that might pertain to his research, and carried the stack back over to his desk.

The first thing that Hudson wanted to confirm was the marriage of his cluster lead's parents, so he started with a small brown book entitled *Wirt County, West Virginia Marriages 1900-1970*. Opening the first pages, he found that it was arranged chronologically, so he skipped through to George Whitlock's birth and then began to work backward. The county was small, and it only took a few seconds of searching before he landed on the correct entry.

Date: Nov 6, 1950

Groom: Morris Whitlock
Age: 29
Residence: Patrick County
Father's Name: John Whitlock
Bride: Jennifer Moran
Age: 28
Residence: Wirt County
Father's Name: Brett Moran

Hudson took a photograph of the entry and copied it across to his pedigree chart. Having confirmed the names and ages of the cluster lead's parents, it was time to move backward on both lines. Since he had a stack of vital records for Wirt County in front of him, Hudson elected to focus first on the maternal side.

He pulled open a thin blue volume that held birth records for Wirt County 1900 to 1970 and began a systematic check of each page. It took just a few minutes to reach the end of the ledger, by which time, Hudson had not recorded a single entry for either the Whitlock or Moran surname.

Switching to the 1950 census, he searched for Jennifer Moran, born around 1922. There was just a single match located in Wirt County, West Virginia.

Viewing a scan of the original census page, Hudson found Jennifer living with her parents, Brett and Cynthia, and Cynthia's widowed father, Richard Riodan. All members of the household were noted as having been born in Virginia—and not West Virginia, where Jennifer's marriage had taken place—which explained why he'd found no trace of her birth.

Stepping back a decade to the 1940 census, Hudson ran a search for the eighteen-year-old Jennifer Moran. He found her easily, residing with her parents in Richmond, Virginia. Was this where she had been born? Hudson wondered as he opened the FamilySearch Research Wiki. He looked up vital records for Richmond and was immediately disappointed to see that no birth records existed online. He switched the search to the Catalog, also finding that there were no vital records on paper or microfilm within the building.

Since he was confident in his research so far, he turned his attention to finding the marriage record for Brett Moran and Cynthia Riodan. According to the Research Wiki, *Virginia Marriages, 1785-1940* were online with Ancestry, MyHeritage and FamilySearch. For no particular reason, he selected the latter and ran a search for the marriage. The top result appeared to be correct. Hudson clicked to view the transcript, smiling at the rich level of genealogical detail that it contained.

Name: Brett Moran
Sex: Male
Age: 21
Birthplace: Richmond
Marital Status: Single
Race: Colored
Father's Name: James Moran
Mother's Name: Duetta Bundy
Spouse's Name: Cynthia Riodan
Spouse's Sex: Female
Spouse's Age: 21
Spouse's Birthplace: Richmond
Spouse's Marital Status: Single
Spouse's Race: American
Spouse's Father's Name: Richard Riodan
Spouse's Mother's Name: Daisy Smith
Event Date: 11 Dec 1920
Event Place: Richmond, Virginia

Hudson saved the image, updated the pedigree chart and then used a combination of the census and marriage records for Richmond to push back on the Moran, Bundy, Riodan and Smith lines. Within an hour, he had taken each back to the great-great-great-grandparent level, where he was satisfied to stop.

Now it was time to focus on the cluster lead's paternal side, Morris Whitlock. Taking the tree back two generations to a fabulously named Napoleon Whitlock, Hudson again found a dearth of online records for Patrick County. Fortunately for him, according to the Catalog, vital records for the county were in book form on the shelves right in front of him.

Returning the stack of tomes for Wirt County to the nearest red *returns* trolley, Hudson made his way back over to the shelves, quickly locating *975.5695*, where he took out an eclectic mixture of sizes and colors of books relating to the county's vital records.

Once back at his desk, he opened *Birth Records of Patrick County, Virginia 1853-1869* to the first page, finding that it was a typed transcript, arranged in alphabetical order. He flipped to the index and ran his finger down the list of surnames beginning with W.

'And here we go,' he said with a smile, having found what he was after. He traced his finger along the line to read the full text.

Child's Name: Whitlock, Napoleon
Father / Owner Name: Whitlock, Flem H.
Race: W
Sex: Male
Mother: Whitlock, Julia A.
Birth Date: 17 April 1865

Hudson took a photo of the page and also noted the key information to the pedigree chart. Then, he opened *Patrick County, Virginia Marriages 1854-1874*, finding that it, too, was a typed transcript in alphabetical order. Close to the back of the volume, he found the entry that he wanted.

31 Jan 1861, Flem Whitlock and Julia Agee. Consent of father, Austin Agee.

Hudson took another photo, added the information to the pedigree, then turned to the previous volume of birth records. Within minutes, he had located the entries for both Flem and Julia.

6 June 1840, Flem Harold Whitlock, son of Jefferson and Pleasant Whitlock
18 Nov 1841, Julia Ann Agee, daughter of Austin and Nancy Ann Agee

Hudson spent some more time confirming the maiden names of Pleasant Whitlock and Nancy Ann Agee, then switched to Napoleon Whitlock's wife, Constant Cannaday, whom Napoleon had married in Patrick County in 1887.

Within forty-five minutes, Hudson had fleshed out all paternal lines from the cluster lead, George Whitlock, back to every great-great-great-grandparent.

With a sigh of satisfaction at his morning's work, he carried the stack of books over to the *returns* trolley, picked up his laptop, notepad and pencil, and then headed over to the elevators.

The air was cold with the threat of the approaching winter as Hudson marched back to the Kearns Building. Eleven minutes after leaving the library, he entered the Venator office.

Maddie was chatting to Ross at his desk as Hudson entered. 'Hey. How did you get on?'

'*All* branches of my cluster lead back to the great-great-great-grandparent level,' he boasted with a smile.

'You didn't happen to see a lost soul wandering the library in search of his native American great-grandmother, did you?'

Hudson looked doubtful. 'I don't believe so, no.'

'Clayton's taken up genealogy,' Maddie explained. 'He's in there again today.'

Kenyatta suddenly whipped around. 'Oh! And? How did it go last night? I forgot to be nosey and ask all about taking your date home to meet the family.'

Maddie sighed. 'It was a mess, truth be told. Mom was *not* having one of her ever-rarer good days, so spent most of the night making inappropriate comments and asking what on earth Michael would think.'

'Oh dear,' Kenyatta said.

'That must have been really awkward,' Hudson added.

'*Very,*' Maddie confirmed. 'Luckily, I'd warned Clayton, and he seems to have taken it all in his stride, somehow. To make things worse still, Trenton decided to be in full provocation mode and was asking when Clayton was going to be moving to Utah.'

Kenyatta grinned. 'Boys will be boys, huh? But…what was his

answer to that question, just out of curiosity?'

Maddie smiled. 'Well... He was very diplomatic, saying that we would have to see how things went before any big decisions were made. But he did say that if the time came that someone needed to relocate, it would be him.'

'Wow,' Kenyatta said.

'So, yeah... It wasn't the best night. Nikki was my one saving grace. She made a fantastic jambalaya, was very welcoming of Clayton and eventually took mom off and kept her entertained.'

'Has Clayton said how he felt it went? Or given you some kind of idea?' Hudson asked as he moved over to the kitchen area to make coffee.

'He texted me a couple of times this morning, actually... Just to say how much he enjoyed meeting everyone and that he wants to do it again,' Maddie answered with a shrug. 'But...what else is he going to say, right?'

'He obviously likes you, Maddie,' Kenyatta said. 'So, let him in.'

Maddie nodded but said nothing.

'Coffee?' he asked her.

'Um... No, thank you. I'm actually heading out shortly to meet Clayton at Eva's,' Maddie said. 'Anyone wants me to bring anything back?'

'No, thank you,' Reggie called over.

'I'm good, thanks,' Kenyatta responded.

'This will keep me going, thanks,' Hudson said, holding up his filled coffee and heading back over to his desk. He woke his computer and began to update George Whitlock's tree based on his findings at the FamilySearch Library. 'Hey, Kenyatta,' Hudson called over to her. 'Where was Mary Poppins born, again?'

'Charlottesville, Virginia,' she replied. 'Why? What you got?'

'Cluster six has links to Richmond, Virginia,' he said, opening Google Maps in preparation for her next question.

'How far away?' she asked.

'Seventy-two miles,' he replied.

'Could be interesting,' she said.

'Yeah,' he agreed, his gut telling him that the two families would likely intersect at some point.

Hudson drank some coffee as he returned to the Venator shared drive and pulled up the CSV file labeled *Cluster Six*. Underneath George Whitlock's name were a healthy eighteen people who shared DNA with both him and the Hollywood Strangler. The second match in the list was given as Joy Atkins, born Messenger, and when Kenyatta had compiled the clusters, she had entered *Yes* into the column relating to the addition of a family tree. It looked promising.

Logging in at FTDNA, Hudson navigated his way through the killer's autosomal matches to Joy Atkins. He clicked the blue tree icon to see that Joy had been born February 17, 1963. He wasn't overly surprised to see that all the other eight names ascending from Joy's were listed as *Private*. He looked around Joy's profile, but the only information of potential use was her Gmail address, which interestingly was fronted with the username *KeithandJoy99*.

Hudson copied the email address and pasted it into the background-search company, Spokeo.

Keith Atkins (possible owner of this email). Age 59. 1 social network.

Hudson scrolled down to the suggested social channel, finding that it referenced the online photograph storage and sharing company, Flickr. He clicked the link and was taken to a profile page with a header containing a photo of a dense woodland. The username associated with the email address from FTDNA was given as *The Joy of Life*, which Hudson assumed was a play on words with her first name.

Clicking on the *Albums* tab, Hudson found four folders headed *Lachlan's 1st birthday*, *Joy's 50th*, *Christmas 2015* and *Ray & Martha Golden wedding party*, respectively.

The cover image of the latter folder interested Hudson the most. It was a black-and-white image of a couple who, Hudson guessed, would have been Ray and Martha standing outside a church at the time of their marriage.

Hudson clicked the cover image and a page containing nineteen photos opened. A subheading read, *Ray & Martha's 50th party @ Billings, June 6, 2012.*

Even though he had no idea who Ray and Martha could have been, or if this Flickr account related to the correct Joy Messenger, Hudson jotted down the potential genealogical details in front of him. Then, he scrolled down the page, looking at each image in turn, being slightly surprised that the owner of this account was happy for the entire world to get a glimpse of this private family moment. The vast majority of the photos were taken at a garden party and key images, such as Ray and Martha cutting a cake, streamers being fired into the air and shots of various people—presumably family and friends—had been captured. When Hudson hovered over each image, a caption appeared in the bottom left corner. Most of the images were simply labeled IMG with a corresponding number, but some had been changed to reflect the content of the photo. He scoured them eagerly, hoping to build up a picture of the family and to get confirmation that he was indeed working along the right lines.

The happy day in 1962 captioned the black-and-white image of the young couple standing outside the church. The next photo was of an older couple at the garden party, holding hands and smiling for the camera. This one was labeled *Mom and Dad*. The resemblance between the couple in each photograph told Hudson that they were one and the same. But could he really assume that they were Joy's parents and not her husband, Keith's? The evidence in front of him wasn't sufficient.

He clicked out of the folder and then went into *Joy's 50th*, instantly receiving the confirmation that he needed from the subheading *Birthday party @ Billings, Feb 17, 2013*.

The date of the party precisely matched the date of birth stated on Joy Messenger's FTDNA profile. There was little doubt, now, that Hudson had identified the correct family.

He spent a little more time working within the Flickr account, extracting potential names and dates, before starting to broaden his search.

Opening the GenealogyBank website, Hudson ran a search for the marriage of Ray and Martha Messenger.

Your search did not match any items.

Switching to Newspapers.com, he ran the same search, selecting *Marriages* from the *Categories* tab. The top result was for an article in the

Montana newspaper, *The Billings Gazette*, March 2, 1962. Hudson clicked to see a scan of the original newspaper page.

Miss Martha Louise Olmstead became the bride of Raymond Messenger at American Lutheran Church with the Rev. L.B. Hippe officiating. The bride is the daughter of Mr. and Mrs. Aubrey Olmstead of 1056 LaBrea St. The bridegroom is the second son of Mr. Donald and the late Mrs. Messenger of 134 Custer Ave…

Hudson continued reading the article, but it didn't contain any further genealogical information that would help his investigation into the two families. He added Raymond's and Martha's fathers' names to the tree and then saved the newspaper story to each of the relevant profiles.

Knowing that the family had been living in Billings, Montana for at least two generations, Hudson pulled up the 1950 census and ran a search for Donald Messenger. The top result appeared to be the right one. The household was comprised of Donald Messenger, noted as a widower, and three sons, Raymond, Atticus and Jimmy. Evidently, Donald's wife had died at some point prior to 1950. Not knowing how Joy Messenger had been related to the cluster lead, George Whitlock, meant that Hudson needed to know the name of the deceased woman.

Returning to Newspapers.com, Hudson ran an obituary search, locating a short one in the June 21, 1945 edition of *The Billings Gazette*.

MESSENGER—The funeral service for Mrs. Grace Anna Messenger, wife of Donald Messenger, will be held Saturday afternoon at 3:30 o'clock at Smith's Funeral Chapel. Interment will be in Mountview Cemetery.

Having saved the information, Hudson set about trying to identify Grace Anna Messenger's maiden name before pushing back further generations.

Hudson hit pay dirt minutes before Maddie called the afternoon's briefing. Since there was so little time left, he decided not to pursue any new lines of inquiry. Instead, he made himself another coffee and checked his personal emails.

His heart jumped a beat when he saw a new email from Wanda Chabala with the subject *Brandon Blake*. Hudson quickly read the message.

Hudson, The judges are in deliberation. A result on freeing Brandon Blake is expected this evening.
Regards, Wanda

Hudson checked the KARE11.com website and, sure enough, the top story was the Minnesota Supreme Court going into the deliberation and decisions phase of the case. Wanda herself was quoted in the short article, arguing in favor of Brandon's release.

Now it was a waiting game.

'Okay, let's get this briefing underway, shall we?' Maddie said, marching into the main office.

'Will Becky be joining us?' Kenyatta asked.

Maddie shrugged. 'Not that I've heard, no. Ross, do you know anything?'

Ross walked over with his laptop, ready to type up the meeting notes. He shook his head as he sat down. 'She's been a little quiet. I haven't heard from her since the weekend.'

'I hope she's okay,' Maddie mumbled. After she'd logged in on the spare computer, she asked, 'Anyone wants to volunteer to go first?'

'Sure,' Hudson said, standing up as he shared the pedigree chart for George Whitlock that was on his screen. 'This morning at the FamilySearch Library, I managed to close every branch to the great-great-great-grandparent level and—'

'That's impressive,' Kenyatta interrupted.

'Yeah, they were a pretty settled family, and the library had a lot of records that I needed,' Hudson explained, switching to another tab which displayed the pedigree chart for Joy Messenger, and which was also complete to the great-great-great-grandparent generation.

'Have we ever closed down *every* branch on two names within a cluster before?' Maddie asked.

'*I* certainly haven't,' Kenyatta replied with a laugh.

'So, did you find the common ancestors?' Reggie asked.

'Indeed, I did,' he answered, drawing a circle with his mouse around Herman Olmstead and Gertrude Tapinala. 'This couple hailed from Richmond, Virginia. Only about seventy miles from Kenyatta's cluster two.'

'That could be interesting,' Maddie said. 'So, moving on to tackle your third cluster already, Hudson?'

He nodded.

'Excellent work,' Maddie praised. 'Kenyatta, do you want to go next?'

'Sure,' she answered, sharing the pedigree for Jean Adams that she had shown at yesterday's briefing. Now it was much more filled out. 'This is not quite as good progress as Hudson...but I have managed to close down several lines. I think, with a bit more work tomorrow, I'll be as done as I can be with Jean, then it will be over to triangulation. Most of her lines are from the Deep South, particularly Louisiana.'

'Thanks, Kenyatta,' Maddie said. 'Reggie? Do you want to fight me to go next?'

Reggie smiled, stood up and tapped on his keyboard to mirror his screen. 'Well, after starting over at square one with a third person from within cluster four, Clement Easton, I've made *some* progress. His maternal great-grandparents were all born in Scotland and his paternal side I'm still struggling to push back in Australia. I think they might have been among the first non-natives to arrive, which isn't making life easy.'

Maddie frowned and surveyed the room. 'We don't have any connections to Scotland, do we?'

'I don't think so,' Ross answered, checking on his laptop, then confirming, 'Nope.'

'Just keep going,' Kenyatta said.

'That's all we can do,' Maddie agreed, sharing her progress on the digital whiteboard. 'So, after writing up a tentative orange slip for Samuel Moreno yesterday, today I started work on cluster five. As you can see, not a huge amount of progress. But I have identified the parents and grandparents. I've got Nevada, Arizona, California and Wyoming as possible locations.'

Hudson studied the surnames on the whiteboard but none of

them were familiar.

'If nobody has any more to discuss—?' she let the question hang in the air for a moment '—then you can all head home and enjoy your evening. Thank you.'

Hudson closed his computer and filled in an orange slip for Herman Olmstead and Gertrude Tapinala. He took it over and fixed it to the whiteboard, then packed up his things to leave. 'You coming home, Reggie?' he asked.

'Sure am, man,' he answered. 'I've got a date with Leon.'

Hudson's eyes widened. 'Leon? Okay. So, do I finally get to meet him?'

Reggie laughed. 'Leon Sierra.'

Hudson rolled his eyes. 'Right. Let's go.'

He said goodbye to the rest of the team and then headed out of the office with Reggie for the forty-five-minute walk home.

Hudson was in bed scrolling through social media, pointlessly fighting against his desire and evident need to sleep. He closed Instagram and saw that he had notification alerts for the Fiorry app. He ignored them and, instead, opened the internet on the KARE11.com website for the tenth time this evening. The main story about the judges entering deliberation had barely changed details across the day. But now it finally had. *Brandon Blake Free*, the headline exclaimed.

Hudson let out a long, weighty breath. Despite his deep regret over the whole situation, at least one good thing had come out of it: an innocent man would now be released from jail.

Chapter Eighteen

Wednesday, November 9, 2022, Salt Lake City, Utah

Reggie Snowwolf was sitting at his desk in the Venator office, eating his tuna sandwich. He'd set aside his work on cluster four and was about to do a little more on Leon Sierra, but first he pulled up the live stream cameras for the Brighton ski resort. He grinned at the four displays showing the bottom of the Milly Express lift, the empty parking lot, the Majestic chairlift and a wide view of the snow-covered mountains from the Great Western chairlift. God, how he longed to get back up there on his board. Three more days.

With some degree of reluctance, Reggie minimized the tab and opened the file on Leon Sierra, where he was starting to make some solid progress. On Sunday, he had discovered the slave-owner David Woods' probate record, which showed that his estate had been divided between his two sons. Reggie had been researching the elder son, James, and the slaves that he had inherited upon his father's death in 1857, when he had spotted that the other sibling, Richard, had been bequeathed possession of four *other* slaves, and among those four enslaved people was Sally Belling, Malik Johnson's great-great-grandmother. It had taken Reggie a lot of analysis to come up with a hypothesis that fit. It was far from evidenced, but he had theoretically produced a common ancestor to Leon Sierra, Malik Johnson and Elijah Benton.

Reggie had input the information that he had had into the WATO—What Are The Odds—tool on DNA Painter. The algorithms had analyzed the amount of shared DNA against Reggie's hypothesis and, although the data was weak, had broadly agreed that the most recent common ancestor to the three men was none other than the slave owner himself, David Woods. Reggie suspected that Thomas Cristmas had been born from a relationship—consensual or otherwise—between David Woods and one of his slaves, Henrietta Cristmas. After David's death, his property, which included the enslaved people, was divided between his two sons, James and Richard. It was Reggie's belief that Richard Woods had followed in his father's footsteps and impregnated his slave, Sally Belling. If his working theory were correct, then Richard Woods would be one of Leon Sierra's direct ancestors. But it was difficult because Reggie had no idea how many children Richard might have had who had remained undocumented.

The irony of possibly achieving the difficult task of connecting the DNA between three black men because of a white slave owner was not lost on Reggie as he considered what more he could do to prove his theory.

On-screen in front of him was the profile for Richard Woods, which contained every official document that Reggie could find. From his investigation so far, he had found no trace of a marriage or children, so he was now concentrating on the enslaved women and girls in Richard's household.

Reggie pulled up the list from the 1857 probate document.

Frances Brown, 18
Hannah Brown, 16
Sally Belling, 10
Betsy Adley, 6

He started by fleshing out what Maddie had already started on Sally Belling's line. His aim was to produce a comprehensive list of every single one of Sally's descendants and then do exactly the same for Frances and Hannah Brown and Betsy Adley. He didn't have the luxury of multiple clusters; he only had this one and he had to hope that he could find a place where Leon Sierra might fit. He banished thoughts of other undocumented children who might have been fathered by Richard Woods and focused instead on Sally Belling's family tree.

'Oh, you're back on Malik's tree?' Maddie questioned as she walked behind him and noticed what he was doing.

'Yeah,' he confirmed. 'Just while I eat my lunch.'

'Did I make a mistake?'

'No, I'm fleshing the tree out some more. I've got a theory I'm working on.'

'Talking of theories,' Kenyatta said, looking over from her

computer. 'How did Clayton get on at the library yesterday? Did he find his tribe?'

'No,' Maddie answered. 'He's back there today *and* he's ordered a DNA test.'

'Wow, you'll have to show him the ropes. Train him up and give him a job here.' Kenyatta quipped.

'No chance,' Maddie answered.

'Hey, you planning on taking him skiing?' Reggie asked. 'Brighton opens in two days, you know. I literally cannot wait until Saturday.'

'He doesn't ski. So, I'll have to wait until he's gone back home before I get up there.'

'Well, in my eyes, that right there is a deal breaker... unless he learns,' Reggie said with a grin, turning to see Ross's mock scowl. Reggie gave him a cheesy wink and then turned back to his computer to do a bit more on Sally Belling's tree before his lunch break was over.

Half an hour later, with no sense of obvious progress, Reggie headed over to the kitchen area to make himself some coffee. 'Anyone wants a drink?' he called to the office.

'Me, please,' Ross accepted, while the rest of the team declined.

'Coming right up,' Reggie replied.

He made the drink and carried it over to Ross's desk, placing it down in front of him. Ross thanked him and smiled. 'Is it me or Leon tonight?'

Reggie rubbed his chin, then said quietly, 'Hmm, that's a good question. Tricky...'

Ross rolled his eyes. 'Well, I've got pizza, beer and season five of *The Crown* which is out today on Netflix. Your choice.' He turned back to his computer with an exaggerated flounce.

'*The Crown?*' Reggie said a little too loudly, drawing the attention of the other staff. He lowered his voice and continued, 'Leon can wait. *The Crown* cannot. I will be at your place at six o'clock. Don't watch any of it without me.'

Ross laughed quietly.

'And now...back to reality and identifying the Hollywood Strangler,' he said, walking over to the kitchen where he poured himself some fresh coffee before returning to his desk.

Reggie pulled up the speculative tree that he was working on for Clement Easton and navigated through to his maternal great-grandmother, Amelia Barclay, who had been born in Scotland around 1900.

Logging in on the ScotlandsPeople website using the Venator credentials, Reggie clicked to search the 1901 Scottish Census for Amelia. Three results: a thirty-five-year-old, a nine-year-old and a one-year-old. Reggie clicked on the latter, using six credits from the Venator account. A black-and-white copy of the original census loaded in front of him. It was for a place called Barrhead, a town just south of Glasgow.

Alastair Barclay, head of household, married, age 26, draper, born Barrhead, Renfrewshire
Bonnie Barclay, wife, married, age 25, dressmaker, born Barrhead, Renfrewshire
Amelia Barclay, daughter, age 1, born Barrhead, Renfrewshire

The father's name matched that on Amelia's marriage certificate. Reggie updated the tree and saved the source before turning back to the main search page on ScotlandsPeople and clicked *Statutory registers*, which included birth records from 1855. He entered Amelia's name and a five-year search window around her 1900 birth, and then hit the search button. One result. He confirmed the use of another six credits and a scan of the original birth certificate immediately loaded.

Name and Surname: Amelia Barclay
When and Where Born: November twenty-seventh 1900, 265 Main Street, Barrhead
Sex: Female
Name, Surname & Rank or Profession of Father: Alastair Barclay, draper
Name, and Maiden Surname of Mother: Bonnie Cameron
Date and Place of Marriage: 1899, June 12th, Barrhead

Reggie added the extra detail from the certificate, grateful to have a lead on the date and place of Alastair and Bonnie's marriage. With luck, that too would be rich with genealogical detail.

Clicking *Search marriages*, Reggie entered the details for Amelia's parents and the precise year that the marriage had taken place. One result, which cost another six credits to view.

When, Where and How Married: twelfth day of June, 1899 at Barrhead after publication according to the forms of the free Church of Scotland.
Signatures of Parties: Alastair Barclay
Rank or Profession: Draper
Whether Single or Widowed: Bachelor
Age: 25
Usual Address: 265 Main Street, Barrhead
Name, Surname, and Rank or Profession of Father: Andrew Barclay, deceased
Name, and Maiden Surname of Mother: Margaret Barclay, previously Banks

The groom's side alone provided a lot of information. Reggie added it to Clement Easton's growing family tree and then looked at the bride's details.

Signatures of Parties: Bonnie Cameron
Rank or Profession: Flax mill worker
Whether Single or Widowed: Spinster
Age: 28
Usual Address: 201 Main Street, Barrhead
Name, Surname, and Rank or Profession of Father: Bryce Cameron
Name, and Maiden Surname of Mother: Aisla Cameron, previously Baird

'I love the Scottish record keeping!' Reggie declared.
Kenyatta sat back with a groan. 'Oh, don't. To have a universal, clear system across the whole country *and* to fill the records with so much information. If only the rest of the world was so organized.'
'Yeah, but have you found what you needed to triangulate the cluster?' Hudson asked.
Reggie shook his head. 'Still nothing. And it's so annoying. I don't know what I'm missing here.'
'Keep digging,' Kenyatta encouraged. 'Maybe while you have such good records, really flesh out the Scottish side. You'll either find the

link or feel pretty confident that it's not in that part of the tree.'

'Good idea,' he said, checking that the company still had credits left to spend on ScotlandsPeople. They were almost out. Reggie stood up and walked over to Maddie's office. The door was open, and she was sitting behind her desk, looking at her computer.

'Hey,' she said, looking up with a warm smile. 'How's it going?'

'Generally, or with this cluster?' he asked.

'Both.'

'Generally... Great,' he replied. 'I love it here and I love the work you're doing. On the cluster... Not so good. I'd like to fill out the Scottish side some more, but we're almost out of credits.'

'No problem,' Maddie responded. 'I'll top it up right now.' She tapped at her keyboard, then looked up and said, 'A hundred and sixty credits for forty pounds enough?'

'More than enough. Thanks,' Reggie answered.

'You're welcome.'

Reggie headed back to his desk and picked up with more in-depth research into the Barclay and Cameron families, starting with the census of 1871, the first after Bonnie had been born. With all the information that he had, finding the family proved easy. They were living at 37 High Street, Renfrew.

Bryce Cameron, head of household, married, 25 years old, cabinet maker, born Renfrew
Aisla Cameron, wife, married, 23 years old, born Renfrew
George Cameron, son, single, 3 years old, born Renfrew
Laura Cameron, daughter, single, 3 years old, born Renfrew
Bonnie Cameron, daughter, single, 1 years old, born Renfrew

Reggie updated the family tree, saving the census entry against each name, before running a search within the same census for the Barclay family members. He took a long breath in, trying to quell his growing frustration at not finding the link between Clement Easton, Jonas Crawford and Jennifer Hatter, all of whom should share at least one common ancestor. He was starting to worry that the genealogy and the genetic genealogy were never going to match up.

Several hours later, Maddie opened the afternoon's briefing. Reggie had barely concluded his research into the Scottish side of Clement Easton's family. He'd worked exhaustively, adding every census, birth, marriage and church record that he could lay his hands on. He'd built out a solid tree but there was simply no discernible overlap with the other two people within the cluster.

His disappointment was evidently etched on his face when Maddie asked who wanted to go first. 'Obviously not you, then, Reggie.' She said it with a laugh, and he knew that anyone working in the field of investigative genetic genealogy—or genealogy at all, for that matter—regularly hit brick walls. He just didn't want to hit this one quite so soon after taking on the job—and especially not after all the fanfare of his interview task.

'I will,' Hudson volunteered, pulling up his screen and sharing a pedigree for the cluster seven lead. 'I've made a good start. Here are some of the names involved.' He circled the four paternal great-grandparent names with his cursor. 'Nothing obvious as of yet location-wise that might link it up to another cluster.'

Reggie looked at the names, desperately hoping that he could spot something that would move his own tree along, but there were no overlaps. Here he was, having not closed down a single cluster, while Hudson was well into his third.

'Thanks, Hudson,' Maddie said. 'I'll go next.' A few seconds later, Maddie's screen appeared on the digital whiteboard. 'So, I think *I* might be competing with Reggie for slowest progress of the day. I've managed to identify all four paternal great-grandparents for the cluster lead, but I'm really struggling getting anywhere on the maternal side. Any of these names familiar?' she asked hopefully.

When the rest of the team failed to spot any possible connection, Maddie handed over to Kenyatta.

'Okay, well,' she began, a pedigree for her cluster lead, Jean Adams, appearing on-screen, 'I think I've done all I can with this lady's tree. I've got a few gaps on the paternal side, but I think it's time to concede on those. The family is still rooted firmly in and around Louisiana. Tomorrow, I'll start work on triangulation.'

'Well done,' Maddie said, turning to face Reggie. 'Sorry... But it's your turn.'

With an exaggerated sigh, Reggie stood up and shared his screen. 'I guess I've made progress since yesterday. Although it doesn't feel like it, as I still can't find the connection between the people in cluster four. Anyone see anything I'm missing here?' he asked, clicking on Andrew Barclay's profile, followed by Margaret Banks, then Bryce Cameron and, finally, Aisla Baird. 'Since the other side is in Australia with their paucity of open records, I think I'm looking at having to pick a *fourth* person from the cluster.'

'Wait,' Ross said, looking up from his laptop. 'Go back to Bryce and Aisla Cameron's profile page, specifically their kids.'

Reggie frowned but did as he was asked. What had Ross seen that he had missed? The profile appeared.

George Cameron 1868 - 1922
Laura Cameron 1868 -
Bonnie Cameron 1870 - 1944
John Cameron 1872 - 1879

'Go into Laura Cameron,' Ross directed with an authority that surprised Reggie.

Reggie clicked Laura's name, noticing that there was nothing recorded against her name after the 1881 census. Suddenly, his chess-playing brain moved the pieces and saw what Ross had seen. 'Laura Waldon.'

Ross grinned. 'Does it fit?'

'I think it just might, yeah,' Reggie replied, searching within the tree and finding a Laura with no surname and no birth date or place. It had to be her. When her profile loaded it was obvious. The first record that he had for Laura in the U.S. was her marriage in 1887. From thereafter, she had been recorded religiously on every census until her death in 1952. He had found no official documentation for her prior to 1887 and no documentation post 1881 for Laura Cameron in Scotland. The evidence was pointing to the possibility of the two women being the same person, thereby making Bryce Cameron and Aisla Baird the common ancestors for cluster four. 'She was born in Renfrew, Scotland, not Arkansas!'

'Once you've confirmed it, that right there will be an orange slip for you, Golden Boy,' Kenyatta said.

'I think so, too, but I need to run some more checks,' Reggie replied. He looked over at Ross with a wide smile. 'How did I miss that? Thank you so much, Ross.'

'That's what I'm here for. You can thank me later,' he said.

'Great catch, Ross. Another fantastic day's work, team,' Maddie said, standing in front of the whiteboard. 'Now go home and relax.'

Reggie didn't want to leave until he was certain, one way or the other, that the two Lauras were indeed one and the same person. He started by checking the hints associated with the profile and then gradually saved extra documents, which were usually superfluous at this stage of building a quick and dirty tree. By the time Maddie came to close the office some forty minutes later, he was sure of his findings, and he completed that elusive orange slip for Bryce Cameron and Aisla Baird.

Reggie was sitting beside Ross on the sofa in his apartment, pouring out two bottles of beer into glasses. 'Cheers,' he said. 'And thank you for your help today. I don't think I would have closed the cluster down without you.'

'Not just a pretty face,' Ross answered, raising his glass in the air and then taking a sip.

Two pizzas lay before them on the coffee table, one a roasted vegetable and one a barbecue chicken, and the opening scene of the first episode of *The Crown*, season five, was tantalizingly paused on-screen. Life was pretty good for Reggie right now. He took a slice of pizza and sat back, ready to watch TV, but his brain had other plans. It started thinking about Leon Sierra and the next steps in that case. After taking so long over cluster four, he wanted to show the rest of the team that he was up to the job.

'Do you mind if I do a little work on Leon after we've eaten?' he asked Ross.

'Yes, I do mind. Leave Leon outside for tonight.' He put on a posh British accent and added, 'There will not be three of us in *this* marriage.'

Reggie conceded, grinned, hit the play button and took a mouthful of barbecue chicken pizza.

Chapter Nineteen

Thursday, November 10, 2022, Salt Lake City, Utah

Kenyatta looked up as the main office door opened. She smiled to see Clayton Tyler entering with takeout bags from Eva's. It was the first time that she'd seen him since he'd presented his case to the team back in 2020. He was wearing navy pants, a gray woolen sweater and a bomber jacket. He looked a little smarter and trimmer than she remembered. She guessed—and hoped—that he was dressing sharper now that he was in a relationship with Maddie. Since Kenyatta had started dating Jim, he'd also taken more care of himself. It was sweet.

'I come bearing gifts,' Clayton announced, holding up the bags.

'If you've come to give us lunch, you're too late,' Kenyatta called over to him.

'Actually, it's dessert,' he replied. 'Or…a mid-afternoon snack to keep you going. Whatever.'

'Oh, hey,' Maddie said, stepping out of her office. 'What you got for us?'

'French macarons, chocolate eclairs, sticky buns and some croissants,' he said, offering Maddie the bags.

'Well, as long as you don't tell my dietician, maybe I can have a sneaky bite of something sweet,' Kenyatta said, watching on with a filled, warm heart as Clayton leaned in and kissed Maddie on the lips. She deserved some happiness in her life and from the little that she knew about Clayton, he seemed like one of the good guys.

'Okay. Let's all of us have a break, team,' Maddie said, taking some plates from the cupboard under the counter.

When Hudson and Reggie wandered over to the kitchen area, she added, 'Whatever next? Coffee and croissants at three in the afternoon… Don't get used to this, guys.'

Kenyatta saved the document that she was looking at and then joined the rest of the team in a loose circle in the kitchen area. Hudson, Reggie and Ross were chatting while Maddie was setting several delicious-looking cakes out onto two large plates.

Kenyatta stood beside Clayton and asked, 'I hear you've been at the library, lately. Were you there again today?'

Clayton's eyes lit up. 'Yes, I sure was. I'm really into this genealogy thing now. I was on the phone to my mom last night, telling her everything I'd found out. So, get this. This morning, I discovered my great-grandpa was imprisoned for a bigamous marriage back in the 1920s. I'm not sure if my mom will be excited or horrified when I tell her.'

'See what you've gone and done, Maddie?' Kenyatta said. 'You've gone and turned him into one of *us*.'

'What about you guys?' he asked, widening his stance to include the rest of the team. 'Getting any closer to identifying this mysterious high-profile serial killer?' He looked at each team member in turn, and Kenyatta was certain that his detective brain was reading their expressions and body language for clues about which case they could be working.

'Don't tell him *any*thing,' Maddie warned as she handed everyone a small plate. 'But *do* help yourselves to cake.'

'Thank you so much,' Kenyatta said, taking a small pink macaron.

'Hey, I only asked if you were getting closer,' he said, subtly glancing over in the direction of the three case boards as he transferred a chocolate eclair to his plate.

'Well, yes, we are getting closer,' Maddie admitted. 'And I can see that you're trying to look at the boards, there.'

Clayton grinned and duly turned his back to the boards.

'So, are you happy with how things went with Wayne Wolsey?' Hudson asked Clayton, referring to the serial killer from Chester Creek in Pennsylvania that the team had successfully identified using investigative genetic genealogy back in 2020.

'Oh, yeah, for sure,' he answered. 'As part of his plea deal to avoid the death penalty, he confessed to all twelve murders. So, he is never getting out of jail.'

'And how are you getting on identifying those other victims?' Kenyatta asked, recalling that when Wolsey had been arrested for the three Chester Creek murders, detectives had discovered trophies in the form of hair cuttings from eight other women, one of whom turned out to be his own missing wife.

'Wolsey claims not to have known all of their names or what he did with their bodies, so it's still an open case while we try and figure out who the victims were.'

Maddie passed her plate to her left hand, and then leaned over and offered Clayton her right hand to shake. 'Hi, my name's Maddie. I run an investigative genetic genealogy business, and I might just be able to help with those identifications you mentioned.'

The team laughed, as did Clayton.

'Yeah, it's more of a budget issue,' he explained. 'Because the hair samples are rootless, it's apparently more complex and more expensive to get tested. So, my boss wants us to pursue it the old-fashioned way.'

'I guess whether it's cheaper or not all depends on how many man- and woman-hours you're giving it,' Kenyatta commented.

'Not anywhere near enough,' he admitted. 'Now Wolsey's put away for life and nobody's banging on the station door demanding answers, the case just isn't a priority, unfortunately.'

'If you can get the extraction and testing done, then I'm happy to add the cases to the pro bono pile,' Maddie offered.

'That's very generous of you,' Clayton said. 'Thanks.'

'Well, you've certainly done a lot for me.'

Kenyatta finished the macaron, watching the interaction play out between Maddie and Clayton, positive that she was referring to more than just what his relationship might have done to help her move on with her life. There was something that had bubbled under the surface to do with Michael's disappearance, but Maddie had always kept her cards close to her chest on that front.

'Okay,' Kenyatta said, putting her plate into the dishwasher. 'Thank you so much for the naughty mid-afternoon snack, but I must get back to my work. Nice to see you again, Clayton.'

'You're welcome. It was good to see you, too,' he replied.

Kenyatta headed back to her desk, took a sip of water and then continued with her work. She was trying to build out on the second name within cluster eight, Kevin Biddlecombe. She had so far managed to track down all four grandparents and all four paternal great-grandparents, and she was now focusing on the maternal side. On-screen in front of her was the profile for Kevin Biddlecombe's maternal grandfather, Allen Sullivan. So far, all Kenyatta knew about him was his name and that of his wife, Susan Jayne, which she had gleaned from their daughter's 1988 marriage certificate.

Kenyatta opened Newspapers.com and ran a search for the couple's marriage. She found an article dated September 5, 1965, in the *Anderson Daily Bulletin* that appeared to be correct.

Susan Jayne Grant and Allen Sullivan will marry at 2 p.m. September 8 at Sacred Heart Church in Detroit, Mich. The bride-elect is the youngest daughter of Daryl Grant, 454 Washington Blvd., and Rose Steinbrecher, Madison Heights, Mich. She is a former Anderson resident and a graduate of Lamphere High School in Madison Heights, Mich. Her fiancé is the son of Mr. and Mrs. Richard Sullivan, Madison Heights, Mich. He is also a graduate of Lamphere High School and is now employed by Fischer Buick-Subaru in Troy, Mich.

The article tied precisely with what Kenyatta already knew. Now she added the names of Richard Sullivan, Daryl Grant and Rose Steinbrecher to the speculative tree. The addition of Rose's name as separate from that of her husband implied divorce, which Kenyatta would look into later. But right now, she wanted to identify Allen Sullivan's mother, which would give her the names of all eight great-grandparents ready for the afternoon's briefing.

Opening up MyHeritage and accessing their *U.S. City Directories 1860-1960* document collection, Kenyatta ran a search for Richard Sullivan in Madison Heights, Michigan. She hit the top result.

Name: Richard Sullivan
Residence: 1960, Madison Heights, Michigan
Address: 858 East Lincoln Avenue
Residence status: Homeowner
Spouse (implied): Catherine
Marriage (implied): Before 1960
Occupation: Shipping
Workplace: Bixby Off Sup

Kenyatta saved the record, then ran a search for the family on the

1950 census. The document provided approximate birth years for Richard, Catherine and ten-year-old Allen Sullivan, and confirmed that they were all born in the state of Michigan. Moving back a decade, the 1940 census showed Richard and Catherine together with a two-year-old daughter, Rose, just months prior to Allen's birth, but there was nothing that pointed toward Catherine's maiden name or the precise location of her birth.

Turning to the Research Wiki at FamilySearch, Kenyatta looked for marriage records within the state of Michigan. She spent some time checking in each of the major databases from Ancestry, FamilySearch, FindmyPast and MyHeritage, finding no record of the union among their collections. The same was true in Newspapers.com and GenealogyBank, and Kenyatta was starting to think that she was not going to find Catherine's maiden name.

Time was ticking. The briefing was just over forty minutes away.

She paused for a moment while she allowed her mind to concentrate on other documents that might reveal Catherine's maiden name. She glanced over at the kitchen area, just as Clayton was preparing to leave. She overheard him saying that the leftover cakes could be thrown in the trash.

'Hey! Don't throw anything away,' Kenyatta called over. 'I'm heading out to the homeless kitchen later. I know a few people who will enjoy those.'

'No problem. I'll leave them right here,' Clayton said. He kissed Maddie on the lips, called his goodbyes to the office and then left.

Maddie smiled, abashedly. 'I guess I'd better get some work done,' she mumbled.

Kenyatta gave a dismissive wave and mouthed the words, 'Relax.'

Hoping that she could track down Catherine's death certificate, which might reveal her maiden name, Kenyatta once again ran searches in all the major databases but, as before, drew a blank.

Switching to Find a Grave, Kenyatta finally had some luck. She found Richard Sullivan buried in Oakview Cemetery and, when she clicked *Family Members*, could see that buried in the same grave was Catherine *Kendall* Sullivan 1915-1989. By scrolling down to *Family Members*, she could see that the couple had been buried with their nine-year-old daughter, Rose, confirming that she had found the correct family. Also, in the *Family Members* section under the subheading of *Siblings*, Kenyatta found an older brother for Catherine, named Worlie W. Kendall. A family member had uploaded a photograph and a mini biography for him, which named Catherine as his sister.

Satisfied that she was working on the right lines, Kenyatta updated the speculative tree with all the new information. She was about to work on pushing back on some of these new names, when Maddie strode into the office declaring that the briefing would take place in two minutes.

'Does anyone want any more cakes before I pack them up for Kenyatta to take with her?' she asked.

Everyone declined, making Kenyatta feel bad that they had probably done so because of the idea that they could be taking the cakes out of the mouths of the local homeless and hungry. 'Go ahead and eat them if you want,' she insisted. 'We've got plenty of food down at the kitchen. It was really only if they were headed for the trash.'

'I'm good,' Reggie replied.

'And I already had two macarons,' Hudson said. 'Which is two more than I usually have mid-afternoon.'

'Well, I'm not about to disclose how many I've eaten,' Maddie said. 'But suffice it to say that I don't require any more food for the foreseeable future.'

Kenyatta chuckled, then turned back to Kevin Biddlecombe, displaying his pedigree ready for the briefing. She sat back, drank some water from her bottle and waited.

'Okay. Let's get this thing underway, shall we?' Maddie said, typing into the spare computer so that the screen was mirrored on the large central whiteboard. 'Well, I guess I've made more progress than yesterday. As you can see, I've almost filled out the paternal side of the cluster lead, but still getting nowhere fast with the maternal.' She sighed. 'I'll give it a little more time tomorrow morning, but I think I might need to move on to triangulation and hope that the link is on the paternal side. The family is still in the west—Nevada, Arizona and California in particular. Keep an eye out for them to save me from failure.' She laughed and glanced around the room. 'Kenyatta, please bring us good tidings of your day.'

Kenyatta shared her screen and stood up with a smile. 'So, I'm still triangulating within cluster eight. No connection established yet, but I've got all eight great-grandparents pinned down. Any names familiar here?' she asked hopefully, zooming in to the surnames.

The question was met exclusively with blank faces.

'Okay. That's me about done, then,' she said with a laugh, sitting back down.

'Thanks, Kenyatta,' Maddie said. 'Hudson, your turn.'

Hudson stood up, shared his screen and said, 'Well, I think my lucky streak might be over. Let's just say, it's been a slow day. My cluster lead's maternal grandmother seems to have suddenly appeared on this planet solely for her marriage, but literally not a single record for her prior to that. Nothing.' He zoomed in close to the name of the offending woman, Joyce Masterman. 'I've still got more work to do on the rest of the pedigree, which I'll hopefully get done at some point tomorrow, then on with triangulation.'

'Great. Thanks,' Maddie said. 'And last but not least, Reggie.' Maddie looked over at Ross and quipped, 'Ross, are you getting ready to bail him out again?'

'Very funny,' Reggie said, standing up as his screen overrode Hudson's. 'After Ross saved me yesterday—again, thank you, Ross—I managed to confirm that, yes, Laura Cameron and Laura Waldon *were* actually one and the same person, making Bryce Cameron and Aisla Baird the common ancestors to cluster four. Today, I've started work on cluster nine, which is one of the weaker ones. The lead, Henry Dandzila, only matches with forty-eight centimorgans, but I have managed to get all paternal lines back to the great-great-grandparent level. It's likely, though, that the generation of connection is actually the generation above. They're based in and around California and Arizona at the moment, so possible overlaps with the other clusters in those states. That's it.'

'Excellent. Thank you,' Maddie said. 'Another day closer to catching this guy. Thanks for all your efforts. Enjoy your evening and I'll see you tomorrow.'

On the scrap paper beside her keyboard, Kenyatta made a note about which lines to focus on first in the morning, then shut down her computer and packed up to leave.

'Don't forget the cakes,' Maddie called, as Kenyatta passed by her office door.

'Thank you so much!' she replied, picking up the paper bag and peering at the five cakes inside.

'Make sure Jim gets one,' Maddie said.

'Only if there's any left,' Kenyatta replied, making her way to the door and on out of the building.

'Hey, what you got cooking?' Candice asked, struggling to walk a straight line as she headed over toward Kenyatta. She leaned heavily on the table, her eyes barely open.

'Chicken and vegetable,' Kenyatta answered.

Candice shrugged. 'What?'

'Chicken and vegetable,' she repeated.

'Chicken. Vegetable.'

'Want some?'

'Sure,' Candice replied, swaying at the edge of the table and reminding Kenyatta of a feeble sapling struggling in the wind. Except there was no wind. Her struggles were against something else entirely.

Kenyatta was about to mention the fact that when she had last been here, Candice had declared herself a vegetarian, but she thought better of it. Getting her to eat something—anything in the state that she was in right now—would be an achievement. Kenyatta filled a bowl generously and buttered her a roll. 'Candice, we've got a counselor here tonight. He could maybe help get you off the streets. What do you think? Why don't you have a little talk with him? He's sitting down over at that desk right there.'

Without opening her eyes, Candice laughed in response. 'Yeah, I'll be sure to do that.'

'Here's the soup,' Kenyatta said, holding it out.

Candice reached for the bowl, said thank you, and then threw it directly at Kenyatta. The bowl hit her below the chin, the contents pouring down her jacket. 'I don't like soup. You hear me?'

Kenyatta looked cursorily at the lumpy liquid coursing down her front. She took a steadying breath, picked up a handful of napkins, and began to clean herself up. Then she opened the take-out bag from Eva's and withdrew a croissant and promptly offered it to Candice. 'Here, at least eat this. And if you wait a second, Jim'll be back with the bottled water. You need it, honey.'

Candice took the croissant, and, for a moment, Kenyatta thought that she was about to have that thrown at her too, but instead, Candice took a bite and then sat down on the sidewalk, talking to herself.

Kenyatta took another napkin to wipe more soup from her jacket.

'Hey, Kenny, did you go and throw up over yourself?'

Kenyatta looked up to see Lonnie standing in front of her with a wide grin spread across his face.

'It ain't a good look,' he added. 'You're gonna get complaints for letting the neighborhood down. Need to be more professional-like.'

Kenyatta couldn't help but smile. 'I had an accident. How are you doing, Lonnie?'

Lonnie shrugged, noticing what Candice was eating. 'How come she got that?'

'Want one?' Kenyatta asked, holding the bag open.

Lonnie peered in with a suspicious air, and then said, 'Ain't they a bit fancy compared to what you pious people normally give us?'

'Do you want one, or not?'

He tentatively pulled out a sticky bun and proceeded to lick at the glaze, right across the top.

'Sorry,' Jim said, arriving with two stacks of water bottles. I got stopped talking to—' he broke off from his story, noticing Kenyatta's jacket. 'What happened?'

'She barfed up over herself,' Lonnie explained with a throaty laugh.

'I had an accident. It's really no big deal,' she said, carrying a bottle of water around to the front of the table. She crouched down beside Candice, who seemed on the verge of passing out. Kenyatta placed her hand gently on her shoulder. 'Candice... Candice...' she roused her gently. 'I've got you some water.'

Candice opened her eyes, her pupils fully dilated and not focusing on Kenyatta.

Kenyatta opened the water and held it to Candice's mouth, managing to get some in before she raised her hand to block the bottle.

'I'm done,' Candice muttered, pulling herself up from the ground.

'Candice, please go and talk to Marko about getting yourself some proper help,' Kenyatta pleaded.

Candice smiled at Kenyatta. 'There's no point to any of it.'

Kenyatta watched her stagger across the park, disappearing into the city's shadows and underbelly, wishing desperately that there had been more she could have done to help.

Chapter Twenty

Friday, November 11, 2022, Pétion-Ville, Port-au-Prince, Haiti

Becky Larkin was sweltering in her apartment. She was sitting by the open window in just her underwear, trying to keep cool. Outside it was almost ninety degrees and the occasional breeze only served to waft in more humid air. She was working on her laptop at the desk, reviewing the speculative family tree that she and her charity colleagues had created for V38. She was looking for an oversight or an error that must exist on her paternal side—the one belonging to the UN Peacekeeper. The team strongly believed that one of six brothers, with the surname Fonseka, from the Jaffna region of Northern Sri Lanka, was the grandfather to the man who had fathered V38. The problem was that the descendants of each brother had been carefully traced and eliminated.

Becky pulled up the profile for Martin Fonseka, the youngest of the six brothers and the only one not to have married or had children. The only documents that existed against his name were his birth and death record, both of which had been harvested from the *Sri Lanka, Civil Registration, 1768-1990* collection on the FamilySearch website. Becky reviewed the original black-and-white scan of the birth record, which was written in Sinhala, English and Tamil. Except the obvious differences, the document was identical to his brothers' birth records.

Closing the image, Becky selected his death record and carefully re-read the document for the third or fourth time.

Province: Northern
District: Jaffna
Date and Place of Death: Fourteenth May 1960, Kasthuriyar Road
Name in full: Martin Fonseka
Sex and Nationality: Male. Ceylon Tamil
Age: Thirty-six years
Rank or Profession: Blacksmith
Names in full of Parents: Sinnathiar Fonseka. Ammankutta Sabapathy.
Cause of Death, and Place of Burial or Cremation: Double pneumonia.

Komlyannarel
Name in full and Residence of Informant: Olaganather Thangam, Kasthuriyar Road. Housekeeper. Present at death.

Becky's eyes lingered on the name of Martin Fonseka's housekeeper, who had informed of his death: Olaganather Thangam. Becky was sure that she'd seen that surname somewhere before. Could it have been in one of the victim files?

She opened a password-protected Word document that ran to more than 500 pages, containing much of their organization's work and research to date. She used the search function to check the entire document for the name Thangam. No results.

She momentarily considered searching through the stack of anonymized manila files on the desk but quickly remembered that everything in those files had been duplicated—and with more detail recorded—in the Word document that she had just checked.

Re-opening the file, Becky played around with the spelling of Thangam. But still no results.

She gazed out of the window, watching two young children happily skipping along the sidewalk toward the park, seemingly unaware of the country slowly imploding around them. What Haitians needed desperately right now was international assistance but, given the sinister and insidious previous interventions, the implementation and monitoring needed a total re-think. She and Aidan had spent many evenings gazing out over Pétion-Ville, wondering how long they had remaining here before they would have to evacuate, and what the long-term solution might be for the beleaguered country.

'Free and fair elections,' was always Aidan's starting point. 'Get a new government in who requests specific outside intervention. And big payouts from the UN to fund a robust local law enforcement to get the gangs back under control.'

Becky didn't need to point out to Aidan how those noble sentiments were almost impossible to achieve in reality.

'Thangam. Thangam,' Becky said to herself. Then, an idea occurred to her. Pulling up her own DNA account at Ancestry, Becky clicked *View Another Test* and scrolled down past the many accounts to which she had access, finally selecting *V38* from the long list of victim profiles that she managed. She navigated through to *DNA matches* and typed *Thangam* in the *Surname in matches' trees* box.

No matches found.

Again, she altered the spelling but received the same negative result.

Opening a new tab at MyHeritage, Becky logged in on V38's account there. Having selected *DNA Matches*, she typed *Thangam* into the *Name or ancestral surname* search box.

Showing 1-4 of 4 DNA Matches found for 'Thangam'

Becky smiled as she clicked on the first match, a man by the name of Valan Thangam, who shared 30.6 centimorgans of DNA with V38. It was low, but it was enough to support a working theory evolving in Becky's mind that perhaps V38's biological grandfather had been the product of a liaison between Martin Fonseka and his housekeeper, Olaganather Thangam. But a search for children born to the housekeeper produced no results in the birth index.

Becky spent some time skipping between the DNA matches and the vital records on FamilySearch, the only online repository that she had found for Sri Lankan genealogy. But the records there were patchy, and many were written in Tamil or Sinhala, which required the continual use of Google Translate.

After several hours, she had managed to construct a very limited speculative tree for Martin Fonseka's housekeeper. The tree had tenuous links to Valan Thangam, the top DNA match with that surname, but it was a million miles from the Genealogical Proof Standard. She needed much more evidence.

A crack of distant gunfire drew Becky's attention to the window. The people down on the streets of Pétion-Ville paid the gunshot little heed; random sniper murders had become part of daily life here, inching slowly out of the city center into the suburbs.

With a protracted sigh, she turned back to her screen, wondering how she might prove her theory. She had an idea, but it was a long shot that would take time and might end up leading nowhere at all.

Returning to the Sri Lanka civil registration record set on FamilySearch, Becky ran a birth search from 1940 to 1960 with no names included, just a birth location of Jaffna, Northern Sri Lanka. There were 751 results across 38 pages. Becky switched the number of results from 20 per page to 100, bringing the total number to check down to just eight.

As she expected, the page was dominated by a mixture of Tamil and Sinhala, which were Brahmic scripts bearing no relation to the English alphabet, meaning that the vast majority of the results pages were illegible to Becky. As she had needed to do several times during her investigations in Haiti, she right clicked the page and then hit *Translate to English* and the entire page became re-rendered and mostly understandable.

Slowly scrolling down, Becky carefully checked each result, knowing that there would likely be many errors with the translation. Page one yielded nothing, so she clicked on to page two. Once again, she had the page translated into English and systematically checked each entry. Page three and four were the same. Close to the bottom of page five, Becky stopped scrolling. She'd found something. On 4 June 1947 the birth of a child named Benevolent had been registered to Olaganather Thangam.

Becky hurriedly clicked to see the full entry. The translation wasn't perfect, but it told Becky what she needed to know.

Province: Northern
District: Jaffna
Date and place of Birth: Fourth June 1947, Kasthuriyar Road, Jaffna
Name: Benevolent Thangam
Sex: Female
Name and Surname of Father: —
Name and Maiden Name of Mother, and Nationality: Olaganather Thangam, Tamil
Rank or Profession, and Nationality of Father: —

Were Parents Married? No

Becky was certain that Benevolent Thangam was Martin Fonseka's daughter. If she was right, then Benevolent would go on to have a son who had been a UN peacekeeper and who had raped V38's mother.

With a surge of excitement that she might just be able to name V38's biological father after all, Becky ran a search for the marriage of Benevolent Thangam. *No Results Found.* Undeterred, Becky changed the search parameters for births in Jaffna from 1960 onward, translating each results page as she went.

When Aidan entered the apartment a while later, he found Becky sitting at the table with a wide grin on her face.

'What's happened?' he asked, leaning in to kiss her.

Becky handed him a small piece of paper with four names written on it.

'Vairavan Subpan, Kuhu Subpan, Sri Subpan, Nandhini Subpan,' he read. His eyes met hers, still not understanding. 'Should I know these people?'

'Martin Fonseka's grandchildren,' Becky explained.

'What?' Aidan questioned. 'Martin Fonseka didn't have any kids...'

'He had a girl, Benevolent Thangam, with his housekeeper. Those four names are Benevolent's children.'

'So, any one of these could be V38's bio father?' he asked, unable to contain the rising excitement in his voice.

Becky nodded. 'Actually, *only* one of them. Vairavan was the only male.'

'Crikey,' Aidan said, looking again at the piece of paper. 'So, the UN wasn't giving us their usual BS when they said there was no peacekeeper here with the surname Fonseka from Jaffna. I need to get this name over to legal, right now. Listen, just how confident are you that he's our guy?'

'Very,' she replied, handing him another piece of paper. This one she'd printed from the files that had been amassed since their time in Haiti.

'Crikey,' he repeated, looking at an annotated photograph of a dozen UN peacekeepers. It was a picture taken by one of the locals. The men, wearing full UN peacekeeper uniforms, were standing casually behind a shack, ominously chatting to a group of teenage girls. Above each man's helmet was a handwritten name. The third man in from the left, who had turned almost face-on to the camera at the moment the shot had been captured, was listed as *Vairavan Subpan*.

'We need to push the UN to get him to take a paternity test,' Becky said. 'I'm going to go and see V38's mother this afternoon to see if she can confirm it's him.'

'Aren't you jumping the gun, Becks?'

Becky shrugged. 'Really, Aidan, what are our chances that the UN will actually force this guy to take a paternity test? It's low, right?'

Aidan nodded, then looked up at her. 'There's nothing more going on with this, is there, Becks?'

'What do you mean?' she said, feigning ignorance but knowing full well what was coming next.

'V38 says she knows something about an international abuse ring operating outside of our remit,' he said.

'Why does it need to be outside of what we do, Aidan? Abuse is abuse, period. Does it matter whether it's at the hands of aid workers, sex tourists or criminal gangs?'

'We simply can't take on every case, Becks. But, if we can highlight what's happening here, maybe we'll get more funding and resources to widen the scope of this thing in the future.'

'Look, I'm going to see V38 and I'm going to ask her mom to confirm my findings—and that's it.'

'When are you going?' he asked.

'Now.'

Aidan took in a long breath. 'I'll come with you.'

'*Eskize m, kote legliz Baptise la ye?*' Becky asked an elderly woman in her broken Haitian Creole. She and Aidan were standing on Rue Hubert, trying to find their way to the translator's house, only knowing that she lived opposite the Eglise Baptise Source De Paix.

The woman took a moment to realize that she was being spoken to. '*Legliz batis la? Konsa*,' she said, pointing down an unmarked dirt alley running between two lines of tin shacks.

'*Mèsi*,' Becky said.

'*Pa dekwa*,' the old lady replied, shuffling off.

'Let's get a move on, Becks,' Aidan said, vigilantly checking all around them. 'I don't like this one little bit.'

'It won't take long,' she said, trying to convince herself as much as him. Becky had been in a lot of stressful and difficult situations in her life, and she enjoyed taking part in extreme, adrenalin-firing sports, but nothing had ever come close to being this life-endangering as her work had been here in Haiti. Every time she came to the city, she risked her life; it was as simple as that.

Aidan put his arm out to hold her back from crossing the street while he checked up and down the road several times. 'Okay, run,' he directed.

Becky did as he instructed, running a zigzag line that would make it harder for snipers to take accurate aim. They reached the other side and crossed quickly into the narrow alley. Becky instantly felt more vulnerable as they passed amid an overcrowded settlement of tin homes. An involuntary shudder ran down her spine as every cell in her body told her that she was not safe here.

She could hear the sounds of normal life—children laughing, people chatting, dogs barking—but it was all happening inside the houses that they passed; the surge in extreme violence had rendered the streets almost deserted. There was just a single car in the alley, burned out with bullet holes in the windshield.

'Which way?' Aidan whispered when they hit another junction.

Becky shrugged, searching the skyline for something resembling a church, but there was nothing.

Aidan took her hand and pulled her back behind the trunk of a neem tree. At that moment, Becky spotted a young boy standing in the open door of a house. She repeated her question about the church.

The boy appeared stunned, and Becky asked the question again.

'*Dwat*,' he said eventually.

'*Mèsi*,' Becky said, giving him a big smile. She squeezed Aidan's hand. 'Come on.'

They jogged around to the right and then spotted the church. It was rust-colored and made of tin, standing slightly apart from the neighboring houses and being only fractionally taller. A small wooden sign, replete with several bullet holes in it, bore the name *Eglise Baptise Source De Paix*. There was only one house directly opposite and, as Becky led them toward it, she desperately hoped that it would be the correct place. The house—made from a chaotic mix of tin, wood and stone—had obviously been cobbled together from any materials possibly at hand at the time.

Becky tapped on the wooden door.

'*Kiyès sa?*' a gravelly male voice demanded.

'*Padon. Map chache Fabienne,*' Becky said, attempting to sound coherent, clear and in control when she was actually feeling none of those things.

Her answer was met with silence.

Becky wondered if they had the wrong house or whether her version of Haitian Creole had not been intelligible.

'*Alo?*' came a female voice.

Then, the door opened and Fabienne stood in front of them, surprised. 'What are you doing here?'

'I need to see her—V38,' Becky explained. 'It's important.'

'Her mother is very unwell,' Fabienne reported. 'I do not think that it will be a good idea for her.'

'Please—as I'm sure you realize—we wouldn't have come if it hadn't been urgent.'

Fabienne took a moment to consider the predicament. She turned inside the house, said something that Becky didn't understand and then said, 'We will need to run there and what it is you have got to say needs to be said very quickly.'

Becky nodded.

'It is this way,' Fabienne said, closing the door and beginning to jog along the street.

Becky and Aidan followed in single file, zigzagging down the alley in an erratic manner and using the large trees dotted along the road as extra protection. After a few minutes of running, Fabienne slowed down, then turned ninety-degrees up a gravel path to a one-room metal shack. Without knocking, she pushed open the door, saying something in Creole to the occupants.

For the briefest of moments, Becky wondered if they'd been set up and led into a gang's lair, but then she took in her surroundings and realized that in a city where the gangs had control of practically any building they cared to commandeer, this place would not even have been considered.

The single front window was boarded up and the only light came from a candle burning on a plastic crate off to the side in the room.

V38 was kneeling over a gas camping stove at the back of the room. She was staring at them as they entered the house.

Becky glanced around the gloomy home. Two single beds, almost pushed together, dominated the space. There was a simple wooden dresser with a handful of pots, pans, plates and cups, a large wooden crucifix fixed to the tin wall and a camping stove with something cooking in the corner.

As her eyes adjusted, Becky noticed that one of the beds was currently occupied—presumably by V38's ailing mother.

V38 stood up. '*Èske gen yon bagay ki te pase?*' she said to Fabienne.

'*Yo jwenn yon bagay sou papa ou,*' she answered.

'*Kisa?*'

Fabienne turned to Becky. 'She wants to know what you have found.'

Becky nodded, slid her backpack off her shoulder and took out a document wallet that had been carefully curated in case it fell into the wrong hands. 'Is your mother well enough to look at this photograph and see if the man who raped her is on it?'

Fabienne translated and V38 stared for a long moment at the photograph, then looked across to her mother who appeared to be deeply asleep.

'*Manman,*' she whispered, sitting down on the edge of the bed. '*Èske ou ka louvri je ou?*'

Her mother stirred, gently rolling her head from side to side. Then, she opened her eyes and took a sharp breath.

V38 touched her mother's hand and said something that Becky assumed was to reassure her that she was safe.

Becky watched a short, barely audible interaction between mother and daughter. Then, V38 turned to Fabienne and spoke.

'She says to show her the photograph,' Fabienne said to Becky.

Becky hurriedly opened the document wallet and removed an unannotated version of the picture, which she handed to V38.

'*Mèsi*,' she said quietly. She studied the picture of the peacekeepers for some time, saying nothing, then held the image above her ailing mother's face.

The reaction was instant. She gasped and cried out, '*Oh, Bondye! Ede mwen.*' Between heaving sobs, she managed to utter something to V38.

'We shouldn't have come,' Aidan whispered behind her. 'This is just plain awful.'

V38 lowered the photograph, looked at it again for a long moment and then handed it back to Becky. '*Twazyèm nonm ki soti bò gòch la.*'

'The third man from the left,' Fabienne translated.

Becky turned around to face Aidan. V38's mother had identified Vairavan Subpan as her attacker.

'*Men, te gen lòt gason,*' she said weakly.

'But there were others—other men—who also attacked her,' Fabienne said.

Becky nodded, hoping that somehow those men, who had not left children behind but who had also committed these crimes, would eventually also face justice.

V38 spoke and Fabienne translated it. 'Do you know the name of this man?'

Becky nodded. 'Vairavan Subpan.'

V38 touched her watery eyes. 'Thank you,' she said in English. 'Thank you.'

Becky pulled V38 into a hug.

'We'll make damn sure he's held accountable,' Aidan said with false confidence.

Fabienne added a further layer of assurance in her translation.

'*Mèsi*,' V38 said, adding an extra sentence that Becky couldn't understand.

'She said she will ask the woman—the person you requested about before—she will ask her to speak to you,' Fabienne relayed.

Becky smiled. '*Mèsi anpil.*'

'*Pa dekwa.*'

'Becks, we really need to make it back before it gets dark,' Aidan said.

Becky took one further look at V38's mother, now soundly asleep, and said goodbye.

'*Orevwa,*' V38 said, seeing them to the door.

'We need to run again,' Fabienne instructed. 'I will bring you back to the main street. Follow me.'

Becky and Aidan did as directed, almost sprinting behind her back to the church.

'Are you okay to get back from here? Fabienne asked.

'Yeah, we'll be fine,' Aidan replied. 'Thanks for your help.'

'You're welcome. Goodbye.'

'Bye,' Becky said.

'Let's get home,' Aidan said, breaking into yet another run.

Becky followed behind, thinking over what had just occurred and desperately hoping that Vairavan Subpan and all his predatory friends would face the justice they deserved. But her hopes were not high. Then she thought about what V38 had just told her about contacting the woman from the international abuse ring. Maybe she would finally get some of the answers that she had come to Haiti to find.

Chapter Twenty-One

Saturday, November 12, 2022, Los Angeles, California

Ted Marsden was driving his red Ford Explorer north along Arroyo Seco Parkway, just nudging over the speed limit. Powers was sitting beside him, eating a shrimp taco. It was noisy, messy and the aroma wasn't too great either, but at least it gave Marsden a break from his incessant talking.

'You really think this might go somewhere?' Powers asked, forcing the words out around a mouthful of food, as if sensing Marsden's thoughts.

Marsden glanced across at him, watching sauce drip and run down Powers's chin. 'What? Paying Schnider a visit?' He shrugged. 'I just need to feel I'm doing something on this case. The sooner we close it and I hand in my gun and badge, the better.'

'Still nothing from the forensic gynecologist?' Powers asked, having taken to using that term to describe the IGG process in an attempt at being humorous. The first time Marsden had heard it, he'd laughed; but now it was wearing a little thin.

'No, nothing,' he answered. 'And I'm not chasing again. She gave us some good intel last weekend. Now we just need to let her team get on with it.'

'Uh-huh,' Powers agreed.

On the back seat of the Explorer were the four murder books for the Hollywood Strangler case. Orange Post-it notes stuck out from various points with questions for Bernard Schnider, the retired detective who had first worked it back in the 1980s. It was probably a futile trip and, as Schnider had been eager to point out on the phone, Marsden and Powers were just the latest in a long line of detectives who'd reviewed the case in the last thirty years. All of them had paid a visit to Schnider to see if he'd remembered anything else that hadn't featured in the murder book and all of them had left disappointed. Marsden had had to push hard to get an appointment with him, dangling the carrot of their new leads to hook Schnider's interest. It had worked and they'd been given a half-hour slot this morning.

Marsden turned right off the historic Route 66 that ran through here on its way between Chicago and Santa Monica in LA, on to East California Boulevard, then left onto South Marengo Avenue. 'We're almost there,' he said, glancing across at Powers as he rammed the last bite of taco into his mouth and finally wiped his chin with a napkin.

Marsden hung a right onto Pleasant Street, then slowed down. 'We're looking for seventy-eight.'

They crawled along the quiet residential road, checking the house numbers on each side as they went. It was a good spot to retire to, Marsden thought. Sure, it was quiet and tucked out of the way, but it was close enough to downtown Pasadena and forty-five minutes from downtown LA—traffic depending.

'There,' Powers said. Marsden pulled over, backed up to the curb a little and then killed the engine.

'Get the murder books,' Marsden instructed, wanting to be able to take the lead with Schnider, starting by shaking his hand and explaining where they were at with the case.

'Is that because you're so old and you need my muscle power to carry the files, or because you want me to look like the packhorse and that you're the one in charge here?' Powers asked with a playful smirk.

'Shut up, Powers,' Marsden said, locking the car and striding up the drive toward the house. It was a smart detached place with blue stucco exterior and a gabled roof. It looked to Marsden like some old colonial building from South Carolina. The garden was well-tended, with a mixture of native shrubs and various species of cacti dotted around enticing gravel paths.

As they approached the front door, Marsden noticed the Ring doorbell and did a minor side-step so that Powers might see it before he could potentially say something that they wouldn't want Schnider to hear. He either noticed or didn't have anything to say anyway.

Marsden pressed the bell, and moments later, the door was opened by a bear of a guy who easily topped six feet tall and three hundred pounds. He had unkempt gray hair and a few days' worth of matching stubble on his face. He stared out at them without talking.

'Hi,' Marsden said with a smile, holding up his badge. 'Ted Marsden from RHD. And this is Powers.'

'Come in,' Schnider said, opening the door wide for them to enter.

The house interior was dimly lit and cool. Schnider led them into the first room on the left, which was a large living room that looked as though it hadn't had a vacuum cleaner anywhere near it in several months. It was cluttered with old furniture and stacks of papers and books.

'Take a seat,' Schnider said, pointing to a battered green sofa as he seated himself in an armchair facing an oversized TV.

'Thank you,' Marsden said, sitting down and taking the first murder book from the stack in Powers's hands.

'Listen. Let me save you fellas some time,' Schnider said, seeing the orange Post-it notes sticking out. 'I know those murder books inside out. I've been through them a dozen times—before he was even out of diapers,' he said, pointing to Powers. 'I don't want to sit here answering questions about the chrono and decisions I made decades ago. Why don't you start by telling me what this new information is that you think you got and we'll take it from there.'

Marsden nodded. They'd agreed that under no circumstances would they be discussing the IGG angle, but they also knew that Schnider would need something to get him to talk. 'We've got some new leads that I can't tell you about—'

'Then we're done here,' Schnider said. 'I know I'm a retired detective and should want to help—and, really, let me tell you, I do want this case closed—but I've sat right here opposite a lot of cold case detectives over the years. If I'm not trusted with whatever new leads you guys have, then I've nothing else to say on the matter.' Schnider stood up, making it clear that he was waiting for them to do the same.

'We've got the suspect list down from eighty-six to twenty-two,' Marsden said, holding his nerve and remaining seated.

Schnider sat back down but said nothing.

'We think we're looking for a guy with brown eyes, brown hair and intermediate skin color,' Marsden said, skating over the fact that they'd been warned that these were simply estimates and potentialities at this stage of the IGG process.

Schnider's lower lip curled up, perhaps showing that he was in some way impressed. 'Sounds like you got yourselves a DNA phenotype, huh?'

Marsden didn't want to be drawn into the DNA aspect and said, 'I've got a handful of suspects that I'd like to go through with you, but first, I wanted to talk about a double-bagger on April tenth nineteen-eighty. David and Joyce Peck, murdered in their home at nine ninety-nine Via Arroyo in Ventura. There's nothing in the chrono about it and I just wondered why it was ignored at the time?'

Schnider showed no signs of recognition. 'Why was what ignored?'

'Robyn Stoltman. The first victim lived at that address just a few months before the homicides,' Marsden explained. The more that he'd thought about it, the more he considered the oversight to have been negligent. Maybe the case would have been solved much sooner—perhaps even during the killing spree itself—if the connection had been made to the Pecks at the time of the original investigation.

'I don't know what you're talking about. You're saying that this couple was killed by the Hollywood Strangler?'

Marsden nodded. 'That's right, although detectives at the time thought they were killed by the same person who killed Lyman and Charlene Smith a few streets away.'

'Hang on. Weren't they Golden State Killer victims?' Schnider asked.

'Uh-huh.'

'Was the M.O. similar to the Hollywood Strangler?'

'No,' Marsden confirmed. 'There was no staging of the bodies like with—'

'Why would we have thought it was the Hollywood Strangler, then?'

'Because Robyn Stoltman was living there just a few months before the murders,' Powers answered.

'And how would we have known that? You think with no internal computer system in place we'd just do a homicide tour of the state to find similarities, which you say didn't exist?'

'It was all over the news. Robyn's father even went on *Hour*

203

Magazine to be interviewed about it. It should have been picked up.'

Schnider stood up sharply. 'That's why you're here? To rip holes in my investigation, now that you're sitting down on the high horse of hindsight? It's time you guys left.'

'Please, Mr. Schnider,' Marsden began. 'If we can just run—'

'You deaf? I said, get out of my house.'

Marsden shot a look at Powers, then stood to leave.

Schnider strode down the hallway and opened the front door. 'And do me a favor, Reserve Officers, and put one of your orange labels, there, in the chrono that says never to contact me again about this damned case.'

They walked silently back to the Explorer.

'Well, that went well,' Powers summarized when they reached the car.

Marsden couldn't help but let out a little laugh.

Maddie was running her usual route along the Utah and Salt Lake Canal Trail. She was headed north under State-175, her head throbbing from having consumed too much wine last night. She'd gone out with Clayton to Laziz Kitchen on Ninth Street, where they'd eaten Lebanese mezze and drunk two bottles of American Recordings Chardonnay. The night had ended with a tequila-based cocktail called Morning Fog, which was exactly how she'd felt this morning.

She reflected on the evening and how relaxed she had felt in his company. It was good to have someone in her life again. She was learning to stop fearing and questioning the void that Michael had left and to stop trying to force her growing relationship with Clayton into that same space, where it just did not belong and could never survive. That hole would never be filled by Clayton or anyone else, and that was okay. She was learning how to compartmentalize that part of her life and to allow something new to grow in its own space. Of course, it was far easier said than done, especially with so many lingering questions about what had happened to Michael. Despite the passage of seven years and her emerging relationship with Clayton, she still thought about her husband and what could have befallen him every single day.

Maddie slowed her pace, realizing that her breathing and heart rate had become intense. She took back control, breathed deeply into her lungs, released the air slowly and backed off to a brisk jog.

Her thoughts then turned to something that Trenton had said following the calamitous meal on Monday night. After Clayton had gone home, Trenton had asked to talk to Maddie in his bedroom. His opening question had thrown her off guard: 'Mom, do you think you're less likely to try and find out what happened to dad, now that you're dating someone?'

'No,' she'd immediately responded. 'I will never be able to stop until I know exactly what happened to him. He's your dad and he's still my husband, and there are still a huge number of questions that we need answers to.'

Trenton had nodded, but she could see the doubt in his eyes. 'What about if he asks you to stop looking?'

'Clayton? He wouldn't do that. And don't forget, he's the reason we got the DUI report and the security video from College Park Airport. None of that would have happened without his help,' Maddie had said.

'I know. But at some point—maybe when enough time has passed in his mind—it wouldn't be unreasonable for him to say that enough was enough and it was time to accept things as they are,' Trenton had pushed.

'Trenton. I promise you. I will *not* give up,' she had sought to reassure him.

But now that she was here, running along the tow path with only her own thoughts to consider, could she really say that she had been doing everything in her power lately to find out what had happened to Michael? Maybe not. Maybe she was hitching a lot of hope onto whatever it was that Becky was doing out in Haiti. She wondered if maybe she should call the detective in charge of the investigation or pick up again with her own research. But what other avenues were left to explore? As soon as the pandemic restrictions had lifted, Maddie had gone to Washington D.C. to try to find out more about Emmanuel Gribbin, the employee of Becky's father's company, The Larkin Investment and Finance Group. From the DUI file that Clayton had managed to procure for her, she had had Gribbin's address before his death and had started her investigation there. Her cold calling at the house had been answered by a young female lawyer who had been renting the apartment from the same man that Gribbin had rented it from. The lawyer had been kind and given Maddie the owner's contact details, and she had met him at a nearby coffee shop the following day.

'What happened to Emmanuel's things?' Maddie had asked him, using Gribbin's first name, trying to endear herself to him and to elicit more personal details, potentially. She hadn't told him the full story, just that she was trying to track down Gribbin, whom she'd described as an old friend.

The man owned several properties around the city and had replied, 'Nobody came for his stuff, so I contacted the coroner to get a next of kin, but they said there wasn't one. So, sorry, but I just cleared it all out and took it to landfill.'

Maddie had nodded. 'Do you remember what he had in his belongings?'

The man had shrugged. 'Just the general crap that everyone has. Nothing of any value.'

'No. That wasn't what I was getting at,' Maddie had quickly replied. 'Nothing personal or anything about his family?'

'No, nothing. If there had been anything like that, I would have contacted them and had *them* clear out his stuff.'

The meeting had ended with Maddie knowing nothing more than she had before it had begun. Next, she had approached the Office of the Chief Medical Examiner in Washington D.C. who had informed her that their efforts to track down a next of kin had also failed and, six months after his death, Gribbin had been buried at the expense of the city at Glenwood Cemetery. Maddie had gone directly to the cemetery, where she had been given the reference for Gribbin's unmarked grave. Despite the fact that the plot was unmarked, Maddie had still managed to find it, owing to a fading bunch of red roses placed on the strip of lawn with the inscription, *Emmanuel, Sorely missed. With love, Angelique.* The words had winded Maddie. Someone—and not that long ago, judging by the wilting flowers—had visited this cemetery and known Gribbin's burial spot without a marker. But who was Angelique? Her desperation to find this woman had led Maddie to extend her trip to D.C. and to spend time contacting all the local florists, requesting help in tracking down this mystery woman. But this line of inquiry had gone nowhere, and Maddie still had no idea who she was. Other avenues of her investigation included private security cameras around College Park Airport, but that search, too, had yielded nothing.

As Maddie pushed herself harder along the towpath, she became increasingly satisfied that she *had* pursued every avenue of investigation possible and hadn't simply let the ball drop because of her relationship with Clayton. Despite reaching that reassuring conclusion, Maddie resolved to do two things when she got back home: call Detective Scullion, who was in charge of Michael's case, and ask him for an update; and try and contact Becky to find out exactly what on earth was going on with her in Haiti.

Hudson was sitting down in the Coffee Garden, waiting for his date. He had arrived a full twenty minutes early to make sure that he could get a table in the popular coffee shop. It was one of the hangouts of choice for young work-from-home types, who could make one latte last several hours while they sat with air buds, working on laptops. He'd had to stand around for over ten minutes until a two-person table had become available. Now he sat nervously watching the door for a young woman named Nora Bianchi, whom he had met on the Fiorry dating app. Having completed the comprehensive and highly personal questionnaire, the algorithms had suggested that he and Nora would be a good match. He'd looked at her profile and agreed. Evidently, she'd looked at his profile and had also agreed. Then, they'd exchanged a few messages before arranging to meet. She'd chosen the Coffee Garden in the trendy and thriving Ninth and Ninth neighborhood, which was a good start as far as he was concerned. It was a place that he himself liked to come to sometimes. It had a high vaulted ceiling, exposed brick walls adorned with paintings by local artists and chic rustic tables.

The door opened and Hudson looked over. It was her. He'd heard all kinds of horror stories about people not at all resembling their profile pictures, but there was no mistaking that this was her. She was tall, slim with bleach-blonde curly hair, the longest third of which was dyed bright green. She wore black jeans and a thick rainbow-patterned knitted sweater. She stood in the doorway, surveying the room. He stood and waved, relieved to see her smile when at last she saw him.

Hudson clamped his shaking hands together in front of him as she strode over. 'Hudson, hi,' she greeted, kissing him on both cheeks.

'Hi,' he replied. 'How are you?'

She carried a large raffia bag that she seemed relieved to remove from her shoulder. 'Yeah, great, thanks. 'Uh, in need of coffee, actually. What can I get you?'

'Oh, uh,' Hudson said, taken aback by her unexpected self-confidence in leading the situation. 'I guess I'll get a large oat latte, please.'

'Snap,' she said, clicking her fingers before rummaging in her bag for her wallet. 'Be right back.'

Hudson sank down in his chair, watching her march over to the counter. So far, she was the polar opposite of his ex-wife, Abigail. But maybe that was what he needed.

He took in some long breaths, trying to calm himself as he looked over the art on the walls for distraction. One particular scene, an abstract of a mountain range, especially caught his eye. He looked at it for a long time.

'I got us each a lavender peach Danish, too,' Nora said, arriving back and placing a tray down onto the table.

'I *love* those things,' Hudson replied. 'Thank you.' He couldn't determine the etiquette of whether he should have offered to pay, or now go halves and give her some money. He decided that she didn't seem the type of person who would need to split a small bill and resolved that, if things went well, then he would buy the food and drink at their next meeting.

She sat down opposite him and raised her drink. 'Cheers.'

'Cheers,' Hudson said, tapping his mug against hers and taking a sip. He studied her face as she drank some coffee. She possessed a naturally warm and pretty face, which she supplemented with black eyeliner, a nose ring and bright red lipstick.

'So... Okay, Hudson,' she began, placing her drink down and

holding it on the table between both hands as she met his eyes. 'Your profile says you were born in Maine. What are you doing in Salt Lake City?'

'I guess… Escaping my past,' he replied, wondering if that was a little too honest and a little too serious—or maybe even sounded a little too creepy—for their first interaction.

She smiled and nodded. 'Yeah. That's kind of why I'm here, too.'

'Oh, really? Tell me.'

'Well, I grew up in LA, married a guy from high school, who made a name for himself in the music business and decided he would use his newly found fame and wealth to help young girls into the industry. Specifically, young, beautiful and impressionable girls, who then would have to do whatever he asked.'

Hudson grimaced.

'It's all very MeToo, sad to say,' Nora said. 'I found out on March 19, 2020—the day Los Angeles went into lockdown with the stay-home order. I decided not to stay home. I walked out, leaving everything behind, and drove ten hours up to a girlfriend's just a couple of blocks from here. Stayed there ever since.'

'No regrets?' Hudson asked.

'Only that I didn't find out about what he was up to sooner.'

'So, what do you do here?'

'I'm an artist and photographer,' she answered, turning and pointing at the brick wall behind her. 'Some of those are mine.'

'Oh, that's so great. Which ones?' Hudson asked.

'The two black-and-white portrait photos of the homeless guys, the painting of Death Valley and the mountain abstract at the top.'

Hudson grinned. 'I was really drawn to that painting. I just sat here staring at it. It's the Wasatch Mountain range, right?'

Nora smiled widely. 'You recognized it.'

'I can see that part from my bedroom window.'

'That's cool,' she said. 'So, you're a professional genealogist, right? I Googled you and found some articles you wrote. And you do genetic genealogy, too?'

'Yeah. I work for Venator, an investigative genetic genealogy company downtown.'

'That's using DNA to catch criminals, isn't it?'

Hudson nodded. 'Well, it's that and giving names to unidentified human remains.'

'That must get pretty harrowing and stressful at times.'

'It can, yes,' he said, impressed that she could see beyond the glamorous veneer of catching serial killers. 'Sometimes the cold case detectives share too many crime scene photos or in-depth detail about a serial killer, and I just have to switch that all off and concentrate on the task at hand. We've got one now—' He stopped himself short, realizing that he'd signed an NDA and also that, as someone in her thirties from LA, she would likely be very familiar with the Hollywood Strangler case.

'What?' she asked, narrowing her eyes. 'What were you about to say?'

'I was about to blurt out something to you about the current case, then I remembered that I've signed a non-disclosure agreement about it, so my lips are officially sealed.'

'Fair enough. So, I kind of get the basics of it,' Nora said, 'But I don't get how you go from a DNA sample to a name.'

'Okay, I'll try and explain it real quick,' he said, taking a bite of the Danish first.

'I'm not in a hurry,' Nora replied. 'And I'm actually really interested to know. I'm also getting from you that you're quite passionate about it.'

'I am,' he said with a shy smile. He drank some coffee and then talked Nora through each step of the IGG process. She listened intently, showing genuine and insightful interest through the questions that she asked along the way.

'I did a test years ago at 23andMe,' Nora revealed when he had finished. 'I got it for Christmas one year from my ex, although I haven't looked at it in a long while.'

Hudson was about to ask a question when he was distracted by a familiar voice at the coffee shop door. He turned to see Reggie looking around the room. Hudson internally recoiled, wondering how on earth Reggie could have known where to find him. What did he think he was doing crashing a first date? Hudson's shock and growing resentment was slowly replaced by relief when he realized that Reggie was either looking for someone else or—more likely in this place—a free table. He headed back out the door and Hudson was about to turn back to Nora when he saw Reggie reach out for someone's hand outside. It was his secret date and Hudson was about to find out finally who it was.

The hand, it transpired, belonged to Ross.

'Are you okay?' Nora asked him.

'Sorry, yeah,' Hudson replied. 'The guy who just stepped in is my roommate.'

'Oh. Was he checking how our date was going? Did you guys have a secret password thing going on, to bring it all to an emergency end? Did I fail the test?'

Hudson smiled and shook his head. 'I think he was looking for a table. It appears he's been secretly dating my colleague, Ross, the receptionist from my work.'

'Is that a problem?' Nora asked.

'Of course not. I'm just surprised that he didn't tell me. He's one of the few people in Salt Lake City that I talked to about *my* personal journey. I told him literally everything.'

'I'm sure he has his reasons,' Nora said.

Hudson sat back and drank some coffee, inexplicably feeling the pain of rejection. Then he glanced up at the abstract painting of the Wasatch mountains and brought himself back to the moment and to the enjoyable time that he was having with Nora. He needed to pull himself together and focus on their date.

And, so far, it seemed that perhaps the algorithms had actually got it right.

Chapter Twenty-Two

Sunday, November 13, 2022, Salt Lake City, Utah

Kenyatta had just got in from the City Presbyterian Church. She kicked off her shoes and called out to see if anyone was home. If Jon or Gabe were home, then they were either still asleep or had headphones on, playing games or listening to music. Troy was still not answering her calls or text messages.

She walked along the hall to the bedroom the boys shared to find that it was empty. Although she hadn't set any plans with them, during church she had had the idea that they might all go out for lunch, and afterward maybe, they could watch a movie together. It was at a time like this that she needed to remind herself that the boys weren't little kids anymore.

Feeling slightly crestfallen, Kenyatta headed into the kitchenette, got a glass of water and set Alexa shuffling songs by Billie Holiday. She took out her laptop and sat down on the sofa with a sigh. She opened the screen, undecided about what exactly she would choose to work on. She could continue with the Hollywood Strangler case or figure out what aspect of African American research she would teach for her upcoming class with the Salt Lake Institute of Genealogy, or she could work on her labor-of-love case, the Boys Under the Bridge.

She took a sip of water, considering the three options. The SLIG talk wouldn't take long to prepare, plus she had plenty of time for that. The Hollywood Strangler case was ticking along nicely and would receive the full focus of her weekday energies, whereas the Boys Under the Bridge case went stagnant unless she found the time to pick it up. It was one of a few pro-bono cases that Venator took on every year for the National Center for Missing and Exploited Children. This one—trying to identify two brothers aged around six and four—was a complex case that had lingered on the shelves for several years, owing to the boys' Asian heritage and the accompanying lack of DNA matches in the databases. Kenyatta had struck it lucky a couple of years back when someone had appeared in the GEDmatch database, who had allowed her to find the first set of direct ancestors for the two boys: Arthit and Preeda Tang of Khao Wang in Thailand. Her initial elation had gradually receded into the resignation that tracking down this couple's descendants was a monumentally difficult challenge because there just weren't many records available.

Kenyatta opened the seventy-page document file that she had created for Arthit and Preeda Tang. So far, she had concentrated her efforts on those members of the family who had emigrated to the U.S., including the family of one of the brothers' closer matches, Kanda Phasuk. Kenyatta had discovered that Kanda's great-grandparents had come to the U.S. in the 1930s, settling in Southern California. Over the next thirty years, they had spread east across the U.S., living in several central states. Out of the nine siblings scattered across the country, three had built their lives in Grand Junction, Colorado. These three were the ongoing focus of Kenyatta's research since they had lived just three hundred miles east of Penrose, Colorado. It was on the outskirts of Penrose that the skeletonized remains of the two brothers had been discovered in a dry creek bed with bullet holes in the backs of their skulls. Police believed that whoever had murdered the brothers had dumped their bodies over the side of Colorado-115, known as the Vietnam Veterans Memorial Highway, which ran from the town of Penrose north-east to the city of Colorado Springs. Kenyatta knew the route well; she had used Street View to move along the highway multiple times, searching the vast open fields for any clues, but it was pretty much a wilderness. There was a smattering of houses, an Olympic shooting range, a campground, RV park, the Cheyenne Mountain State Park and, on the outskirts of Colorado Springs, a U.S. Army post, Fort Carson.

Kenyatta pulled up the speculative tree that she had created for Arthit and Preeda Tang, navigating down to the three siblings in question. For the eldest, Kenyatta had successfully traced a living descendent who had been willing to take a DNA test and upload it to GEDmatch, giving the two brothers their closest match with two hundred and forty-five centimorgans, a figure Kenyatta had started to fear that she would never get to see. The match had confirmed her working theory that the boys descended from one of those three siblings in Colorado. The middle child of the three had married twice but only produced one child: a girl who had died at the age of fifteen. The youngest, James Tang, had lived in Grand Junction with his wife, Letitia, and their ten children. Kenyatta was slowly and methodically working her way through those ten, tracing their descendants, any one of whom *could* prove to be one of the Boys under the Bridge's parents. The number of people on the suspect list was over thirty, four of whom she had already approached to take a DNA test and all of whom had refused.

She opened the profile page for the next of James and Letitia's grandsons to be researched: Marcus Tang. He had been born in Grand Junction around 1959, but she had yet to pin down his actual date of birth. Unfortunately for Kenyatta, vital records for the state of Colorado were largely out of the public domain. Birth records were sealed under a one-hundred-year closure rule, death records under a seventy-five-year rule, and the marriage records that were held by the online genealogy companies were mainly indexes rather than the actual records, all meaning that Kenyatta had to rely heavily on other sources for her research.

She turned to the Chronicling America database on the Library of Congress website and clicked *U.S. Newspaper Directory, 1690-Present*. From the drop-down menu, she selected Grand Junction, Mesa, Colorado, and a date range of 1950 to 2022. Just one of the twenty-seven newspapers was in operation for the entire period: *The Daily Sentinel*.

Opening Newspapers.com in a new browser tab, Kenyatta typed the newspaper title into the search box and then added Marcus Tang's name as a keyword, giving her 104 results. She selected *Marriages* from the *Categories* filter. *2 matches*. She clicked the first, dated May 13, 1985. Under a heading of *Couples*, Kenyatta found a black-and-white headshot of a man and a woman, posing and smiling for the camera. The caption below the picture read *Marcus Tang, Lola Brady*. She read the short paragraph underneath the photograph.

Mr. and Mrs. Frank Brady of Bailey announce the engagement of their daughter, Lola Ann, to Marcus Tang, son of Mr. and Mrs. Joseph Tang of Grand Junction. Brady, a graduate of Grand Junction High School, is the manager of the Quick

Chick restaurant at Mesa Mall. Tang is a graduate of Mesa College with a degree in business. The wedding is planned for August 15.

The article was enough for Kenyatta to confirm that she had found the correct Marcus Tang, and she updated his profile on the speculative tree accordingly.

Returning to the second search result, she found that this, too, pertained to the same Marcus Tang. The article was dated June 2, 1987, and featured another monochrome photograph of Marcus, but this time with a different woman beside him.

Christine Etcheverry and Marcus Tang were married May 27 in a garden ceremony at the home of the bride's parents in Helper, Utah. Jim and Regina Etcheverry are parents of the bride. The groom's parents are Joseph and Betty Tang of Grand Junction. The bride is employed as an emergency medical technician. The groom is employed by West Hudson and Company as a management consultant.

The story made no mention of the previous engagement or Marcus being a widower, leaving Kenyatta to assume that the first marriage had either never happened or had ended in divorce. She paused on the year of the wedding: 1987. The eldest of the two murdered brothers was estimated to have been born in 1988. Could Marcus and Christine Tang be their parents? she wondered as she saved the article to Marcus's profile. She returned to the main search menu, switching *Marriages* for *Obituaries*. Kenyatta could see that the single result was for Marcus. The obituary was headed by a headshot, the likeness of which was undoubtedly that of Marcus Tang.

December 19, 1959 - June 29, 2013

Marcus Tang, loving husband and amazing father, passed away surrounded by his family at St Mary's Hospital on June 29, 2013. He was born in Grand Junction in 1959 to parents, Joseph and Betty Tang. Marcus and his four siblings were raised on a ranch just outside the city...

Ordinarily, Kenyatta would skip over the parts about the

deceased's career and hobbies, concentrating solely on the genealogical details, but in this case that information could be important in helping to narrow down the pool of suspects.

...After graduating from Mesa College with a degree in business, he went to work for over thirty years with West Hudson and Company, rising to the position of company manager when he retired in 2010 due to ill health.

Marcus's work life being fixed in one place didn't tie in with the general assumption about the bodies having been dumped by a non-local passing over Colorado-115. It was also much less likely that the news of the discovery of the bodies, which had made the headlines across the state at the time, wouldn't have been tied to the disappearance of Marcus's own kids. But at this stage, Kenyatta was ruling nothing out. The final part of the obit added to the information that the dearth of vital records for Colorado had been as yet unable to provide.

...His parents, Joseph and Betty Tang, and two sisters, Mary-Lou Dern and Tammie Tang preceded him in death. Survivors are his wife, Christine; daughter, Valerie (Mike) Reynolds of Colorado Springs and three sons; Ian Tang of Grand Junction, George Tang of Eagle and Stephen Tang of Fort Stewart, Georgia as well as two brothers, Joe Tang of Colorado Springs and Raymond Tang of Maxwell, New Mexico.

Kenyatta now had confirmation of Marcus's birth, marriage and death dates and, crucially, the names of all first-degree relatives, which she added to the family tree. In the Word document that she had created for the case, she added the names of Valerie Reynolds and Ian, George and Stephen Tang below the heading *Target Testers*. Her next job was to try and track down at least one of those siblings, explain the case to them and ask that they consider taking a voluntary DNA test which would help confirm that she was working along the right lines.

Becky Larkin looked at her watch again. She and Aidan were once more in the makeshift community center opposite the Médecins Sans Frontières Hôpital de Brûlures. Fabienne, the translator, had been due to arrive over forty minutes ago with V38 and a woman who had been the victim of an international abuse ring.

Aidan sighed heavily as he paced over to the window and peered cautiously outside. 'There's still no sign. We'll give them five more minutes, then we really need to leave.'

'We'll give them twenty minutes,' Becky countered. 'That way, we've given them an hour total.'

There followed another loud exhalation from Aidan as he walked back over the dusty wooden floor toward her. 'What are you hoping to achieve from this, Becks?'

'Answers,' she replied. 'Information.'

'Can I ask…? What if you don't get what you're after? Then what?'

Becky shrugged. 'Then, I keep digging. Something's off with my father's company and what his workers were doing here back in 2015. It couldn't have been a coincidence that the three men, who came out here that year, all ended up dead or vanished in mysterious circumstances. I mean, what do you—'

Becky and Aidan were both startled as the doors at the back of the room opened. Fabienne stepped inside, taking a cautious glance around the room.

'It's okay,' Aidan assured her. 'You can come in.'

She entered, followed by V38 and then a timid, fragile-looking young woman. She was dark-skinned with black hair pulled back in a ponytail, and she was wearing a discolored floral dress and battered flip-flops. Becky guessed that she could have been no more than twenty years old.

Becky stood from the table and smiled. '*Bonjou. Mèsi paske w vin isit la.*'

The young woman nodded but said nothing.

'She does not want to be here long,' Fabienne explained. 'What is it that you want to know?'

Becky suddenly bore the pressure of the situation as all eyes fell on her. 'Please, take a seat,' she motioned, trying her best to override her anxiety and appear relaxed and welcoming.

The young girl looked at the door behind her, then slowly moved to sit down with Fabienne and V38 flanking her on either side.

Becky and Aidan sat opposite, both consciously aiming for open body language. Becky picked up her notepad and asked the young girl, 'Can I know your name?'

Fabienne directed the question to V38, and the three women conversed in Haitian Creole before the young girl spoke. 'Lovelie.'

Becky smiled. 'That's such a nice name. Thank you for talking to me, Lovelie.' She waited for Fabienne and then decided that since time was short, she should get straight to the point. 'Where were you living at the time that you were attacked?'

Fabienne translated and then Lovelie answered, '*Mwen te rete Martissant jiskaske yon gang te pran mwen.*'

'She said she lived in Martissant—it's a shanty town south-west of the center. She lived there until she was kidnapped by a gang.'

Becky nodded. 'And then what happened?'

Lovelie answered in a low, quivering voice, and Fabienne said, 'She was taken to a big house—a mansion—to live in Pétion-Ville. She was given a bath, fresh clothes and all she could want to eat and drink. It was paradise.'

Becky said nothing, predicting what was coming.

'And then the white men came, lots of them. They flew in, stayed in the big house and repeatedly raped her.'

'*Mwen regrèt anpil,*' Becky said quietly. She waited a moment and then asked, 'Do you know who the men were? Any names? Where they came from?'

Once Fabienne had translated, Lovelie shook her head. '*Yo tout te Ameriken.*'

Becky did not need to hear the translation to understand.

'Can you describe any of the men?' Aidan asked.

'*Te gen twòp,*' she answered, tears now rolling down her cheeks. '*Twòp.*'

'There were too many,' Fabienne said.

Lovelie spoke again and Becky waited for the translation. 'They called the man in charge Bakas.'

'Bakas?' Becky queried.

'Bakas are malevolent spirits who originate from the deceased who lived wicked lives. They are known for causing misfortune or bringing harm to living people.'

Becky waited a moment. 'How old were you at the time?'

'*Douz*,' she replied.

'She was twelve.'

Becky's pity was morphing into a rising anger. 'How many other girls were there like you at the house?'

Fabienne translated the question and then the answer. 'The girls changed from time to time. There were often ten or more of them. As soon as they became pregnant, they were thrown out onto the streets.'

'All around the same age? Underage?' Becky asked.

Lovelie nodded.

'Jesus,' Aidan muttered.

'You have to remember,' Fabienne said of her own volition. 'Rape only became a criminal offense here in 2005, but still there is nobody here to enforce that law. Rape is just commonplace. Gangs use it as weapon against their enemies. Nobody cares.'

'We care,' Becky said. 'Do you know where these other girls are now? The ones with the babies?'

Lovelie shrugged.

Fabienne told them, 'Abortion is illegal here, so these girls get discarded. Nobody wants a pregnant girl here with a white baby. They go to the street to raise these children with nothing.'

'You don't know any of them?' Becky pushed. 'Where they might be now?'

After translation, Lovelie shook her head and stared at the ground.

Aidan turned to Becky. 'We need to call this. She doesn't know anything else.'

Becky agreed but had one last question. 'Would you come with us to Pétion-Ville and show us which house it was?'

Once again, the three women conversed in Haitian Creole. There seemed to be some disagreement between them. Finally, Lovelie said, '*Wi. Mwen ka fè sa.*'

'She will do it.'

'*Mèsi*,' Becky said, taking out fifteen thousand Haitian Gourde from her jeans pocket and handing it over.

'Becky,' Aidan warned. They weren't supposed to offer money to any of the women whom they were helping.

'It's only about a hundred dollars. And she's not part of the program,' Becky responded.

'Thank you,' Lovelie said. 'Nice American.'

Reggie was driving down UT-190 with a contented smile on his face. He'd just finished a day snowboarding on the Snake Creek and Great Western slopes of Brighton. The snow was perfection and, if he hadn't told Ross that he would be at his apartment by five o'clock, Reggie might well have made a detour to the roundabout on Ninth and Ninth to make an offering at the Church of the Sacred Whale. He laughed out loud as he considered what Ross's reaction would be when he told him that.

He was cruising in a long line of ski traffic making the descent down the mountain pass toward Salt Lake City. The snow line was moving farther and farther away from him, and the snow-dusted pine trees gradually gave way to signs of civilization. A pall of sadness would usually engulf Reggie at this point in the journey, but not today. Although he couldn't wait to get back up there next weekend, he was also really looking forward to seeing Ross. After spending most of last night with him at the Milk+ bar and getting back to his apartment past 2 a.m., they'd decided to spend this evening relaxing and watching more of *The Crown* after Ross cooked them dinner.

Ten minutes later, Reggie parked outside the Sugar House Apartments, walked over to the building intercom and pressed the lighted button marked LARKIN/MOLE. A few seconds later, Ross spoke. 'Hello?'

'Hey, it's me,' Reggie said.

'Come on up,' Ross said, buzzing him in.

Reggie bounded up the stairs, finding Ross holding open the apartment door. 'How were the slopes? Did dropping a stone on a roundabout with a plastic rainbow whale give you good snow?'

'It really did,' Reggie said, entering the apartment and kissing Ross. 'I tell you, man, I was actually going to swing by there and leave another offering, but the traffic off the mountain was pretty heavy, and I thought you might not appreciate that.'

Ross shook his head. 'Can you tell me which roundabout I leave a rock on to guarantee warm sunshine?'

'Don't even think about it until the ski season is over,' Reggie said, removing his boots and thick snowboarding jacket. 'How was your day?'

Ross led them into the kitchen area, where something awesome-smelling was cooking in the oven. 'It was good, thanks. I had brunch with my sister in the Tinker's Cat Cafe and—'

'Is that the one with actual cats roaming freely around the place?' Reggie asked, sitting down at the counter.

'Uh-huh. It's cute,' Ross said.

'Uh, not for my allergies, it's not.'

Ross smiled. 'And then I came back here, read my book, did some chores, and then spent a ridiculous amount of time preparing our dinner. Wine?'

'Sure, thanks.'

Ross poured out two glasses of white wine and handed one to Reggie. 'Cheers.'

'Cheers.'

Just as their glasses chinked together, a noise from the hall drew their attention. It was the sound of a key opening the door.

Ross's eyes lit up. 'Oh my God, is that Becky?' he said, setting down his wine and rushing for the door.

Reggie stood up and tentatively followed.

'Oh, hey, Mr. Larkin. Is everything okay?' Ross asked.

A man—Becky's father, Reggie surmised—strode into the apartment seemingly oblivious to him or Ross. He was a stocky but fit man with short gray hair and piercing eyes, wearing smart clothes. He stood in the open-plan living area, looking around the room. His eyes darted around quickly, as if trying to take in the place as a whole.

'Hi,' Reggie said, offering his hand to shake.

'Mr. Larkin?' Ross said.

'Have you heard from my daughter lately?' the man asked, glowering at Ross and then at Reggie.

'Uh... She calls from time to time, but I haven't heard from her in—'

'And no idea when she's planning on coming back?'

'No, I—'

'Okay, you've got one week to pack up and get out. I've got someone who's going to rent the apartment next Monday,' Mr. Larkin said, spinning around and making for the door.

'Wait!' Ross called. 'What do you mean? This is Becky's apartment.'

Mr. Larkin whipped around. 'No. It's *my* apartment. And I'm informing you that I am renting it out starting next Monday.'

'What will I do?' Ross asked.

'Find yourself somewhere else, I'd say.'

'But what about all Becky's things?' Ross pushed. Reggie could hear that he was on the verge of tears.

Mr. Larkin laughed. 'I really don't care. Send them to Haiti, throw them in the trash...whatever. Just make sure this place is cleared out by Saturday at the latest, so I can get my guys to come in and give the place a once-over. Got it?'

Ross nodded weakly.

'Anything—or anyone for that matter—still in here on Sunday will be removed by my guys and dumped outside on the sidewalk.' He turned around and marched out of the apartment, slamming the door behind him.

'Wow,' Reggie muttered, taking a seat in the living room area. '*That* was Becky's dad?'

Ross nodded as he moved to the couch and sat down with a long, emotional exhale, disoriented. 'I've got less than a week to find a new place. I can't believe it. I have to call Becky.' He leapt up, grabbed his cell phone from the kitchen counter and called her. 'It's ringing.'

'You could always stay at Hudson's—with me—temporarily, I mean,' Reggie suggested.

Ross didn't acknowledge the idea as he paced over to the balcony window. 'Becky! Hey, what's going on? Yeah... Wait... I've just had your dad here at the apartment. Uh-huh. Yeah, right. Well, get a load of this. He's just given me—wait, no, given us—six days to move out. Yeah. He said it was his place and he's got someone else coming in.'

Reggie listened to the one-sided conversation, trying to fill in the gaps. From what he could gather, Becky was as surprised by the eviction as was Ross. As the telephone call continued, Reggie thought about what he'd just offered. He probably should check with Hudson that Ross would be okay to stay in the house, even if for a short while. Would it even work, them all living together? He'd been dating Ross for such a short time, and they were still in the honeymoon period. It might be too soon for twenty-four seven.

Ross ended the call and sat down next to Reggie. 'She said I could fight the amount of notice I've been given, but I'd never win. I'm basically screwed and need to clear out—including all of her things.'

'Jeez,' Reggie said. 'Well, okay. So, let's park *The Crown* and spend the evening looking for a storage unit for you to rent and a moving company to move you out on Saturday.'

'But where am I going to go?' Ross said, his voice cracking with emotion.

'Come stay with me until you get yourself a place,' he reassured.

Ross nodded. 'I hope to God that Becky is out there right now, finding something that will bring that odious man down.'

Chapter Twenty-Three

Monday, November 14, 2022, Salt Lake City, Utah

Maddie was sitting down at her office desk, slowly drowning under the volume of emails landing in the Venator inbox. Ross had called her late last night asking for the next three days off work, which, given the case that they were currently running, she'd been loath to grant. However, once he'd explained that Becky's father had burst into the apartment and given him just six days to get out, she'd accepted his request. But now she was fielding emails asking to schedule interviews and talks, people wanting to know how to get into the industry and, that which made up the bulk of the communications, potential cases. These came both from members of the public, wanting to get a cold case investigated, and from law enforcement, seeking Venator's advice and assistance. Monday mornings were always the worst. Not only had the inbox been unattended over the weekend, but Saturdays and Sundays seemed to be the peak time during the week when people decided to make contact.

Maddie took a sip of coffee, finding that it had gotten cold. She wondered again at the implications of what Ross had told her. She'd pushed for more details about why Andrew Larkin would evict him, but Ross hadn't known. Something was clearly very wrong if he was prepared to throw his daughter's possessions out onto the street. Maddie couldn't help wondering if it was all connected to whatever it was that Becky was doing in Haiti. She'd tried to call her yesterday afternoon but hadn't managed to get through. She had succeeded in talking to Detective Scullion, however, who had given his usual perfunctory BS that Michael's case was still being worked but they were awaiting new lines of inquiry.

She wanted some fresh coffee but, when she saw that it was after 12:15, she thought better of it. She was due to meet Clayton for lunch in forty-five minutes and she was nowhere near clearing her inbox that would allow her to carry on working on the Hollywood Strangler case.

The next email in the list was from Cheri Hudson Passey, asking if Maddie would like to appear on her genealogy YouTube chat show,

GenFriends. Maddie had so many requests for interviews that most got declined, but she always had a blast on GenFriends and, so, accepted the invitation. She hoped that the Hollywood Strangler case would be solved before her appearance so that she would be able to give Cheri an exclusive.

Next was a genetic genealogist asking if Venator had any intern opportunities coming up. Maddie replied that there was currently no availability but that it was something she was exploring for the future—mainly because Nikki was pushing her into creating a role specifically for her when she finished college.

The following email was from a detective from the Las Vegas Metropolitan Police Department, regarding a cold case up at Lake Mead. Maddie read the email with interest. It was a request for help in identifying bodies found stuffed into wooden barrels that had appeared following a drought at the lake. She flagged the email to come back to. Right now, though, she needed to get ready to meet Clayton.

She put her laptop to sleep, pulled on her jacket and headed out into the main office. 'Okay, guys. I'm going out for lunch. I shouldn't be too long.'

'Have fun,' Kenyatta called over. 'I'll redirect switchboard to me.'

'Say hi to Clayton from us,' Hudson added.

'And tell him to bring more fancy cakes!' Reggie chipped in.

'Sure, I'll tell him all of that,' Maddie said, walking through the office and out the door. Down the hall, she rode the elevator to the first floor and walked north up Main Street one block to the City Creek Center. She walked through the shopping mall to the Nordstrom Grill, tucked away at the back of the cosmetics section. It was a contemporary restaurant with subtle lighting and stylish, red leather booths that ran parallel to a long bar.

'Hi,' a server greeted Maddie at the entrance. 'Table for one?'

Maddie craned her neck to see inside. 'Actually, I'm meeting someone. Ah, I see him over in the corner.'

'Here's a menu for you and I'll be over in just a second to take your order.'

'Thanks,' Maddie said, taking the menu and walking over to Clayton.

He stood, smiled and leaned in for a kiss. 'Great to see you, Maddie.'

'You, too. How's your day been? Please tell me you've done something other than hole yourself up in the library again?'

Clayton grinned. 'What can I say? I'm addicted. I've got so much to tell you about what I've found out.'

Maddie held up a hand and said, 'Let's choose first.'

'Oh, I've already chosen: roasted turkey and avocado club, and an iced tea.'

Maddie set down her menu. 'Sounds perfect. I'll just get the same.'

'Okay. So…' Clayton began with an enthusiasm Maddie couldn't help but love. 'My great—hang on, let me get this straight in my head first—my great-great-great-grandma was married and widowed four times. And get this, she actually went to jail for murdering her last husband. Can you believe it? Here, let me show you.'

'Oh, my goodness,' Maddie said, watching as Clayton took a stack of paper from his bag. 'It must be costing you a small fortune in photocopies.'

'Hey, it's worth it.'

'Hi,' a new server greeted. 'Are you ready for me to take your order, or do you need a couple of minutes more?'

'We're ready,' Maddie said. 'Two iced teas and two roasted turkey clubs, please.'

The server jotted it down, smiled and replied, 'Perfect.'

Maddie watched the server strut over to the bar to key in their meals. Suddenly, a wave of uncertainty washed over her, and she felt as though she were living in a parallel universe. 'Clayton, can I ask you something?'

'About my murderous great-great-great-grandma?'

'No. About us.'

'Oh,' he said, putting down the papers that he had been excited to show her. 'This sounds serious.'

'Maybe it is. I mean, all of this—' she pointed to his research, although that really wasn't what she was getting at '—it's great for a vacation but what after that? Where are we headed?'

'I'd like to keep seeing you,' Clayton answered. 'I think we've got something. I hope you do, too?'

'Yes, I do,' she replied honestly. 'But you live two thousand miles away. I've got my kids, my mom, my business…'

'I would move here for you. I mean it,' he said, meeting her eyes.

She hadn't expected that answer. 'Really, though?'

He nodded. 'Well…more for the library, really, but at least I'd be really close by.'

Maddie laughed. 'Be serious, Clayton. You'd really do that…? You'd relocate? What about your work?'

He shrugged. 'I'll find out from Utah POST what they need me to do and—'

'Utah POST?'

'Peace Officer Standards and Training. It's like a transfer process. I'll likely have to undergo a certification review of some kind, but I'll get in,' he replied with confidence.

'So, what time frame are we talking about here?'

Another shrug. 'I'd start the process today, but I guess you also need to answer the question of where we're going.'

Maddie took time to answer. 'I'd like to see where we go…but I'm nervous to ask you to move your life to the other side of the country. Is that even fair? What if it doesn't end up working out for us?'

'Then… I'll either stay here and find myself another investigative genetic genealogist to shack up with or move back home.'

'Let's see if you still feel the same way once you get back home from the vacation,' Maddie said.

The server arrived with their drinks and Clayton raised his glass to Maddie's. 'To our future. To us.'

'To us,' she echoed, trying to let go of all the questions, hopes, fears, doubts and reservations that came with those two simple words. 'So. Let's change the subject, for the moment at least. Tell me all about your wayward great-great-great-grandma.'

Their food arrived while Clayton animatedly talked through his various findings and Maddie's lunch hour turned into two as their conversation switched to a myriad of topics. At the end of lunch, she found herself sad to be leaving his company. 'I take it you're heading back to the library?' she asked him.

'Of course. But I just want to make some calls first. And—just so you know—Utah POST is top of the list.'

'Good luck with that. I was wondering... Could you bear coming over for dinner again this evening?' she asked as she pulled on her jacket.

'Are you kidding? I would love that. What time? I'll be there.'

'Six thirty?'

'Looking forward to it already,' he said, giving her a parting kiss.

'See you tonight, then.'

Maddie strode from the Nordstrom Grill with an inner warmth and a growing confidence that maybe this relationship could work out. She realized then that, since Clayton had been here, she'd thought less and less about what Michael's reaction might have been to how things were turning out for her. What if he were to show up suddenly? What that thought meant unsettled her a great deal.

She walked back to the office much more sedately than how she had rushed to their lunch date, spending the time pondering Michael and Clayton and the complexities of her relationships with both men.

She arrived back at the office at 3:38 p.m., giving her less than one hour to work on her cluster before the briefing. Then, she sat at her desk and saw the twenty-eight new emails that had arrived in her absence. 'Oh, well now, that's just great,' she mumbled, clicking on the first message in the inbox.

At 4:30 p.m., Maddie stood from her desk having achieved nothing on the Hollywood Strangler case at all. She walked out of her office and switched on the digital whiteboard, then set up her laptop ready to do that aspect of Ross's job and take notes from the briefing. 'Is everyone ready?'

When all the team were facing in her direction, she opened with, 'I'll start. I've achieved literally nothing since Friday. Kenyatta, do you want to go next?'

Kenyatta laughed and stood up, waving an orange slip in the air. 'Ta-da! Cluster eight is in the bag at last!'

'Awesome,' Maddie said.

Kenyatta shared her screen and then ran her mouse around a

couple on Kevin Biddlecombe's pedigree. 'Ronald Baldwin and his better half, Margaret Willis, from Tucson, Arizona, are the common ancestors to cluster eight.'

'Right where the Morenos came from—there has to be a convergence there some place. Go put it up on the board,' Maddie said, typing the details into the main case file. 'Hudson, do you want to go next?'

'Sure.'

While Kenyatta attached her orange slip to the board, Hudson stood up and displayed his computer screen for the team to see.

'Well,' he began. 'I was about to complain about my severe lack of headway on cluster seven, but I think Kenyatta might just have handed me the link that I needed.'

Kenyatta paused on her way back to her desk and curtseyed in his direction. 'You're welcome.'

'Look,' he said, bringing up the profile for one of his cluster lead's great-grandfathers.

'Julian Baldwin,' Maddie read out loud. 'From where?'

'Take a guess,' Hudson answered with a grin.

'Tucson, Arizona?' Kenyatta suggested.

'Correct. As you can see, I've yet to identify his parents, but I've got a pretty good idea that they're going to be Ronald Baldwin and Margaret Willis.'

'Wow,' Maddie said. 'That came out of nowhere. You've got some interesting work to do tomorrow, Hudson.'

'Yeah. I would work on it this evening but I'm going out, so it will have to wait.'

'And wait it certainly can,' Maddie agreed. 'Excellent. Reggie?'

'Still slowly pushing on with triangulation within cluster nine,' he informed them, standing up and overriding the whiteboard with his screen. 'I'm working on Lori Fik's tree. Any of these names—Fik, Veneski, Compton or Vabel—familiar to anyone?' He paused and glanced around the office. 'I think one more day of work on trying to link up cluster nine is probably enough with either outcome.'

Maddie nodded in agreement, typing for a moment and then looking up and addressing the team. 'Yeah, I think we're almost at the tipping point into the reverse-genealogy phase here. So, Reggie and I will spend tomorrow trying to close our clusters, but if they're not done by the briefing, we call time of death on them and move on. Hudson, keep going with this possible link between clusters seven and eight. Kenyatta—' Maddie turned to the whiteboard with the common ancestors' details affixed to the top and touched the only blue slip of paper, reminding herself of the names '—start reverse-genealogy for James Fellows and Florence Boicourt. Any questions?'

'Nope. Not from me,' Kenyatta said.

Reggie and Hudson shook their heads, so Maddie closed the briefing. 'Okay. Fantastic work, everyone. We're closing in on him.'

'Amen to that,' Kenyatta replied.

'Have a great evening and I'll see you all back here tomorrow.'

Maddie carried the laptop back into her office and added some final details from the briefing. Given the key point at which the case currently sat, she was anxious to get her cluster closed to join in with the reverse-genealogy phase, but she also needed to get home. It was Katie's night off and she'd told Clayton to come over at six thirty, so she needed to lock up and get out.

Before she closed her laptop, she took one final cursory glance at the Venator inbox. Another forty-seven emails had arrived. She groaned and shut the lid.

Maddie arrived home to find the house unusually peaceful. She stood in the hall listening for any signs of life. Nothing, which was simultaneously a joy and a worry. Then, she remembered that Trenton was at his friend's house for the evening. She took off her shoes and jacket and quietly stepped into the kitchen, finding Katie wiping down the counters.

'Hey,' Maddie whispered, knowing that if Katie had the time for domestic chores, then her mom was likely asleep.

'Hi, Maddie. Your mom's taking a nap in her room.'

'How's she been today?'

Katie screwed her face up. 'Not so good. She was quite vocal this morning and didn't want to do anything, which has pretty much worn her right out. Let her sleep if you can.'

'Oh, I won't wake her,' Maddie replied. 'Well, it's your evening off. So, you go and enjoy it. And, as always, thank you so much for your help.'

'You're welcome. Okay, then. See you in the morning.'

'Bye, Katie,' Maddie said, waiting until the front door closed. Then, she took out her cell phone and video-called Becky. In just a few rings, it was answered.

'Hey, Maddie. Good to see you,' Becky greeted. 'Is everything okay?'

Maddie could see by the surroundings that Becky was in her apartment in Port-au-Prince. 'Yeah, it's all good. How are things with you out there?'

Becky smiled, appearing as relaxed and happy as she usually did. 'Good, thanks.'

'Really?' Maddie countered. 'I keep hearing bad things on the news about the gangs taking over the country. Are you safe there?'

Becky shrugged. 'Well, it's like anywhere. There are good and bad neighborhoods. Some places I wouldn't go anywhere near, others are okay.'

'I worry about you, Becky.'

'You don't need to, Maddie. Honestly. And it's not forever.'

'How long *is* it for?'

Becky sighed, tucked an errant strand of hair behind her ear and answered, 'I'm not sure. Still a while longer.'

'Listen,' Maddie said, wanting to get to the point before the connection could fail. 'Have you found anything out there that links what happened to Michael and his visit to Haiti? And the other two guys?'

'I'm working on it. I don't have any concrete proof yet but, yes, I think there is a connection.'

'Can I ask what it might be?'

'Maddie, what is it you tell detectives who want early answers on an IGG case?' Becky asked. She was smiling but the tone was clear.

Maddie nodded. It was a fair point that didn't need answering.

'I promise that I'll tell you the second that I can,' Becky tried to reassure her.

Given the volatile situation in Haiti, Maddie's thoughts went to a dark place: if something bad happened to Becky, the truth would never come out. But this wasn't a fear that she could readily vocalize. 'Is someone working with you on this?' was the best that she could say to try and allay her worries.

'Uh-huh,' came Becky's vague response.

'Is this connected to your father throwing you and Ross out of your apartment?' Maddie asked.

'I think so, yes. My parents aren't talking to me, so I haven't heard anything directly from them, but I think it's in retaliation for what I'm doing out here. How's Ross coping with it?'

'He'll be okay. I've given him a few days off to get the apartment packed up.'

'Thanks, Maddie.'

'Well, whatever it is you're doing out there, please don't do anything that will get you into danger or trouble,' Maddie said.

'I won't.'

'Okay. Well, you take care and let me know if there's anything that I can do to help.'

'Thanks, Maddie. Goodbye.'

'Bye,' Maddie replied and ended the call. She held her cell in her hand, staring at the blank screen. She was certain that Becky's outwardly happy and positive demeanor was just a brave, thin façade. She also didn't believe that Becky would stay out of harm's way in her quest to get to the truth. Maddie felt helpless about the whole situation. There were so many questions and so few avenues to pursue in search of the answers.

She put her cell phone down and put relaxing jazz music on Spotify as she turned her thoughts over to what she was going to make for dinner, something that she hadn't even considered before inviting Clayton over. Maybe it was a good sign for their relationship that she didn't feel the need to cook to impress. She opened the refrigerator, but the ingredients made no sense. So, she picked her cell phone up again and sent Clayton a message. *Take out good for you?*

He answered instantly. *Perfect.*

Maddie gave his reply a heart emoji reaction. She looked at the time and realized that now she didn't need to cook, she had time to run a bath. She stood up and made her way out of the kitchen just as Trenton burst through the front door, yelling, 'Mom—oh, there you are. I was just going to—'

'Ssshh!' Maddie said as she reached the hall. 'Grandma's asleep and I kind of wanted to leave it that way.'

'Oh, sorry. I was just going to ask if I could stay over at Kevin's tonight?'

'It's a school night.'

'Yeah, but we're working on a science project that is kind of due tomorrow,' he said with a wince.

'Trenton.'

'I know. But we can get it done tonight. I just might be a little tired in the morning.'

'Okay. But this isn't happening again. Next time, it's tough. We're not making a habit of this, you hear?' Maddie said.

'What's all the yelling?' her mom said from the top of the stairs. She was in her night dress with disheveled hair. 'Is father home?'

Maddie didn't bother to question to which father she might be referring. 'No, not yet.'

'That's a real pity,' her mom said. 'I got all dressed up, thinking he was home.'

'Well, you look very nice, Mom. Come down and I'll fix you a drink.'

'I'll have a wine,' her mom said, taking her time to put both feet on each step as she descended. Every day there were signs of a new regression, or some skill or piece of knowledge that slipped into the widening darkness inside her brain.

'Watch her,' Maddie whispered to Trenton as she returned to the kitchen and poured some non-alcoholic wine into a plastic cup. 'Here you go,' she said, handing it over when eventually her mom shuffled into the kitchen.

'Thank you,' she replied. 'Have I got time to change before dinner?'

'There's no need to change, Mom. You're beautiful exactly as you are. I've got Clayton coming over for a take-out shortly.'

'Who?'

'Clayton... The guy I'm dating.'

Her mom raised her eyebrows and took a sip of drink. 'I'm not sure I approve of you dating boys at your age, Madison.'

Maddie couldn't help but grin at Trenton at that comment. 'Well, he's coming over later. How about you wait and see if you like him.'

'I'm going to grab my stuff and head out,' Trenton said, heading for the stairs. 'Good luck, tonight.'

'Thanks,' Maddie muttered, bolting the front door and returning to the kitchen in the knowledge that she would no longer be able to bathe or get ready for Clayton coming over. 'Do you want to do a jigsaw puzzle?'

Maddie's mom smiled. 'Sure, why not?'

'Great. I'll go get that nice kitten one that you like.'

Maddie took the box from a stack of kids' jigsaws and set the twelve pieces out on the table. She feigned difficulty, allowing her mom to take the lead. But that just led to frustration, so Maddie pieced together the top and bottom edges, leaving just four pieces for her mom to assemble.

Twenty minutes later, just as her mom positioned the final piece, the doorbell sounded.

'Yes!' Maddie said, standing from the table. 'Amazing job, Mom.'

Her mom smiled. 'See, I've still got it.'

'You sure have.' Maddie was relieved that her mom seemed to be in a good state of mind and hoped that it would continue for the rest of the evening. She unfastened the multiple locks on the door and smiled when Clayton presented her with a large bunch of red and white roses. Even though he appeared perfectly smart at lunch time, he'd changed into a fresh pair of pants and a white shirt that clung tightly over his biceps. He was definitely dressed to impress.

'I did it,' he said, entering the house.

'Did what? What did you do?'

'I completed the Utah Peace Officer waiver application form.'

'Oh,' Maddie said, taken aback. 'So, that's it? You're transferring to Utah?'

'Well, uh, no,' he answered, obviously registering her surprise. 'It's just the first step. They might not accept my application. And then there's a knowledge exam and a fitness test. Don't worry, I'm not moving here next week, Maddie, and I can always back out.'

She could see that it was just a first step; but it was a *major* first step and one she wasn't sure she was ready for just yet.

Chapter Twenty-Four

Tuesday, November 15, 2022, Salt Lake City, Utah

Hudson was eager to get to his desk this morning. It was 8:49 a.m., and he was standing outside the Venator office, waiting with a growing impatience for Maddie to arrive and open up. While he waited, he looked at a message from Nora that had arrived on his walk in this morning.

I really enjoyed last night. Wanna do it again some time?

Me too and yes, definitely. When are you free? He texted back.

After their first meeting at the Coffee Garden on Saturday had gone so well, they'd arranged dinner last night at the Tsunami Restaurant and Sushi Bar on Harvey Milk Boulevard in the Ninth and Ninth neighborhood. He'd arrived early at the restaurant and, as he'd waited nervously outside, he'd witnessed a bizarre sight at the end of the block: Reggie had darted across the street, weaving through the busy traffic, and placed a small object down on the roundabout beneath the huge whale art installation. Hudson had been utterly perplexed by what he had witnessed but had stepped back to avoid being noticed. He hadn't seen Reggie since to ask what on earth had been going on with him.

Nora had arrived for their date exactly on time. She'd been wearing over-sized bleached jeans, a baggy sweater and a vintage-style lieutenant's cap. The evening had gone well, and he had enjoyed getting to know her over fresh sushi. He'd quickly relaxed in her company and had found that they had a lot in common.

Friday night? Wanna come to my place? I do the best tuna lasagna, Nora replied.

Sounds great! Looking forward to it, he answered with a smile on his face and a smiley emoji on the text.

'Good news?' It was Maddie, arriving at the top of the stairs.

'Yeah, I guess you could say that,' Hudson answered.

'Cool,' Maddie said, unlocking the door. 'I guess you're here early to work on your cluster-seven-and-eight convergence?'

'Exactly. I want to get that blue slip up on the board,' he said, heading over to his computer.

'Can I get you one?' she asked, firing up the overworked office coffee machine.

'Yes, please.' He sat down and started up his computer, opening Julian Baldwin's profile on the family tree. Currently, the two spaces for Julian's parents read + *Add father* and + *Add mother*, which was precisely what Hudson was about to try and do. If the obvious puzzle pieces were to fit into place, then those names should be Ronald Baldwin and Margaret Willis.

Hudson only liked to check the hints listed against individuals once he had conducted his own investigation but, on this occasion, he wanted to shortcut the process. At the top of the list of hints was *Ancestry member trees*, which he very rarely looked at, owing to the shockingly high percentage of inaccuracies. Next in the list was a hint for the 1900 U.S. Census, which he opened.

Ronald Baldwin, head of family, white, male, born March 1870, married 10 years, born Arizona
Margaret Baldwin, wife, white, female, born July 1870, married, three of four children still alive, born Arizona
Julian Baldwin, son, white, male, born November 1891, single, born Arizona
Theresa Baldwin, daughter, white, female, born April 1893, single, born Arizona
Clyde Baldwin, son, white, male, born December 1896, single, born Arizona

Before he saved the entry, Hudson checked the speculative tree that Kenyatta had created and confirmed that Theresa Baldwin was Jean Adam's—the lead of cluster eight—great-grandmother, and Clyde Baldwin was the second in the cluster, Kevin Biddlecombe's great-grandfather.

'Here's your first fix of caffeine for the day,' Maddie said, placing a cup of coffee on his desk.

'Thanks. I think I'll need plenty of that,' he replied, leaning back and showing Maddie the screen. 'I've just found the Baldwins on the 1900 census and it does look like Julian Baldwin is one of the killer's direct ancestors. I just need to shore up the evidence.'

'Excellent, keep going.'

Hudson worked through several more sources, saving them to the tree as he went. The final confirmation that he was working on the right lines came from Julian Baldwin's birth certificate, which he found on the FamilySearch website. The parent details matched those of Theresa and Clyde's identically. All this work served to confirm with absolute certainty that Julian Baldwin was indeed a great-grandfather of the Hollywood Strangler.

Hudson completed a blue slip of paper for Julian, adding his wife's name, Deborah Lippkee, in brackets, as, so far, there was no genetic proof that she was also related to the killer. Time and research would provide certainty.

He carried the piece of paper over to the whiteboard, attaching it beside that of James Fellows and Florence Boicourt. The team were now in possession of three—possibly four—of the killer's eight great-grandparents. Hudson stared at the board, having absolutely no doubt that they were on the verge of identifying one of the most notorious serial killers in U.S. history.

'Admiring your handiwork, huh?' Kenyatta said with a chuckle as she strolled into the office.

'Oh, yes. I've just confirmed that Julian Baldwin was the brother to your Clyde and Theresa.'

'Awesome job!' she congratulated, looking at the board. 'Two blue slips and they're both yours.'

'Hey, it's a team effort,' he said, heading back to his desk. He sat down just as Reggie arrived with his usual morning joviality.

'Good morning, Venator!' Reggie said, clearly imitating the style of Robin Williams's character in *Good Morning, Vietnam.*

'Morning,' Hudson replied, less enthusiastically. He hadn't seen Reggie since he'd set off snowboarding early Sunday morning and he wasn't sure whether to ask about what he'd seen happening at the whale on Ninth and Ninth last night, since it would inevitably lead to questions about what he himself had been doing there. Reggie had also still not told him about his relationship with Ross and Hudson now wondered if perhaps there was nothing to tell because there *was* no relationship. He'd seen Reggie reaching out for Ross's hand, nothing more than that.

'Anyone needs their caffeine levels topped up?' Reggie asked.

'I'm good thanks. The boss lady beat you to it,' Hudson answered, holding up his full cup and then taking a sip before returning to Julian Baldwin's profile. Having married in 1912, Julian and his wife, Deborah, had had six children. One of those, Gabriella, was the grandmother of the cluster-seven lead person, eliminating her from his inquiries and leaving the other five needing to be fleshed out as far as possible. One of those five was highly likely to be the killer's grandparent. The key would be identifying each of their spouses, hoping that a surname from one of the other clusters would appear.

Hudson looked at the five children, opting to work through them systematically in order of their births. First up was Elias Baldwin, who, according to the census, had been born in Tucson, Arizona, in 1913, which Hudson confirmed with his birth certificate. He then pulled up the 1940 census, which was the first where Elias had not been recorded in the family home. There had been several Elias Baldwins recorded in the state of Arizona, but only the top person had been born in Tucson. He clicked to view it and found that it showed a married couple named Elias and Mollie Baldwin, with their two sons, living in the city of his birth. The entry looked to be correct but, before Hudson updated the family tree with the new information, he wanted to be certain that he had the right Elias.

In a new browser tab, he pulled up *Arizona, County Marriages, 1871-1964* from FamilySearch and ran a search for the couple. He hit the first in the list, dated 1936, and clicked *view original document*. It was brief and, unfortunately, didn't name Elias's parents, although it did provide confirmation of Mollie's surname: Parsons.

He wanted to push on, harvesting vital records for Elias Baldwin and his kids, but he still wasn't sure if he had the correct person.

Returning to Julian Baldwin's profile, Hudson ran a search for his obituary. He found nothing at GenealogyBank but had a stroke of luck at Newspapers.com. A short obit had appeared in the August 10, 1949 edition of the *Arizona Daily Star*.

Julian Baldwin, 58, of 45 West Rillito Road, died in a local hospital yesterday morning. He had lived in Tucson his whole life. He leaves his wife, Deborah; three daughters, Gabriella (Fred) Clinton, Frances (Bob) Selmes, Jacqueline Baldwin; and three sons, Elias, John and Terence. Funeral arrangements will be announced later by the Arizona Mortuary.

Hudson saved the document to the profiles of everyone mentioned in the story, then he updated Frances Baldwin's tree to include the name of her husband. The record was invaluable for this point in the investigation, but it still did not tie Elias, the son of Julian and Deborah, with Elias, the husband of Mollie Parsons.

Hudson opened the Word document that Ross maintained for the investigation as a whole. It contained a summary of the key aspects of the case and every name and location that came out of the team's research as it proceeded. The data was presented in a variety of ways: alphabetized, by geographical area and by cluster. Hudson searched the whole document for the name Parsons, but there were no hits. While he had the file open, he looked for any mention of the surnames Clinton or Selmes that had come out of Julian Baldwin's obit but again received no hits.

He finished his coffee, which had gone cold, and considered the implications of the negative search result. If the research to this point had been correct, then one of Julian Baldwin's children *should* have intersected with a family from another cluster. There were plenty of explanations for the lack of convergence, however, so he wasn't unduly concerned for the moment. For now, his attention was firmly on Elias, and Hudson set about searching for him in the 1950 U.S. Census. Adding Mollie as his spouse in the search boxes led to just a single result.

Baldwin, Elias, head, male, white, age 37, married, born Arizona
Baldwin, Mollie, wife, female, white, age 35, married, born Arizona

Baldwin, Phillip, son, male, white, age 13, single, born Arizona
Baldwin, Evan, son, male, white, age 11, single, born Arizona
Baldwin, Deborah, mother, female, white, age 58, widowed, born Arizona

Deborah's presence in the household confirmed what Hudson needed to know. He saved the document, then turned his efforts briefly to the two children, Phillip and Evan. At this stage, he still had Elias's four other siblings to investigate, not knowing which of them was the killer's grandparent, so he didn't want to spend hours working on a potentially dead lead. He checked out the hints for Phillip's and Evan's profiles, looking for any potential spouses. If the suggestions were to be believed—which Hudson might need to confirm later—then Phillip had married someone with the surname Shapiro, and Evan had married someone called Meenan.

He ran a search for the two surnames in the alphabetized list for the case but there were no matches. Although it didn't rule out Elias Baldwin's branch of the family, the lack of evidence made Hudson think that the killer did not descend from this side, and so he switched his focus to the next of Julian and Deborah's children: John Baldwin.

John's birth certificate stated that he had been born in Tucson in 1914. He'd been recorded in the family home on census records from 1920 to 1940, so Hudson looked him up in 1950. He found a possible match in Hamilton County, Ohio, living with a wife, Ruby, and a two-month-old daughter, Patricia. Their marriage certificate, which he found on FamilySearch, confirmed this to be the correct candidate, as his parents were listed as Julian and Deborah Baldwin. He also gleaned Ruby's maiden name, Baylor, from the certificate. But when Hudson ran it through the list of names associated with the case, he once again drew a blank. Undeterred, he used a combination of record sets to build out John and Ruby's family tree. After some time, he had conclusively added four daughters and one son. None of their spouses' surnames were on the list, making Hudson believe that the Hollywood Strangler did not descend from John Baldwin.

The third of Julian and Deborah's children was named Terence, and he was born in Tucson in 1915. Before he got into the research again, Hudson went to get a fresh brew, asking if anyone wanted any as he walked.

'Yes, please,' Reggie replied, adding, 'I might just have broken open cluster nine.'

'Oh, well done,' Kenyatta praised.

'Yeah, let's not celebrate too soon, though,' Reggie countered, 'I'm not quite there.'

Hudson stuck his head inside Maddie's office. 'Can I get you some coffee?'

She looked up and seemed to take an age to answer the simple question. 'Yes, thanks. Did Reggie just say he's nearly done with his cluster?'

'Yeah,' Hudson confirmed.

'That means I need to get a move on. How are you doing?'

'Working my way through Julian and Deborah Baldwin's kids, but I'm getting no overlaps so far.'

'Well, keep going. We've got—' she screwed her eyes up and stared at her laptop clock '—five blink-and-you'll-miss-'em hours until the briefing.'

The clock was ticking and the whole team was starting to feel the mounting tension that always seemed to hit when they reached this part of the reverse-genealogy phase. To get this far was like reaching the top of the rollercoaster ride; the end was in sight, and it would come rushing forward fast.

Hudson hurried through the process of making three coffees. He carried Maddie's into her office. 'Here's your next fix of caffeine for the day,' he said, playing on Maddie's earlier comments to him.

'Thanks, but I need more than caffeine right now. I'll need a miracle to close down this cluster.'

Hudson knew Maddie well enough to know that there was little point in offering her reassuring platitudes or even help; she needed to solve it for herself. Besides which, if *she* couldn't figure it out, then it probably couldn't be done. He wished her luck, backed out of her office and took Reggie his coffee before returning to his workstation.

Following the same pattern with the previous two Baldwin boys, Hudson searched for Terence on the 1950 census.

'Oh,' he mumbled, clicking the top-most result.

Baldwin, Terence, prisoner, white, male, single, born Arizona

Terence had been recorded in the Pima County Jail in 1950. Suddenly, Hudson's thoughts rushed ahead of him with ideas that maybe criminality might run through the bloodline of this side of the family all the way down to the killer. What was Terence imprisoned for and did he have a documented spouse or children? Hudson wondered, taking a sip of his drink and setting about answering those questions.

He spent some time searching online for historic criminal records, only managing to find Ancestry's *Arizona, U.S., State Prison Records, 1875-1929* record set. Despite the fact that Terence would have been fourteen years old at the time of the records' termination, Hudson still searched for him. Unsurprisingly, the result came back negative. Instead, Hudson went looking for a newspaper report of whatever crime had sent Terence to jail. He found it in the April 16, 1948 edition of *Tucson Citizen*.

Escaped Slayer Captured in Ohio
Terence Baldwin, the 33-year-old Tucson resident wanted on a second-degree murder charge following the shooting of George Shorewood is now in a Hamilton, Ohio jail following his arrest by the FBI in that state on Friday. Baldwin, who jumped a $1,500 bond, had been missing since the shooting in January of this year and failed to put in an appearance for his trial. The FBI tracked him to his brother, John Baldwin's, address in Ohio. He will be returned here immediately to face second-degree murder charges in which the county alleges that he shot Shorewood believing him to have been having an affair with his wife, Mrs. Lucinda Baldwin, who strongly denies the allegation.

Hudson saved the story with great intrigue, noting that Terence had had a wife, Lucinda, named in the article. He drank some coffee, wondering if his theory about a criminal family might actually be borne out. He needed to know Lucinda's maiden name and whether any children had been recorded belonging to the couple.

'Yes!' Reggie said, punching the air.

'Cluster nine?' Kenyatta asked.

'Yeah. Everybody, keep your eyes open for the surnames Serano or Soto from California,' Reggie informed them. 'Most recent common ancestors for cluster nine.'

'Will do,' Kenyatta replied.

'Good work,' Hudson commented, making a mental note of the names before resuming his own work. He spent some time in vain trying to track down Terence Baldwin's marriage to Lucinda.

After almost another hour of searching, Hudson had managed to derive Lucinda's maiden name from her Social Security Application. But the surname that it revealed, Conover, didn't show up in the list of people connected to this case. He found more newspaper articles about Terence's criminal career and, by the time Hudson had created a solid biography for the man, he had determined that the couple had died childless, pushing his theory into the realms of serious doubt. Since there were only two more siblings to research, and one of those, Jacqueline, appeared not to have married, Hudson began to worry that they were facing the possibility of a non-paternity event with Terence having fathered a child for which not a shred of official documentation would exist.

Right now, he needed to park that bleak possibility and continue working on Julian and Deborah Baldwin's kids. Next up chronologically was Gabriella, the grandmother of the cluster seven lead. The amount of shared DNA between the cluster lead and the killer ruled out Gabriella's descendants as being potential suspects, so Hudson moved on to sibling five: Frances Baldwin.

Maddie appeared in Hudson's peripheral vision. 'I'm just quickly shooting over to Eva's. Anyone need anything?'

'Are you not going out for lunch today?' Kenyatta asked.

'I was supposed to, but I've cancelled,' Maddie admitted. 'I'm way behind on my work and, with Ross off, I simply can't justify it. I'm sure Clayton's secretly pleased, though, as it means he gets to spend more time in the library. So, does anyone want anything?'

Hudson had brought lunch from home but was still very tempted to get something from the bakery. He thought about it but declined her offer, as did Reggie and Kenyatta.

He returned his focus to Frances Baldwin, finding her birth

recorded in Tucson in 1918. He'd already saved her appearance in the family home on the 1920 to 1940 censuses to her profile. According to her father's 1949 obit, Frances had married someone by the name of Bob Selmes and, using the combination of the two names, Hudson easily found them living in California in 1950.

He was intrigued to see that Bob's occupation had been listed as a *studio grip*, which he took to mean working in the movie industry. He looked at the precise address, 5788 Kraft Avenue, Los Angeles, and put it into Google. 'Wow,' he muttered.

'Wow what...?' Reggie asked.

'One of the Baldwin kids lived smack dab in the middle of Hollywood in 1950,' Hudson said.

'So, you found the convergence point?' Kenyatta asked.

Hudson shook his head. 'No, not yet. And, so far, no recorded kids.'

'Well, you've got three hours until the briefing,' Kenyatta said with a laugh. 'Knock yourself out.'

Hudson returned to the Word document for the case and, rather than run a *Find* search for the whole file, went to the alphabetized list of all surnames and slowly checked it in its entirety for any possible spelling variations of Selmes. He found nothing even remotely similar.

Something was off, but Hudson couldn't put his finger on it.

He used the Research Wiki on FamilySearch to locate marriage records for Frances Baldwin and Bob Selmes, and then worked through the various links, finding nothing. Feeling the growing weight of pressure from the looming briefing, Hudson looked at the family tree suggestions offered in the hints for Frances's name. None of the member trees included a spouse or children.

He found the dates of Frances's and Bob's deaths but couldn't find an obit for either person. Find a Grave recorded that they had been buried together in Mount Sinai Memorial Park, close to the Warner Brothers Studio. Hudson Googled the park, which informed him that it was the final resting place of several Hollywood stars, including Bette Davis, Carrie Fisher, Debbie Reynolds and Stan Laurel.

The more Hudson searched and gradually added tidbits of genealogical information to Frances Baldwin's profile, the more convinced he became that her address in North Hollywood was a red herring and that, actually, her brother, Terence, was the person he should be concentrating on. He still had the final sibling, Jacqueline, to research, so perhaps it was neither who was the killer's ancestor.

With the briefing just minutes away, Hudson switched to Jacqueline's profile hints, quickly scouring the results for any mention of a spouse or children. There was nothing obvious.

Maddie stepped out of her office, saying the words that he was not at all ready to hear. 'Five minutes, team!'

Hudson sat back in his chair, taking stock of all six of the Baldwin siblings. If he had to triage them right now, he would put Terence at the top because of his criminal background, closely followed by Frances because of her geographical area. Out of all the siblings, one of those two was the most likely to have had a child with someone from another cluster.

'Hey, Reggie,' Hudson began. 'Where did your cluster nine MRCAs come from?'

'San Diego,' he replied.

California. The link had to be there.

As he watched Maddie switching on the digital whiteboard, Hudson pulled up Frances Baldwin's profile, wondering if Terence's criminal history had given him a confirmation bias toward him, while Frances was the most obvious candidate. At the briefing, he would raise his thoughts and theories and ask Maddie to request that the detectives running the investigation search records closed to the public for a child born in California to Frances Baldwin, but who had been adopted.

As Maddie opened the briefing, Hudson sighed at having devised a plan to move his stalemate forward.

'Well,' Maddie said to the team. 'In what appears to be becoming a shameful habit, I don't have much to say.' She was sitting at the vacant desk close to the board with her laptop open in front of her. She clicked to share her screen. 'I've tried everything to link the genetic families together, but the paper trail just isn't there. Any of these names familiar?' She scrolled slowly down the list of direct ancestors for her cluster lead, then repeated it for two other people within the cluster. As she had clearly found, there were no duplicate surnames.

Her team members were apologetically silent.

'Okay, then I'm calling time of death on cluster five. Reggie, wanna show me up with your work on cluster nine?'

'Sure,' he said, overriding her screen with his. 'As I think I might have mentioned earlier, I finally broke this genetic network wide open.' He ran his cursor in circles over the names of the two most recent common ancestors. 'Ramon Serano and Anita Soto from San Diego, California. Immigration from Mexico—plus several divorces—made this a tough one to crack, but I got there in the end.'

'Well done,' Maddie said. 'With my failure, that's all clusters finished. We're now very much into the reverse-genealogy phase. How have you got on with that, Kenyatta?'

Kenyatta took in a long breath and stood up, sharing her screen which displayed a vertical family tree for James Fellows and his wife, Florence Boicourt. 'Anyone see the problem I'm having here?'

Hudson grinned. As he had found previously, the pair had had twelve children. He watched the board as Kenyatta clicked each profile once, which revealed a multitude of birth and death locations, but Hudson's thoughts had hooked into something that Reggie had just said about his cluster and what had made it hard to solve. He replayed the sentence in his mind: *Immigration from Mexico, plus several divorces.*

He glanced up as Kenyatta was explaining about the trouble she was having with pinning down James and Florence Fellows's children, while he discreetly pulled up *California, County Marriages, 1850-1952* from FamilySearch. When the search box opened, he subtly clicked *More Options* and typed in Frances's first name with no surname and a date range from 1933 to 1949. *Filtered Results (408,561).* Far too many to sort. He clicked to add a spouse, typing in Selmes. *Filtered Results (21).*

'Thanks, Kenyatta,' Maddie said. 'Hudson. Your turn.'

'Uh, one second. The wait could be worth it,' he said, quickly scanning down the list of marriages, hoping that by not stipulating Frances's surname he might hit upon a previous marriage.

Halfway down the page he found it. He clicked the entry to see a scan of the original marriage certificate for *Robin Selmer*—the misspelling having been part of the reason for his failure to find it previously—then shared his screen, zooming in on the bride section.

Full name: Frances Moreno
Residence: 1596 Chickasaw Ave, L.A.
Color or Race: White
Age at last birthday: 19
Single, Widowed or Divorced: Divorced
Number of Marriage: 2
Birthplace: Tucson, Arizona
Name of Father: Julian Baldwin
Birthplace of Father: Tucson, Arizona
Maiden name of Mother: Deborah Lippkee
Birthplace of Mother: Tucson, Arizona

'Her first marriage was to a *Moreno*?' Maddie stammered.

'Uh-huh,' Hudson confirmed. 'But I don't have his name as of yet.'

'But you've just identified one set of the Hollywood Strangler's grandparents.'

'It sure looks that way, yeah.'

Chapter Twenty-Five

Wednesday, November 16, 2022, Salt Lake City, Utah

Reggie was cradling his mug in his hand as he stared at the digital whiteboard. It was just after nine in the morning and Hudson had requested a briefing to explain his rushed findings from last night. It was inevitable that following his discovery of Frances Baldwin marrying someone from the Moreno family that he would continue his work once he got home.

On the screen was a scanned original of Frances Baldwin's Los Angeles marriage certificate. It wasn't the same one that Hudson had shown them at the briefing yesterday; this was for her first marriage, to one Joe Moreno.

'Come on, Hudson. You're killing me,' Maddie said with her fists clenched. 'Does Joe Moreno fit into my cluster three or not? Is his father, Emilano, the son of Samuel Moreno?'

Reggie also wanted him to cut to the chase. 'And I see his mother is listed as Rita Cameron. Is that the Cameron family from my cluster four? The Scottish link?'

Hudson grinned, clearly enjoying the building up of drama that he was causing his colleagues. 'Patience, my fellow genealogists. Patience.'

'Lord, give me strength,' Kenyatta said.

Hudson pulled up Joe Moreno's family tree profile and hit *View in tree*. All of their questions were immediately answered.

'And there it is, right there,' Reggie said, seeing the results of their individual work being dramatically pulled together. Joe's paternal line went through Emilano to Samuel Moreno, the MRCA for cluster three; while his maternal line ran through Rita, her father Peter, to his parents, Bryce Cameron and Aisla Baird, the MRCAs Reggie had identified for cluster four.

'Perfect,' Maddie said. 'So, now click *Joe's children* and let's see what we're looking at. Come on.'

Another grin from Hudson as he clicked the small arrow below Joe Moreno's avatar. Six children appeared.

'*Lenore, Margarita, Delia, Carlos, Fernando and Christina Moreno,*'

Maddie read out. 'One of those six people is the Hollywood Strangler's parent. This is fantastic work, everyone. We now know *a lot* about one side of the killer's family. Hudson, I need a green slip of paper with Joe Moreno and Frances Baldwin on it, please.' She turned to the static whiteboard and began to move the orange, purple and blue slips of paper, dividing them into two separate groups, representing the two established sides of the killer's family. 'Obviously we don't yet know which side is paternal and which side is maternal, but clusters three, four, seven and eight all link up on this one side of his family, giving us all four great-grandparents and both grandparents.'

'Here you go,' Hudson said, presenting her with the requested green slip of paper containing the names of Joe Moreno and Frances Baldwin.

'Thanks,' she said, arranging the papers like an inverted pyramid with the orange slips at the top, purple below those, then blue and finally the green slip that Hudson had just given her. She half-turned so that she was angled toward both the team and the board. 'We're still looking for how clusters one, two and six relate to each other. We *should* have a convergence between a Serano and an Olmstead descendant, and then one of *their* children should converge with a child of James Fellows and Florence Boicourt.' She smiled. 'We're so close. Really close. Okay, let's assign jobs for the day. Kenyatta, are you happy to focus on the children of James Fellows and Florence Boicourt?'

'Sure thing. I'm on it,' she answered.

'Hudson, I think you need to continue working on the six Moreno kids. Reggie, can you take Ramon Serano and Anita Soto's offspring?'

'Yes, ma'am,' he replied, pleased to be picking up again with his cluster nine.

'And I—for all the use I seem to be to you all, right now—will work on Herman Olmstead and Gertrude Tapinala's kids and then grandkids from cluster six. Any questions?'

Although the team was silent, there was a palpable buzz of energy in the air. Despite this being Reggie's first IGG case, he knew that they had reached a pivotal and decisive moment.

'Oh, before you get on with Joe and Frances's kids, Hudson,

could you run Moreno, Olmstead and Fellows through the Y-DNA database, please?'

'Already did last night,' he replied with a smile. 'Negative on all three.'

Maddie nodded, knowing that a negative result didn't mean that they had made a mistake or were on the wrong tracks. There were various reasons why the killer's own surname might not appear in the Y-DNA match list.

'Okay, let's go,' Maddie said, scooping up her laptop and retreating to her office.

Reggie opened the tree for Ramon Serano. He and his wife, Anita, had been born in Mexico in the 1860s, then entered the U.S. in 1888, with him working as a miner in Yuma County, Arizona. Reggie had found them living in San Diego on the 1900 census with their five children, Joaquin, Sofia, Miguel, Lucia and Rafael. Of those five, Joaquin and Lucia were ruled out from the killer's direct line, as the shared DNA was too little and they were the pair who had linked the genetic network together, giving their parents, Ramon and Anita as the most recent common ancestors. Sofia, Miguel and Rafael needed deep investigation to try and find the point of convergence with another cluster.

Reggie clicked on Sofia's profile. Everything that he knew about her came from the 1900 U.S. Census where she was recorded as having been born in July 1889 in California. She was not in the family home ten years later, so he opened the 1910 census and ran a search for her there. Of the thirteen results presented, all except one—which he now selected to view—were spelling variations. The entry was correct but unrevealing. Sofia was living as a boarder in the home of Santa Ana Romero and her daughter, Rosario. Reggie was confident from the given information about her and her parents' birthplaces that he had found the correct person, so he saved the entry to her profile and then moved on a decade to 1920.

As he scanned down the list of results, he saw his cell phone light up on the desk beside him. He picked it up to see that it was a text from Ross.

Hi. Have you had a chance to ask Hudson about me moving in for a short while until I get a place?

Reggie felt a wave of guilt at his not yet having asked Hudson. Although it was true that he'd not seen much of him in the past few days because he'd been busy helping Ross to pack up his apartment, Reggie guessed that he had also been putting it off in case Hudson said no, as Ross had predicted that he might.

Not yet, he texted back. *I'll do it today, promise. How's the packing going?*

Slowly and painfully, came the response a few seconds later.

Reggie answered, *I'll help again tonight. Don't stress.*

Ross came back with a thumbs up and Reggie returned his attention to the 1920 search results. None of them seemed obviously correct, but he clicked on several to double-check. Having gone through several of the results, Reggie theorized that Sofia might have married or died in the intervening decade.

Opening up the links to vital records for California on FamilySearch, Reggie worked his way through the four marriage indexes, searching for Sofia but finding nothing.

'Come on,' he whispered to himself, conscious of time passing with nothing yet to show for it. He turned back to the main record set, *California, County Marriages, 1850-1953*, and hit the *How to use this collection* button. He wasn't seeking guidance on how to use it, but rather to get a look at the *Coverage Table* which detailed precisely how many records for each county were included in the database. He scrolled down to San Diego and found the answer: *0*.

'Great,' he said, flipping back to the 1920 census and trying a new tactic. He edited the search by removing Sofia's surname and adding a birthplace and residence in 1920 of San Diego, then hit *search*.

1-50 of 1,536,771

It was a hopeless number to cross-check. He sighed, got up and went across to Maddie's office. 'Hey, have you got anywhere yet with the Olmsteads?'

Maddie looked as frustrated as he did. 'Nope. Two hours now, and nothing. I'm really starting to think I've lost my touch.'

'Is any gender more likely on the Serano side to help me narrow my focus?'

She shook her head. 'I've managed to eliminate one girl who died in infancy, but that's it. I'm working on a son at the moment, but he appears to have had just one marriage. I took a quick look at his kids, as they're the ones who we should find interacting with a Serano, but nothing jumps out. I'll shout as soon as I know something either way.'

'Me too,' he said, hurrying back to his desk.

He checked in the various death indexes for California to see if Sofia had died between 1910 and 1920 but found nothing. Hints for her name also contained nothing beyond that which he had already discovered.

Reggie closed his eyes and consciously caused his mind to stop thinking about the problem altogether, allowing his brain some minutes to analyze the conundrum in the background.

After a while, Hudson asked, 'Aww. Has your mystery date been keeping you up at night? You poor tired thing.'

Reggie smiled but didn't open his eyes. 'I'm letting my mind do its thing and work the Snowwolf magic.'

Hudson groaned.

The moment of detachment gave Reggie the clarity that he was getting nowhere fast with Sofia. His thoughts pushed him to Sofia's parents. He opened his eyes and clicked on Ramon Serano's profile. He'd found no obituary for him or his wife, Anita, but he had found their burial locations on BillionGraves.com. Reggie navigated via the link in Ramon's profile to his entry on the website. It contained a photo of the simple headstone and details of the inscription. He looked for any mention of other family members or public comments that might have been made on the page, but he found none. Under the photograph of the headstone was a hyperlink for *Mount Hope Cemetery*, which he followed, landing on the main page for this San Diego burial location. According to the cemetery details, there were 45,454 records for interments there. In the search boxes in the top menu, Reggie entered Sofia's first name, leaving the other fields completely blank.

Five results, but only two were spelled correctly. Reggie clicked on the first, Sofia Caruso, and read the associated details. She was the wife of Antonio Caruso and had been born 10 May 1932, which didn't fit with what he knew about Sofia Serano. He hit the back button, selected the second person and read the inscription.

Sofia Vargas
Born: 3 July 1889
Died: 19 September 1982
Age: 93

Reggie smiled. The month and year of birth tied with what he had found on the census. He checked who else was in the burial plot and found her husband, William Vargas. It looked as though he'd found Sofia, but he wanted confirmation. He went back to the open 1920 census tab in his browser and edited the search parameters based on what he'd just found. One result.

Vargas, William, head, male, white, 31, married, born California, father born California, mother born California
Vargas, Sofia, wife, female, white, 31, married, born California, father born Mexico, mother born Mexico

It had to be her. She was even buried in the same section of Mount Hope Cemetery as her parents. He followed her life through the 1930, 1940 and 1950 censuses to make sure that there were no other marriages or complications. As far as documented genealogical evidence was concerned, Sofia Serano was off the list as being one of the killer's direct ancestors.

Reggie returned to Ramon and Anita's children. Mentally, he crossed off Joaquin, Sofia and Lucia from the list. Just Miguel and Rafael were left.

He suddenly realized something, jumped up and hurried over to

Maddie's office. 'You're looking for a female converging with a male Serano,' he informed her. 'I've just crossed all the females off my list.'

'Excellent,' Maddie said. 'That will really help. I've just finished fleshing out Herman and Gertrude Olmstead's four kids. Between them they have *ten* children, but now I can discard the four boys—thank you. Any locations that might help find the link sooner?'

'Just San Diego so far.'

'Excellent. Thanks.'

'You're welcome,' he said, heading back out to the main office. As he strode over to his desk, he suddenly felt the familiar bite of hunger in his stomach and he looked at his watch: 12:58. He glanced at Kenyatta and Hudson, both intently staring at their computers; nobody had realized that it was lunchtime. 'Anyone need a drink or anything,' he called, fetching his salad box from the refrigerator and making himself a drink.

Kenyatta gazed over, looking as though she'd just woken up. 'Uh, no thanks.' She noticed his lunch box and added, 'Wait. What time is it?' She answered her own question. 'Oh, my! It's high time I got my blood moving, is what it is. My doctor would *not* approve of me sitting down on my big behind for this long.'

Reggie carried his lunch and coffee back to his desk as Kenyatta marched two brisk loops around the office, collected her lunch and sat back down, evidently satisfied with her brief burst of exercise. Without taking her eyes away from her screen, she opened her lunchbox and fed herself some carrot sticks. Hudson also seemed oblivious to anything in reality, except for whatever it was he was doing on his computer.

'Want anything, Hudson?'

'Huh?' he said without looking up.

'Do you want anything,' Reggie repeated. 'It's lunchtime.'

'No. I'm good, thanks.'

'Suit yourself,' he replied. He wanted to say that he'd like to talk tonight, but Reggie could see that now was not a good time to get Hudson's full attention. He fired off a message to Ross, asking again how the packing was going, then pulled up the profile for the next of the Serano children.

Miguel Serano had been born in San Diego in 1890 and was living in the family home for the two censuses following his birth. The family trees that were found in the hints for his name generally agreed that he'd married a woman named Michelle Blasczyk and that he'd died in 1963. Given the point that they were at in the case, Reggie wondered whether to abandon Miguel already and move on to the last sibling, Rafael, who, through a process of elimination, was now the top of the list of candidates. But he decided to stick with researching Miguel in order to be able to rule him firmly out.

Reggie ran the Blasczyk surname through the list of names currently associated with the case, drawing the anticipated blank. Then, he ran a search for Miguel on the 1920 census, the first where he was not at home. The first result included his wife, Michelle.

Serano, Miguel, head, male, white, 30, married, born California, father born Mexico, mother born Mexico

Serano, Michelle, wife, female, white, 28, married, born California, father born Virginia, mother born Virginia

Serano, Matias, son, male, white, 6, single, born California, father born California, mother born California

Serano, Gloria, daughter, female, white, 4, single, born California, father born California, mother born California

Serano, Leandro, son, male, white, 2, single, born California, father born California, mother born California

As Reggie looked down the entry, he noticed the location at the top of the page. *California > Los Angeles.* Tilting his head to one side, he read the street address which was written vertically down the side of the page. North Grand Avenue. He typed the address into Google and hit *Maps*. It was right in the middle of downtown LA.

There was something more in the entry that piqued his excitement. Michelle's father had been born in Virginia. Reggie hurriedly pulled up the Word document for the case and scrolled down to the summary of each cluster that had been identified. The MRCAs for cluster six, Herman Olmstead and Gertrude Tapinala, had lived in Richmond, Virginia.

Reggie almost hit a run as he went over to Maddie's office. 'Sorry.

Me again.'

'What you got for me?'

'Miguel Serano married someone called Michelle Blasczyk. And her father was from Virginia.'

Maddie frowned. 'I don't have a Blasczyk in the tree so far. Do you have Michelle's parents?'

Reggie realized at that moment that, in his eagerness, he'd jumped the gun; he hadn't yet searched for Miguel and Michelle's marriage, which might well confirm or refute his theories. 'Not yet. I'll go and search out the marriage now.'

'You're looking for Ella, Joyce or Barbara,' Maddie called after him. 'They're the only ones I haven't filled out.'

'Got it,' he said, scuttling quickly back to his desk.

He searched for Miguel in the *California, County Marriages, 1850-1953*, hoping that he hadn't married in San Diego which wasn't included in the record set. Reggie was in luck; there was a record of the marriage. He grimaced as he selected to view a copy of the suggested entry, hoping that the pieces were about to fall into place.

He examined the certificate, then stood up, about to head over to Maddie's office. But there was no need, she was heading his way already, and so, he sat back down.

'Did you find anything?' she asked.

Reggie rolled his chair sideways, letting her see the screen.

'Get it up on the board,' she directed. 'Hudson, Kenyatta, we've got a development. Reggie, explain what you've got.'

Reggie stood up and shared his screen. 'This is Ramon Serano and Anita Soto's son, Miguel. He married in Los Angeles to a Michelle Blasczyk. Her mother was Ella Olmstead from Virginia.'

'That's the link!' Kenyatta shrieked! 'Great job.'

'Blue slip, Reggie,' Maddie said, walking over to the whiteboard, where she started to rearrange the genetic networks to fit the new information.

Reggie wrote the cluster information on the paper and rushed it over to Maddie. She fixed it up beside the blue slip bearing the names of James Fellows and Florence Boicourt.

'Okay,' Maddie said, turning away from the board. 'Reggie, have you found any children to Miguel and Michelle yet?'

Reggie pulled up the tree for Miguel for everyone to see, scrolling down so that the names of his children became visible on the right-hand side. 'I've only got these three so far from the 1920 census. There may be more.'

Maddie nodded. 'Well, Matias, Gloria, Leandro or another yet-to-be-identified sibling converged with one of James Fellows and Florence Boicourt's offspring. Kenyatta, anything from you on that front yet?'

'Yeah,' she said. 'Shall I share? Are we having an impromptu briefing?'

'I guess we are,' Maddie answered. 'Go ahead and share.'

Kenyatta displayed her screen. 'Of James and Florence's twelve kids, I've got very solid biographies for ten of them. They scattered all over the country, two went over the border to Canada and one had four marriages.' She ran her mouse over the two youngest children as she said, 'Just these two left, Fred and Anna Fellows.'

'One of each,' Maddie commented. 'Hudson, how are you getting on with the other side of the tree?'

'I've worked up the first three of the Moreno kids. So far, all California-based but no overlap with a Serano, Blasczyk, Fellows or Boicourt.'

'Who you got left?' Maddie asked.

'Uh,' he began, glancing down at his screen. 'Carlos, Fernando and Christina Moreno.'

'Okay, so let's...' Maddie looked down at her watch. 'Wow, okay. It's past three already and I've not had any lunch. I suggest we *all* have a short break. No screens for fifteen minutes—and I mean it. I'm going to Eva's to see what they've got left. When I get back, I'll switch to helping you, Hudson.'

'I'll come with you,' Kenyatta said, sliding out from her desk and standing up to stretch. 'If only to get my steps up.'

Maddie asked Reggie and Hudson if they wanted anything and then pointed at them both. '*No* screens. Do you hear me?'

'Yes, ma'am,' Reggie said, giving a mock salute.

When the main office door had closed behind them, Reggie rolled his chair around to Hudson. 'I've been wanting to talk to you. So, maybe this is as good a time.' He tried to sound upbeat, but his words came out like the preamble to a break-up.

'Uh-oh. Sounds ominous,' Hudson said, turning his chair to face Reggie.

Reggie smiled. 'No. No, it's not. It's about the person I'm in a relationship with.'

'Ross. Yeah... What about him?' Hudson said.

'What? How do you even know that?' Reggie countered. There was no way Ross would have told him.

'I saw you together,' he said. His tone was neutral, but Reggie knew him well enough to know that something negative was underlying his words.

'Hudson, I had every intention of telling you, man,' Reggie assured him. 'I just wanted to see where it went, first. If it was going nowhere in the first few weeks—like so, so many of my past relationships—then there would be nothing to tell.'

Hudson nodded, then said, 'It just felt a little cold, after I confided in you with my stuff...about being trans and all.'

'I get it. I totally get it. And, hey... You're still the first person that I've talked to about it. Honestly. The intention wasn't to keep it a secret but to just see where it went.'

'So, it's going well, then?'

'Yeah, it really is.'

Hudson smiled, looking Reggie in the eyes. 'Good, and I'm happy for you,' he said, sounding genuine. He started to turn back to his workstation.

'Actually, I've got a favor to ask, regarding Ross.'

'Go on.'

'Becky's dad is being an asshole and throwing Ross out of the apartment—'

'Is that why he's off?'

'Uh-huh. And I was wondering if he could move in with us...temporarily. Just while he finds himself a place. He's got to be out of the apartment by Saturday, tops.'

'Does Becky know about this?'

'Ross has told her, yeah.'

A short silence hung between them. Hudson was staring at the floor, evidently mulling it all over.

'So, is it okay if he stays for a short while? What do you say?'

Hudson exhaled, clearly not really happy with the situation. 'I guess so, yeah.'

'Thanks, man,' Reggie said, rolling his chair back to his desk where he messaged Ross the good news. It would at least ease his mind in the short term.

Thanks, Ross replied with a red heart.

Ten minutes later, Maddie and Kenyatta were back in the office and everyone's focus had switched back to the case.

Reggie started with finding Miguel and Michelle Serano on the 1930 census. They were still at the same address on North Grand Avenue, Los Angeles. In addition to Matias, Gloria and Leandro, there were two more children.

'Just FYI,' Reggie said to Hudson and Kenyatta, 'I've got two more kids for Miguel and Michelle for you to watch out for: Robert and Rosenda.'

'Got it,' Kenyatta said.

The 1940 census saw no new additions to the Serano household, but the two eldest children, Matias and Gloria, were no longer living in the family home. Before Reggie started to search for their whereabouts, he skipped on to the 1950 census to be absolutely certain that Miguel and Michelle had indeed had no more children.

Reggie was just returning to the 1940 census, when Kenyatta broke the mesmerized silence of the office by clapping her hands together, almost startling him out of his skin. 'It has to be Anna Fellows. All the rest are out,' she declared, looking at Reggie. 'Anna Fellows must have had a child with a Serano. Who am I looking out for?'

'Matias, Leandro or Robert,' Reggie answered, entering Matias into the 1940 census search. 'It *is* Anna,' he quickly confirmed. 'Come take a look.'

Kenyatta hurried over to his workstation and together they studied the entry.

Serano, Matias, head, male, white, 26 years old, married, born California
Serano, Anna, wife, female, white, 25 years old, married, born California
Serano, Eugene, son, male, white, 6 years old, single, born California
Serano, Kathleen, daughter, female, white, 4 years old, single, born California
Serano, Eliza, daughter, female, white, 2 years old, single, born California

'That's it,' Kenyatta said. 'All four of the Hollywood Strangler's grandparents are in place. Now we just need to figure out which of Matias and Anna's kids was the parent.'

'Maddie and I only have Carlos and Christian Moreno left on our list,' Hudson confirmed.

'Meaning we're looking for a female Serano,' Reggie added. 'Kenyatta, do you want to take Kathleen, and I'll take Eliza just as soon as I confirm that there are no other kids we should be on the lookout for?'

'Yeah, I'll just go and update Maddie, so she knows where we're at.'

With a bubbling internal excitement, Reggie ran a search for the family in 1950. There were no more recorded children born to Matias and Anna.

Serano, Matias, head, white, male, 36 years old, widowed, born California
Serano, Eugene, son, white, male, 16 years old, single, born California
Serano, Kathleen, daughter, white, female, 14 years old, single, born California
Serano, Eliza, daughter, white, female, 12 years old, single, born California

Reggie took a few seconds to register the significance of that census entry. Matias's widowhood limited their search to just Kathleen and Eliza Serano. One of those two sisters was the Hollywood Strangler's mother. 'There are no more kids,' he told Kenyatta.

'I don't think it's Kathleen,' she replied with a shake of the head. 'I think I've found a marriage for her on the Reclaim the Records site for New York.'

Suddenly, Maddie burst out of her office. 'Fernando Moreno married Eliza Serano. Was she one of the possible candidates?'

Reggie and Kenyatta both replied affirmatively.

The team shared complete silence for a moment as each person absorbed the news.

'Fernando and Eliza Moreno are the Hollywood Strangler's parents,' she said finally, picking up a marker pen and writing the names on the glass board under the heading *SUSPECT'S PARENTS*. Below that, she wrote *SUSPECTS*. 'Now we need the names of their children.'

Chapter Twenty-Six

Thursday, November 17, 2022, Salt Lake City, Utah

Just like the rest of the team, Kenyatta was sitting down at her desk, ready to work at eight fifty. While she waited for Maddie to open a short briefing, Kenyatta looked at the colored slips of paper attached to the whiteboard. The two inverted pyramids representing the paternal and maternal sides of the Hollywood Strangler's family now converged in one yellow slip: that of his parents, Fernando and Eliza Moreno.

Kenyatta's eyes lingered on the names, wondering if they could have had any inkling—any sign at all—that one of their children would grow up to become a monster. Was he born that way? Were any telltale behaviors there when he was growing up? Did they wonder when the horrific murders were reported that their son might have been responsible? Becky was often reminding the team that multiple psychological studies suggested that twenty percent of what made a person become a serial killer came from genetics, while the remaining eighty percent came from environmental sources, most often a traumatic childhood.

Kenyatta thought of her own three boys and how different they each were, despite having had the same upbringing. Although she wouldn't admit it to anyone else, she was terrified about Troy and the path that he seemed to be taking in life. She took out her cell phone and sent him a message.

Miss you, Troy.

She held the phone wistfully for a few seconds, then put it away and looked over to the glass board at the word *SUSPECTS*. Following the discovery of the killer's parents yesterday afternoon, the team had worked doggedly to identify the names of their children. The two females' names had been struck through, leaving the four males as their remaining potential suspects.

~~Juanita Moreno~~

José Moreno
~~*Simona Moreno*~~
Andrés Moreno
Santiago Moreno
Angel Moreno

Kenyatta stared at the six names, still not quite able to believe that one of those men was the notorious Hollywood Strangler.

It had taken some time yesterday to confirm those names and the team hadn't left the office until after seven. Because of that, Maddie had insisted that nobody work the case last night and, instead, they had all been primed to get a good night's sleep and return today with fresh eyes.

'Okay,' Maddie said, strolling to the front of the room. 'I'll keep this briefing...well, *brief*, as I know you're all anxious to get moving on it. As usual, we need to know every last detail that we can about these four brothers. We need all vital records, obits, public documents, photos, social media—basically, anything at all that can help build a biography for them. Kenyatta, you take José. Hudson, you take Andrés. Reggie, you take Santiago. And I'll take Angel. Questions?'

There were no questions and the team quickly turned to their computers. With a spot of luck and a lot of hard work today, they might just unmask one of America's most infamous serial killers.

Kenyatta opened the family tree profile for José Matias Moreno, wondering if perhaps his middle name was for his maternal grandfather. The records that they had pulled last afternoon had suggested that he had been born around 1959, although no official birth record had been found for him.

Given the point that they were at with the case, Kenyatta's first step was to run a general Google search for José. The results, for multiple people with that name, ranged across social media accounts, YouTube videos, newspaper stories and genealogy websites around the globe. She clicked on some of the links as she moved down the list. When nothing was immediately forthcoming, she added *Los Angeles* to the search. The top result was for a family tree on Geneanet, which stirred Kenyatta's interest. But when she clicked through to read it, she found that it related to a man born in 1818. She backed out to Google and looked at another result. This was from the *San Diego Reader* and was about a series of love letters between two people in the 1850s and 1860s. It took a moment for her to find the causal link to her search criteria: a shipwrecked whaler in California named Joseph Matthew Brown had changed his name to José Matias Moreno. He wasn't the guy that she was looking for.

Moving back to the Google results page, Kenyatta gradually sifted her way through the suggestions, reading in more detail some that looked as though they could fit the bill. After searching for a while, she decided to call it until she had something more specific to go on.

Back on Ancestry, Kenyatta looked at the two hints for José's name. The first was *U.S., Public Records Index, 1950-1993, Volume 2*, which she opened to read.

Name: José Moreno
Birth Date: 19 Aug 1959
Address: 6500 Romaine Street #5
Residence Place: Los Angeles, California, USA
Zip Code: 90038

The record by itself was not yet enough to prove that this was the correct person, but Kenyatta copied the address over to Google and hit *Maps*. 6500 Romaine Street was situated off-center of a circle which had Sunset Boulevard, Santa Monica Boulevard, the Hollywood Walk of Fame, Paramount Studios and Hollywood Forever Cemetery at different points of its four-block circumference. It couldn't have been more Hollywood if it had tried.

Kenyatta wrote the address on some scrap paper and carried it over to the whiteboard, where Maddie had affixed the map that Becky had prepared showing a large purple circle pulled over a map of Hollywood. It covered a vast area, and it took Kenyatta a few moments of searching to locate Romaine Street. She found it very close to the center of the circle.

She returned to her desk, reminding herself not to get ahead of herself in the thrill of the chase. At this point in time, she didn't know if the public record related to the correct person. She clicked to view the source of the data.

Original data: Voter Registration Lists, Public Record Filings, Historical Residential Records, and Other Household Database Listings.

Above the record was the question *Does the José Moreno in this record match the person in your tree?* Kenyatta hit *Maybe*. Not only could she not confirm if it was the correct person, but the date range for the record set ran for a large span of years from 1950 through 1993. She needed something much more precise and opened the background-check website, BeenVerified. As expected, there were multiple José Morenos currently living in Los Angeles. When she filtered the results for those born around 1959, the number dropped to thirteen. She could see that just one of those men also had the middle name Matias. She looked at the result. This guy had been born in 1959. There were no family members listed under *Relatives*, so she continued down the profile to his address history. It was much more detailed than the one suggested at Ancestry, giving a good chronological breakdown for the past forty years. All the addresses were situated in Los Angeles, the most current being given for Durand Drive.

She looked more closely at the period from 1980 to 1986, when the murders were carried out, and found that this man was indeed living at 6500 Romaine Street.

Returning to Google Maps, Kenyatta dragged the little orange Street View man from the bottom-right corner and plopped him down in the middle of the road outside that address. She found herself looking at a run-down two-floor apartment block on the corner of Romaine Street and Wilcox Avenue. The building itself was a dirty shade of ochre with a flat roof. Most of the windows were barred with red grills. At the bottom of her computer screen were various other dates displaying the same location. She scrolled along to the first date, May 2009, and clicked in. The only substantial differences were rolls of barbed wire along the front-facing balcony and two dense palm trees that rose either side of the front door. She took a screenshot of both the earliest and most recently dated images, and then pasted them into a suspect file that she would compile on José.

Despite still not knowing if she had the right person or not, she copied some of the key information across from BeenVerified to the file before continuing to examine this man's background. As she did so, she couldn't shake off the feeling that he had lived right in the heart of where the killings had occurred and right where Becky had theorized the killer would live.

She felt a growing nervous excitement inside as she selected the *Criminal & Traffic* tab, expecting to see a full history of criminal convictions. But there was nothing. This José Moreno had no criminal activity attached to his name. How likely was it that someone could commit such brutal attacks but have no criminal record whatsoever? It was possible, just unlikely in her experience. She also considered the fact that the address history for this man ran right up to last year, going against the police theory that the killer had died not long after the final murders in 1986. The initial flurry of excitement that she might be onto the killer began to dissipate.

Even though it had drawn a negative result, Kenyatta added the criminal record check to the profile that she was building, as it might become significant when the team would later triage the four brothers.

Next, she looked at José's work history on BeenVerified.

Warner Bros Studios - runner
TLP Productions - assistant
Paramount Studios - grip
Simms & Fry Productions - grip
Reel of Dreams - manager

His work life had clearly been dominated by the movie industry, which could be highly significant, given the killer's M.O. However, much of the population of LA was involved in or connected to the movie industry in some way or another. She copied the information across to the profile and then moved on to *Social Media*. There was just one suggestion linked to this man's email address and it was for Facebook.

Kenyatta clicked through, hoping that it was an open profile which contained enough personal information to confirm that *this* José Moreno was the person that she should have been pursuing.

It turned out that it was the type of page that Kenyatta hated. The person had gone to the trouble of setting it up but never got around to using it. There were just two posts, both in June 2010 when José had joined Facebook. The first was of a photograph of the famous Hollywood sign and the other was of a circular sign that might appear hanging from a shop façade. In the center of the circle, over a blood-red background, was an old-fashioned movie camera, and arced over that in white letters was written, *Reel of Dreams: The Hollywood Film Odyssey Museum*. Neither image had any emoji reactions or comments.

Other than those two images, the Facebook profile was empty. Kenyatta clicked to view his friends, finding that there were just five names there. But one of those names made her sit up: Eliza Moreno. Could it have been the mother? Kenyatta wondered, moving into her profile, which instantly seemed fuller and more recently active. The *Intro* provided evidence that this might be the correct person.

Wife and mother to six kids. Grandma to ten! Great-Grandma to 3!

Kenyatta copied the information over to the Word document, even though it was still insufficient evidence to tie the two Facebook profiles back to the José Matias Moreno that she was investigating. She had reached this point before in cases, only to discover something that proved that she had in fact been working on the wrong person.

She continued down the page, which was largely dominated by pictures and posts of flowers, food hacks, plants and life-affirming memes. Wanting to get to something more substantial, Kenyatta clicked *Photos*, which allowed her to see all the images that Eliza had posted in rows of six. Now she was able to scroll down the page quickly through the images, pausing when there were photos of people. She hit on a picture—that was clearly taken a long time ago—of a grinning man and woman looking at the camera. Cradled in the woman's arms was a tiny baby. The date of the posting was August 19, 2019. There was just one comment on the photo by someone named Arlene Swift, who had asked, *Which of the lovely boys is that?* Eliza Moreno had answered with the words, *My José* along with a red love heart.

Kenyatta looked again at the date of the posting, noticing that it was on José's sixtieth birthday. She had found the link, which confirmed that the background check had hit on the right person. With a smile, she dragged more information to the suspect file and then carried on data harvesting from within Eliza Moreno's Facebook page.

By lunchtime, Kenyatta had some good, solid biographical material in José's profile. She had taken her salad box back to her desk and picked up her cell phone to see if she'd had any messages. Much to her surprise, Troy had replied.

Miss you too Mom. Are you home tonight?

I'll be at the SLC kitchen right after work then home, she responded.

She wasn't sure what to say next. Should she directly ask him to come home? She didn't want to push. Was he saying that he wanted to come home? She stared at the screen, but nothing came back, even though she could see that he'd read the message.

'How are you getting on?' Reggie asked her.

She set her cell phone down and looked at him. 'Good, I think. It took a while to confirm that I was working on the correct person, but I got there in the end.'

'How's he looking?' Hudson asked, wheeling his chair around to sit nearer to her. 'Suspect-wise, I mean.'

'I haven't found a photo of him yet to compare EVCs, but his address history for the times of the murders is smack square in Hollywood. He also worked in the movie business, so he certainly ticks some of the boxes. However, he's still alive and living in the area and has zero criminal history. What about yours?'

'Andrés doesn't seem at all likely,' Hudson reported. 'EVCs are a definite match but the rest is way off the mark. I don't know how he compares to the other brothers, but he would be bottom of the pile, based on what I've found. His address history is solid San Francisco. He's gay, politically very active and seems to have been with the same male partner for over thirty years. No criminal history. Interestingly, there's nothing of the Moreno family on his socials. That all seems to be more about him, his partner and their friends.'

'Job?' Reggie asked.

'Charity work and teaching, as far back as the murders.'

'What about Santiago?' Kenyatta asked Reggie. 'How's he looking?'

'EVCs gets a red flag,' he replied. 'Location also gets a red flag: he lived within the purple circle of doom.'

'Interesting,' Kenyatta said, as Maddie strolled into the office, carrying a piece of paper which she attached to the glass board.

'Mugshot for Angel Moreno,' Maddie informed them.

'Rap sheet?' Hudson called over.

Maddie's eyes widened. 'Oh, yeah. As long as my arm. I'll tell you more at briefing, but I'd be surprised if the other brothers can top this guy.' She paused on her return to her office. 'Are you all good?'

'Just comparing notes over lunch,' Kenyatta replied.

'Good, I'm glad you're stepping away from the screens.'

When Maddie was back in her office, Hudson said, 'But we only have three and a half hours until the briefing. So, I'm going to get back to my screen,' as he rolled himself back to his workstation.

Kenyatta laughed, ate a forkful of salad and then checked her cell phone to see if Troy had replied. He hadn't. But Jim had sent a message saying that he was looking forward to seeing her tonight. She smiled and then turned her attention back to the suspect file for José. The profile was good. She had exhausted all the background-check websites and had followed various tangents and fallen down several social-media rabbit holes in the pursuit of the information.

She returned to the second and final hint against José's name at Ancestry. It was for *U.S., School Yearbooks, 1900-2016*. The suggestion provided a thumbnail of a black-and-white photograph, with name, birth year and residence typed beside it. Kenyatta clicked the title for further information.

Name: José Matias Moreno
Estimated age: 16

Birth Year: 1959
Yearbook Date: 1975
School: North Hollywood High School
School Location: North Hollywood, Los Angeles, California
Grade Completed: Sophomore

Kenyatta clicked to see the entry in the context of the yearbook.

A page containing thirty black-and-white images of school students loaded in front of her. A photo in the second row down, second from left, had a green box highlighted around it. An accompanying green box was around the words *José Matias Moreno* in the list of student names to the right of the photos. Kenyatta zoomed in to the picture so that it filled her screen. The boy staring out at her seemed older than his sixteen years, she thought. He was wearing a smart suit, white shirt and tie. Just like his male classmates, José had what was evidently the hair style of the day: a thick sweep-over from a side parting, covering his ears and touching the edge of his shirt collar. By comparison to those around him, who were beaming widely, José was only half-smiling.

Kenyatta looked in the file notes for the case quickly to remind herself of the killer's purported EVCs: *Brown eyes, brown hair, intermediate skin color.* She returned to the yearbook and zoomed out slightly. As the image was black-and-white and not the best quality, it was hard to determine José's phenotype precisely. He definitely had dark hair and, judging by a comparison to an African American girl and an obviously white girl with blonde hair, Kenyatta considered him to have intermediate skin color. His eyes were harder to read. They looked dark, but then so did every other person's on the page.

She was confident that this was the right José Matias Moreno, but since she had not found a single photograph of him as an adult, she had nothing to compare it to. She looked at the bottom of the yearbook image and noticed that it totaled two hundred and forty-five pages. She typed *1* in the page number box, and it jumped to the yearbook front cover, which was of a group of students standing under a tree, taken from a second-floor viewpoint. To the right, in cream-colored letters were the words, *El Camino 1975*. The image of the students had been made to look like a jigsaw puzzle with one piece, at the top of the tree, missing. How ironic, Kenyatta thought with a smile as she hit the right-hand arrow and began to work her way through the entire book, not sure what she was looking for exactly.

She moved through the usual shots depicting life at North Hollywood High School: sports events, academic life, music concerts, parades, art exhibitions and the social sides of student life. On page twenty-three was a photograph of a smiling lady sitting at a desk. The headline and caption beside it read, *ADMINISTRATION. NEW LEADERSHIP. Striking a blow for women's lib, North Hollywood High School acquired its first female principal, Mrs. Eva Kirby. Mrs. Kirby's feminine influence was evident during a massive clean-up campaign…*

'Go, Mrs. Kirby,' Kenyatta muttered to herself, pushing on through the next pages, which showed each department and its staff. This was followed by some student poems and art. Then the class photos began, starting with the sophomores and followed by pictures from various sports teams. Despite the images being annotated, there was no sign of José. She began to move through another section of student poems when she suddenly noticed his name below one entitled *Stars*.

In '75, beneath the Hollywood sign,
A reel of dreams spins out of line.
Stars walk the earth, in daylight gleam,
Silk and glitter, a silver screen dream.

Lucille's whisper, a siren's song,
Bogart's shadow, bold and long.
Dean's rebel yell, echoes still,
Monroe's smile, a pillowed thrill.

Sunset Boulevard, a starlit trail,
Casting calls in every mail.
The flicker of film, a dance of light,
Starlets chase fame into the night.

Tinseltown tales of love and strife,
Cut through celluloid, slice of life.
Golden era, fading fast,
In cellulose frames, forever cast.

As pages turn in high school halls,
Hollywood's echo softly calls.
In every yearbook, dreams await,
Stars of tomorrow, through the gate.

'Wow,' Kenyatta said, impressed by his poetry skills. Her eyes returned to the first verse. *A reel of dreams...* The name of the museum where José worked. There could be no doubt that this was the right person.

She took a screenshot of the poem and then saved it, along with the yearbook picture and information, to the suspect profile. She sent a full-size copy of José's photograph to the printer, which she then took over to the glass board and affixed beside those of his siblings, Angel, Santiago and Andrés. It was weird to look at them all lined up like that, trying to guess which looked more like a cold serial killer. Kenyatta had to agree with Maddie that Angel's mugshot stood out from the other brothers. There was a definite family resemblance, though, and she could see that they all fit the bill in regard to EVCs. It would be their suspect files that would be key in isolating one of the siblings as the most likely candidate.

Back at her computer, Kenyatta finished her check of the high school yearbook, finding no further reference to José.

There were no more hints for his name at Ancestry, so Kenyatta started a methodical check of each of the big genealogy websites.

At 4:30 p.m., Maddie called them all to the briefing. She had already shared her laptop screen on the digital whiteboard, which showed a suspect profile for Angel Moreno.

'Ross. Good to have you back. Welcome. You ready to take notes?'

He nodded and offered a weak smile as he sat down with his

laptop. Kenyatta had no idea what was going on that had necessitated him taking time off at such a busy time for the team, but he sure wasn't himself right now.

'Okay,' Maddie said. 'Where to start with Angel? I guess by saying that he was very far away from being an angel.' She moved down the page from a blown-up image of his mugshot to a series of smaller mugshots, clearly taken at different times in his life. 'At the time of the murders, he was living on Clinton Street, a block over from Paramount Studios and right in the center of the circle where Becky thought the killer would live. As I mentioned earlier, he has a *very* long rap sheet. We've got convictions for robbery using a firearm, GBI, battery, disturbing the peace, drug charges, traffic violations and—'

'You mean, there's more?' Kenyatta asked.

Maddie nodded emphatically. 'And murder.'

'Oh,' Hudson commented.

'And it was in downtown Hollywood in 1987,' Maddie said, scrolling down to a newspaper story.

Although the text was too small for Kenyatta to read, the headline was very clear: MURDERER CAUGHT IN CAR WRECK.

'I know you can't read the story from where you're sitting, so I'll just give you a summary,' Maddie said. 'It's saved in Angel's suspect profile if you want to read it in full. So, witnesses saw Angel murdering a sex worker in downtown LA. He got away, but then law enforcement caught up with him a couple of days later in a car with one of his brothers. They gave chase and the car hit a wall, flipped over and caught on fire.'

'Which brother was it?' Reggie asked.

'The story doesn't name him, but what is significant about that is that only Angel was arrested at the scene. After trial, he was sent to California State Prison—sumptuous home to the likes of the Night Stalker, Richard Ramirez, the Dating Game Killer, Rodney Alcala and, of course, Charles Manson.'

'He's in good company, then,' Hudson said.

'Not good enough for Angel, apparently,' Maddie answered. 'He committed suicide in July 1990.'

'It all fits date-wise,' Kenyatta said.

'Yeah, it really does. The problem we now have, though, is that he was cremated. I can't find any record of a spouse or children. So, if he does end up as our number-one suspect, the detectives are going to need to get DNA from the other siblings. Which, I guess, is a good segue over to you guys. Who wants to go next? Anyone think they're onto a better suspect than Angel?'

When nobody spoke, Kenyatta said, 'Well… José has several red flags, but nothing compared to Angel and, some of those flags, like the EVCs and his address at the time of the murders, seem to be equally applicable to several—if not all—of the other brothers.'

'Show us what you've got,' Maddie said, taking a seat at the spare desk and turning to face the screen.

Kenyatta overrode Angel's suspect profile on the digital whiteboard with her own screen. 'I've struggled to find any up-to-date pictures of José but, as you can see from his high school yearbook photo, his phenotype appears to fit the bill.' Kenyatta then went through the whole profile, outlining all of her findings so far, ending with the *Stars* poem.

'It's actually a really good poem,' Maddie said.

'It is,' Hudson agreed. 'I'd place him second in line as the suspect. He's clearly had a fascination or obsession with the movie industry since high school at least. He's got the right EVCs and address at the time of the murders, but he's nowhere near as high up the list as Angel.'

'I agree,' Reggie chipped in.

Maddie nodded. 'Anything else, Kenyatta?'

'That's all for today,' she said, sitting back down. 'But there's still a lot more work to do on him tomorrow.'

'Yeah, I'm not done with Angel yet, either. Reggie, what have you found out about Santiago?'

Reggie shared the suspect profile for Santiago. Considering it was his first time pulling one together, he'd done a good job with it. It started with a full-size photo of Santiago, the same one he'd printed out and stuck to the glass board. It was a selfie showing Santiago on a sandy beach with his arm around a pretty young Latina woman who was the person taking the picture. Like his brothers, he had an exact match for the EVCs.

'I feel as though I've barely scratched the surface with this guy. He's prolific on almost all socials. He runs a chain of gyms in LA and also offers life-style coaching, personal training—that kind of thing. He's got a lot of celebrity endorsements, running right back to the mid-to-late eighties. I've seen photos online that show the insides of his gyms and there are pictures on the walls of him standing beside Richard Burton, Paul Newman and Rock Hudson, to name but a few stars of the day.'

'In other words,' Maddie chipped in, 'he also has a connection to the movie industry.'

'Uh-huh,' Reggie agreed. 'He moved around a lot during the murder period, bouncing in and out of the circle of doom.'

'How about any criminal history?' Kenyatta asked.

'Just a traffic violation back in 1992. Because of his profile in the Hollywood set, there are countless newspaper articles that mention him, so I'm nowhere near done.'

'Hudson, what have you got for us with Andrés?' Maddie asked.

Hudson shared his screen and stood up. 'As I told Kenyatta and Reggie a while ago, Andrés is *very* unlikely. Compared to the other brothers, he's very much the rainbow sheep of the family. There's no rap sheet, no connection to the glitz and glamour of Hollywood. Only his EVCs fit the bill.' Hudson talked through the suspect file, sharing all the evidence that strongly pointed to Andrés being bottom of the suspect pile.

'I agree,' Maddie said when he'd finished. 'This is going to be a tough one to call between the other three. Fortunately for us, we don't have to. We just need to finish these suspect profiles and hand them over to the detectives. If nobody else has anything to say, then we'll call this briefing over and carry on tomorrow. Good work, everyone.'

Kenyatta shut her laptop and started to get ready to leave.

'We're *so* close,' Reggie said with an excited glint in his eye.

Kenyatta grinned. 'Right... This is your first suspect case. Well, let me tell you now, they're not all as big and juicy as this one.'

'I still can't believe we're working the Hollywood Strangler case; it's totally mind-blowing.'

'Well, go home and get some rest, and maybe tomorrow we can figure out which of these Moreno boys did it,' Kenyatta said. 'I'm off to spend the evening freezing my hiney off in Pioneer Park. Thankfully, there's no snow.'

'Well, I hope there is…above ten thousand feet,' Reggie replied.

Kenyatta rolled her eyes, said goodbye to the team and left the office.

'Here she is, the woman of my dreams!' Jim greeted her from behind the two long trestle tables holding the soup pots and bread baskets.

Kenyatta fought back a big smile and waved a hand dismissively. 'Oh, behave yourself, now.'

He leaned in and kissed her. 'How was your day? Have you caught your mystery serial killer yet?'

'We're down to four suspects,' she revealed.

'That's impressive,' Jim said. 'But you still can't talk about it?'

Kenyatta mimed a zipper going across her lips.

'Well, if it is the case that Lonnie thinks it is, then I sure will hear about it on every news outlet in America.'

Kenyatta sucked in a long breath, hoping and praying that the case wouldn't be such a big deal, but knowing really that it was going to be major news across the world for a long time. 'How do you feel about taking a trip out to Cedar City this weekend?'

'Sure,' he answered with a slight frown. 'Why Cedar City?'

'Well, I need to go see a potential test-taker for the Boys under the Bridge case but that won't take long, and I thought, once we were there, we could take a hike in one of the canyons nearby.'

'That sounds great,' he said. 'I'll let you work out all the details.'

Kenyatta kissed him. 'Thank you.'

'Every damned time,' a voice barked from behind the table. 'What is it with you two, making out in public, every chance you get?'

Kenyatta turned to see Lonnie appearing from behind the table, wearing his usual dirty suit, shirt that had once been white, and blue tie.

'Oh, hey, Lonnie,' Kenyatta greeted. 'How you doing?'

He shrugged. 'I was doing okay until I saw you two at it again. You're like two disgusting teenagers.'

'Young love,' Jim said.

'Guess you heard about Candice?'

'No, what about her?' Jim asked.

'She's dead,' he said matter-of-factly.

'What?' Kenyatta said. 'No. What happened to her?'

'OD'd...behind a dumpster in some parking lot.'

'Oh, that is so sad. That poor girl,' Kenyatta said, raising her hand to her mouth.

'When did this happen?' Jim asked.

'Last night. Found this morning. What's the soup, Kenny?'

'Uh...it's,' Kenyatta started to answer, then looked at Jim. 'What is it tonight?'

'Just plain old tomato.'

'Sure, I'll take some,' Lonnie said. 'And if I like it, I'll get Candice's share, too.'

Kenyatta frowned at him, and he shrugged. She was desperately upset about poor Candice and wondered if she could have done more to encourage her to get the help she needed and get off the streets.

'So, who's the Hollywood Strangler, then?' he asked in a deliberately loud voice.

'Ssshh!' Kenyatta urged. 'I never said that was the case I was working on.'

A wide, toothless grin spread over Lonnie's face. 'No, but old Lonnie here can read Kenny like a book. I keep looking in the newspapers to see if he's been arrested but I ain't seen anything yet.'

'Lonnie, I can't talk about the case I'm working on. And, you know, even if I could, I—' she stopped mid-sentence when she saw someone approaching the table. 'Troy.'

He briefly looked up from the ground and met her eyes. 'Hey.'

'What are you doing here? How have you been? Do you want anything to eat?' She didn't know what was different about him, but something definitely was. He didn't look right.

'Yeah, please,' he muttered.

'Hey,' Lonnie barked. 'That food ain't meant for just any folk's family and friends. He ain't getting Candice's share. That's for me.'

'Lonnie, calm down,' Jim tried to soothe. 'There's always some left over because some folks are just too picky.'

'Hmm,' Lonnie mumbled, grabbing a bread roll and shuffling off, talking to himself all the while.

'Where have you been?' Kenyatta asked Troy.

'Just around.'

'Come home with me tonight,' she said.

Troy didn't answer.

'Take him home now,' Jim insisted. 'If you want.'

'You sure?'

He nodded. 'Go. I'll see you on the weekend for our big adventure.'

'Thank you,' she said, touching his arm and kissing him. 'Come on, Troy. Let's get you home.'

Chapter Twenty-Seven

Friday, November 18, 2022, Salt Lake City, Utah

'Oh, my God,' Maddie exclaimed. She was sitting down in her office continuing to work on the suspect profile for Angel Moreno. Having considered what Kenyatta had found yesterday in the North Hollywood High School yearbook, Maddie had been slowly working her way through the 1979 edition of *El Camino*, where she had already found Angel Moreno's graduation photograph. Now, she was looking at the school's academic, sport, music and drama achievements, which were apparently not included in the yearbook indexing. On a page titled *The Inside Story* were several monochrome photos of students acting on a stage. One of them was clearly Angel Moreno. But it had been the short description that had taken Maddie aback.

The 'Drama Monsters' stomped into the Fall semester by entering several competitions and debuting an alumnus version of 'West Side Story.' The Fall Festival competition was held at Reseda High with over 68 schools participating in a variety of performances. All students performed excellently and were a credit to the school. The main roles of Riff, Tony, Bernardo and Maria were played by Dean Robinson, Damon French, Angel Moreno and Tracie Satchell respectively. The musical, especially the acting, received outstanding reviews.

Angel Moreno had acted in a school play with one of the Hollywood Strangler's final victims. Maddie took a screenshot but, before she did anything else, returned to the pages containing the student photos. She quickly found Tracie Satchell's picture and confirmed that she was indeed the same person as in the file shared by Detective Marsden. Maddie added the new information to the suspect file and then sent it to her printer.

Picking up the piece of paper, she headed out to the kitchen area, where Reggie and Hudson were making themselves drinks.

Hudson caught her eyes and he said, 'I've just found a blog online that says Andrés Moreno was working in Nigeria in 1984, which was when Natalie Van Derlyn was murdered.' He shrugged and added,

'Obviously, this isn't categorical proof—the blog might be a lie or mistaken, or he could have flown home in that time, committed the murder and then returned to Nigeria, but…'

'Yeah, it's unlikely,' Maddie said. 'And look what I just found.' She held up the extract from the yearbook.

Hudson's eyes widened as he read it, and Reggie gasped.

'What? What? What?' Kenyatta demanded, leaping up from her chair and hurrying over to see what all the fuss was about. She read the short article. 'Oh, my goodness me. Talk about smoking gun.'

'Yeah, this could be what links all the victims to the killer,' Maddie said. 'I'm going to switch focus for a moment and see where all the other victims went to school.'

'Good idea,' Kenyatta said, taking a Coke Zero from the refrigerator.

'Wouldn't that have been an obvious line of police inquiry at the time of the murders?' Hudson asked.

'Yeah, you'd think by now someone would have looked at that angle,' Maddie agreed. 'But they wouldn't have been able to cross-refer the victims with Angel Moreno.'

'True,' Hudson said, pouring coffee for himself, Reggie and Maddie.

'Thanks,' Maddie said, taking the mug back into her office and then typing the name of the first victim, Robyn Stoltman, into *U.S., School Yearbooks, 1900-2016*. There were just sixty-five results but, as Maddie scrolled down the page, she found only one in Los Angeles. She clicked the entry, finding that it pertained to the right person. Robyn Stoltman had graduated from Theodore Roosevelt High School in Los Angeles. Maddie quickly Googled the distance to North Hollywood High, finding it to be seventeen miles to the northwest.

She saved the entry to a new document, then searched the entire yearbook from cover to cover, looking for any mention of acting, drama performances, the other victims or anyone from the Moreno family. Her search came up blank, and so she repeated it for the second victim, Tiffany Winters. When there was no sign of her, Maddie opened *U.S. Yearbooks Name Index, 1890-1979* at MyHeritage and found Tiffany had attended the Hollywood Hills High School. She could find no mention of the other victims or of any Morenos, so she moved on to the third victim, Kevin Hoang.

After more than an hour of searching, Maddie had found high school yearbook entries for all the victims apart from the fourth, Natalie Van Derlyn. The information for the other victims, however, had not pushed the investigation forward and Maddie found herself wondering if she had wasted precious time on a wild goose chase. But her gut instinct told her that there was some kind of a connection there, which might help to consolidate the growing evidence that was mounting against Angel Moreno, firming up his being their main suspect in the case.

With a sigh, she decided to take some time to conduct the cross-referencing within the newspaper search engines that the company had access to and, if nothing was forthcoming, then she would return to developing Angel Moreno's suspect profile.

Just before lunchtime, Maddie hit an article in the December 8, 1978 edition of *L.A. Weekly*, whose tagline was *The Publication for News, People, Entertainment, Art and Imagination in Los Angeles*. Something in that newspaper had referenced both Angel Moreno and Natalie Van Derlyn.

MURDER IN THE FOG, mystery set in a gentleman's club in London. Wordy through the first act, but neatly wraps into a tight package by the final curtain. Good work by actors Angel Moreno, Ross Smith and Natalie Van Derlyn. Matrix Theatre, Thurs-Sat, 8:30. Call 852-9411

Maddie was shocked to find another piece of evidence that tied Angel Moreno to another of the victims. She took a clipping of the paper and added it to the suspect file, along with the source information.

She was about to carry on with the other victims when her phone pinged with an incoming message.

Coming for lunch??!

'Damn it,' she said, realizing the time. Clayton was due to fly home tomorrow night, and she'd agreed to meet him for lunch today at Eva's. She quickly replied to him that she was coming, grabbed her jacket and purse, and headed out of the office.

Minutes later, she found Clayton sitting on a stool at a narrow, corridor table, right opposite the counter. He was looking at her in the mirror in front of him as she approached.

'Admiring yourself?' she said with a smile, leaning in to kiss him.

'Admiring *you*, actually,' he replied.

'Well, what can I say?' Maddie said, taking off her jacket and flicking her hair.

'How's your morning been?' he asked. 'Identified him yet?'

'Honestly,' Maddie squashed an inch of air between her thumb and forefinger. 'We are *this* close.'

Clayton raised his eyebrows. 'I know you can't talk about it because of the NDA, but am I going to see this on the news in Pennsylvania?'

Maddie nodded.

'Wow,' he said. 'I'm pretty sure I know which case it is, but I won't push.'

'My lips are sealed,' Maddie returned, picking up the menu. 'Have you decided what you're eating yet?'

'Roasted chicken salad.'

'Me too,' she said, putting down the menu.

'That was easy,' Clayton said, taking her hand in his. 'For a tougher question, where are you on the whole me-transferring-to-Utah thing?'

Following Clayton's bombshell that he'd started the application process to get a transfer to Utah law enforcement, Maddie had been in a deep quandary, flitting back and forth between its being a great idea, to its being the worst idea. Over dinner on Monday, Clayton had tried to reassure her that he was simply applying to transfer to the state of Utah, nothing more. If he were successful and she wanted it, he would then get his own place somewhere in Salt Lake City, and they'd take it from there. Maddie had consulted with all three of her kids and their verdict was unanimous: let him move closer and see where the relationship goes. Jenna had gone one step further and repeated her pragmatic opinion that it was time to have Michael declared dead.

Maddie was about to answer when a waiter came over and took their order. Once he was behind the counter, punching in their choices, she answered. 'I think you should go ahead with the application to transfer.'

Clayton grinned. 'You're sure?'

Maddie nodded, which was not one hundred percent honest. She still had her doubts but also knew that all the while Michael's disappearance remained a mystery, there would always be doubt.

Clayton pulled her into a hug. 'I love you, Maddie.'

The words hit her like a punch in the stomach. It was the first time that he'd said it, and it was the first time anyone had said it to her for seven years. The feelings were there, and she wanted to reply that she loved him too, but the words simply refused to come out.

Maddie spent the afternoon trying to finish Angel Moreno's suspect file. It was probably the most crucial part of the investigation, and she needed to concentrate, but her mind kept wandering back to the two interwoven thought-tracks of Jenna's wanting to have Michael declared dead and Clayton's telling her that he loved her. When she hadn't reciprocated, he'd squeezed her hand and said that she didn't need to say it back; and with that the moment had slipped away, the words left unsaid.

Despite her fluctuating levels of concentration, by mid-afternoon, Maddie had reached a point in the process of building the suspect file where she had exhausted all the major lines of inquiry in the genealogy databases. She checked in with the rest of the team and, when she found that they were all in a similar place, she decided to call an early briefing.

'So, I think we're at the point in the investigation where we need to cross-check each other's work. Go back to the original match list and make sure the shared DNA is correct, then work through the suspect profiles looking for any mistakes, inconsistencies or anything that challenges or disproves our findings. Reggie, you and I will swap. Kenyatta and Hudson do the same. Questions?'

When no questions were asked, Maddie went back into her office, took a deep breath to try and clear her thoughts, and then opened the file, labeled *Cluster Four*, from the shared drive. The cluster lead name was Jennifer Hatter, who matched the killer with seventy-two centimorgans of DNA. Reggie had identified Bryce Cameron and his wife, Aisla Baird, from Scotland as being Jennifer's great-great-great-grandparents. If the team's work was correct, then Bryce and Aisla were also the same distance from the Hollywood Strangler, making the killer and Jennifer Hatter fourth cousins.

Switching over to the DNA Painter website, Maddie selected the Shared cM Project Tool and then typed 72 into the search box. The relationship of fourth cousin was a possibility, coming in at fifteen percent of all relationships with that quantity of shared DNA. Maddie was happy to move on and check his sources, and then finally the suspect file for Santiago Moreno.

She spent some time analyzing his results. She was impressed. Considering it was Reggie's first suspect case, he'd conducted a thorough and meticulous investigation. Maddie couldn't fault his lines of inquiry. Santiago's EVCs, address at the time of the murders and his occupation meant that he was still on the table as a suspect, but there was really no comparison to all that she had found implicating his brother, Angel.

Maddie closed all the files down and took a moment to calm her breathing. If the others had also found no errors, then she would be sending the four names over to Detective Marsden and, at some point in the near future, all hell would undoubtedly break loose. She also intended to send everything over to Becky for her assessment.

Closing her eyes, Maddie tried to shut everything out. But her thoughts kept coming back to what she was going to do about Michael and Clayton.

After some time, Kenyatta knocked on her door. 'Sorry, am I disturbing?'

'No, not at all. Come in. I was just trying to clear my head.'

'Everything okay?'

Maddie nodded. 'Yeah, just a lot going on, as usual.'

'Well, if you want to talk, you know where I am.'

'Thanks, Kenyatta.'

'Sure. We're all done with the cross-checks.'

'Excellent. Me too,' Maddie said, sliding her chair back and standing up.

She followed Kenyatta out into the main office. 'Okay,' she said, summoning some positive energy. 'Let's get on with what might possibly be our last briefing on the Hollywood Strangler case.' When she had everyone's full attention, she continued. 'So, I've cross-checked Reggie's work and—as we've all come to expect in the short time that he's been with us—everything is thorough, sourced and comprehensive. I don't have any issues. Reggie, I am slightly hesitant to ask. Did you find any oversights or mistakes in my work?'

'No, all good,' he replied.

'That's a relief,' she replied with a laugh.

'And your theory about Samuel Moreno fathering Maria Trilby checked out, too.'

'Good. Hudson, everything okay with Kenyatta's work?'

'Spot on,' he answered.

'Great. Kenyatta, Hudson's work?'

'Perfecto as usual.'

Maddie paused for a moment. 'So, does everyone agree that the four Moreno brothers are our prime suspects and that we would suggest that the detectives start their inquiries with Angel Moreno?'

Nods of agreement came from the whole team.

'I'll do that right now. And I'm also going to send it to Becky to get her critical interpretation. Fantastic work, everyone. Take the last couple of hours off and go home and relax.'

Maddie returned to her office, picked up the phone and called Detective Marsden.

'Hey, it's Maddie...from Venator,' she said when he picked up.

'Oh, hey, Maddie. You got news for me?'

'I have. I've got the names of four brothers who are the main suspects.'

'Really? Not relatives...?' he replied. 'The actual suspects? Are you kidding me?'

'No, I'm not kidding. The DNA points to José, Andrés, Santiago and Angel Moreno, but it can't distinguish between them. That part is over to you. We have got very detailed files on each of the brothers and there is a lot of evidence pointing to one brother in particular.'

'Go on.'

'Angel Moreno. I'll send you everything we've got but, briefly, his phenotype matches the killer, he lived in the right area, he acted in high school with Tracie Satchell and performed in another play with Natalie Van Derlyn, and he had a list of convictions as long as your arm.'

'Oh, my God. I don't think this name has shown up anywhere at any time involved with this investigation. Incredible. But I notice you said *had*. Is he dead?'

'Yeah, I'm afraid so. He died in California State Prison in 1990.'

'What was he in for?'

'Murdering a sex worker.'

'Holy cow. This is… I don't know what to say, Maddie. It's just…incredible. I honestly didn't think we'd ever get here…to this point.' Marsden fell silent for a few seconds, then said, 'You do realize the size of this, don't you? Just a heads up… If we can get the final confirmation from CODIS, you're gonna get the world's media on your doorstep.'

'Yeah, I know,' she answered.

'Wow. It looks like we might be heading for an exhumation to prove it was him.'

'He was cremated,' she said.

'Oh. Any kids?'

'It doesn't look like it, no.'

'Damn. Well, I guess we can get some DNA from one of the brothers. Can you send me over what you've got right away?'

'Give me two minutes and it'll be in your inbox.'

'Jeez, this is just incredible. I can't begin to understand how you… Thank you.'

'You're welcome, Detective. Keep me posted on the investigation. Good luck.'

Detective Marsden thanked her again and then ended the call.

Maddie zipped up all the suspect files into one folder and sent them to Marsden's email address. As he had just said, they needed a CODIS hit to be one-hundred-percent certain, but, as far as she and her team were concerned, the Hollywood Strangler case was now over, and they had just handed over four potential names for one of the most notorious serial killers in the U.S.

She slumped back in her chair, exhausted. She needed the night off. Picking up her cell phone, she sent Clayton a message.

I'm done at the office. Dinner at your hotel?

He came straight back with, *See you in the bar. Korean street tacos and a white wine await!*

She smiled, finding it sweet that he had remembered what they'd eaten when they'd met there two years ago. The case being closed left a new void in her mind, affording her some room for clarity on her other problems, and she made a decision about her future.

Chapter Twenty-Eight

Friday, November 18, 2022, Pétion-Ville, Port-au-Prince, Haiti

Becky and Aidan were standing under the shade of a mango tree, high on the hills of Pétion-Ville. They were staring at a high stone wall topped with a spiked metal fence. On Monday, they had brought Lovelie to Pétion-Ville to identify the mansion where her abuse had taken place. She had brought them here, to Château Lwa, situated behind the stone wall in an affluent part of the Pelerin 5 neighborhood. The former prime minister, Jovenel Moïse, had been assassinated last year just a few properties down the street from where they were now standing. It had been in the mansion behind the stone wall in front of them that Lovelie claimed her captivity and abuse had been perpetrated.

'Come on,' Becky said, reaching for Aidan's hand and leading him over to the huge double gates. They were made from solid metal, yet someone had vandalized them, somehow managing to peel back the bottom left corner like a can of dog food.

A rotatable video camera was positioned on a pole just inside the compound. It was facing in their direction, but both Becky and Aidan believed that the evidence, including the damaged gates, the smashed video entry system, the broken name plate and the thick weeds on the driveway, pointed to the place having been abandoned.

Becky crouched down and peered through the gap in the gates. Overgrown shrubs and trees that lined the driveway inside provided the mansion with further protection from prying eyes, but she could just see the top floor of a white building.

'Do you see anything?' Aidan asked.

'Not really,' she answered, lowering herself down onto her stomach.

'What are you doing, Becks?' he said, reaching down and grabbing her arm.

'What does it look like I'm doing? I'm going inside for a better look,' she replied, shaking off his grip and starting to wriggle through the hole.

'Becks! You can't. I can't fit through that gap,' he said, reaching for her left leg.

'Aidan, get off. I'll be okay. I might even be able to unlock it from this side if you just let go of my leg.'

'Do not go towards that house,' he directed, letting go of her leg. 'I flamin' mean it, Becks.'

Becky slithered on the dusty ground through the hole in the gate and then stood up on the other side. Although they had both agreed that the property had likely been abandoned by its rightful owners, there was a big chance that such a grand mansion like this would be an ideal place to be taken over by one of the city's many gangs.

Becky looked at the inside of the gate. Three large metal bolts were driven across the center and padlocked into place. 'Three huge gold padlocks,' she said, crouching down to the hole.

'Then, you come back through this side, and we'll see if we can find another way in,' Aidan said.

'I'm just going to take a sneak peek up the drive. I won't go all the way up to the house,' she said.

'No. Becks! Come back out here,' Aidan said. 'If anything happens to you, I can't get in there. What do you want me to do, call the cops if you get into trouble?'

'Aidan, calm down. Nobody's been here for a long time,' she said, looking at the weeds that had risen up through the cracks in the block-paved drive.

'Crikey, Becks. This is so not okay,' he shouted.

Becky knew that it wasn't okay, and she knew that if she did encounter any nefarious persons within the compound, she was on her own. Aidan wouldn't be able to help her, and the police certainly wouldn't be able or even willing to help her.

With Aidan's vociferous protests continuing behind her, Becky cautiously made her way up the drive. It seemed to have been deliberately created to wind its way between dense areas of shrubbery, keeping a distance from the house. Becky's suspicious mind assumed that, given what had gone on here, it provided further security and cover for the house. She wasn't surprised to find that the driveway terminated at a large turning circle in front of a four-bay detached garage, still with no full view of the house. So far, what Becky was finding matched Lovelie's description perfectly.

Her eyes ran from the garage to a brick wall that was at least ten feet high. Lovelie had said that the entrance to the house had been through a metal gate in that wall. She'd also told them that all the girls held here had been forbidden from passing through that gate, which had always been kept locked.

Becky slowly walked around the final curve in the drive, which gave her sight of the gate. Just like the one at the entrance, it was solid metal, but this one hadn't been bent open. She stood still for a moment, just listening for any signs of life. All she could hear were the distant calls of the Hispaniolan Trogon, the national bird of Haiti. As she approached the metal gate, Becky was confident that she was alone here. Despite this belief—which might just have been thinly disguised hope—she walked with a light step, ever more vigilant as she grew closer.

When she reached the gate, she tried to turn the metal knob, but it was locked and there were no cracks or gaps through which to see the other side.

Becky took a step back and looked at the problem as though it were one of the climbing walls at The Front in Salt Lake City, where she had been a frequent visitor. She quickly mapped out a route and, before she talked herself out of it, hoisted one foot up onto the doorknob, then reached one hand up and grabbed a tiny ledge created by a damaged brick. Next, she swung her other foot up and managed to brace it on the metal hinge before lastly using her free hand to grab the top of the wall.

'Ahh!' Becky yelped, her hand landing on a proud shard of glass. Despite the pain, she moved her hand along to a spot where there was no glass and then hauled herself up, using all of her upper body strength to get up onto the edge of the wall. Only now could she see that the entire top of the wall was lined with broken glass, fixed into a bed of cement as an extra deterrent. Becky wondered if the heavy security was to keep the girls in or to keep prying eyes out. Both, probably.

She winced as she opened her left hand, finding it deeply lacerated and bleeding heavily. She had nothing with her with which to stem the flow, so she just clenched her fist and hoped for the best.

Becky finally took in the view of the Château Lwa. It was exactly as Lovelie had described. A huge white building with stunning views over the city of Port-au-Prince. It was like nothing she had seen in Haiti before. Even though it was showing signs of decay, the house was spectacular. The architecture gave her the impression of art deco merged with Spanish villa style. There were balconies on several of the rooms and large bay windows that overlooked the hills. She looked inside the windows closest to her, but the rooms appeared empty. Whatever had gone on here before appeared now to be over.

Becky looked from the glass line embedded in the wall to the ground below. If she stood up carefully and managed to step around all the glass, there was a chance she could find a spot from which to dangle over the edge and drop to the other side. But if someone were here, it would be a huge risk, and she would be totally trapped. She settled on the decision that there was little to gain by getting any closer to the house.

Taking one final look around the compound, Becky unclenched her fist and tentatively placed it down onto the wall, yelping as fresh pain stabbed at her from the laceration. She had no choice but to push through the soreness as she lowered herself back down the side of the wall, dropping the last few feet to the ground.

From somewhere nearby there came the crackling of gunfire.

Becky ran as fast as she could back up the drive toward the gate. 'Aidan?' she called, panic rising inside her.

But there was no response.

She reached the front gates and threw herself to the ground, crawling through the gap and repeating her call for Aidan. On the other side, she stood up, half-expecting to see him lying in a pool of blood, but he was nowhere to be seen. 'Aidan!' she called, walking toward the car. He wasn't inside, so she started to walk quickly up the road beside the stone wall that edged Château Lwa.

Then, he appeared, jogging around the corner.

'Jesus, Becks!' he yelled angrily. Then he looked down at the trickle of blood running out of her palm and his manner switched.

'What happened?'

'Sliced it open on a glass-topped wall,' she said, spinning around. 'We need to get out of here.'

'Did you find something?'

Becky shook her head. 'No, but it fits exactly with how Lovelie described it. The security and privacy inside is incredible. We need to figure out who owned it back in 2015.'

'That's more easily said than done,' Aidan said.

They got in the car and quickly drove away from Château Lwa, Becky thinking about the name of the villa in light of what they now knew. *Lwa* referred to the powerful spirits of Haitian Vodou, the intermediaries between the human world and Bondye, the supreme God. Whoever was running the abuse ring here back in 2015 certainly likened themselves to the role of a supreme God. Becky had a terrible, haunting feeling about who that might have been.

Back in the apartment, Aidan dressed her cut hand. He had been adamant that she should go to the hospital to get it checked out, but Becky had refused.

She was now sitting down at the table by the open window, gazing out over Pétion-Ville, wondering how they were going to find out who had owned Château Lwa in 2015.

'Becks, I really think we've pushed our luck here,' Aidan said, sitting down opposite her. 'We've done all the groundwork. Everything else, all the genetic genealogy, all the legal work, *every*thing else can be done remotely. We don't need to stay here in Haiti.'

'I'm not done here,' Becky retorted, turning to meet his gaze with her own clear resolve.

'How about…we just hop over the border to the Dominican Republic? Work there and come back as and when we need to.'

She knew that Aidan was right, they had pushed their luck to the limit, and the country was spiraling rapidly toward outright anarchy. But if they left and other agencies also pulled out, who would stay to help fight for those innocents left behind? And Becky knew that if she left, she would likely never get the answers that she desperately wanted about what had gone on at Château Lwa.

'I'll think about it,' she finally accepted.

From the bedroom, she heard her phone beep with another message. It was probably from Ross, who was struggling to pack up the apartment prior to the eviction deadline tomorrow. When he had called her to tell her about her father's malevolent appearance at the house, she'd tried to contact him, but he hadn't picked up. Every day she'd tried calling both of her parents' cell phones, the house phone and even resorted to calling her father at work. She never got through and all she could do was to tell Ross to treat the threat seriously and to get out of the apartment. Becky was certain that the dramatic turn of events was directly related to what she was doing out here in Haiti. It was more than just another verbal warning from her father.

She started to get up, but Aidan held out his hand. 'I'll get your phone, you stay there.'

Becky rolled her eyes. 'Aidan, I've cut my hand. I'm not incapacitated.'

He ignored her, took her cell phone off the charger and placed it into her good hand. The message hadn't come from Ross, it was from Maddie, asking her if she could run a critical analysis over the four suspect profiles that the team had created for the Hollywood Strangler.

She eagerly opened up her laptop and downloaded the files, seizing the moment while she had internet connectivity.

While Aidan cooked them *diri shela poul fri* for dinner, Becky worked her way through the suspect profiles, occasionally checking things online for herself. By the time that Aidan had dished up the dinner, she was satisfied that one of the Moreno brothers was indeed the serial killer.

But Becky disagreed with Maddie and the rest of the team about which one.

Chapter Twenty-Nine

Saturday, November 19, 2022, Los Angeles, California

Ted Marsden was sitting down at his desk in the LAPD Police Headquarters Facility, re-reading everything that had come through last night from the IGG team over in Salt Lake City. Even though they'd set out with the sincere hope that the killer's DNA alone would be able to close the case, he was still blown away by what the team had been able to discover. And all in under three weeks. It was beyond incredible. Maddie had been clear over the phone and in her email that the DNA could not distinguish between the four Moreno brothers, and, therefore, it could have been any one of them. However, having read through the reports that she and her team had compiled on each of the siblings, Marsden was very much inclined to agree that Angel Moreno was the prime suspect.

Marsden had run all four brothers through the crime index computer, supplementing the criminal records already found for Angel Moreno with additional arrests for GBI and battery. He had also cross-referenced the Moreno name against the suspects and persons of interest in the four murder books, but the name had never come up anywhere in association with the case.

Marsden slid his chair back and addressed Powers who was sitting in his cubicle beside him. 'So, since this guy is long-deceased and was cremated, I figure we go after one or more of his brothers for their DNA.'

Powers nodded his agreement and held aloft his own hard copy of the paperwork sent over from Venator. 'Given all we've got here, it shouldn't be too hard to get a current address for the two living in LA. Do we need to go after the one in San Francisco, too?'

Marsden thought for a moment. 'We may need to, yeah. If getting trash DNA from Santiago and José just eliminates them but points to another of the brothers, then we've gotta remove Andrés from the frame, too. But let's start with the two based in LA.'

'Hey, guys,' Detective Supervisor Mitzi Roberts greeted, strolling by their workstations. 'What brings you two in so early on a Saturday?'

Marsden held up the suspect profiles. 'The IGG came through. We got a name.'

'What? Already?' Roberts said. 'That's amazing.'

'Well, it's four names, actually,' Powers corrected. 'Siblings, but one stands out a mile.'

'Come on, then. Tell me,' she said.

'Angel Moreno,' Marsden said.

Roberts thought for a moment, then shook her head. 'Doesn't mean anything to me. Was the name in the murder book?'

Marsden shook his head. 'Nope. Not one mention.'

'City of Angels, huh?'

Marsden smirked at the pun.

'So, what's your intended next step?' Roberts asked, folding her arms.

'He's dead. Killed himself in Cal State back in 1990, cremated and no known kids. So, we're going after the brothers' DNA. One of them's got a gym downtown and the other works in some cheesy Hollywood museum. We're going to scope them out today.'

Roberts nodded. 'What about the blood card?'

'What blood card?'

'If this guy died in Cal State, then a blood card would have been taken. Get his DNA off that and you won't need the brothers,' Roberts said.

'Damn it. I should have thought of that,' Marsden replied. 'I guess that's why you're the boss.'

Roberts grinned. 'Glad to help. I guess that means I share the main credit now with catching the Hollywood Strangler?'

'Hey, don't push it,' Marsden said. He looked at Powers. 'Why didn't I think of the blood card?'

'Because you're like super old,' Powers suggested. 'What even is a blood card?'

'When a prisoner dies in a California prison, they're automatically given an autopsy, no matter what the cause of death. Their blood is taken and put on a filter paper and, as soon as it's dried, the sample gets stored.'

'So, where is this sample now?'

'At the coroner's office,' Marsden answered. 'I'll get it FedExed over right away and then we can get it into CODIS.'

'Hang on. It's Saturday. Will they be open?' Powers asked.

'Damn,' Marsden muttered. 'I don't think so. Let me check.' He opened the website for the Los Angeles County Department of Medical Examiner-Coroner. 'Closed weekends.'

'Shall we go pay a visit to Santiago and José while we wait for Monday?' Powers asked.

'Yeah, I'd like to see these guys in person,' Marsden answered.

'Take one each?' Powers suggested.

Marsden nodded. 'Which one do you want?'

'I'll take Santiago. I can go in and talk fitness and gyms.'

'And I'll take José and talk Hollywood,' he said without much enthusiasm.

Marsden shut down his computer, grabbed his bag and walked over to the elevator with Powers.

'So, you think if we solve this case, you're still going to retire?'

Marsden pressed the call button and looked at him as though it were the dumbest question. 'Of course. The shit this case is going to throw up in the air, *big time*. I'm definitely out of here.'

'Right, playing golf every day and taking old-people vacations to…' Powers fake yawned and then rocked forward, meeting the elevator door with his forehead, pretending to have fallen asleep.

'Anything that gets me away from you,' Marsden retorted.

The door opened and the two men stepped inside, riding down to the first floor. 'Text me when you're done,' Marsden said. 'Let's meet up somewhere to grab a bite.'

'Got it,' Powers said, offering a mock salute.

Marsden walked to his Ford Explorer and programmed the address for the museum into his Sync Navigation System. Rather predictably for the nature of the place, it was on Hollywood Boulevard in Thai Town.

Marsden headed northwest on Sunset Boulevard. The traffic was uncharacteristically light and, just fourteen minutes after leaving the LAPD Police Headquarters Facility, the Ford Sync's female voice informed him that he was one hundred yards away from his destination. With nothing behind him, Marsden slowed the car as he approached. On either side of the five lanes of vehicle traffic were two-story buildings, fronted by a variety of shops, including a tattoo parlor, a hairdresser and several empty units. According to the map, the museum was down the boulevard between a rotisserie chicken joint and a music shop. Marsden pulled into the empty lot and took one of the first of ten parking spots. At the end of the parking lot was a drab, gray building that looked more like a warehouse than a museum.

Before he got out of the car, he removed his tie and jacket, and pulled his shirt out to try and look less like a cop. He got out and, pretending to type into his cell phone, took a surreptitious photo of the building. Pocketing his phone, he walked through the parking lot toward the museum, still not certain that he was headed to the right place. As he got within twenty feet, he saw a faded, red sign announcing *Reel of Dreams: The Hollywood Film Odyssey Museum*. Below the sign was a wooden door with a central glass pane surrounded by peeling red paint. It was little wonder that the parking lot was empty.

Marsden pushed open the door and stepped inside a small reception area that was maybe ten feet by ten feet and painted in the same shade of red as the door.

'Morning,' a man said cheerlessly from behind a wooden counter that was fronted by cheap plastic movie-themed souvenirs and postcards of iconic movies. On the walls behind him were framed posters from some classic movies, including Marsden's own favorite, *Casablanca*.

'Hi,' Marsden replied, taking a good look at the man. He was in his sixties and had a thin, drawn face. He had lank shoulder-length brown-gray hair and dark eyes. Marsden's assumption that this was José Moreno was confirmed by the identifying lanyard around his neck.

Marsden couldn't quite believe that he was staring at the brother of the Hollywood Strangler.

'Can I get a ticket?' Marsden asked.

Moreno shrugged. 'Sure. You a veteran or a cop?'

Marsden balked at the unexpected question, then quickly realized he was asking because of a discount. 'No, just a regular ticket, please.'

Moreno nodded, tore off a red paper ticket and handed it over.

'Ten bucks.'

Marsden took a ten from his wallet and gave it to Moreno, realizing at that moment that the man was in a wheelchair and had no legs.

'It's through the *Psycho* shower curtain,' Moreno said, nodding his head toward a white plastic curtain on the opposite wall.

Marsden grinned. 'Nice. Is it the actual one?'

Moreno sighed and shook his head with the tired annoyance of a man who'd had to answer the same question countless times over the years.

Marsden had been hoping for some dialogue to get the measure of the guy, but, when he could see that that wasn't forthcoming, he turned and walked through the shower curtain.

The room that Marsden entered was like the props room on a movie set. It was a cold and vast open space, containing a myriad of junk, collectibles and memorabilia from a large variety of movies. He glanced around, unable to find any logic to the layout or a sensible place to start. Not that he needed to look around, really. He wasn't especially into the movies and, having grown up in LA, was apathetic toward the whole industry. What he really wanted was to talk to Moreno. So, he started walking through the maze of junk in search of a plausible topic of conversation. He passed a row of locked glass cabinets displaying Oscar statuettes for actors and directors that he'd never heard of, then came to a full-size old-model Mini that had apparently been used in *The Italian Job*. 'Now, that *was* one cool movie,' he acknowledged, as he continued past a series of costumes in cabinets that ranged from period pieces to familiar superheroes, until he came to a huge model shark that he correctly guessed was one of the props from *Jaws*. He ignored the sign and touched the side of the shark.

'It says *Don't touch*,' a voice said from out of nowhere behind him.

Marsden turned to see Moreno in his wheelchair, just a few feet away. There was definitely something about the guy that creeped him out. 'Sorry. I just couldn't resist,' he said with a wide and fake smile. 'I mean. It's *Jaws*, right.'

'Yeah, it is. But, like I said, it says not to touch it,' Moreno said flatly.

'Sorry. Won't happen again,' Marsden promised. 'Hey, do you have anything from any of the *Star Wars* films, here?'

'No,' Moreno replied. 'The props are too expensive and too highly sought after.'

Marsden nodded in agreement. 'Sure. So, this your place?'

'Yeah, that's right.'

'Been here long?' Marsden asked.

'Since eighty-eight,' he answered. 'Got it with the insurance money from my accident,' He tapped his hands on the front of his wheelchair in the place where his legs should have been.

'What happened?' Marsden asked, remembering that Angel Moreno had been involved in a car wreck in 1987 that had led to his incarceration. 'If you don't mind me asking, that is.'

Moreno shrugged. 'Car accident, not far from here on Sunset.'

'I guess you could say some good came of it, if you ended up with this great museum,' Marsden said.

'Are you interested in early cinema? I've got one of the Lumière brothers' first cameras back there.'

Marsden noted the sudden change of topic. 'Sure, I'd like to see that,' he replied, not having ever heard of any of the Lumière brothers.

'I'll show you,' Moreno said, moving his motorized chair in front of Marsden. 'They were the pioneers of cinema. Apparently, their film, *The Arrival of a Train*, caused mass panic when the audience watched a huge train coming toward…'

Marsden stopped listening and stopped walking, having been distracted by a glass cabinet beside him. It contained a pair of white lace panties and the caption read, *Part of a costume worn by Natalie Van Derlyn in Echoes of Yesterday, 1984.*

A cold shiver ran down Marsden's back.

Moreno turned his chair to face him.

Maddie looked at the dining room table, pleased with her efforts. She hadn't put this much work into Thanksgiving for a very long time. Clayton was flying back home this evening, so she'd decided to celebrate with him five days early. Since it was on a weekend, it also meant that Nikki was able to come home and join the feast.

'Whoa—this is impressive,' Clayton said as he entered the room and looked at all the food. The table was dominated by a large turkey in the center, surrounded by a range of home-cooked dishes. He kissed her on the cheek. 'Thanks for doing all this, Maddie. It's awesome.'

'This is probably the peak of my culinary skills, by the way. Just so you know, it'll only go downhill from here.'

'I can cope with that. Want me to get the kids and your mom in?'

'Sure. Thanks,' she replied, lifting the foil from the side dishes.

Moments later, they all trooped into the dining room.

'Jeez, Mom,' Trenton said. 'You never did this when it was just us three.'

Maddie shrugged. He had a point.

'Amazing job,' Nikki commented, sliding in beside her brother.

'What are we celebrating?' her mom asked as Maddie guided her into a chair.

'Early Thanksgiving.'

'Oh. And who's this man who's joining us?' she asked, pointing at Clayton.

'That's Clayton.'

'Well,' her mom said. 'The only Clayton I know was in *Dallas*, but he doesn't look anything like him.'

Maddie and Clayton exchanged a smile as she began to serve up the dinner.

'This mashed potato doesn't look as good as I used to make it,' her mom informed her as she prodded the food with her fork.

'No, it very likely is *not* as good,' Maddie admitted.

'I'm sure it will be amazing, Mom,' Nikki said, turning to Clayton and, probably in an attempt to change the subject, asked, 'So, how's your trip to Salt Lake City been? Mom said you've spent most of your time locked away in the library.'

Clayton laughed. 'Yeah, pretty much. I visited Antelope Island and did a few touristy things in the city, but I've really gotten a kick out of this genealogy stuff.'

Maddie looked at the kids and her mom as she dished up the food. She'd been procrastinating about telling them about Clayton's intention to transfer, fearing any adverse reaction. For some unknown reason, she decided that now would be the perfect time to tell them. 'So, Clayton's loved it so much that he's going to put in for a transfer to Utah.'

Nikki smiled. 'Excellent!'

'Oh, you should definitely move to Utah,' her mom said.

Trenton nodded at the news, picked up a stuffed mushroom with his fingers and shoved it into his mouth, whole. 'Grandma, could you pass the gravy, please?'

'Sure,' she said, handing him the jug.

Maddie looked at the three of them, then at Clayton. Another smile passed between them. Her fear about her family's reaction had turned out to be baseless and their response had amounted to them thinking nothing at all negative. Given this fact, she considered if maybe she herself had wrangled over the idea rather more than had been necessary.

After a few minutes of passing dishes and bowls around, everyone at last had a full Thanksgiving plate.

Maddie stood up, clasped her hands together and said, 'So, as we gather around this beautiful, if slightly over-cooked, turkey, I want to just take a moment to reflect. First, to my beautiful kids—' She looked between Nikki and Trenton with a smile '—Thank you both and Jenna for keeping life exciting, our home full of energy and the fridge eternally empty. You make me very proud. Mom, even though you don't always remember everything, know that we always remember your love and the warmth you've brought into our lives. Clayton—' she looked at him just as her mom interrupted.

'I can remember a lot,' her mom said. 'I bet none of you can remember the name of your kindergarten teacher. I can. It was Miss Beacham.'

'You know, you're right. I really can't,' Maddie agreed, then continued with her speech. 'Clayton.'

'Maddie,' he returned with a grin.

Then, Maddie's cell phone began to ring. She sighed, pulled it out of her pocket without caring to see who was calling and put it on silent. 'No phones. Clayton.'

'Maddie.'

'I just want to thank you for your patience. I realize I come with a *little* baggage, but not only are you willing to put up with that, you're actually helping me deal with it. And you've brought me to a happy place that I really didn't believe I would ever get to again. So, thank you and I really am excited about what the future will bring for us all. So, here's to a Thanksgiving filled with love and laughter. Thank you all.'

'Happy Thanksgiving,' the table toasted in return.

Maddie took a sip of her white wine, aware of her phone vibrating on the table. She picked it up to see who was calling. Becky. And there were six missed calls from her.

'Guys, I know I just said no phones, but do you mind if I take a real quick call? I think it might be urgent,' Maddie said, taking the phone and stepping out of the room. By the time she'd got herself out into the hallway, Becky had stopped ringing.

Maddie hit to return the call.

'Sorry, Maddie,' Becky said. 'Is it a bad time?'

'No, it's fine,' she lied. Becky calling at all meant that it was probably important. Calling seven times meant that it was *definitely* important.

'Listen, I've been through the suspect files. And, well, I think you're mistaken about who the Hollywood Strangler is.'

'What? Are you kidding?' Maddie asked, knowing full well that she would not be joking about this.

'I don't think it was Angel. I think it was José.'

'I don't understand. The whole team went through all the profiles as usual, and we all agreed that Angel was the most likely suspect. True, José hit some red flags but nothing in comparison to Angel. What did we miss?'

'Well, at first I was thinking the same thing, that Angel's criminal record made him the obvious choice, but then I started to drill down into his criminal history and all of his crimes were anger-driven; there was nothing sexual there at all.'

'Becky, he killed a sex-worker.'

'Yeah, but the report said he killed her because she tried to steal his wallet. He didn't kill for sexual gratification. It's a totally different

M.O.'

'But you're the one who's usually always pointing out that M.O.s can shift and change over time.'

'This is two different people, Maddie. None of Angel's crimes were premeditated or organized by any stretch of the imagination. I don't need to remind you of the type of planning that went into the Hollywood Strangler murders.'

Maddie went silent for a moment as she thought about what Becky was telling her. 'What about the fact that Angel acted alongside at least two of the victims?'

'My guess would be that José met them through Angel. Maybe they came to the house to rehearse, or he went along to watch the performances, and that started the infatuation. Remember, these murders were sexually driven. His obsessions could have started years before.'

'Yeah, I see that. So, apart from the EVCs and the Circle Theory, which several of the brothers shared, what else raised José above the parapet for you?'

'His work history in the movie industry and obvious liking for all things Hollywood is interesting but fairly circumstantial; LA is full of people like that. But the fact that he worked as a grip raised a red flag for me.'

'I don't really know what a grip does. Is it something to do with electrics?'

'Sort of. Moving, setting up and striking lighting equipment. And, crucially here, building rigging. This guy's job at the time was literally building frameworks to hold or support heavy objects.'

'Right,' Maddie said, seeing the pieces starting to fall into place. She needed to call Marsden right away. 'Is there anything else?'

'Yeah,' Becky said. 'José was in the car crash with Angel, and he lost both his legs. Remember this was 1987, five months after the final victims, Tracie Satchell and Christian Lofthouse, were murdered. He was probably on the lookout for his next victim at the time of the crash.'

'And he lost his legs...which would have brought his killing spree to an end.'

'Exactly. I really think he's the main suspect, not Angel.'

'Okay. Thanks, Becky. I have to get off the call. I need to get in touch with the detectives right away.'

'Let me know how it goes,' Becky said.

'Yeah, will do. Thanks again. Take care of yourself,' Maddie ended the call and immediately dialed up Detective Marsden. The call went to voicemail, so she left a message. 'Hey, it's Maddie from Venator. I think we may have prioritized the wrong brother: you need to start with José. Call me back.'

Maddie stared at her cell phone for a moment, wondering if Marsden might call straight back. She was annoyed at herself for reaching a wrong conclusion, essentially through confirmation bias, something that she was well aware needed to be guarded against in Venator's line of work. It was a stark reminder to her to be led by the evidence. It was also a reminder that she needed Becky on her team. Reggie was proving to be a real asset and was unquestionably an excellent genetic genealogist, but Becky's degree and master's in criminology was a knowledge base, skillset and an insightful edge that none of the rest of the Venator team possessed.

Maddie pocketed her cell phone and then returned to the dining room to try to enjoy her Thanksgiving dinner with Clayton and her family.

Ted Marsden walked away from the Hollywood Film Odyssey Museum. With his hands slung in his pockets, he strolled along at a slow pace, as if he were in no hurry to leave, when in fact his body was alive, coursing with adrenalin. In his right hand, he was holding his vibrating cell phone, but he didn't want to pull it out in view of the museum, in case he spooked José. He thought that he'd screwed up by staring at the display of Natalie Van Derlyn's underwear for too long. José had seen him, had registered his interest but had continued leading him to an exhibit on early cinema at the rear of the museum. Marsden had tried to play it cool, acting as though nothing had changed, but in reality, he had known that he was making small talk with the Hollywood Strangler. He'd lingered, feigning interest in several displays on the way out, despite being desperate to leave.

He climbed into his car, started the engine, pulled out of the parking lot and then turned onto Hollywood Boulevard. He drove a short distance and then pulled into a parking space outside a real estate office and took out his phone to call Powers. He saw that he had two missed calls from Maddie.

'Where are you?' Marsden asked when Powers finally picked up.

'Just leaving Santiago's gym. I sounded him out and I don't—'

'Venator got the wrong brother. It's José,' Marsden interrupted. 'He's got Natalie Van Derlyn's panties from *Echoes of Yesterday*. And he's got no legs.'

'Are you kidding me? He's actually got the panties…on display in the museum?'

'Uh-huh. I'm really hoping he didn't notice me paying them more attention than I should have. It just took me aback and I froze for an instant. Listen, we need to get his DNA right away.'

'Meet back at headquarters and write up a search warrant?' Powers asked.

'I don't think we've got probable cause,' Marsden returned. 'We get his DNA, we get a match in CODIS, then we get a search warrant.'

'You got a plan?'

'Uh-huh. Can you swing by a Target and pick up two bags of heavy groceries and an envelope—not the self-sealing ones, the type you need to lick shut.'

'Does it matter what size envelope or what type of groceries?'

'About nine by twelve. And just make the grocery bags look heavy.'

'Got it,' Powers said.

'I'll meet you outside *RD White's Real Estate* on Hollywood.'

Marsden ended the call and sat for a moment with his thoughts swirling as the reality of the situation hit home. They faced a mountain of work and further investigation to tie José to the crimes, but nothing could happen without the CODIS match. Being a Saturday, it was unlikely that the lab would be open, but Marsden couldn't wait until Monday to get the process started. So, he called up Cathy Winthrop who was in charge of the forensics lab and who also happened to be a good friend of his wife.

'Hey, Cathy. It's Ted,' Marsden greeted, calling her at home.

'Is Judith okay?' Cathy asked, concern rising in her voice that he would be calling her.

'Yeah, she's good,' Marsden answered. 'Doing too much, even though I tell her not to. You know what she's like.'

'But the treatment's going well?'

'The doc's cautiously optimistic. We're keeping everything crossed.'

'So, I'm guessing this isn't a social call, then?' Cathy intuited. 'Even though you're calling me at home…on Saturday.'

'You guessed right. I've got a *really* big favor to ask.'

Cathy groaned. 'Listen, Teddy. I've got the weekend off. My friend from out of town is here. We have plans. What can't possibly wait until Monday? Have you got exigent circumstances?'

It was a tough one to answer. Strictly and legally speaking, exigent circumstances meant that it was an emergency situation where there was imminent danger to life, which clearly was not the case here. He took a gamble in his answer. 'Cathy—what I'm about to tell you has to go no further, not even to Clive—we're about to get a DNA sample that we think is the Hollywood Strangler.'

'Oh, my God,' Cathy said.

'Yeah, and I need a rush-through on the testing, big time.'

'I get your eagerness, Teddy, but it's not exigent circumstances, is it?'

'No, Cathy. It's not. But I just can't wait until the lab opens on Monday. Plus, I think I might have spooked the guy and there's a risk he might take off.'

He heard Cathy take in a long breath as she weighed the situation. 'Okay, Teddy. You've got it. I'll do it.'

'Thank you so much. Can you meet me at the lab in an hour?'

'I'll do my best.'

Marsden terminated the call. Then, while he waited for Powers to arrive, he phoned Judith to check in on her.

Fifteen minutes later, Powers pulled up behind him in his black Jeep Cherokee. Marsden got out of the car at the same time as Powers got out of his.

'Did you get the stuff okay?'

Powers nodded and took two filled plastic bags from the car.

'Where's the envelope?'

'Right here,' Powers answered, taking it from one of the bags and handing it over.

Just as Marsden had directed, the envelope was not a self-seal. Marsden turned to lean on the Cherokee hood.

'Hey, watch the car,' Powers warned.

Marsden ignored him, took a pen from his pocket and wrote a name and address on the front of the envelope.

'Who's Jemma Wentworth?' Powers asked.

'Your sister. You're going to go into the museum with one bag in each hand and the envelope under your arm. At the counter in the entrance to the museum is a rack of postcards. You're going to tell Moreno that your sister sent you in for a set of the classic Hollywood cards. You buy them, then you ask him nicely if he would put them in the envelope for you. Then you ask him to seal it.'

Powers smiled as he understood the plan. 'Got it.'

'He's in a wheelchair, wearing a lanyard, but just in case, he's in his sixties, long brown and gray hair, brown eyes, maybe a hundred and eighty pounds.'

'Minus a few pounds for the lost limbs,' Powers added.

Marsden ignored the joke. 'Don't spook him. We've got to get that DNA. And you *have* to watch him lick it. Don't let him leave your sight while he does it. Are you ready?'

'Sure. Where am I going?'

'That way,' Marsden directed. 'Down a drive between a chicken place and a music shop. Good luck.'

Powers winked at him, positioned the envelope under his arm and strolled along to the drive entrance and then disappeared. Marsden watched him go, wondering if the plan was a smart one. He'd used it before in another cold case and it had worked perfectly. But that was him running it, not Powers.

Several minutes passed and Marsden began to worry that something terribly bad had happened in there. Just because the guy was in a wheelchair, it didn't make him incapable of doing something horrific. He started to imagine Powers overacting the part and arousing Moreno's suspicion. Maybe he had been in too much of a hurry and he should have gotten someone more experienced from the unit to do it.

He cursed himself and began pacing the sidewalk nervously, looking every few moments at his watch.

Then Powers appeared with a wide grin on his face. He moved one shopping bag to the other hand and offered Marsden the envelope. 'Jemma will be very pleased. He did a lot of licking to get that baby stuck down.'

Marsden smiled. 'Good job. I'm going to get it over to the lab right now. I've pulled some strings, and a friend of mine is going to start the sequencing right away.'

Marsden climbed into the car and placed the envelope on the passenger seat beside him. With luck, they would have the results on Monday, and finally, after thirty plus years cold, they might be able to arrest the Hollywood Strangler.

Chapter Thirty

Sunday, November 20, 2022, Cedar City, Utah

'Okay, it's that house over there,' Jim said, pointing through the windshield at a small redbrick bungalow on Shakespeare Lane. It was a quiet residential street in Cedar City that terminated a few hundred yards away at a large red mountain dusted with snow. They'd driven three and a half hours south of Salt Lake City so that Kenyatta could try and convince Valerie Tang Reynolds, who lived in the red brick bungalow, to take a consensual DNA test. Even though Valerie had agreed to the meeting, Kenyatta would need to tread very carefully.

She leaned over and kissed Jim on the cheek. 'Why don't you go on into town and get some coffee, and I'll call you when I'm out.'

Jim looked mortified at the idea. 'No way. I'm waiting right here until you're done. And if I don't hear anything within an hour, I'm coming over there.'

Kenyatta laughed. 'This isn't a suspect's house, Jim. This is just a regular lady who I'm hoping will take a DNA test for me and give me some information.'

Jim shrugged. 'It's still a stranger's house and someone who might be related to a person who killed those two boys.'

'It's fine, Jim, honestly. I won't be too long, and then we can head out to Cedar Breaks,' she said, getting out of the car with her purse containing a notebook, pen and MyHeritage DNA kit.

'Good luck,' Jim called after her. 'I'll be watching.'

Kenyatta rolled her eyes at Jim treating the situation as though he was on a stake-out surveillance mission for a dangerous criminal. It was sweet, she supposed, as she crossed the street to the little house.

She reached the door and checked the time, finding that she was five minutes early. She pressed the bell, put on a warm smile and waited. Moments later, a young woman who appeared to be in her early thirties opened the door. She had brown eyes, dark hair pulled back into a ponytail and intermediate skin tone that hinted at her Asian heritage. She smiled and asked, 'Kenyatta?'

Kenyatta nodded. 'That's me. And you must be Valerie Tang?'

'Yes,' she confirmed, standing to one side. 'Come on in.'

Once inside, Kenyatta followed Valerie through a bright yellow hall into a living room at the back of the house. Although the room was small, it was nicely furnished, and a large floor-to-ceiling window gave a view over a small dusty yard and beyond to the rich red and white mountains that surrounded Cedar City.

'Take a seat,' Valerie said, gesturing to one of two sofas.

'Nice view,' Kenyatta said, sitting down and taking out her notepad and pen.

'Yeah, it's not bad,' Valerie agreed, sitting down opposite Kenyatta. 'So, you said you were working on a John Doe case—two boys that you think might be distantly related to me?'

Kenyatta nodded. Although she had laid it on thick in her email about the two boys' tragic situation, she had been deliberately vague about how she thought Valerie might be related. She started by repeating the facts about the two boys and their discovery in a dry creek bed in Penrose, Colorado.

'How awful for them,' Valerie said when Kenyatta finished. 'And how do you think they're related to me?'

And there was the killer question. As tempting as it was to give some nebulous answer that would mean Valerie would be more inclined to take a DNA test, Kenyatta needed to get informed consent. She needed total transparency. 'The DNA led me down from Arthit and Preeda Tang of Thailand through their kids who emigrated to the U.S., to three siblings who settled in Colorado. Two I have managed to eliminate, leaving the third, James Tang.'

'My great-grandfather?' Valerie asked. Her question sounded to Kenyatta like she was checking that she was following correctly, rather than incredulity that her family might be involved.

'Uh-huh. I don't know how much you know about your family history, but James Tang and his wife, Letitia, had ten children and it's my belief that a descendant of one of those is a parent of the Boys under the Bridge.'

Valerie's eyes widened. 'And that includes my dad and his brothers and sisters?'

'Yes, it does,' Kenyatta confirmed. 'But, those ten children of

James and Letitia Tang had *thirty* kids between them and the only way I can narrow that pool down is to get people to take a voluntary DNA test.'

'Which is where I come in,' Valerie concluded. 'I'm happy to take the test. I'd like to help.'

Kenyatta was relieved to hear her say it, but she was not yet fully informed.

'That's great to hear. But you do need to be aware that the test might implicate your own father, or an aunt or uncle in this case. It may also reveal something that you didn't know about your own close family.'

'Meaning my dad might not be my dad?'

'Exactly that kind of thing. But it could show up all kinds of unexpected results. I've worked with people who have discovered through testing that they were adopted, full siblings were actually half-siblings, they've discovered extra siblings, or found that parents or grandparents weren't who they thought they were, that they were donor conceived—'

'You sound like you're trying to talk me out of it,' Valerie interrupted.

Kenyatta smiled. 'I'm definitely *not* trying to do that. Solving this case relies on people taking consensual tests, but they need what we call informed consent. You have to be aware of the implications. Four people—your distant cousins—have already refused.'

Valerie nodded. 'I get it. Honestly, I've wanted to get one of these tests anyway for some time. I want to find out more about my Thai family. Here's the deal: I'll take the test voluntarily, knowing that I might get unexpected results, in exchange for you sharing what you know about my Thai family.'

'I will happily share what I know with you, whether you take the test or not,' Kenyatta replied.

'Do you have a kit with you?'

'I sure do,' Kenyatta confirmed, taking the MyHeritage kit from her purse. 'Do you want to take the test now?'

'Sure.'

'You haven't eaten or had anything to drink in the last thirty minutes, have you?'

Valerie shook her head, and Kenyatta opened up the test kit and handed the swab over.

'You need to open the pack and then swab the inside of your cheeks,' Kenyatta instructed.

Valerie took out the swab and began to rotate it around the inside of her cheeks.

'So, do you mind sharing a bit about your aunts and uncles on the Tang side?' Kenyatta asked. 'Like, who they married, kids, where they lived... That kind of stuff.'

'My father, Marcus Tang, had four siblings: Mary-Lou, Tammie, Joe and Raymond. We were pretty close with Tammie and Mary-Lou before they died but not very close to Joe, and I've only met Raymond once when he showed up unexpectedly at my dad's funeral. He never stayed in one place very long.'

Kenyatta's pulse quickened as she thought about the police view on the boys' deaths and how nobody seemed to have missed them.

Valerie screwed the cap tightly shut on the tube and handed it back to Kenyatta.

'Thanks,' Kenyatta said. 'We'll go ahead and get the kit registered to you in just a moment. Could you start by telling me what you know about Raymond?'

'Well, it'll be very brief. Based on what my dad told me, he had several girlfriends and kids along the way. He was pretty transient, moving from state to state, looking for work, then blowing all his money on having a good time.'

'Any idea of names of his girlfriends or children?'

Valerie shook her head. 'I can ask my Uncle Steve, Mary-Lou's husband. He might know, possibly.'

'That would be really helpful, thanks.'

'Do you want me to try and call him now?' Valerie asked.

'Well, sure, if you don't mind.'

Valerie nodded and picked up her cell phone from the coffee table. 'There's no time like the present, or so they say.'

'I'll get this kit registered to you while you're calling,' Kenyatta said, completing the registration details on her cell phone.

Valerie tapped the screen of her phone, then held it to her ear. She moved toward the window and stared out at the snow-capped mountains while she waited for the call to be answered.

Kenyatta watched her, deeply grateful that she had taken the DNA test, which would at the very least hopefully confirm that she was working on the right lines by focusing her attention on the descendants of James and Letitia Tang.

Valerie moved the phone from her ear and said to Kenyatta, 'Voicemail.' Then she raised the phone again and said, 'Hey, Steve. It's Valerie. I'm starting to do some family tree research into the Tangs, and I was wondering if I could pick your brains on my dad and his siblings sometime. I'll call again, or you can get back to me. Thanks, bye.'

'Thank you for doing that,' Kenyatta said. Once the results are in, it would be really useful to me if you could download them and then upload them to GEDmatch, which is a third-party website that allows comparisons of DNA kits from across the major companies. That way I can see how closely related to the two boys you are.'

'Got it. No problem—I might ask you to help me with it when the results come through.'

Kenyatta passed her cell phone to Valerie. 'If you can put your email and a password in there then it's all done.'

Valerie took the phone, added her details and then handed it back to Kenyatta. 'Shall I fill you in with what I know about the rest of my father's generation?'

'That would be great, thank you,' Kenyatta replied, picking up her pen and preparing to take notes.

Valerie talked extensively about her father, his two sisters and the little that she knew about her uncle, Joe. Kenyatta was grateful for the information but felt that they were unlikely to have been the parents of the Boys under the Bridge. It just didn't fit. They each had stable, well documented lives and their children had all grown into adulthood.

Widening the net, Kenyatta asked if Valerie knew anything about her grandfather's siblings and their descendants, but she knew almost nothing of use.

When Valerie could think of nothing more to say about her

family, Kenyatta packed away her things and put the DNA swab into the plastic envelope. 'Thank you so much for your time and for taking the test. I'll email you a link to the family tree that I created when I get back home. And you can always get back to me if you think of anything else about your family.' She stood up, put her things into her purse and shook Valerie's hand.

'No problem at all. I'll let you know when the results are posted, and you can talk me through getting the DNA onto GEDmatch.'

'Thanks again,' Kenyatta said, heading to the front door with Valerie walking behind her. 'I'm heading off to Cedar Breaks now...' Her voice trailed off as Valerie's cell phone began to ring.

'Excuse me,' Valerie said, taking the phone from her pocket. 'Oh, it's my uncle Steve. You might want to wait a moment. Hey, Steve. Yeah, that's right. I'm interested in the Tang line that goes back to Thailand. No, I realize you don't, but I want to start from me and work backward. Um, I've got pretty good information on my dad, Tammie and Mary-Lou, but Joe and especially Raymond I'm pretty sketchy on. Uh-huh. Right. Right. Oh, okay.'

As hard as she tried, Kenyatta failed to follow the one-sided conversation. But, as they continued talking, one thing became certain: Valerie was surprised by whatever her uncle was telling her.

The call lasted more than five minutes and, when it ended, Valerie looked shaken. 'It could be him—the man you're looking for. I think it's my uncle Raymond.'

Hudson was in his bedroom with the door shut. He could hear Ross and Reggie laughing in the living room and he found himself wondering if he was going to cope with having an extra roommate, even on a temporary basis. He was sitting down on his bed, gazing at the painting he had just hung on the wall opposite. It was the mountain abstract that he'd liked when he'd seen it on the wall of the Coffee Garden before Nora had told him that she had painted it.

Hudson took a selfie with the painting behind him and then typed out a short message.

Obsessed by this amazing painting that I bought today!

He sent the photo and message to Nora, stood up, took in a long breath, and then walked out of his bedroom and into the living room. Reggie and Ross were sitting on the couch, holding hands and watching *The Crown*. It was a surreal moment that reminded him of happier times doing exactly the same thing with Abigail.

'Hey, man,' Reggie said, releasing Ross's hand and pressing pause on the TV. 'Do you want us to get out of your way? Or do you want to watch this with us? Or maybe we could all watch a movie together?'

Hudson offered a reassuring smile. 'I'm good,' he insisted, aware that Reggie was trying to make the situation as easy as possible for all three of them.

'Thank you so much for letting me stay,' Ross said. 'I honestly really appreciate it, but I won't overstay my welcome. As soon as this episode is done, I'm going to get back on to looking for an apartment.'

'It's okay. Take your time,' Hudson replied. 'Just relax. It's Sunday. You had a crappy day yesterday. Chill out.'

'Yesterday *was* pretty awful,' Reggie agreed. 'Being harangued out of Becky's place by those heavies was totally out of order. They could see we were doing our best and in the process of leaving. They really didn't need to throw the rest of the stuff out onto the parking area like that.'

Ross agreed, tears welling in his eyes again. He'd arrived at Hudson's house yesterday, sobbing from the way that he'd been treated, all of it happening under Becky's father's watch from a car parked across the street from the Sugar House Apartment building. Whatever kind of message Andrew Larkin was trying to send to Becky, Hudson was fairly sure he'd achieved it, and Ross had paid the price. He hadn't liked to press the issue but, reading between the lines, gathered that something big was going on between Becky and her father, and that somehow it involved Maddie's missing husband.

'Keep watching,' Hudson insisted, pointing at the TV. 'I've got stuff I need to work on.'

'We don't mind going out or going into my room, or whatever,' Reggie said.

'No. You live here. It's fine,' Hudson said, turning and heading back to his bedroom. He closed his door and sat back on the bed. It was kind of true that he had stuff to do, but he didn't have the desire to do it. What he wanted to do was hang out with Nora, but he didn't want to appear desperate and scare her off.

He looked at his cell phone and found that he had a message and a missed call. The message was from Nora, and he felt the surge of an unfamiliar warmth as he read it.

Hudson! That's so sweet. Love it. Wanna come over for the evening?

Before he replied, he dialed up his answerphone and listened to the message. It was from an unknown number.

'Hi, Hudson. I know you don't want your name publicly linked to my story, but I just wanted to say how much I truly appreciate all you've done for me. I can't put what it means into words, but I hope you know that you've literally given me a second chance at life.' There was a short pause during which Hudson figured out who had left the message, then it was confirmed. 'It's Brandon Blake, by the way.'

Hudson listened to the message again as he stared at Nora's abstract painting of the Wasatch Mountains. He'd beaten himself up endlessly over the mistakes that he'd made with taking on the Chabala case, but he now accepted that it was over, and justice had finally been served. Just like the other mistakes that he'd made in his life, it was time to let it go and move on. He typed out a message to Nora.

I'm coming over right now.

Becky Larkin was sitting down in her apartment at the table by the window. She was finalizing her report into V38's biological father and the genealogy that had led her to identify him as a Sri Lankan UN Peacekeeper named Vairavan Subpan. The investigation needed to be watertight, meticulously referenced and unequivocal in its conclusion. The organization's legal team would push the UN hard to force Subpan to take a paternity test and face the consequences of his actions. She wasn't optimistic about its outcome, but she had to try.

She glanced out of the window at the relative normality of Pétion-Ville, thinking once again about Aidan's desire to leave the country before it was too late. The balance of her decision swayed between selfishly wanting to get out as fast as possible and feeling compelled to stay as an advocate for these women who had already endured so much. She looked at the pile of manila folders on the table, all of them abuse victims of the UN peacekeepers and all of them open cases. Could they really work them properly out of the country? She wasn't sure.

For the second time, Becky re-read her report, actively searching for errors, inconsistencies or anywhere that enough doubt over her work could be cast so that the legal team might choose not to go after Subpan.

She finished reading the report and made herself a glass of fresh mango juice. As she was drinking it, Aidan entered the apartment.

'G'day,' he greeted, bolting the door and kissing her on the lips.

'Hi,' she replied, noticing that he was holding a stack of official-looking papers. 'What's that?'

Aidan grimaced. 'Something you want to see but won't want to see.'

'Cryptic,' she said. 'What is it?'

'Copies of the deeds of the ownership of Château Lwa from 2010 to 2020.'

Becky gasped. 'How did you get those? And on a Sunday?'

'Good old-fashioned bribery.'

Becky held out her hand, but Aidan didn't pass them over. 'Let me see it, then.'

Finally, Aidan passed her the papers. With a sinking feeling, she looked at the first page. It took a matter of seconds to identify the owners of Château Lwa: The Larkin Investment and Finance Group. She looked up at Aidan with tears in her eyes.

'It's your dad's company, right?'

Becky nodded as her stomach contorted, making her feel instantly nauseous.

'Crikey. But it doesn't mean he's implicated, Becks. I've looked on each page and it's just signed by a woman called Angelique Miller. Your dad's name is nowhere to be seen. A big corporation like his must have stacks of offices, buildings and houses around the world. He can't know everything about all of them.'

Her father's name might not be on the title, but Becky now knew that he was implicated. His reaction to her inquiries and his overreaction to her coming out to Haiti clearly demonstrated that he was scared of what she might find. There was no doubt in her mind that her father knew what had gone on at that property. She just desperately hoped that he hadn't been directly involved. She thought of Maddie and her search for answers about Michael. A feeling of nausea rose inside her as she considered what she could tell her. As things stood, there was no confirmation that Michael, Artemon Bruce or Jay Craig had ever set foot in Château Lwa but the potential implication hung unspoken in the air.

Becky sent the file on V38 to the printer and then opened a password-protected document that she had been compiling on her investigations into her father's company.

'What are you going to do now?' Aidan asked.

'Find out who was involved at Château Lwa,' she replied, enlarging photographs of Michael Barnhart, Artemon Bruce and Jay Craig and sending them to the printer.

'And how are you going to do that?'

Becky swiveled her laptop in his direction. 'I'm going to show these photos to Lovelie and see if she recognizes them.'

Aidan sighed but said nothing, turned and headed into the bedroom. He didn't need to talk; she knew of his deep reservations about her investigation.

In a motion that felt as though it sliced into her heart, Becky scrolled down the document to a corporate headshot of her father. She enlarged it to fill the screen and sent it to the printer.

'Daddy,' she whispered, staring him in the eyes. 'What have you done?'

She closed the file, picked up her cell phone and called Fabienne. She picked up almost instantly. 'Hello, Becky.'

'Hi. I need to see Lovelie right away. I have something that I need to show her.'

Fabienne took a moment to answer. 'When do you want me to arrange a meeting?'

'Today—this afternoon,' Becky replied. 'It's important.'

'I will see what I can do. Let me call you back.'

'*Mèsi*,' Becky said.

Becky and Aidan were waiting anxiously inside Fabienne's shack. They had traveled into the center of Port-au-Prince again to meet with Lovelie. They were each sitting on a wooden stool, gazing at the closed door. As with most houses in the city, the shutters were closed over the solitary window, giving the room a gloomy atmosphere. The mood was made all the darker by the presence of a toothless old man sitting in the corner of the room, staring at them and occasionally barking at them in Haitian Creole. Fabienne, standing beside the locked door and peering out through a finger-wide crack that ran down its length, had explained that her father was not happy about their presence in the house. 'It could attract attention from the gangs,' she had translated.

'Tell him we won't be long, and we won't come back,' Becky had said, which had seemed to quiet the old man.

And now they were all waiting in silence.

Becky was tapping her knee as her anxiety about the situation grew. She was nervous that Lovelie might not show up, but she was even more nervous about the implications if she did show up. It was going to be a decisive moment.

Aidan placed his broad hand over Becky's and gave it a firm squeeze, which helped to calm her slightly. 'It'll be okay,' he whispered.

Becky nodded but, if her suspicions were right, then the situation would be very, very far from okay.

'I spoke to Dickie Stones this morning, and he thinks it's a good plan to hop over the border into the Dominican. He said he'll set the wheels in motion first thing tomorrow.'

Becky met his gaze, not sure what to say. Dickie Stones was their line manager and, since the assassination of the prime minister, he had been putting pressure on the team to leave Haiti.

'I don't know, Aidan,' Becky replied quietly.

'She's coming,' Fabienne announced, unlocking the tin door and pulling it open.

Lovelie stood at the entrance and peered inside, squinting as her eyes adjusted from the harsh light outside.

'*Bonjou*,' Becky said, standing up and trying to offer a warm smile. 'Thank you for coming.'

'Hello,' Lovelie replied, stepping inside so that Fabienne could close and lock the door behind her.

Becky noticed that she was wearing the same discolored floral dress and tatty flip-flops as the last time that they had seen her.

Becky wanted to ask how she was but could see from everyone's faces that they just wanted the meeting over with before it had even started. 'So, we've been making inquiries and we found out who owned Château Lwa. It's a company called The Larkin Investment and Finance Group,' Becky said, pausing so that Fabienne could translate. Lovelie had no reaction to the news, so Becky continued. 'It's an American company.' She'd toyed with the idea of full disclosure about her connection to the company but, following discussions with Aidan, she had decided to keep that information quiet for the moment.

Fabienne translated but, again, there was no reaction from Lovelie.

'I have photographs of some of the staff in my bag,' Becky said. 'I believe they came out to Haiti in 2015. May I show them to you?'

Once she had heard the same in Haitian Creole, Lovelie nodded.

Becky opened her bag and removed the papers. On the top was a color photograph of Jay Craig, which she passed over.

Lovelie took the image and studied it for a few seconds before nodding. '*Wi. Li te nan kay la*,' she said quietly.

'Yes, he was at the house,' Fabienne said.

Becky felt sick as Lovelie spoke more. She talked fast and Becky couldn't follow anything of what was being said. She glanced from Lovelie to Fabienne, waiting for the translation to come.

'He was at the house, but he did not go near any of the girls. He came with some other men, but they were not expected, and all the girls were made to hide away until they were gone. But Lovelie saw them,' Fabienne explained.

Becky passed Lovelie the photograph of Artemon Bruce. Lovelie quickly responded with, '*Se menm bagay la.*'

'It's the same thing,' Fabienne said.

Lovelie spoke more and Becky waited.

'He came to the house with the last man, but it is the same situation: he did not take part in the assaults.'

Becky nodded, then showed her the photograph of Michael Barnhart, holding her breath in anticipation. In the few seconds that it took for Lovelie to study the image, a whole age seemed to pass in Becky's mind, as she thought about what she would be telling Maddie.

'*Li te ak de lòt mesye yo. Li te sanble fache anpil kont Bakas yo,*' Lovelie said.

Becky's nausea worsened as she heard the word *Bakas*, recalling that the abuse victims had given that name to the evil man in charge of what had occurred at Château Lwa.

'He was with the other two men. He seemed very angry at the Bakas,' Fabienne relayed.

The relief was instant. Michael was not the Bakas. 'Do you know what they were arguing about?'

Once translated, Lovelie immediately shook her head.

'Did they stay long?'

Lovelie again shook her head.

Becky had one piece of paper left in her hand. It was the photograph of her own father, Andrew Larkin. The idea of not showing the picture flitted into her thoughts. Perhaps life would be simpler if she didn't know of her father's involvement. But she crushed the idea and handed it over to Lovelie. She simply had to know.

The reaction was immediate and horrific.

Lovelie gasped and then screamed loudly, making the man in the corner of the room leap up and shout.

'*Se li! Se li! Se Bakas yo,*' Lovelie shrieked.

Becky didn't need the translation, but Fabienne provided it. 'It's him. The Bakas.'

Fabienne put her arm around Lovelie, who was now sobbing uncontrollably, clearly retraumatized by the image.

'I think we need to leave,' Aidan said, standing and touching

Becky's arm.

Becky agreed.

'*Se li ki banm ti bebe a*,' Lovelie said between sobs.

Becky looked at Fabienne to understand.

'She says, he's the one who gave me the baby.'

Becky's breath caught in her throat and her heart felt as though it had cracked in two.

She now knew that she had to stay in Haiti.

Chapter Thirty-One

Monday, November 21, 2022, Los Angeles, California

Ted Marsden was sitting at his workstation in the LAPD Headquarters, exhausted. He'd spent most of the night backgrounding Moreno and writing a strong affidavit that now ran to forty-two pages. He'd extracted a lot of information from the crime index and DMV databases about Moreno's life during the period that the murders took place. The case against him was already good and he was sure that it would get even stronger once they were legally permitted to search his house and the museum.

On his desk was the affidavit for the arrest and search warrant that he had prepared for José Moreno and his properties. He was triple checking that it was good to go the moment that he had the confirmation from the forensics lab that José's DNA, extracted from the envelope, matched with the profile in CODIS. The affidavit had been approved by Detective Supervisor Mitzi Roberts and an attorney from the prosecutor's office. Although more investigation would be needed, they all agreed that, with the DNA confirmed, they will have proved probable cause.

Marsden slid his chair back and addressed Powers, who was sitting down beside him going through the murder book for the Hollywood Strangler case, making notes in light of the IGG findings. After the arrest, they would need to work hard and quickly to prove the case beyond a reasonable doubt. 'Do you want to go through this affidavit again?' Marsden asked him.

Powers screwed up his face. 'Honestly, it's there, Marsden. It's solid. It doesn't need more work. Which judge are you taking it to?'

'Judge Bones,' he replied, having already looked up the judge who was on duty for signing warrants today and finding that it was a person with whom he was unfamiliar. With a case of this magnitude, he did not want to waste the time from all the additional questions that would likely stem from the unfamiliarity. Instead, he was going to try his go-to judge, William Bones. Marsden had worked with Judge Bones on numerous occasions in the past and he felt that he trusted his work to the point that the judge rarely read the affidavits presented to him in full.

Marsden put the affidavit back down on his desk and stood up to go and get some coffee. Powers was right; it was solid and good to go. 'Have you found anything new from the murder book?'

'Not much. I'm just making notes for new leads to pursue.'

'Anything from EDD?' Marsden asked, referring to the Employment Development Department for the state of California, whose database was capable of producing ten years of work history.

'It just gives the museum,' Powers replied.

'That's probably a good thing,' Marsden conceded. 'We just need to tear his house and the museum apart for any other souvenirs he might have taken.'

'If he's brave or stupid enough to have a pair of Natalie Van Derlyn's panties on public display then he's—'

Marsden's cell phone began to ring on his desk. He answered it quickly. 'Marsden.'

'Hey, Teddy. It's Cathy.'

'Oh, hi, Cathy. Do you have news for me?' He said, putting the call on speaker so that Powers could hear.

'I do indeed,' she answered.

'Come on, already. Tell me. Is it a match?'

'It is,' she confirmed.

Marsden took a moment, staring at Powers as the reality of the situation kicked in. 'You're sure about that, Cathy?'

'It's a straight match. The chances of it being someone else is over five octillion times.'

'Wow. Not that I know what that number means.' It was the news that Marsden wanted and was fully expecting to hear, but still it took his breath away. They had done what many had considered impossible and had identified the Hollywood Strangler.

'Teddy, are you still there?'

'Sorry, Cathy. Yes, I'm here. Thank you so much for working after hours on this. I really appreciate it. I owe you.'

'You're welcome. Give my love to Judith. And good luck with the case.'

Marsden thanked her again and ended the call.

'We did it,' Powers said, offering his hand for a high-five.

'Not yet,' Marsden said, declining to slap Powers's hand. He'd seen plenty of investigations throughout his career fail at the last hurdle. 'Let's get this affidavit signed and get Moreno into custody before we celebrate.' Marsden opened the contacts on his cell and scrolled down to the judge. It was picked up in just a few rings. 'Hi, Judge. It's Ted Marsden from LAPD.'

'Oh, hi there,' Bones greeted. 'I'm taking it that a call at eight o'clock Monday morning isn't going to be social?'

'You'd be right about that. I've got an affidavit to sign. It's a big one. You're going to like it.'

'You want to do a telephonic search warrant?' Bones asked.

'I'd prefer to come over and see you in person, if that's okay?' Marsden said. A telephonic search warrant involved a recorded three-way phone conversation with the addition of a prosecutor from the District Attorney's office. It was much quicker to obtain but involved a lot more paperwork after the event.

'Sure. I'm home for the morning if you want to swing by.' Bones said.

'We're leaving right now,' Marsden said, thanking the judge and terminating the call. 'Let's go.'

Marsden and Powers arrived at Judge Bones's home on Sunset Boulevard in Beverly Hills twenty minutes later.

'Man, am I in the wrong job,' Powers exclaimed as Marsden parked his Ford Explorer on the drive to a sprawling gray-brick mansion.

Marsden ignored the comment, climbed out of the car and hurried toward the door, which opened as they approached.

'Was that good, pre-rush-hour traffic or were you parked around the corner when you called me?' Judge Bones asked, offering a thin smile. He was a tall African American with short black hair, matching moustache and a stern demeanor.

'Good traffic,' Marsden answered, shaking the judge's hand. 'Good to see you.'

'And you,' Bones replied, shaking Powers's hand and inviting them both inside.

Marsden elbowed Powers as he whistled at the grand entrance hall with marble floors, high ceilings and a wide mahogany staircase over which hung a large chandelier.

As he always did when Marsden approached him at home rather than in court, Judge Bones directed them into a library off the hall. The walls were lined with floor-to-ceiling bookshelves and in the center of the room was a long dark wooden table. Judge Bones sat at the head but didn't invite Marsden and Powers to join him. Instead, he raised the pair of reading glasses hanging on a chain around his neck and held out his hand.

Marsden silently passed the judge the thick stack of paperwork and watched as he skipped over the front page, known in LAPD as the hero sheet, which detailed Marsden's training and experience in law enforcement, and instead, began to read about the case in question. Just as Marsden had expected, he quickly looked up at the two men. He removed his glasses and said, 'Remarkable.'

'I said it was a big one,' Marsden said with a grin.

The judge repositioned his glasses and continued reading through the chronology of the steps taken to reach the point of naming José Matias Moreno as the killer.

Marsden glanced across at Powers, knowing what he was thinking: the judge was taking much longer than he usually took to read the statement. The longer that it went on, the more worried Marsden became, and his hopes that the delay was caused by the case being high-profile and forty-two pages long began to slip away. Had they been too hasty in getting to this point? Should they have conducted more of an investigation to take the case past beyond reasonable doubt?

Suddenly, the judge looked up and removed his glasses. 'I'm satisfied that what you've outlined here establishes probable cause. Please raise your right hand and swear that the facts set forth in this affidavit are true.'

Marsden took a long breath, raised his right hand, and responded, 'I, Edward Marsden, do solemnly swear that the facts set forth in this affidavit are true and correct to the best of my knowledge and belief.'

Judge Bones nodded, flipped the affidavit to the correct page and slid it over to Marsden to sign.

'Thank you, Judge,' Marsden said, signing his name.

'Good luck with it. You've got ten days to execute the warrant,' Judge Bones said, adding his own signature to the bottom of the document and standing up to signal that the meeting was over.

Marsden took the paperwork, thanked the judge again, and then headed to the door and back out to the car.

'I thought he was never going to sign it,' Powers said with a nervous laugh. 'Can we just code three it over there and make the arrest already?'

Marsden rolled his eyes at Powers's half-serious idea of a gung-ho approach to blue light it over to Moreno's house to make the arrest right now. 'This may be Hollywood, but it isn't *Hollywood*,' Marsden answered, pulling out onto Sunset Boulevard, which was steadily getting busier with commuter traffic. They needed to get back to headquarters and set the plan in motion. He'd already discussed what would happen next with Detective Supervisor Mitzi Roberts. Now he just needed to put it into action.

Chapter Thirty-Two

Monday, November 21, 2022, Salt Lake City, Utah

Maddie checked her emails, cell phone and then the *LA Times* website, searching for any mention that José Moreno had been arrested. But there was nothing. She'd tried to call Ted Marsden several times yesterday and again today to check that her message that they'd made the wrong call with Angel Moreno had been received, but he hadn't gotten back to her. The silence made her nervous and unable to concentrate on her work. It was exactly the same for her team and, for that reason, she had given them a couple of days to work on their own side cases while they waited for news about the Hollywood Strangler.

From the outer office, she heard Kenyatta arrive back from the funeral of one of the homeless people she worked with at the SLC Kitchen.

Maddie went out to find Kenyatta removing her jacket. 'How was the funeral? Are you okay?'

Kenyatta turned with a sigh, revealing that her eyes were bloodshot and puffy. 'Just awful. Apart from me and Jim and the vicar, there was nobody there. Not a single other person. How sad is that? The service was short with nothing personal about Candice, because nobody knew her life before she became homeless. Then, it was all over.'

Maddie touched Kenyatta's arm. 'I'm sorry.'

'I just feel so helpless,' Kenyatta said.

'You help more than most people. You touch their lives in ways you can't imagine.'

Kenyatta wiped her eyes. 'But it's not enough. The city is going to pay for a pauper's funeral. She won't get a headstone. Nobody will mourn her. It just breaks my heart.'

Maddie pulled her into a hug, not knowing what more she could say to reassure Kenyatta that she was just a good person living in a sometimes-bad world. 'Why don't you take the rest of the day off?'

Kenyatta dried her eyes. 'I'm okay. Jim's being very sweet. He wants to take me to Hawaii. Can you imagine?'

Maddie shrugged. 'You should take him up on it. Go.'

'I can't do that,' Kenyatta countered. 'There's the job, the kids, the homeless kitchen.'

'The kids are old enough to look after themselves. There are enough helpers at the kitchen to cover you and, as for your job, I insist that you take a vacation.'

Kenyatta thought for a moment, then shook her head. 'No. It's okay. I'm okay. Have you heard anything from the detectives about the case?'

'Not yet. I've tried calling him but he's not picking up or getting back to me. I don't know what to take from that.'

'I guess it means that he's busy—hopefully making an arrest.'

'Yeah,' she agreed absent-mindedly.

'So, what are we all working on today?' Kenyatta asked.

'Your own cases,' Maddie replied.

Kenyatta's face lit up. 'I've got an update on the Boys under the Bridge, but I'll save it for this afternoon. I need to do some more investigating.'

'Glad you've made some progress,' Maddie said. 'I look forward to hearing all about it.'

Maddie returned to her office and sat down with a protracted sigh. She checked her phone and emails once again, but there was still nothing. What was going on with the Hollywood Strangler case?

Unusually for Maddie, the afternoon dragged. Her concentration levels were at an all-time low and she flinched every time her phone beeped, or a message pinged into her inbox. She wasn't usually this distracted by a case, but she knew that this one was going to generate a huge amount of publicity and she wanted to be as forewarned as possible. She'd tried calling Marsden twice more during the day but had reached his voicemail on both occasions. She was getting the picture that, for whatever reason, he didn't want to talk to her right now.

At 4:30 p.m., Maddie called a briefing. She had no expectations of her team, as they were all working cases that had so far proven difficult to crack. But it would be an opportunity to talk through what they were up to, and then everyone could go home a little earlier than usual.

'Anyone desperate to share anything?' Maddie asked, taking a seat close to the front.

'I've been working on the Cleveland Cannibal, but nothing to report,' Hudson said. 'One day…'

'Well, I have a very important update on the Boys under the Bridge,' Kenyatta announced, rising from her seat and sharing her screen on the digital whiteboard. It showed a descendant's tree for Joseph and Betty Tang.

'I'll just start with the caveat that I'm waiting on the results of a DNA test by this young lady here,' Kenyatta said, circling her mouse over one of Joseph and Betty's grandchildren, Valerie Tang. 'The kit is on its way to MyHeritage right now, but it's my belief that one of Joseph and Betty's children is the mother or father of the two boys.'

'That's amazing, Kenyatta,' Maddie congratulated. It was her pet case that she'd been working hard to solve for a very long time. Getting to this point was a fantastic achievement.

'Thank you,' Kenyatta replied. 'That's not all. Valerie gave me a lot of background for this generation and most of them had stable and well-documented lives that I've managed to confirm for myself. All except one, that is.'

'Well, don't keep us in suspense,' Maddie said. 'Which is it?'

'Raymond Tang,' Kenyatta revealed, clicking on his profile. By Kenyatta's normal standards, it was sparse, containing a birth year and location but no marriage or death information. Down the right-hand side, three spouses with limited biographical detail were listed.

'Raymond was itinerant and never stayed in any one place for more than a couple of months at a time. He had multiple girlfriends, wives and kids all around the States. All of his known partners were Asian, which, if I'm right, would explain the high proportion of that ethnicity in the boys' DNA. Raymond didn't keep in regular contact with the rest of the family but would show up randomly, then disappear again for years on end. I think he could be the boys' father.'

'That's great work, Kenyatta,' Maddie praised. 'It's a great example of not giving up on a case because of low matches.'

'Yeah, I just need to wait with bated breath for the MyHeritage results to show up and then get her DNA onto GEDmatch so I can compare it to the boys'.'

'Have you told the detective in charge of the case that you've made progress?' Maddie asked.

'Not yet,' Kenyatta replied. 'I didn't want to get ahead of myself.'

'Well done,' Maddie said.

'Thank you. I won't rest until there are two names on the headstone and someone is behind bars,' she said, sitting back down.

'Reggie, do you have anything to bring to the table?'

'The Snowwolf magic strikes again,' he said, rising from his chair and sharing his screen. 'Say hello to Wind River Doe or Leon Sierra as he's sometimes known.'

'What? That's him?' Maddie shrieked, looking at a monochrome photograph of a smiling black man, standing on a deserted beach and posing for the camera.

'Uh-huh,' Reggie confirmed.

'Who was he?' Maddie pressed, heartened to know that this man had had family or friends somewhere out there who might be missing him.

Reggie closed the photograph and returned to Leon Sierra's profile. At the top of the page was his name.

'Hector Lewis,' Maddie read, drawing it out as a sense of satisfaction that he'd finally been identified pervaded her body. 'Tell me about him.'

'So, Hector Lewis was born in Mississippi in 1949. He moved to New York to study photography and then, at some point in the 1960s, he moved to Kansas City, where he worked as a wedding photographer. On March 18, 1978, he left his apartment and disappeared. His sister reported him missing but he was never seen again. Here's his NamUs profile.'

Reggie switched tabs to the National Missing and Unidentified Persons System website, where a biography was open and waiting.

Missing Person: Hector Lewis
Missing From: Kansas City, Kansas
Missing Age: 29
Current Age: 73

Height: 5' 8"
Weight: 176 lbs
Race: Black / African American
Date of Last Contact: March 18, 1978
NamUs Case Created: July 15, 2018
Circumstances of Disappearance: The missing person left his apartment in Kansas City on the morning of March 18, 1978 to go to his job as a photographer's assistant but never made it there. He has never been seen since.
Clothing: Black jacket, black cap, white shirt

'I can't believe you did it,' Maddie said, her eyes moistening with emotion. 'Was it difficult?'

Reggie nodded and explained the steps he'd taken to reach his conclusion. His theory about Leon Sierra descending from the white slave owner, Richard Woods, and one of his slaves, Betsy Adley, had been borne out. The link between Leon Sierra and his DNA matches, Malik Johnson and Elijah Benton, was through David Woods, the slave owner.

'I'm so happy,' she said, dabbing her eyes. 'I'll get in touch with the two law enforcement agencies so they can link the cases and let Hector's family know about his death. Hopefully this new information might shed some light on how he died.'

'It'll be a bittersweet moment for the family,' Kenyatta commented, adding her congratulations to Reggie.

Maddie stood up, just as Ross walked over to her and whispered, 'Detective Marsden is on the phone for you. I thought you'd want to take it.'

'Thank you,' she replied. 'Put him through to my office.' She turned to the team and said, 'Well done, everyone. You're all amazing. I'm so proud of you all. Really. We're done for the day. Please go home and rest, and I'll see you tomorrow.'

Maddie hurried into her office and closed the door. She hoped that she hadn't been too abrupt with the staff but ideally wanted them gone to avoid any questions that might arise about this phone call.

'Hello?' Maddie said.

'It's Ted Marsden here,' he said. 'Sorry I haven't been able to take your calls.'

'No, it's fine. I just wanted to make sure you got my message about José being the main suspect.'

'Yeah, I got the message, thank you,' he said flatly. 'Was there something else?'

'Uh, I guess just to know how you're getting on.'

'I'm afraid I can't tell you anything right now. I will, but I can't right now.'

'Sure, I understand,' Maddie said.

'I really need you not to talk about this case *at all* with anyone for the next twenty-four hours, okay? That includes partner, kids, office staff, best friend. The NDA is still in place.'

'I get it,' Maddie answered.

'Goodbye,' Marsden said, terminating the call.

Maddie stared at her phone, assuming that within the next twenty-four hours, José Matias Moreno was going to be arrested and named as the Hollywood Strangler.

Chapter Thirty-Three

Tuesday, November 22, 2022, Los Angeles, California

Ted Marsden was sitting beside Powers in the back of an unmarked white Chevrolet Express van. They were parked on Canyon Lake Drive, opposite the entrance to Lake Hollywood Park, renowned as being one of the best spots to photograph the Hollywood sign. Even though it was just after 6 a.m. on a chilly November morning, there were already tourists standing on the worn patches of grass, taking selfies as the sun rose over the adjacent hill, illuminating the huge white letters.

Marsden looked out of the blacked-out windows, adrenalin already firing through his veins at what was about to go down. On the opposite hill to the Hollywood sign, he could see the rear of Moreno's property, perched high up on Durand Drive. It was ironic that an estimated eight million dollars and over two hundred thousand man-hours had been spent looking for the Hollywood Strangler, and all along he'd been living directly opposite the iconic sign, while running a museum on Hollywood Boulevard dedicated to the industry. This guy was a new level of psychopath and, for that reason, a detailed plan involving twenty-six personnel from LAPD had been hatched for his take-down.

Owing to the steep and narrow nature of Durand Drive, three of the eight vehicles involved were parked at the bottom of Canyon Lake Drive and two further along the road above but well out of sight of Moreno's property. Just one vehicle, a dark blue Toyota Sienna, had a view of Moreno's house. Inside it was a two-man surveillance team that had been monitoring the front of the house for several hours. Although there had been no positive sightings of Moreno so far this morning, the surveillance team had reported that several lights had gone on and off at the property and that they had seen movement behind a window. The Ford Bronco registered to Moreno was parked in front of the house.

'This feels like the longest morning of my entire life,' Powers complained. 'Can we get an UberEats delivery here?'

Marsden glared at him.

Stevenson, the operation commander from SWAT, was sitting up front in the passenger seat, studying Moreno's house through binoculars. Since their arrival two hours ago, he had said very little. He was in his early thirties with a thick neck and broad, muscular shoulders. He was wearing the black SWAT outfit and helmet, ready to go. Beside him was another team member who'd not been introduced but who kept one hand poised by the engine start button and one hand on the wheel.

The car fell back to silence and Marsden watched a group of high school kids pour out of a minibus into Lake Hollywood Park, every single one holding up their cell phones and taking pictures of the sign. He took a deep breath to try and subdue the adrenaline rush. He was definitely too old for all this. After he'd talked over the arrest plan with Mitzi Roberts, he'd handed in his resignation from the cold case team. She'd said that she was sorry to see him go but totally understood that the timing was right. He had said he'd stay on to help get the case ready for prosecution, then he would be done.

'Confirmed sighting of the suspect,' Stevenson's radio suddenly announced. 'Suspect in wheelchair moving toward the vehicle. Appears to be alone, no visible carry.'

'All teams, green light. Go!' Stevenson yelled into his radio.

Marsden gripped the seat as two black armored BearCats whizzed past at high speed. Directly behind them, a patrol car with lights flashing but no sirens parked across the street at an angle that completely blocked the road.

'Go!' Stevenson shouted to the driver, who hit the accelerator and followed the BearCats up the road toward the house.

'It's happening,' Powers said, as they flew up the road.

Seconds later, they parked behind the two BearCats, which had been joined by the other two that had driven down from above the house. At least a dozen SWAT officers, dressed fully in black with bullet-proof vests, were aiming Colt M4 Carbine assault rifles, moving steadily up the drive and surrounding Moreno in his wheelchair.

Marsden held his breath as the SWAT team slowly moved toward Moreno, shouting commands for him not to move. Marsden had seen plenty of occasions when suspects at this point had reached into their jackets for a gun and been instantly killed by a shower of bullets. He'd also seen it when a suspect had reached into his jacket for nothing at all, knowing what was coming and preferring the firing squad to a lifetime in jail.

Moreno raised his hands in the air as the first SWAT officers reached his wheelchair.

From the car, Marsden could hear they were yelling at him but couldn't hear what they were saying.

Moreno leaned forward and one of the officers slapped a pair of handcuffs behind his back and then proceeded to conduct a thorough search of his body and the chair.

'We're clear,' a voice said over the comms.

'Alpha team move to the house,' Stevenson replied. He waited and watched as half the personnel on the drive proceeded toward the house with their weapons drawn and ready. The entry team with various tools, including a battering ram, followed closely behind.

Stevenson turned around to face Marsden and Powers. 'You want to do the honors?'

Marsden nodded and they stepped out of the car, following Stevenson across the street and through the gates.

Moreno was sitting in silence with six members of the SWAT team standing over him, their weapons pointed at his head and chest.

Moreno looked up and a thin smile of recognition spread over his face when he clocked Marsden and Powers. 'I thought you guys might be cops.'

Behind him, the entry team smashed open the front door to the house.

Moreno glanced over his shoulder. 'I would have given you the key, if you'd asked.'

Marsden stepped closer, the weight of what he was about to say heavy on his shoulders. 'José Matias Moreno, you are under arrest for murder and conspiracy to commit murder. You have the right to remain silent. Anything you say can and will be used against you in a court of law. You have the right to an attorney. If you cannot afford an attorney, one will be provided for you. Do you understand these rights as I have recited them to you?'

Moreno said nothing, and Marsden saw his cold and lifeless eyes up close for the first time.

'Do you understand your rights, Mr. Moreno?' he repeated.

'Murder of who?' he asked, swishing back his greasy hair.

'I can't talk until you confirm that you've understood your rights.'

'I understand my damn rights.'

'The murder of Natalie Van Derlyn,' Marsden answered.

Moreno gave a grotesque grin, but there was nothing in his dead eyes. 'It was her panties, wasn't it?' Moreno gave a hollow, haunting laugh. 'They've been on display in that museum for over a decade and nobody even noticed. Then *you* swing by and, of all the exhibits I got going on, you notice a pair of panties. I guess that says something about you, huh, Detective?'

'I noticed them because I'm working this case and knew that the killer had taken them,' Marsden said.

'Sure,' Moreno said with a grin. 'Natalie was a Hollywood Strangler victim, but you're not charging me with the murders of the other victims. Why is that Detective?'

'Natalie's just for starters,' Marsden retorted, disgusted by Moreno's reaction. Since the only evidence that they had besides the DNA was Natalie's underwear, it had been agreed only to arrest Moreno initially for her murder, in the hope that evidence for the other victims would turn up in the house and museum.

'So, just because I got her panties on display, that makes me the Hollywood Strangler? I've got an animatronic shark in the museum, but it doesn't make me Spielberg. I'm a collector, Detective. It's called Murderabilia. I've also got prison art by Dahmer, signed photos of Richard Ramirez and letters from Ted Bundy and John Wayne Gacy. It don't make me a serial killer, though; it makes me a collector.'

'We've got your DNA,' Powers said.

Marsden watched the blood drain from Moreno's face, his mask of confidence gone in that instant. 'The envelope,' he muttered, nodding slowly.

'Yeah, the envelope,' Powers confirmed.

Moreno looked at Marsden. 'Guess I'd better take the fifth.'

Marsden was sickened. He turned to Stevenson. 'Take him downtown.'

Stevenson nodded and began to prepare the team to transport Moreno to the LAPD Headquarters, where their role in the arrest would end.

'Can we go inside the house?' Marsden asked.

'Not until it's cleared,' Stevenson replied.

Marsden and Powers watched as Moreno was transferred from his wheelchair into the rear of a black Mercedes-Benz Sprinter van. 'They'll make a movie of this someday,' Moreno called.

Marsden was in no doubt about that. He watched as the sliding door was closed and the Sprinter took off down the hill.

'Now do we get to high-five?' Powers asked, holding up his hand.

Marsden slapped his hand.

'We did it,' Powers said.

'Yeah,' Marsden said. 'But really, it was the Venator team who identified him. And even that wouldn't have been possible had Dr. Speth not taken the duplicate rape kit. I need to call him and let him know what his dedication back in the 1980s just did.'

'It's a team effort,' Powers conceded.

'The house is clear,' a voice barked from Stevenson's radio.

'Okay, you're good to go inside,' Stevenson said. 'We're going to move out, and I'll get the patrol cars up here to wait until you get forensics here.'

'Thank you,' Marsden said, shaking his hand.

He and Powers walked up the drive as the SWAT team exited the house, their weapons down.

'Here,' Marsden said, handing Powers a pair of latex gloves. He put his own pair on and then stepped inside the property.

He didn't have a clear idea of what he expected the Hollywood Strangler's house to look like, but this wasn't it. The entrance hall, hexagonal in shape, was clean, bright and modern with black polished-granite floor tiles. Including the front door, there were six open doors, one centered on each wall. Marsden instinctively walked toward the one back right, where the most light was coming from.

'Wow,' Powers said, following him into what was evidently a

living room. The ceiling was pale blue, the walls were painted to resemble the Hollywood hills and framed perfectly into the rectangular window was a view of the Hollywood sign.

'Freaky,' Marsden commented, checking out the rest of the decor. Perhaps unsurprisingly, the carpet was bright red and the two black sofas, resembling movie theatre seats, faced a huge TV screen that took up most of one wall. The back wall was filled entirely with shelves crammed with VHS movie tapes and DVDs.

'Check this out,' Powers said, standing in front of a framed picture. It was a poster for *Garbo's Wishes*, Tracie Satchell and Christian Lofthouse's final movie.

Marsden moved back into the hall, walking through the open door between the living room and the front entrance. Inside the dimly lit room were six glass cabinets about the size of chest freezers but, from his position in the doorway, Marsden couldn't determine what was inside. He stepped into the room to the first cabinet and found that it contained a perfect miniature re-creation of the famous scene from Robyn Stoltman's movie, *Fleeing to France*.

'God,' he whispered, crouching down and taking in the perfect detail of the display. He quickly realized that this wasn't actually a re-creation of the scene from the movie, but a haunting re-creation of Moreno's own horrific tableau. The Barbie-sized figure representing Robyn was sitting on a sofa, drinking and smoking in her own bedroom, suspended by fishing line from a wooden frame that Moreno had constructed.

He stood up, stunned.

He shifted along to the next cabinet, finding that it was a perfect miniature version of the scene Moreno had created from *Moonlit Desires*, again with a Barbie-esque figure appearing in every way as the actress, Tiffany Winters, had appeared in the movie, right down to her clothes and hair.

The third cabinet contained a re-creation of the film noir, *Diamonds in the Rough*, with the actor, Kevin Hoang, AKA Jack Fairbanks, being represented by what appeared to be a customized Action Man figure. The staging was scaled perfectly.

Marsden turned to the three cabinets behind him, seeing instantly that they were the grotesque homages to Moreno's work on the final victims. He bent down to look closely at the miniature set of *Garbo's Wishes*. It was exactly as he had remembered it. The wallpaper, the bed linen, the carpet and every item of furniture was just how it had been.

He shuddered and suddenly needed to get outside and away from the macabre freak's museum. He turned to the open front door and took in a long breath of fresh air. Then, he noticed the room directly opposite the one he'd just left.

Crossing the hall, he entered the dark room and switched on the light. Every single inch of every wall, even the window and the ceiling, was covered in newspaper and magazine cuttings, all of them dedicated to coverage of the Hollywood Strangler, going all the way back to the 1980s.

Marsden gazed across years of headlines, photographs and newspaper extracts, unable to take in what he was seeing. Then, his eyes settled on the creepiest part: a single red chair in the center, the only piece of furniture in the whole room.

He slowly walked over to the chair and sat down. It faced six images running in a vertical line of each of the victims in their grotesque post-mortem poses. The Polaroids were identical to those left at each crime scene but for one thing: standing beside each of the victims was a naked man, grinning. That man was indisputably José Moreno.

Marsden had investigated a lot of disturbed individuals throughout his career but, as he gazed around the room in disbelief, he realized that he was ending his career on the most depraved psychopath he'd ever encountered.

Chapter Thirty-Four

Tuesday, November 22, 2022, Salt Lake City, Utah

Maddie pulled onto her driveway, switched off the DNA: ID podcast that she'd been listening to all the way home and headed into the house. She kicked off her boots, hung up her jacket and bolted the front door.

'Mom!' Trenton yelled, rushing from the kitchen. 'You're never going to guess what's happened.'

Maddie's heart began to pound as all manner of possible scenarios ran through her mind. Bizarrely, at the forefront of her thoughts was the idea that Michael had returned. Then she wondered if something had happened to her mom, but Trenton seemed to be in disbelief rather than panicked.

'What?' she finally asked.

'They've arrested the Hollywood Strangler!' he answered, hurrying back into the kitchen.

Maddie followed and saw that Katie and her mom were both seated in front of the TV, as though they were in a movie theatre. ABC4 Utah was showing a press conference live from Los Angeles. A police chief, flanked by several officers, was talking to the camera.

'...*the suspect, José Moreno, was identified through investigative genetic genealogy.*'

Trenton frowned and slowly turned to face Maddie. 'Mom?' There were dozens of other IGG companies out there who could have solved it, but he could see in her face that it had been Venator that had cracked it. 'No way!'

Maddie couldn't help but laugh.

'What's so funny?' her mom asked.

'Mom's company was the one to identify the Hollywood Strangler!' Trenton cried. 'I can't believe you didn't tell us. This is *huge*, Mom!'

'Yeah, I know.'

'He doesn't look like a strangler,' Maddie's mom commented as the news channel showed a mugshot of José Moreno. 'He looks like a nice guy. Are you sure it's him?'

Maddie nodded. 'Oh, it's definitely him alright.'

'Are you going to have to testify in court?' Trenton asked.

'Possibly,' she replied, not looking forward to the media storm that would ensue.

The news broadcast had moved on to relaying aerial shots of Moreno's Hollywood home, where he'd been arrested early this morning, and exterior shots of the Reel of Dreams Museum.

'I've got some urgent calls to make,' Maddie said, although none of the three appeared to have heard her and continued watching the broadcast.

In the privacy of her home office in the basement, she called Becky, who had messaged Maddie earlier in the day, asking her to phone when she got a moment. The message contained nothing more than that simple request, yet Maddie had an ominous feeling as she waited for Becky to answer.

'Hey, Maddie,' Becky greeted. 'I see they've arrested José Moreno. Congratulations.'

'Wow, that news got to you quickly,' Maddie responded.

'Not really. It hasn't made the local news here. I just got a message from a friend in LA, asking if I had had anything to do with it.'

'Thanks for your help on the case.'

'You're welcome—glad to help.'

'Talking about the news,' Maddie began, 'what I'm hearing out of Haiti isn't good. I really think you should come home.' It wasn't her place to say it, but Maddie was growing increasingly worried about her.

'It's not as bad as the news makes out,' Becky replied.

'Can you not do the work you're doing somewhere else?'

'Yes and no,' she answered. 'My work with the charity can happen out of the country, I guess, but I'm working on other things, too. That's what I wanted to talk to you about.'

'Go on,' Maddie encouraged.

'I found something out about Michael and the other two men.'

The words hit Maddie like a gut punch. At last, there was some information.

'I think Michael, Jay and Artemon were sent to Haiti to work on an infrastructure package for my dad's company.'

'Uh-huh,' Maddie agreed. This was not new information.

'But I think they visited a place owned by my father's company. A place called Château Lwa,' she said, her voice cracking with emotion. 'It was a mansion where young local girls were kept against their will and subjected to sexual abuse on a massive scale.'

'What?' Maddie gasped, slumping down into her office chair. She couldn't believe it. Not Michael. There was no way.

'From what I can gather, Michael and the other two weren't involved in the abuse, and I think they were on the verge of blowing the whistle on the whole thing, when…' Her sentence trailed off, but Maddie knew where it ended. Becky was crying uncontrollably.

'My God, I can't believe it,' Maddie muttered. 'You're sure they weren't involved in it?'

'I don't think so,' Becky stammered. 'I've spoken to one of the girls who remembered Michael, Jay and Artemon visiting the house unexpectedly. She said they didn't take part in the abuse.'

Maddie couldn't think straight. 'Do you think your father knew what was going on in this…château?'

Becky took a long time to answer. 'He was in charge of the whole thing, Maddie.'

'Oh, Becky. I'm so sorry.'

'I'm staying out here to find out—'

The call ended and Maddie tried to phone her back, but it went straight to voicemail.

Clutching her cell phone, Maddie considered what she'd just heard. Michael and his two friends had been about to blow the lid off an international abuse ring. It fit with the dark mood that Michael had returned in from his trip to Haiti. She felt sad and guilty that she hadn't pushed more to find the truth. But it wasn't too late. She would talk more to Becky, and together they would come up with a plan to find out exactly what had happened and bring justice to the three men and, hopefully, to the victims of Andrew Larkin's abuse ring.

Before she returned upstairs to hear the latest on the Hollywood Strangler case, Maddie called Clayton.

'Hey. I was just going to call you,' Clayton said. 'I take it this arrest is thanks to you, right?'

'Well, mainly my team, actually,' Maddie replied.

'That's amazing. Like most people in law enforcement, I didn't think the guy was still alive, or that he'd ever be identified. Well done.'

'Thanks. I was just calling to ask if you'd heard anything about your application to join the police in Utah yet?'

Clayton laughed. 'It's only been a week. Wait, do you want me to withdraw?'

'No, I don't,' she replied. 'I want you here.'

'That's nice to hear, Maddie. I'm desperate to be with you.'

Maddie had to fight to hold back her tears.

'Mom!' Trenton shouted down the stairs. This time he sounded annoyed. 'There are a whole bunch of reporters gathering on our driveway.'

'I've got to go,' she told Clayton. 'Talk to you later.'

'Okay. Love you.'

'Love you, too,' she replied, taking a breath and preparing to face the media circus that was about to engulf her life.

Acknowledgements

As with the other two books in the series, this book required a great deal of assistance to get many crucial aspects of the storyline correct. I'm very grateful for the willingness to help shown by so many individuals. Although this is a work of fiction, I aim to make it as realistic as possible, which would be unachievable without these valuable contributions.

My first thanks must go to Dr. Peter Speth who spent several hours talking to me on Zoom and via email about his fascinating career. I first learned about Dr. Speth from Barbara Rae-Venter's brilliant book, *I Know Who You Are*. It wouldn't be overstating the point to suggest that the Golden State Killer would not have been identified were it not for Dr. Speth's commitment to his job and diligence in taking duplicate rape kits. All of the procedures depicted in the prologue were conducted by Dr. Speth in his investigations, including on Charlene and Lyman Smith, who transpired to be victims of the Golden State Killer. I thank him for his lifetime's work and for generously appearing as himself in this book.

Similarly, I would like to offer my sincere thanks to Detective Supervisor Mitzi Roberts from the LAPD cold case team. Her commitment to law enforcement has resulted in the closure of many cold cases and the capture of the most prolific serial killer in the U.S., Sam Little. Detective Roberts willingly answered my questions and agreed to appear as herself in the book. Any mistakes, errors or exaggerations are all mine. One procedure point to note, here, is that LAPD routinely use the FBI for their investigative genetic genealogy work, not Venator.

I would like to extend my thanks to Professor Andrew MacLeod for taking the time to share his insight into aid agency / UN abuse with me. What I have depicted happening in Haiti is tragically based on reality. The abuse that is happening is on an unbelievable level. This book only scratches the surface. More information can be found at the following links:

- https://www.independent.co.uk/news/world/americas/un-haiti-peacekeepers-child-sex-ring-sri-lankan-underage-girls-boys-teenage-a7681966.html
- https://www.theguardian.com/world/2019/oct/01/haiti-cholera-2010-un-us-supreme-court
- https://www.tandfonline.com/doi/pdf/10.1080/13533312.2019.1698297?download=true
- https://www.abc.net.au/news/2023-04-17/abusers-in-the-aid-sector/102223176

Thank you to Allison Peacock from FHD Forensics for answering several of my questions regarding IGG procedures and to Dr Shelley Murphy for sharing her expertise over several emails with links and assistance for African American genealogy.

My thanks go to Maria Tegtmeier for information regarding studying genealogy at BYU and to Angie Bush for all of the Salt Lake City restaurant recommendations and for the Sacred Whale information.

Thank you to competition winner, Linda Carranza Rawlinson, who provided the Hollywood Strangler with his name: José Matias Moreno. Linda's real Moreno relative was actually the same whom Kenyatta found on Google, the shipwrecked whaler named Joseph Matthew Brown who changed his name upon arrival in California, translating directly word for word.

My thanks as always go to Patrick Dengate for his awesome cover and for gently guiding me away from impractical ideas.

To my wonderful group of early readers, I give my deep gratitude. You really do help to make the book significantly better, and you all bring different things to the table. John Lisle, Cheri Hudson Passey, Ruth Wilmore, Helen Smith, Laura Wilkinson Hedgecock, Mags Gaulden, Natalie Levinson, Pat Richley-Erickson, Crystal Cuelho, Celeste McNeil, Connie Edwards, Lorna Cowan, Nairet Jacklin, Heather Choplin, Dr. Karen Cummings, Elizabeth O'Neal, Heather Choplin and Mia Bennett, I really appreciate the huge amount of time you all put in to commenting to make the book better and flag any tpyos.

I'm indebted to all the various individuals, companies, businesses and genealogy societies who have supported and promoted this series; it is very much appreciated.

Final thanks must go to Robert Bristow for his usual help and guidance with the book, and for assisting with location-hunting in Los Angeles and Salt Lake City.

Further Information

Website & Newsletter: www.nathandylangoodwin.com
Twitter: @NathanDGoodwin
Facebook: www.facebook.com/NathanDylanGoodwin
Instagram: www.instagram.com/NathanDylanGoodwin
Pinterest: www.pinterest.com/NathanDylanGoodwin
LinkedIn: www.linkedin.com/in/NathanDylanGoodwin

The Chester Creek Murders
(Venator Cold Case #1)

When Detective Clayton Tyler is tasked with reviewing the formidable archives of unsolved homicides in his police department's vaults, he settles on one particular cold case from the 1980s: The Chester Creek Murders. Three young women were brutally murdered—their bodies dumped in Chester Creek, Delaware County—by a serial killer who has confounded a slew of detectives and evaded capture for over thirty-eight years. With no new leads or information at his disposal, the detective contacts Venator for help, a company that uses cutting-edge investigative genetic genealogy to profile perpetrators solely from DNA evidence. Taking on the case, Madison Scott-Barnhart and her small team at Venator must use their forensic genealogical expertise to attempt finally to bring the serial killer to justice. Madison, meanwhile, has to weigh professional and personal issues carefully, including the looming five-year anniversary of her husband's disappearance.

'Both educational and entertaining, this fast-paced glimpse into an entirely new technology is a must-read for anyone interested in genealogy, law enforcement, or mystery'
Blaine Bettinger

'This is a novel for all family history fans. The plot unfolds with twists and turns, keeping us guessing to the end. I thoroughly look forward to the next book…'
Family Tree magazine

The Sawtooth Slayer
(Venator Cold Case #2)

April 2020, Twin Falls, Idaho. A serial killer is on the loose. A nameless man is kidnapping young women from their own homes, taking them out of the city to kill them before returning their bodies to random locations around the city. Detective Maria Gonzalez heads up the investigation but has very few leads to pursue. As time passes and fears rise that the killer might strike again with a fifth victim, Maria turns to Venator—an investigative genetic genealogy company—in the hope that they can identify the killer from his DNA alone before he has the chance to take yet another life. Despite her initial reticence to take on the company's first ever live case, Madison Scott-Barnhart and her team in Salt Lake City agree to try to reveal the identity of this barbaric serial killer. In the midst of the global pandemic that has closed the Venator office and posed both personal and professional problems for Madison, time is running out on this case.

'Gripping to the point of being un-put-downable, the core story is fascinating to anyone who enjoys crime novels, and particularly those with an interest in the use of DNA in genealogy research'
Family Tree magazine

'Highly recommended'
Who Do You Think You Are? magazine

'Once you start reading you won't want to stop – though that's what I've come to expect from this author. Highly recommended!'
LostCousins

Printed in Great Britain
by Amazon

5e84c1a8-ecda-4b05-8a5d-80fa4c0cb99aR01